the exception

NAN A. TALESE

DOUBLEDAY

New York

London

Toronto

Sydney

Auckland

A NOVEL

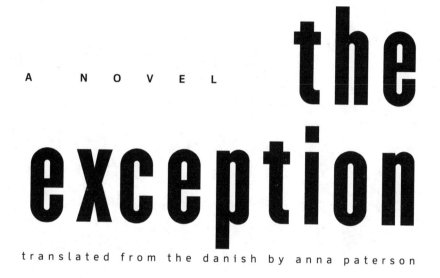

the exception

translated from the danish by anna paterson

christian jungersen

PUBLISHED BY NAN A. TALESE
AN IMPRINT OF DOUBLEDAY
a division of Random House, Inc.

DOUBLEDAY is a registered trademark of Random House, Inc.

This book is a work of fiction. Any references to real people or organizations are
intended only to give the fiction a sense of reality.

The Exception was first published in 2004, in different form, under the title
Undtagelsen in Denmark by Gyldendal, Copenhagen.

Book design by Ellen Cipriano

Library of Congress Cataloging-in-Publication Data
Jungersen, Christian.
[Undtagelsen. English]
The exception : a novel / Christian Jungersen ;
translated from the Danish by Anna Paterson.
p.   cm.
I. Paterson, Anna. II. Title.
PT8176.2.U47U7313 2006
839.81'38—dc22
2006022907

ISBN 978-0-385-51629-7

PRINTED IN THE UNITED STATES OF AMERICA

1   3   5   7   9   10   8   6   4   2

First Edition in the United States of America

the exception

iben

chapter 1

d on't they ever think about anything except killing each other?" Roberto asks. Normally he would never say such a harsh thing.

The truck with the four aid workers and two of the hostage takers on the tailgate has been stopped for an hour or more. Burned-out cars block the road ahead, but it ought to be possible to reverse and outflank them by driving right through the flimsy small shacks.

"I mean, what are we waiting for? Why don't they just drive on through the crowd?"

Roberto's English accent is usually perfect, but now, for the first time, you can hear that he is Italian. He is struggling for breath. Sweat pours down his cheeks and into the corners of his mouth.

The slum surrounds them. It smells and looks like a filthy cattle pen. The car stands on a mud surface, still ridged with tracks made after the last rains, now baked as hard as stoneware by the sun. The Nubians have constructed their grayish brown huts from a framework of torn-off branches spread with cow dung. Dense clusters of huts are scattered all over the dusty plain.

Roberto, Iben's immediate boss, looks at his fellow hostages. "Why can't they at least pull over into the shade?" He falls silent and lifts his hand very slowly toward the lower rim of his sunglasses.

One of the hostage takers turns his head away from watching the locals to stare at Roberto and shakes his sharpened, one-and-a-half-foot-long panga. It is enough to make Roberto lower his arm with the same measured slowness.

Iben sighs. Drops of sweat have collected in her ears and everything sounds muffled, a bit like the whirring of a fan.

Garbage, mostly rotting green items mixed with human excrement, has piled up against the wall of a nearby cow dung hut. The sloping three-foot-high mound gives off the unmistakable stench of the slum.

"O glorious Name of Jesus, gracious Name," the youngest of their captors intones. "Name of love and power! Through You, sins are forgiven, enemies are vanquished, the sick . . ."

Iben looks up at him. He is very different from the child soldiers she wrote about back home in Copenhagen. It's easy to spot that he is new to all this and caving in under the pressure. Until now he's been high on some junk, but he's coming down and terror is tearing him apart. He stands there, his eyes fixed on the sea of people that surrounds the car just a short distance away; a crowd that is growing and becoming better armed with every passing minute.

Tears are running down the boy's cheeks. He clutches his scratched black machine gun with one hand while his other hand rubs the cross that hangs from a chain around his neck outside his red and blue I LOVE HONG KONG T-shirt.

The boy must have been a member of an English-language church, because he has stopped using his native Dhuluo and instead is babbling in English, prayers and long quotes from the Bible, in solemn tones, as if he were reading a Latin mass:

"Surely goodness and mercy will follow me all the days of my life. And I will dwell in the house of the Lord for the length of all my days . . ."

It's autumn back home in Copenhagen, but apart from the season changing, everything has stayed the same. People's homes look the way they always did. Iben's friends wear their usual clothes and talk about the same things.

Iben has started work again. Three months have passed since she and the others were taken hostage and held prisoner in a small African hut somewhere near Nairobi. She remembers how important home had seemed to all of them. She remembers the diarrhea, the armed guards, the heat, and the fear that dominated their lives.

Now a voice inside her insists that it was not true, not real. Her experiences in Kenya resist being made part of her quiet, orderly life at home. She can't be that woman lying on the mud floor with a machine-gun nozzle pressed to her temple. She remembers it in a haze, as if it were a scene in some experimental film seen long ago.

This evening Iben has come to see Malene. They are planning to go to a party later, given by an old friend from their university days.

Iben mixes them a large mojito each. She waits for her best friend to pick something to wear. Another track of the Afro funk CD with Fela Kuti starts up. After one more swallow, she can see the bottom of her glass.

Malene emerges to look at herself in the mirror. "Why do I always seem to end up wearing something more boring than all the outfits I've tried on at home?"

She scrutinizes herself in a black, almost see-through dress, which would have been right for New Year's Eve but is wrong for a Friday-night get-together hosted by a woman who lives in thick sweaters.

"I guess we just go to boring parties."

Malene is already on her way back to the bedroom to find something less flashy.

Iben calls out after her: "And you can bet tonight will be really dull. At . . . Sophie's!" She pauses, as if the mere mention of Sophie's name says it all, and hears Malene adopt a silly voice: "Oh, yes . . . at Sophie's."

They both laugh.

Iben sips her drink while she looks over the bookshelves as she has done so many times before. When she arrives somewhere new she always likes to check out the books as soon as she can. At parties she discreetly scans the titles and authors' names, filtering out the music and distant chatter.

She pulls out a heavy volume, a collection of anthropological articles. Clutching it in her arms, she sways in time to one of the slower tracks. Her drink is strong enough to create a blissfully ticklish sensation.

She holds her cold glass, presses it against her chest, and gently waltzes with the book while she reads about the initiation ritual to adulthood for Xingu Indian girls. They are made to stay in windowless huts, sometimes for as long as three years, and emerge into the sunlight plump and pale, with volumes of long, brittle hair. Only then does the tribe accept them as true women.

Also on the bookshelf is the tape that Malene's partner, Rasmus, recorded of the television programs on which Iben appeared when she returned from Kenya. It sits there on the shelf in front of her.

Nibbling on a cracker, she puts the tape into the machine and presses Play without bothering to turn down the music. As the images emerge on the screen, she takes a seat.

Now and then she laughs as she observes the small puppet-Iben, sitting there in front of the cameras of *TV2 News* and *TV Report*, pretending to be so wise and serious as she explains how the Danish Center for Information on Genocide, where she works as an information officer, lent her to an aid organization based in Kenya. There is a short sequence filmed in a Nairobi slum before the camera records the arrival of the freed hostages at the American embassy for their first press conference. She studies these images. Every time she sees them, they seem just as fresh and unfamiliar.

Malene comes back, trailing a faint scent of perfume and wearing a gauzy chocolate-colored dress. Dresses suit her. It's easy to understand what men see in her. With her thick chestnut hair and lightly tanned skin, she looks positively appetizing, like a great smooth, glowing sweet.

Malene realizes at once which tape Iben is watching and gives her friend a little hug before sitting down next to her on the sofa.

Iben turns down the music. Roberto, still in Nairobi, is addressing a journalist: "In captivity it was Iben who kept telling us that we must talk to each other about what was happening, repeating the words over and over until they were devoid of meaning, or as near as we possibly . . ."

He smiles, but looks worn. They were all examined by doctors and psychologists, but Roberto took longer than anyone else before he was ready to go home.

"Iben explained that there were a lot of studies demonstrating how beneficial this could be in preventing post-traumatic stress . . ."

TV Report cuts to Iben speaking in a Copenhagen studio. "If you want to prevent post-traumatic stress disorder, it's crucial to start debriefing as soon as possible. We had no idea how long we were going to be held. It could have been months, which was why it was a good idea to start trying to structure our responses to what we were experiencing during captivity . . ."

Safe in Malene's apartment, Iben groans and reaches for her drink. "I come across as . . . totally unbearable."

"You're not the tiniest bit unbearable. The point is, you knew about this and most people don't."

"But it's just the kind of stuff that journalists are always after. I sound like such a psychology nerd . . . as if I had no feelings."

Malene puts down her drink, smiles, and touches Iben's hand. "Couldn't it be that they were simply fascinated by the way you managed to stay in control inside that little cow dung hideout? You were heroic. No one knows what goes on inside the mind of a hero, and you certainly weren't used to being one."

Iben can't think of anything to say. They laugh.

Iben nods at Malene's dress. "You know that you can't turn up at Sophie's in that."

"Of course I do."

The next recordings are Iben's appearances on *Good Morning, Denmark* and *Deadline*. On screen she looks like somebody quite different from the old stay-at-home Iben. Normally her shoulder-length blond hair is thick but without the sheen that the sun brings out in most blondes. The African light, however, has been strong enough to bleach her hair. Since then, she has had her hairdresser add highlights to maintain her sundrenched appearance.

She had also wanted to hang on to her tan, which, in the interviews, was almost as good as Malene's. And she felt that the usual rings under her eyes were too visible for someone not yet thirty, so she had followed Malene's lead. She went off to a tanning salon, but it didn't take her long to realize that frying inside a noisy machine was not for her. Now her skin is so pale and transparent that the half-moon shadows under both eyes look violet.

At the time, her story suited the news media down to the ground. Whatever Iben said was edited until it fitted in with the narrative they were after: an idealistic young Danish woman confronting the big, bad world outside and proving herself a heroine. She was the only one who had managed to escape from the hostage takers. Afterward she had left her safe hiding place to run back to the captives in an attempt to make the brutal policemen change sides in the middle of a brawl.

The papers loved quoting the other hostages when they described Iben as "the strongest member of the group." A tabloid phoned one of them and didn't leave him alone until he admitted that "without Iben the outcome might well have been less fortunate." The media chased the story for a week and then totally lost interest. The group's captivity had lasted just four days, which meant that Iben didn't rank among seriously famous hostages. By now, the journalists have forgotten her.

Iben realizes that Malene is trying to sneak a look at her face to find out if something's the matter.

"Malene, I'm fine. Why don't you go and change?"

"Are you positive?"

"Yes. Sure."

Malene and Rasmus's apartment is in a state of transition. Draped over the backs of two cheap IKEA folding chairs are Indian throws from a fair trade shop. Like the cheap Polynesian figurines on the pine shelves, the blankets are reminders of the time when Malene was studying international development at university. Three years have passed since Malene received her graduate degree and a well-paid post at the Danish Center for Information on Genocide. Now their furniture includes a pricey new Italian sofa and two sixties Danish Design armchairs. Both Malene and Rasmus make decent money, and little by little they've been able to afford more upscale pieces.

There's little evidence, however, of Rasmus's taste. After receiving a university degree in film studies, he couldn't find a job, so now he sells computer hardware at trade shows all over Europe, requiring him to spend more than half the year on the road.

The telephone rings. Iben answers and recognizes the deep male voice with the Jutland accent. She has listened to Gunnar Hartvig Nielsen so many times on the current affairs program *Orientation*.

Iben calls Malene, who is presently sporting jeans and a fashionable, colorful silk shirt. It looks like her last bid in the dressing-up stakes, because she has put on some makeup.

Iben hears Malene turn down Gunnar's suggestion that they should meet for dinner and invite him to join them at Sophie's instead.

When Malene hangs up, Iben wonders aloud: "Could he really be bothered to come to Sophie's?"

"Why not?"

"But what's he going to do there?"

"Meet people, talk to me. Have a good time. Like we are."

"Yeah . . . of course."

Iben switches off the television and follows Malene to the bathroom, where Malene finishes putting on her makeup.

Iben had heard Gunnar Nielsen's name for the first time when she was still a student. Everyone in her dorm shared a daily copy of *Information*, which published Gunnar's stream of articles on international politics. They scrutinized every word and particularly admired and debated his reports from Africa.

Like Malene, Gunnar had grown up in rural Denmark. At nineteen, he joined a development project in Tanzania, where he taught himself Swahili, and then stayed on in Africa, traveling around for three and a half years. When he came home, he wrote a book about the continent, *The Rhythms of Survival*. It not only had become required reading for young backpackers, but also was taken seriously by people concerned with international issues.

By the time he was twenty-five, Gunnar was a well-established journalist. He had gone back to Africa several times. At one point, he had tried to combine university studies with his *Information* assignments to cover summit meetings and conferences, but the dull world of university life couldn't compete with the excitement of being at the center of things, so he had dropped out of the course after little more than a year.

Iben and Malene were still at university when Gunnar's newspaper pieces suddenly stopped. His fame as a star left-wing writer quickly faded.

Four years ago, when she was a student trainee at the DCIG, Malene had found out what had happened. She had managed to get hold of him for an interview about the horrific but at the time unrecognized genocide in the Sudan. Gunnar had taken a job as the editor of *Development*, a magazine published by Danida, the Danish state organization for international development. He had told her that, after his divorce, he needed a steady income to pay child support and to rent a new apartment with enough space for his children's visits. His articles were as good as ever, but they went almost unnoticed by people outside the circle of Danida initiates.

Iben, who was studying comparative literature at the time, felt envious of her friend, who always met such exciting men through her work, and was good-looking enough to attract many of them. Her envy deepened when Gunnar invited Malene out to dinner.

More meals followed. Malene and Gunnar explored restaurants in every corner of the city, but did nothing else. Gunnar's stocky frame, his "disillusioned Socialist" attitude, and, above all, the fact that he was in his midforties meant that Malene thought the chemistry between them wasn't right, much as she loved dining out with him. Now and then she would tell Iben about how weary she felt when she saw the pleading in his large eyes.

Once Iben spoke out. "It isn't fair to keep going out with Gunnar and letting him pay for one meal after another. He's in love with you and you don't even want to sleep with him."

"Oh, come on. We always have such a good time together. And he's said that he isn't expecting anything more—you know, like love or sex."

"But he's got to pay for you all the same?"

"No, it's not like that. It's simple: he enjoys eating in restaurants and so do I, but I'm broke. If he couldn't afford it and I could, I'd pay for him."

When Malene met the younger, cooler Rasmus and became his girlfriend, he too tried to stop her evenings out with Gunnar. Iben overheard Malene say, "Rasmus, there's nothing sexual between Gunnar and me. We're just good friends." Still, Rasmus had insisted that she should pay her share.

Before leaving, as Iben and Malene talk about who they'll see tonight, they wolf down some leftovers. In the hall, Malene quickly changes to another pair of her expensive orthopedic shoes, which she needs because of her arthritis. They drain their mojitos—and leave.

Iben and Malene hang up their coats in the narrow passage of Sophie's apartment. The air is heavy with the smell of fried food, wine, and people.

Sophie comes over to meet them. After the hugs and cries of "So good to see you," she notices Malene's clothes and makeup. "But Malene, it's not that kind of party . . ." Some of her other guests are drifting out through the living room door and bump into her. Distractedly, she finishes the sentence: " . . . it's just, you know, the same old crowd coming round for a drink. You know I'm off tomorrow, don't you?"

When she phoned about the party, Sophie, who had lived in the same student housing as Iben and Malene, explained that she was leaving Denmark to join her boyfriend, a biologist working in Canada on a two-year project.

Someone in the living room calls out: "Hey, look, there's Iben. The heroine has arrived!"

"Went back to protect the others instead of just looking after number one," another old college friend adds.

Iben smiles. God only knows how many times she's explained it all before. "I had no idea what I was doing. Everything was so confusing. I just didn't think about the outcome."

"But that's precisely what makes what you did heroic, Iben. You had the right instincts. Or whatever it is that kicks in when you've got to make a split-second decision."

Sophie gives Iben another little hug and looks her in the eye. "Most people would have run for it."

The living room is full of familiar faces. A few years ago they were all students together, in their early twenties. Iben remembers how they would laze around on the grass in Fælled Park when there was a concert on. Almost all of them have finished with education by now. Some have jobs, but many more live on welfare, full-time or part-time. Despite failing in the job market, they still feel less poor now, because the unemployment payments are quite an improvement on student grants. Individual lives are being pushed in utterly unforeseen directions along career paths, sometimes along straight routes and sometimes up blind alleys. Some of them already have children.

They are everywhere, standing or sitting, drinking beer or red wine, chatting in the low light from a few dim lamps. Three young mothers drift around with babies in their arms. Iben and Malene exchange glances. Obviously, dancing isn't an option.

There are more questions about Nairobi, but Iben only smiles. "I've been asked about all that so often I can't even bring myself to discuss it any longer. Some other time. Look, what about you?"

She does the rounds of the room and then tucks herself away in a corner where she can half sit, half lean on a table. A man starts reminiscing about nights spent clubbing. He's a dentist, fresh from his qualifying exams and already well on his way to becoming an alcoholic.

She looks up and, across the room, sees Gunnar. Malene once spoke of him as "such a big guy" and Iben got the impression that he was John Goodman–sized. Now she realizes that he is more like the young Gérard Depardieu.

Iben sees Malene get up from an inflatable armchair and walk toward Gunnar; the dentist turns to watch.

Iben crushes a chip between her teeth. Some women, she thinks, would be bloody irritated if their friend had that sort of effect on every single guy they met. She observes Malene lead Gunnar away to the relative peace of the hallway.

Later, Iben and one of Rasmus's best friends end up side by side on the sofa. He wears a neon blue jacket with contrasting seams and is proudly telling her that he landed a job as a copywriter in an advertising agency. His voice sounds louder than it used to be, and his laughter seems more mechanical.

"Human rights and art—great stuff, but there's no money in it!"

He sees the expression on Iben's face. "Sure, it's not so bad being more or less broke. But unemployment, that's something else. It's awful. I mean, just look at the way you're treated by your prospective employers. They couldn't give a fuck. They know perfectly well they can take their pick from thousands of graduates." Some of the people standing nearby are listening in, and he turns to them as well. "But in a good agency you get treated differently. The bosses know how few there are who have both the talent and the stamina to put up with that line of work." He smiles. "Like, watch the style, fuck the substance."

He mentions the name of his agency and Iben is obviously meant to recognize it. "We've been on TV. Like you."

Iben pours fruit juice into her plastic cup while keeping an eye on Gunnar, who has come back into the room. He isn't surrounded by any female admirers. Maybe because by now they're old enough to feel self-conscious or because they think that, in the flesh, he doesn't quite live up to their fantasies. Or maybe because he is just too old.

Rasmus's friend is still working his story. Now he's telling everyone about how his agency paid for him and the rest of the crew to take a three-day Christmas break, partying in Barcelona, and how it was worth it, given the firm's investment in their salaries.

Maybe it's the impressed looks on the listeners that prompt Iben to jump in and defend traditional values, such as "Money isn't everything" and "You can't buy happiness." In no time she realizes that this discussion is just a rerun of their old debates, as if they are all battle-worn politicians in the last days of an election campaign, able to predict their opponents' arguments.

Avoiding eye contact, she deliberately turns away from the discussion and tries instead to eavesdrop on the conversation of the two strangers sitting opposite.

But Rasmus's friend hasn't finished. "Iben, your job is different. I would've liked it myself. You investigate serious stuff. Humanitarian issues. That's really worthwhile. It means something." He pats his bright blue jacket. "You try to make the world a better place, sure. But I'm not convinced that will ever happen. It's not at the top of the agenda." He breaks off, apparently amused by his own paradox.

Later, Iben finds herself standing next to a child's folding cot, all aluminum and nylon, like a tiny piece of camping equipment. She is balancing a glass of red wine and three broken crackers.

Suddenly Gunnar materializes at her side. "What's it like to be back home?"

That calm voice of his.

She looks at him. He has gray-blue eyes. "I'm not sure if I am back."

They laugh.

Iben doesn't know where to look. Sophie has put on one of her Buddha-Bar CDs. At the other end of the room Malene walks over to a wooden chair and sits down. Only Iben knows exactly how Malene looks when her feet begin to hurt. She will want to go home soon.

Gunnar is telling her about being in Dar es Salaam to interview Habyarimana, the former Rwandan president. Not long afterward the presidential plane was shot down and his widow touched off the alleged revenge, killing 500,000 of the country's Tutsis. Gunnar speaks of when he handled one of the heavy nail-studded wooden clubs used to break human skulls.

"I'm sure you know that a lot of the murdering was done inside churches, where many of the Tutsis sought refuge. It was hard work killing human beings with whatever was at hand—mostly household implements and agricultural tools. Faced with hundreds of victims, the Hutus found it expedient to cut the Achilles tendons of their victims straight away. Then they could take their time about the slaughter—days, if necessary."

In his company Iben finds it easier to recall the three months she spent in Nairobi before being captured. She tries to express how surreal it all was. Most people are bemused, but Gunnar knows Africa.

They withdraw to one side and lean against one of Sophie's bookshelves. She loses track of time. Then somebody passing by accidentally bumps into Iben and she discovers that she's been standing there with her mouth half open a bit too long, gazing up into Gunnar's regular features and drinking in his long, absorbing explanations. She gives herself a little shake, like a dog that's clambered out of the water.

I'd better go and talk to someone else, Iben tells herself. But she sees Malene heading over to join them. This is not good.

Malene doesn't look at Iben, only Gunnar, when she tells him about meeting one of his journalist friends at the Center and what a funny encounter it was.

Iben wants a glass of water. She turns to go, but Gunnar grabs hold of her wrist.

"Who knows—I might run into you one day at the Metro Bar."

"Metro Bar?"

"Don't you know it? I was sure I'd seen you there. It's the café next to Broadcasting House. I go there several times a week."

"No, I don't know it."

Iben realizes what he has just said and quickly looks over at Malene.

Malene pats Gunnar's broad shoulder. "Look, I really came over to tell you that I'd better leave. My feet . . ." She smiles a big goodbye without finishing the sentence.

Gunnar and Iben nod in silence, looking at her arthritic hands and feet.

Malene smiles again. "Iben, are you coming?"

The Danish Center for Information on Genocide, or DCIG for short, was set up to collect data about genocide and make it available, both in Denmark and abroad, to researchers, politicians, aid organizations, and other interested parties. Over the years, the organization has accumulated Scandinavia's largest collection of books and documents on the subject.

The DCIG is housed in a restored old red-brick building, along a lane in Copenhagen's central Østerbro district. Its offices and library take up the entire attic floor, a space once occupied by the city council archives.

The library is expanding all the time. Gray steel shelves cover the walls almost everywhere—in the kitchen, the hallway, and the space they call the small meeting room. They have also invaded the largest room, which serves as a shared office for Iben, Malene, and Camilla. Wider and heavier industrial-style shelves, steel lacquered dark green, have been tucked into less accessible corners and are laden with cardboard boxes full of documents such as diplomatic reports and transcripts of foreign court proceedings.

Only five people are employed to manage the Center and handle the mountains of printed material. In addition to Iben (the information officer) and Malene (the project manager) are

Paul, the head of the Center, Camilla, Paul's secretary, and Anne-Lise, the librarian.

Apart from Paul's room, the spacious main office is the brightest and most pleasant. Iben and Malene sit facing each other at ergonomically correct desks. Although most of the walls are lined with books, the shelving is not as tightly packed as it is in the library. Malene has put potted plants on the sills in front of the three windows, which is why the office is lovingly referred to as the "Winter Garden." The point of the joke is, of course, that the room will always look like a library, regardless of how much vegetation is crammed into it.

Iben and Malene have tried to make their office look homier in other ways as well. They have put up a notice board and with time it has become covered with photos, conference invitations, newspaper cuttings, and postcards with teasing messages about the sender having a great holiday while the rest are slaving away in an office.

It's the Monday morning after Sophie's get-together and Iben and Malene are at work as usual. They sometimes chat with each other, sometimes with Camilla, whose desk is at the other end of the large room, next to Paul's door.

Iben can sense something—something in Malene's eyes.

At one point, Malene sighs audibly and Iben looks up. "What's the matter?"

"Oh . . . nothing."

Malene prints out a piece that she's been working on and starts correcting it, first with a green marker and then with red. After a while she sighs again.

Iben looks away from the screen, hesitates, and tries a little smile. They are such good friends that Malene can't help smiling back.

"What's up?" Iben asks.

Malene slams the printout down on the wrist support in front of her keyboard.

"I just can't get it right. Not the way I want it."

"What's the problem?"

"I've got to get the text ready for at least three posters about how Danes rescued lots of Danish Jews. It's for the exhibition. It's so hard . . . Whatever I write sucks. It sounds so self-satisfied and so . . . evangelical!"

Iben leans forward, pleased that Malene seems to have forgotten about the slight awkwardness at Sophie's party.

"I've rewritten the whole thing four times, but it's just . . . How do I avoid writing stuff like 'the only country in the world' and so on?"

"Why not add something about the restrictive asylum policy toward foreign Jews during the 1930s?"

"I thought of that, but it doesn't fit in with the main theme of the exhibition. Besides, what I wrote sounded like crap as well." Malene starts writing again.

Iben gives up and returns to her own screen. She can't quite put Malene out of her mind, even though she knows that there's no real conflict between them and Malene is probably just having a bad morning.

They are both working on an exhibition based on an idea that Malene had while Iben was away in Africa. Malene thought that many people might share her own sense of weariness at all the evil deeds in the genocidal world out there and want to know more about the heart-warming exceptions. She thought up a theme for a poster exhibition that would celebrate the small minority of good and brave people in Nazi-controlled regions—people who saved lives during the Holocaust. She talked to Paul and he liked the idea. The Copenhagen City Library agreed to allocate space and time, and afterward the exhibition would be made available to schools and any other interested institution.

Something occurs to Iben. "Maybe it would work better if you described the civil servants behind the thirties asylum policy? It would fit in with your approach of looking at the individuals behind the rescue stories."

Malene takes her time to reply, and Iben doesn't want to seem bossy.

"Look, it's just a thought."

Iben's job is to research the background for Malene's posters. She is revising her notes on the story about the Polish shepherd Antoni Gawrylkiewicz. He risked his life by digging underground shelters, where he housed sixteen Jewish survivors of the ghetto massacre in Radyn. The Jews had managed to escape by hiding in an attic. When the Germans were searching the house, a Jewish father had to strangle his youngest child, a little boy, because he started to cry.

As so often at work, Iben feels hopelessly spoiled. How could anyone possibly think that what she had experienced in Nairobi was of any consequence? She had been kept prisoner for four days. When she came back home, she was offered all the counseling she needed, paid for by the aid organization she worked for. Antoni Gawrylkiewicz had never gotten any kind of support or care.

True, her supposedly therapeutic talks hadn't been particularly helpful. The therapist had asked about the depression and panic attacks that had hit Iben after the death of her father nine years ago. At that time, talking to friends and to a psychologist had actually helped, but after Nairobi, with the new therapist, it seemed to her that nothing at all came up that she didn't already know.

Those who challenged the system during the war were left terrifyingly alone with their fears. Iben had found another item about a man, a passerby, who was suddenly shot dead in the street by an SS officer. The man's crime was to hand a jug of water to the prisoners in a Jewish transport.

Regardless of the terror, Antoni Gawrylkiewicz, and others like him, had fed and housed Jewish strangers for years. Night after night they must have fallen asleep knowing that the family might be woken up at any time by hammering on the door and be deported to a concentration camp, together with their secret houseguests.

No one dared tell anyone else about the deadly risks they were taking. For two years Antoni Gawrylkiewicz cooked for sixteen Jews and, to make sure there were no signs of their existence, carried away their excrement from the earth shelters where they lived. Many of the units in the Polish resistance movement were as driven by anti-Semitic hatred as the Nazis, and one local unit suspected Gawrylkiewicz of hiding someone. He was tortured but revealed nothing.

After the liberation the Jews he had saved were at last free to return to their homes. Even though resistance fighters kept up their murderous attacks against Jews, at the end of the war there were many survivors because of him.

And as it is said in several religious creeds, including Judaism: "He who saves one life, saves the entire world."

Iben misses the laughter she usually shares with Malene. Ostensibly there is no problem. They talk, as ever, about work-related topics. They haven't really fallen out with each other. If anyone has the right to be cross, Iben feels it should be her. Malene, always so sure of being attractive to men, is making a big fuss over nothing.

Camilla's gentle voice floats across the room from her desk. "Paul called to say he won't be in this afternoon. He'll be in tomorrow morning."

"Thanks, Camilla."

Camilla is at least ten years older than Iben and Malene. She has little in common with the two younger women, but Iben likes her. Camilla is generous and brilliant at her job, always happy to share a joke.

Iben wants to stretch her legs. She goes to the kitchen, fills the thermos with coffee, and returns with an idea. "I thought maybe the exhibition could be called something like 'Everyone Can Make a Difference.' It would refer to what the exhibition aims to do, which is to make people want to create a better future, not just dwell on the past. The name would highlight that."

Camilla is quick off the mark. "That's a fantastic idea."

After a moment, Malene responds. "Aha . . . Right . . ." She looks up from her writing, which is obviously still frustrating her. Clutching the knuckles of one hand with the other hand, Malene swivels on her chair to look first at Camilla, then Iben.

"I'll add it to my list. We'd better run our ideas past Paul soon."

Paul has a terrific talent for formulating concise and arresting sound bites that always go down well with the media. He once said in a television interview that the DCIG should survive because "the purpose of the Danish Center for Information on Genocide is to develop a vaccine against what, in the past, has been the worst form of political disease. Our goal is to encourage resistance in the communities of the future."

Paul is in his thirties, lean and fair. His hair is very short and he almost always wears a black sweater. Sometimes he dresses up by adding a black jacket. He plays the role of politically engaged, media-savvy intellectual to perfection. During a typical workday Paul spends more time networking over a lengthy lunch than he spends in his office. His top priority is to increase the public's awareness of genocide, and he goes about it by making sure he's part of the current affairs coverage. He has excellent relationships with a whole string of editors and journalists, which helps him secure amazing amounts of free publicity.

Iben once told some of her friends that Paul, despite coming across as a black-suited embodiment of sobriety, drives an Alfa Romeo and keeps his cell phone on when he's out jogging in Hare Woods, the best nature trail in the city.

Her friends instantly labeled him a fraud. But Iben disagrees with them. It is Paul's job to fit in, and he conforms one hundred percent because he cares passionately about the cause. Without Paul, the new right-wing government would have put the Center under tighter control immediately after the election. They might even have closed it down, as they did so many of the other social-democratic projects. But it didn't happen, probably because Paul spent several days in town, lunching with the right people in the right places at the right time.

Iben already has a vision of him promoting their exhibition in some news feature, and imagines the kind of sales pitch he would give based on the slogan "Everyone Can Make a Difference":

"It is increasingly common to hear people say that it is pointless for individuals to act. The DCIG's new exhibition sends a crucial message: personal responsibility still matters. What you decide to do can make a huge difference."

Malene has worked for the DCIG the longest. As a student trainee she was exceptionally capable, and after graduating she was offered the post of project manager. One of her chief responsibilities is to look after the academics and civil servants who contact the Center.

Two years ago, when the information officer's post became vacant, Malene recommended Iben but didn't tell the selection committee that she was her best friend. She had met Iben at college, she told them, and worked with her in a few student societies. In Malene's view, Iben was unusually bright, efficient, and easy to work with.

Once Iben was short-listed, Malene briefed her carefully, giving her insider advice about the right things to say. In the end, Iben landed the job ahead of 285 other applicants. She and Malene took care not to show how well they knew each other and tried to make out that their close friendship had developed in record time once they started working together.

After a few weeks Paul stopped at their desks, chatted for a while, and then paused, smiling as he looked at them. "You two have learned to get on quickly. Good!" He tapped on Iben's new computer. "It's a match I'm proud of. It bodes well!"

Iben's job at the Center had been her reward for standing by Malene over the years.

One night six years earlier, Malene had been woken by a stabbing pain. Three of her fingers were red and inflamed. It had grown worse, and by four in the morning the fingers were grotesquely swollen and immobile. She had walked along the corridor and knocked with her other hand on Iben's door. Iben had phoned the doctor on call. The diagnosis was a sudden onset of rheumatoid arthritis, and Malene had been kept in the hospital for several days.

She had recovered, but was told that she must have frequent checkups and that the illness had no effective cure. It would come and go for the rest of her life. It could target any of her joints, for variable lengths of time, but especially those in her hands, feet, knees, elbows, and shoulders. The affected joints would become stiff and very sore.

Afterward a kind of pattern developed. For a few days every second month or so, Malene was incapable of doing things like using her computer keyboard or grasping the handlebars of her bicycle. Taking painkillers helped, but her hands were so weak that Iben had to help her carry shopping bags and so on.

The booklets from the hospital hadn't mentioned a decrease in appetite, but Malene lost weight quickly. Over the following six months the pretty but rather plump Jutland girl with radical attitudes was transformed into Socialist Barbie.

While her friend's pain came and went, Iben felt like Malene's squire, always ready to help and support her. Only Iben was allowed to know when Malene wasn't capable of twisting the lids off jars, of buttoning her shirts, or of unlocking doors by herself.

Just before lunchtime, Malene phones Frederik Thorsteinsson, the suave and sophisticated head of the Foreign Affairs Ministry's Center for Democracy as well as the deputy chairman of the DCIG board. Today is his birthday.

Malene knows Frederik best and is on easier terms with him than Paul.

She's bantering with Frederik when Iben calls out, loudly enough for him to hear her: "Happy birthday, Frederik!" She gestures for the others to come and sing "Happy Birthday!" into the receiver. Camilla joins in at once, but then Malene waves them away and carries on talking.

After lunch, the afternoon is busy. Iben writes a review of a new book called *Systematic Torture as a Method of Oppression: Chile 1973–76*, finds a translator for an article in Latvian about the classification in international law of six and a half million murdered Soviet kulaks (are they a social class or an ethnic group?), and goes on to test new software designed to help export texts to the DCIG Web site. She has also created the invitations to a talk, "The Significance of Gender During the Bosnian Genocide." As the day wears on, Iben begins to feel a little moody and wants to be left alone.

Just before going home, however, Camilla discovers a new episode of the popular radio show *Chris and the Chocolate Factory* on the Internet and turns the volume up so that everyone can listen. Anne-Lise comes out of the library and they all gather around Camilla's desk. Together they pick a few more skits, laughing as they hear Chris do his funny telephone voice. As usual, he is spinning out new reasons for skipping work.

"Right, boss . . . but you see, there's this other thing that stops me from coming in today. It couldn't be more unfortunate, almost . . . but, listen, what else could I do? Eh, boss? . . . The thing is, I've gotten stuck in my hammock. I can't fight it. I'd like nothing better than to get out of it, but what can I do?"

Malene, who has always been brilliant at voices, joins in, improvising Chris's words. From time to time she entertains everyone with parodies of the Center's clients, members of the board, or Paul at his most self-satisfied. It's one of her best impersonations. Smiling, she knocks on Camilla's computer with her knuckles and then announces: "You two learned to get on quickly. Am I right or am I right? It's a match I'm really proud of." She snaps her fingers and shakes her head lightly. "It bodes well!"

It's very amusing. Even Iben cracks up laughing.

by seven o'clock that evening Iben is the only one left in the office. At eight o'clock she drags two large bags of groceries into her apartment. She has stocked up on her staples: rice, honey, toilet paper, three packets of organic crisp-bread that was on special offer, yogurt, and vegetables. For supper she chops a handful of greens, adds seasoning and olive oil, puts in today's special—a frozen block of cod—and shoves the batch into the microwave.

So far, she hasn't done much to her apartment. The walls are still white, as they were when she first moved in. Her few pieces of furniture are either inherited or bought secondhand.

While the microwave hums she checks her answering machine. No messages. Once the oven has beeped, she opens her e-mail. There's only one new entry:

YOU, IBEN HØJGAARD, ARE FOR YOUR ACTIONS RECOGNIZED AS
"SELF-RIGHTEOUS AMONG THE HUMANS"
IT IS THEREFORE MY PRIVILEGE AND MY JOY TO
BRING YOU TO DEATH
NOW

What's this? She leans forward, reads it all again. Without formulating the thought, she instinctively knows that she mustn't touch anything.

This is a death threat. No question. Stay calm and think. There have been stories going around about journalists receiving threatening messages from neo-Nazi teenagers. Now it's her turn. Maybe.

The sender's address is "revenge_is_near@imhidden.com." The English is reasonable and the spelling is correct, which exempts just about all the young local neo-Nazis. The expression "self-righteous among the humans" is an attempt to play on the phrase "righteous among the nations," part of the citation for the highest honor awarded to foreign nationals at Israel's national Holocaust memorial. A foreigner who knows something about the history of genocide might have written that.

Her first reaction is pure sorrow, nothing more. She can feel her face dissolving, and her whole body seems to crumple.

That terrible African sun bears down on her again. It could be one of Omoro's friends or family, she thinks. Or a Luo tribesman. She feels dizzy; it's the heat and the smells. She sees the prison hut, the flies, the militia, the tall trees, and his blood. The Luos have found out what happened. They know who she is and have come here from Nairobi. She'll have to accept being killed if that is what they have decided.

She looks around. The bedroom door is open. She hasn't been in there since she came home. And she closed the door this morning.

Standing motionless, she scans the room. Nothing unusual about the stack of books or the cupboard or the bookshelves. What about her desk? The pile of papers looks tidier than she left it. Someone has been through her papers.

No sounds, except her own breathing and faint noises from the television set in the apartment below. Her nostrils feel dry, like when the hot dust blows in the wind. The air smells of the angry, sweating men, alert to danger.

She cannot tell why, but she is convinced that someone is hiding in her place.

Don't switch off the computer. Don't run to grab a coat from the hall.

Instead she walks calmly to the kitchen. She tries to convey that she is relaxed, on her way to do something completely ordinary. Takes her supper out of the microwave oven, which is on top of the fridge, next to the door leading to the kitchen stairs.

Breathe slowly, deeply.

She picks up her cell phone from the kitchen table, moves to the stair door, and opens it gingerly. No one is waiting for her on the landing. She shifts gears and flies down the narrow stairs, her feet barely touching the steps. It's important to outrun the man in her apartment, but also to be quiet enough to delay him discovering that she's gone.

She doesn't close the door, doesn't even give it a push.

She's underdressed for the crisp October evening.

The door to the yard. She stops, just a few steps away.

It isn't likely to be one of Omoro's friends. Something made her jump to conclusions. She must be sensible, ask herself who else it could be. There are plenty of suspects to choose from, she knows that. Not that it helps. Iben has always tried to forget the obvious fact that all surviving war criminals, the very ones she keeps writing about for the DCIG Web site, can access the site too. They can Google their own names from anywhere in the world and, in seconds, her articles—in English as well as in Danish—will flash up on their screens. The writer sits in a modest Copenhagen office with no special security features while her contact details—home address, phone number, e-mail address—are easily displayed.

But would an experienced mass murderer take the trouble to travel to Denmark? Of course he might. The airfare wouldn't be much for a professional soldier. And wouldn't an experienced soldier position himself right there, on the other side of the door to the yard? He'd have a direct escape route into the street, making it easier to cover his tracks. Maybe he intended to make her dash downstairs and open that door.

She listens. Not a sound.

Then a click as the stairwell light switches itself off. All too quickly, as usual. It's very dark now. But her eyes don't have time to grow used to the darkness. Above her on the stairs someone switches the light on again.

She waits for a second, badly wanting to believe that she is safe—that no one is in her apartment, and that whoever is on the top landing isn't coming after her.

The sound of heavy male boots on the stairs. Before she has even turned the lock the footsteps have reached the next landing. No time to think. If someone is waiting for her outside, she'll have to take him by surprise.

Above her the man has passed two more landings. A deep breath. Iben yanks the door open and, in the same movement, starts sprinting across the pavement.

She scrambles over bicycles and garbage cans, and over the fence into the neighboring yard. One more yard to go before she finds an unlocked gate. She runs out into a street that is not her own.

After about a hundred yards she stops to look behind her. There are people, but none of them seems to be in pursuit. Here she will be harder to spot.

Whom has she written about recently?

Barzan Aziz, a small dentist with a large mustache, who lives in a penthouse apartment and has a history of personally having taken the lives of at least 120 Kurds and many Iraqi journalists and intellectuals. Aziz strangled his victims with a steel wire, except in some cases when he hammered nails into their skulls.

Romulus Tokay, an ex-member of the Romanian secret police, was put in an orphanage at the age of eighteen months. He escaped after killing one of his teachers and is currently employed in Colombia, where his usual practice has been to hang people upside down in trees and light fires under their heads.

And what about George Bokan? He was raised in the United States and played football in college, but he went back to Serbia in the early 1990s to help fight the war. Bokan trained snipers, one hundred men at a time, in the skill of killing innocent civilians from vantage points in the hills around Sarajevo.

There are so many more. Iben has summarized the witness statements and other evidence of the activities of mass murderers such as Najo Silvano, Bertem Ygar, William Hamye, and others, who between them have killed hundreds of thousands of their fellow men. It is all on the Web site, as are her condemnations of a whole array of military units, regimes, and power-mad dictators.

Have they been hunched over their PCs in Serbia, the Philippines, Iraq, Turkey—wherever—studying her accounts of their crimes?

She looks around in all directions as she walks toward Nørrebro Street. The autumn air is cutting through her thin blouse and the sweat is beginning to dry on her skin, adding to the chill. She overtakes a pale girl with a ring through her nose, military boots, and pink highlights.

Iben dials 112—emergency services—on her cell phone and tries to explain quickly to the woman at the other end what has happened.

"Hold on, please. You say that someone sent you an e-mail and now you've run out into the street?"

"Yes . . . no. Not exactly. It was a death threat. The sender is probably a war criminal. Maybe from Iraq!"

The woman's voice is dry, tight: "This is an emergency number. It is reserved for serious calls. I have to ask you to get off the line. Tomorrow you can phone your local police station—if you still feel this matter is important, that is."

Iben tries to explain that it's her job to write about international war criminals and that the threat is not just a practical joke played by an ex-lover, or whatever the woman is imagining. But she is not convinced and replies abruptly: "You're blocking an important emergency line. That's an offense and you may be fined. I can see your number in front of me. If you don't end this call, we'll have to fine you."

Iben is about to reply when the woman hangs up.

Is she right? Iben asks herself. Is this an attack of hysteria? It would be good to think so. Then she could simply turn around and walk back home.

She's walking quickly now, keeping an eye out for suspicious-looking men. The trouble is that they are everywhere. Small gangs of swarthy men are driving up and down Nørrebro Street in souped-up cars and hanging out in the many Middle Eastern takeout places. Men in black leather jackets walk toward her, follow behind her.

Who knows how a war criminal reacts when he first reads the description of himself on a Web site? Is it a blow to his sense of honor? Might not his claim for asylum in some European country or his pending court case be affected? Some of these men would slit her throat as easily as they'd swat a fly. She has seen photos of massacred people and listened to survivors speaking at conferences. These men do not murder because they hate: even being vaguely irritated is enough.

But why should a killer take the trouble to go after her? Iben is so insignificant. Or is she? Her articles and abstracts describe events involving many hundreds of thousands of men, all experienced killers and mentally unstable. If just one of them is "irritated" enough, her fate is probably sealed.

There are no police patrol cars around, and by the time she's reached Nørrebro Circus she decides to phone the emergency number once more. She'll try to explain things better this time and insist on talking to somebody who's prepared to listen.

At that moment her cell phone rings. It's Malene. "Iben! I've tried to phone you at home. Where are you?"

"At Nørrebro Circus. Without a coat. I'm freezing." Iben begins to describe what has happened, but doesn't get far before Malene interrupts her.

"I've had a threatening e-mail too! It says I'm evil and must die. I only just opened it!"

Iben can't help shouting. "You mustn't stay in your apartment!"

Malene sounds confused. "I can't stay here? I don't know . . . I didn't take it that seriously. Should I have?"

Iben hesitates. It's a comfort that someone else has been threatened too. Everyone in the Center might have received one of these e-mails, and perhaps dozens of people in similar organizations abroad.

"Malene, I was so sure there was someone in my apartment. It could've been . . . I mean, if there was nobody in your place . . . Anyway, they could just be trying to scare us. If they really wanted to kill somebody, it'd be silly to send an e-mail first."

"That's what I thought."

Iben is perfectly aware of what her friend Grith, a trained psychologist, would say about her reaction: it is a response conditioned by her experiences in Kenya, one of exaggerated watchfulness—"hyperalertness"—which is the lasting effect of previous exposure to danger.

A thought suddenly strikes Malene: "Iben. Do you think your reaction is because of Nairobi and all that?"

"I suppose . . ."

"Listen, find a taxi and come on over. I'll wait for you in the street and pay for the cab."

"But if these people break into your apartment, they'll find both of us."

"Iben, I don't think so. Look, it won't happen."

Iben doesn't answer, so Malene hesitates. "Okay. What do you suggest then?"

"What about meeting in a café?"

"But we'll have to go back to our own places afterward."

Iben hates playing the part of the weak female, especially with Malene, but suggests that there are lots of people's places where they could crash until they have a better idea of the danger they're in.

"Oh, Iben. Okay, I'll come." They agree to meet at Props Café.

Iben feels she has been leaning too heavily on her friend, and can't quite bring herself to ask Malene to make sure that she isn't being followed.

Iben sets out toward the café, along the road by the Assistens Cemetery. Suddenly, for no reason, she starts running. She never cared for sports of any kind, despite her friends' attempts to persuade her, but now running feels right. She overtakes pedestrians on the broad pavement, where deep shadows are pierced by shafts of light from shops and passing cars.

A white car skids to a halt not far ahead, and two men jump out so quickly that a cyclist almost collides with one of them. He calls out angrily. The men shout back in reply, and Iben slips through the slow-flowing stream of cars to reach the other side of the street.

It is time to calm down and take stock. She turns to get a look at the two men. They're standing in the street talking to a third man, whom they must have spotted from the car. All three have dark sideburns and one of them wears metal-framed glasses with small round lenses.

She starts off again, jogging now. The pavement is narrower here and cluttered with a greengrocer's stall, bicycle racks, and advertising boards.

It occurs to her that the e-mailer might not have had far to travel. There are thousands of political refugees in Copenhagen, all of whom have had terrible experiences and whose family members or friends have been victimized in armed conflicts, persecution, torture, and murder. Some may have carried out acts of violence themselves. If Iben has exposed someone, this might be his response.

She feels breathless and slows down. Ahead of her is a tall, sickly-looking man with messy pale blond hair, wearing a torn camouflage jacket.

Over the last ten years, almost five hundred journalists have been killed worldwide, mostly in undemocratic states. Did any of them receive e-mails from revenge_is_near@imhidden.com? Iben hasn't heard of them being tracked down in Western Europe. Who would be well informed about this?

Gunnar would, of course.

When the traffic lights change, an old BMW accelerates, its tires screaming, and races to the next intersection. The lights turn against it and the driver has to brake again. A passerby laughs.

Iben wants to phone Gunnar right away.

She had a strange feeling about him all weekend, speculating about what his apartment might be like and his lifestyle. The fantasy of moving in with him gives her an odd but comforting sensation. She would fit right in, she felt. But how could she know?—a man whom she has met just once and spoken with for an hour at most? But then, she explains to herself, over the years his writings must have taught her so much about the way his mind works, what his favorite words are, and the nature of his thoughts.

She swerves to avoid a group of noisy teenage boys.

Then she thinks about the word "self-righteous" in the e-mail. It seems they used different words in Malene's e-mail.

Iben begins to run again.

malene

malene is in the train, on the way back from a lecture tour in Jutland on behalf of the DCIG. Her lectures have gone well, but she's used to that.

Rasmus is away on one of his sales trips, so back home their apartment stands empty. Iben is in Nairobi. She has been away for a month, and so much is happening to her that for days on end she hasn't answered Malene's e-mails or phone calls. Three of Malene's best friends have had babies during the last year; all of them have moved out of the center of town and are completely absorbed in their new families.

Nothing else for it: Malene must expand her circle of friends. There's no way she can just hang on for two more months, waiting for Iben to write or phone. Which is why Malene is getting off in Odense before going on to Copenhagen. She has arranged to see Charlotte, a contact she made through the Association for Young Arthritic People, which offers volunteer "buddies" as a means of support. They have never met, but they have exchanged lots of e-mails and spoken on the phone. Charlotte's fighting spirit is tremendous. At last they have a chance to meet.

Malene steps from the taxi in front of a small terraced house of bright yellow brick. She rings the doorbell. Sheltering under the roof of the porch stands a well-cared-for plant in an old blue enameled pan. Behind the glass in the door hangs a little wreath made of straw, suspended by a silver ribbon.

Charlotte's face is pale under her mass of blond curls. In her baby blue blouse she looks pretty but bland, like a catalog model, and completely unlike any of Malene's friends.

They smile and hug.

"Oh, how smart you are. So chic! You can tell you're from the city."

Strange to meet someone you've written to so often. Charlotte keeps smiling. Her lips are glossy with rose lipstick.

"Let's make ourselves more comfy."

Malene leaves her coat in the hall. Charlotte leads the way, moving slowly and hesitantly. The living room is too warm.

"Please sit anywhere you like. The coffee is ready."

Malene settles down on a cream upholstered armchair opposite a matching sofa. A large framed poster is hanging on the wall behind the sofa. Just as in her e-mails and on the phone, Charlotte is bursting with energy and optimism and there is something basically open and friendly about her. But Malene notices that Charlotte is finding it difficult to get over to the sofa.

"I'm sorry . . . today is one of your tough days."

"Not at all. You mustn't worry about me. I'm fine. Let's just enjoy this."

Charlotte smiles again, drawing back her small, prettily shaped lips over perfect teeth.

"But it must be . . ." Something makes Malene stop.

Her eyes travel quickly around the room. The furniture is more spread out than normal. She sips her coffee, thinking about what she sees. The gaps are the same everywhere, between chair and table, chair and chair, chair and wall. The simple answer is that this room is furnished to suit someone who often has to use a wheelchair to get about, even at home. There is no wheelchair to be seen, but it could be elsewhere. Maybe in the bedroom.

She notes that the light switches are operated by string-pulls. She has seen that kind of thing in shops selling gadgets for the disabled. People with severe joint problems find pulling a string easier than turning a switch. And what about the cushions on the sofa? There are lots, not in absurd quantities, but too many to fit in with the plain furnishings and very subtle colors of the room. The cushions, piled up, would allow Charlotte to half sit, half lie on the sofa.

It baffles Malene to find Charlotte so much more badly afflicted than herself. How can Charlotte carry out her job at Odense City Council? Why did Malene believe that they were more or less in the same shape? Discreet questioning about the job reveals that it is a specially designed post of only twenty hours per week, personally devised for Charlotte. As Charlotte speaks, Malene feels that she has heard this before, probably in one of their phone calls. As likely as not she has simply forgotten about it, the bad news being outdone by all the good, cheerful stories from Charlotte's life.

The conversation moves on. They talk about a series of documentary programs on the radio and the best way of chopping almonds when your hands hurt and how good it would be to have Wellington boots designed for arthritic feet.

It is cringingly awful. Why, Malene asks herself, do I know so little about this woman? Especially since I imagined that we share so much. I must've been chatting away on the phone without asking the right questions, without listening properly.

Charlotte snickers when she admits that she can take time off work without any questions being asked. Like today. Meanwhile, Malene has taken in other little things about this room that looks as if it is shared by a young woman and her grandmother. Woolen joint bandages lie neatly rolled up within reach, as does a collection of pop CDs. Charlotte is a couple years younger than Malene, but she has suffered from arthritis for eight years compared with Malene's six.

Still speaking as vivaciously as ever, Charlotte is describing AYAP's social calendar—the parties and seminars. The membership has such a great time together on their weekend jaunts, when they make their aching bodies play about in hotel gardens during light summer nights. Then she asks about Rasmus and Malene wonders how much she should tell.

At this point Charlotte speaks in a flatter tone, clearly self-conscious about not having a boyfriend. They have talked about it on the phone, but Malene has always assumed that it's just a matter of time before Charlotte finds someone. It can't be more serious than that. Now, watching her, Malene can see how ill she is. Maybe Charlotte will never find anyone.

Malene realizes that she has just come out with some tired old cliché to the effect that there is a Mr. or Miss Right for everyone.

Charlotte puts on a happy face and straightens up. "That's true, I know. And while I'm on the lookout, I won't waste my time complaining." She dunks a cake delicately in her coffee.

Thoughts fly into Malene's head. How do they manage, the ones who are seriously disabled? How do they endure it all without jumping off a bridge? Charlotte will never get a man and she knows it. She'll never escape this social housing hellhole. And how would I cope? I could never be so happy with so little.

Charlotte in the flesh is no different from the person who wrote the e-mails. It's just that finding her here, among her cushions and special aids, changes Malene's perception of her. For Malene, this realization is all the harder to take because of the worsening situation between her and Rasmus. As they put it in *Seinfeld*: "Breaking up is like knocking over a Coke machine. You can't do it in one push; you've got to rock it back and forth a few times." Malene has noticed that Rasmus is definitely rocking.

Soon it will be my turn, she thinks. I will smile mechanically as I tell people that Rasmus and I aren't together anymore. Never mind, I'll say, there are so many fun things to do when you're single.

She gets up, excuses herself, and goes to the bathroom. Inside, she weeps noiselessly among all the special bath aids and handles that Charlotte requires in order to be able to wash on her own. Or does someone come in to help her? Will Malene's own bathroom look like this in a few years?

Malene takes her time. She pinches some of Charlotte's foundation to pat into the skin under her eyes. Better that than have to explain to Charlotte that just being with her makes Malene want to cry.

She takes a few deep breaths and opens the door. Baffled, she recognizes the smell even before she sees Charlotte. This sweetish, resinous scent is just about the last thing she expected. Charlotte is sitting in her big armchair, puffing vigorously on a large joint.

"Oh good, there you are. I was worried. Thought I might have to blow some smoke under the door to tempt you to come out."

Malene has listened to other arthritic people speaking about the advantages of smoking hash. Drinking wine often causes stiffening and pain, and can react unpredictably with medicines. She sits back in the soft armchair and starts to munch on a little chocolate-dipped cake. Might be just as well to leap into the world of the disabled here and now, she thinks.

Charlotte hands her the joint. "The longer you hold the smoke in your lungs, the more you get out of it. Don't even think of coughing!"

"Thanks. Lots of my friends used to smoke. I've tried it too. Trouble was, it had no effect on me."

Malene inhales heartily. That should be enough to get me stoned, she thinks.

But, as before, smoking pot seems to do nothing for her. They light another joint a little later and she tries again. Still nothing, except for the sweating, and that's mostly due to the overheated room.

It isn't until she stands up to leave that she finally notices her head feels distinctly strange.

They embrace.

"Lovely to meet you at last!"

"Yes, it really was. I'll e-mail you from the office tomorrow."

"Maybe I'll mail you sooner. While you're on the train back home."

One more hug.

There isn't much waiting for her in Copenhagen: when a friend has been as supportive as Iben, you can't reasonably expect more, like her remembering to e-mail you from Nairobi. Not even if you've written to tell her that you are worried about your relationship with the man in your life.

Malene's hands and feet are tingling. Any moment now she might tip over into the unknown. Collapse in unstoppable laughter, perhaps.

If I hadn't gone out of my way to fix Iben up in that job, it would've been me who went to Africa. And then I would have had all the exciting new experiences and made all those international contacts.

Malene is crying in the restroom on the train. The cannabis has hit home and the air is bubbling up against her face. The dingy white plastic surfaces seem to float upward, the filthy gray floor too, followed by metal handles, and then signs, smells, sounds. Everything is rushing up, up, even faster, past the electrical cables. Or perhaps it's the other way around. Inside the rumbling of the train, Malene is falling.

On the Monday after Sophie's party, Malene is at her desk in the office, working on the text for three posters that will feature stories about Danish people helping Jews to escape during the Second World War. The subtext is that people should have the courage to confront any persecution of a minority, but the fact that thousands of Danes risked their lives and saved more than ninety percent of Denmark's Jews gives yet another dimension to Malene's project.

Gunnar once expounded on the subject while he and Malene nibbled olives, waiting for a menu.

"The mass rescue of Jews strengthened the sense of national self-satisfaction. All nation-states hang on to beliefs like 'This country of ours is special' and 'We're the decent ones.' The Danes simply indulge in this kind of thing more than most and they feel justified. History tells us that we're without evil, and so without guilt."

Malene doesn't want her exhibition to bolster this national lack of insight. And, as usual, Iben is full of suggestions. Malene considers countering with Gunnar's quote but decides against it.

She leans forward in her ergonomic chair, bought to alleviate the pain from her arthritis, and tries to concentrate on what she is writing. "Bispebjerg Hospital had registered two hundred

Jews as patients under false, non-Jewish names when the Germans surrounded the hospital . . ." She knows perfectly well that she mustn't allow herself to fret about Iben and Gunnar.

Iben is actually in top form today. Normally Malene is glad to have her back in the office—the atmosphere was much duller while she was away in Kenya. At first Malene had worried about her brainy friend coming to work at the Center. For one thing, with only five colleagues, it could have been slightly claustrophobic. Also, supporting Iben's job application could have ruined the friendship Malene had come to depend on so much.

The first things she had noticed about Iben when they met were her clear blue eyes and the sharp little crease between her eyebrows. In those days Iben's skin was paler and her manner more earnest. Still, it was easy to make her laugh, dissolving into the bubbling loud giggle that made her look so charming. Afterward she would compose herself quickly, ready to debate any issue seriously.

But Iben is also a perfectionist. Everything has to be well thought out, executed to perfection, one hundred percent. Anything less seems worthless to her. Apparently Iben needed therapy for panic attacks after her father's death. Malene didn't know her then, but it's always been obvious to her that Iben is fragile.

Probably no one but Malene knows that Iben can't stand having her head and body under water at the same time. Iben keeps her head dry when washing her body and remains fully dressed when she washes her hair. That has to be a symptom of something or other.

They were all astonished to learn how Iben behaved during the hostage business. She would have wanted to do "the right thing" of course, but to act so dramatically—well, that was unexpected. She said herself that she had been "someone else" in Kenya. That's why Frederik called her "Batgirl." He must have thought it was flattering to suggest that she had a secret identity. But he had enough sensitivity to see how much Iben detested the idea and stopped his joking at once.

Two years ago, for all her doubts, Malene had felt she had to support Iben for the DCIG post. All the students of literature had hoped to land jobs as editors or book reviewers or journalists writing on the arts. Instead, and regardless of how brilliant they were, they received at best low-paid freelance commissions, supporting themselves with unemployment benefits. Decent public jobs were few and far between. As Iben scouted around, her lack of office experience turned out to be a major drawback. She would come back from the employment offices with gruesome tales of graduates who had been in the system for years. They were game for anything, but would-be employers labeled them "overqualified."

"You can spot them at once. Ten seconds is enough. These guys are broken, and no sensible boss would dream of employing them. And they know it too."

When the post as DCIG information officer was advertised, Iben didn't go for it. She didn't even mention it. Instead she applied for every other job with a whiff of desperation.

Malene knew the risks when she phoned Iben and urged her to apply. "When we receive your application, I'll tell everyone how talented you are and what a hard worker you are. And I'll tell them how much I look forward to the pleasure of working with you."

"Come on, they won't consider your best friend."

"I won't tell them that. I'll say that we were students together and that I got to know you when we lived in the same dorm. And that I remember you were fantastically efficient and reliable. That's only the truth."

"We're not letting on that we're close friends, then?"

"Well, no—not close friends. But 'friendly.' "

"I still won't get the job. I'll be up against thousands of more experienced people."

"I'll brief you on exactly what you should say to the different board members in the final interview. That'll help."

Silence.

"Iben! It's a job. It's the job of your dreams!"

By lunchtime Paul still hasn't come back. Iben, Malene, Camilla, and Anne-Lise lunch together on a fresh rye loaf from the baker, two different cheeses, and low-fat liver pâté—Camilla's special. No different from so many other days.

Camilla is slightly overweight, but not so plump that she needs to wear the long, floppy tops she likes to hide beneath. Both she and Anne-Lise are hovering around forty years of age. It makes them older than Iben and Malene by only ten years or so, but there is a marked generation gap.

Camilla and Anne-Lise seldom stay in town to go out. They live quietly in the suburbs with their respective husbands and children. Things like new films or music hardly matter to them.

Camilla is talking about how much she's saving by going to the dentist in Sweden. "And if you take into account that Finn is going there too, we saved more than three thousand kroner last year." Camilla has developed her telephone voice over many years of secretarial work, and everyone comments on its cheerfulness, unexpected in an office dedicated to human tragedy. Still, optimism is important if the routine work of the Center is to be endured.

They talk for a while about a particular journalist from an evening paper who interviewed Iben about her time as a hostage.

Then Camilla is off again about the family trips to Sweden. "You see, once we've had our teeth fixed in Malmö, we go for a drive. Sometimes we simply pack a picnic and pile the kids into the car. Last time, we went to the Dinosaur Park. It's such fun . . ." She glances at Malene and hesitates. "At least, anyway . . . if you're there with children."

Malene gets up. "Now we'd better be good."

This signals that the lunch break is over. They pour themselves fresh mugs of coffee and go back to their desks.

Later that afternoon Camilla finds some new Internet clips from *Chris and the Chocolate Factory*. They laugh so hard that Anne-Lise comes out from the library to join them.

Malene has sensed tension between herself and Iben all day. Iben probably thinks that she will try to prevent her from seeing more of Gunnar. Malene decides to amuse them with a few impersonations.

"You know, I think having fun together now and then is really important. It unites people." She turns to Camilla, her voice still full of laughter. "Imagine if someone sponsored a kind of reconciliation project where stand-up comics went to entertain mixed groups of Serbs and Bosnians, just so they could experience laughing together."

Anne-Lise stands over by the library door and turns to Malene. "There are twelve million Serbs and four million Bosnians."

Malene wants to be nice to her and smiles. "Oh, it was just a thought. A bit of fun. I didn't mean it literally."

· · ·

That evening Malene finds an e-mail waiting for her on her home computer:

YOU, MALENE JENSEN, HAVE SWORN TO YOUR SECRET EVIL, AS LEADER
AND CHANCELLOR OF YOUR REICH, LOYALTY AND BRAVERY.
YOU HAVE PLEDGED TO EVIL AND THE SUPERIORS APPOINTED BY EVIL,
OBEDIENCE UNTO DEATH.*
SO HELP YOU GOD.

*DEATH, WHICH I WILL BRING YOU VERY SOON.

Nothing happens when she double-clicks on the sender's address, which is revenge_is_near@imhidden.com.

She recognizes many of the words from the oath of allegiance sworn by SS officers to Hitler, but changed so that "Hitler" is replaced by "your secret evil" and so on. She walks over to a window facing the street, looks out, and then closes the curtains.

After getting a piece of chocolate, she phones Rasmus in Cologne, but he must be in a meeting or something because his cell phone is switched off.

Instead she calls Iben. It turns out that Iben has had a threatening e-mail too and has completely freaked out. She ran out without a jacket and is somewhere on Nørrebro Street.

Malene thinks Iben's reaction is over the top, even given their place of work. It was just an e-mail, after all. She tries to empathize and calm Iben down at the same time. However, she finds herself listening for sounds in her own apartment, though she can't take herself seriously.

Going out into the cold night doesn't make her happy. She has just started the washing machine and the apartment is a mess. Still, she agrees to meet Iben at Props. Afterward she intends to sleep in her own bed; Iben can stay where she likes.

Before leaving, Malene phones Paul. He is giving a lecture out of town, but luckily she gets hold of him during a coffee break.

He seems untroubled by her news. "It's the kind of thing you expect if you're involved in anything political. You just have to learn to put up with it. Of course, we'll look into these threats, but on the other hand, don't let them scare you."

Malene doesn't feel scared. "So you've had e-mails like this too?"

"Yes."

"People threatening to kill you?"

"That's right."

"Are they sent by war criminals, do you think?"

"No, I don't. It's mostly right-wing idiots who write to me—neo-Nazis and what have you. Everyone in our kind of job gets threatened sooner or later. All you can do is ignore it."

Malene is breaking off small pieces of her chocolate bar but isn't eating any of them. "I've just talked to Iben about it. You know, about how seriously we should take the threats."

"It's unpleasant, I know. Is Rasmus at home now?"

"No, he's in Cologne. At a trade fair."

"That's not so good."

Malene doesn't answer. She can hear the voices of Paul's audience in the background.

Props is nearly empty. It's too early in the evening. A couple of years ago, Malene and Iben started going to Props, where most of the regulars are men, often creative types with slightly haggard faces. Many have made a pass at Malene across the café tables, which look like relics from a 1960s summer house.

Iben waves Malene over.

Even before Malene has a chance to sit down, Iben starts speaking urgently, as quickly and matter-of-factly as if she were at work. Her voice cuts through the low Steely Dan number that's playing in the background.

"Listen, I've rung Camilla and Anne-Lise. Camilla hasn't received one of the e-mails but Anne-Lise wasn't in. And I phoned Lotta and Henk from the Swedish and Dutch genocide centers. Neither of them has had e-mails like the ones we received, and they don't know of anyone who has." She smiles a little, holding a warm cup of coffee with both hands. "Then I contacted Anders and Karen at Human Rights and Svend at International Studies. And Paul . . ."

"I called Paul too."

"I know. He told me. After you called, he phoned his wife and asked her to check. He hasn't got e-mails like ours. It looks like you and I are the only ones."

Malene had wanted to hug Iben because she'd been so scared, but the stream of words gets in the way. Instead she hands over a sweater she has brought and goes to order another coffee for Iben and a glass of white wine for herself. The two of them agree that Paul would be the likeliest target for a war criminal's threats. Paul is constantly in the media spotlight and signs most of the Center's public statements regardless of who drafted them. So why hasn't he, or someone else prominent in the human rights sector, received the menacing messages?

They try to think of a war criminal they have exposed on the Web, one Paul hasn't mentioned publicly, but no one seems to fit the description.

At a corner table two men in soccer jerseys start arguing loudly. Iben holds her line of thought, and blinks, turning to scan the darkness outside the large window that looks onto Blågård Street. Malene can't help following Iben's gaze, but there is nothing to see. Iben is definitely not herself.

Wearing Malene's coffee-colored sweater, Iben leans forward. What she says gives little away about how she feels. You must watch her eyes and mouth instead.

"Here we are, good people with university degrees. Day after day, we're off to our jobs at the Center or the Institute for Human Rights or Amnesty International or Doctors Without Borders. We discuss the news during our lunch breaks and water plants and put up posters for UN special days. And we don't realize that at any moment we might have to fight torturers or executioners or militia bosses. Because, although we never think about it, we're soldiers at war."

Small muscles twitch around Iben's mouth, indicating, as Malene knows, that what she is saying is paramount.

Malene feels a surge of warmth toward her friend and proposes a toast: "To us. Women at War."

Iben responds eagerly, as if Malene has just uttered the phrase she had been searching for. "Yes, that's who we are! Women at War. We've never realized it until now. None of us ever thought about herself that way . . ."

Iben has said it so loud that the two men in soccer jerseys turn around to look.

"We're not much good at warfare, though. We're so easy to find on the Internet. If notorious war criminals want to know what's been written about them in the media, they can find us, no problem."

It sounds to Malene as if Iben truly believes that her life is in danger. She seems to be going through many of the same feelings Malene has endured for years, ever since learning about her illness. Malene feels more connected to her old friend than ever before. She smiles and says she's going to get another glass of wine. This time Iben wants one too.

Back at the table, Malene quickly checks the dark street outside once again. "Why now, do you think?"

"Because we've challenged somebody."

She sits up straight. "That's it. Someone thinks we're making a difference. Enough for him to feel uneasy."

Malene wants to call Rasmus and goes outside to escape the music. Blågård is a quiet pedestrian street. She looks around for Iben's men with swarthy faces and a military bearing. There are dozens of them. At this time of evening the street is full of immigrants gathered in small groups, almost all of them male.

Rasmus replies this time. He's in a taxi, taking a few clients to a bar.

Malene tells him about the e-mails and Paul's advice. She adds that Iben is taking the threats much more seriously than she might have expected. "I've never seen Iben like this before. At least now she seems ready to admit that there was no one in her apartment."

Two years younger than Malene, Rasmus has a laid-back, boyish style that makes their age difference more pronounced. Nevertheless, he is sensitive to her moods and able to shift instantly from being narcissistic to being supportive. "If only I were at home with you. We could find out more about this together."

They talk for a few more minutes. Malene feels happy because she has someone special to lean on, but she's aware that if she discusses her concerns—even her illness—for too long, Rasmus becomes restless. She hates to thinks about it, but he seems to have less and less patience.

"Would any of your IT specialists know how to trace a sender?"

His voice becomes animated at once. "Actually, I know quite a bit about that. If your sender is smart he'll have e-mailed via an anonymizer site. If he has, we won't be able to trace him so easily. But let's make sure. E-mail his mail header to me. You should be able to find his IP address if you right-click on the mail. Choose Properties and then Details. If he uses a fixed Internet link, we'll have him cornered. If not, it will give us the name of his service provider, so we'll know which part of the world he's mailing us from—unless he uses an anonymizer site, that is. If he does, we'll write a spyware program and send it back to him by using Reply. If we do it right, the spyware will pick up his personal details and mail them back to us."

"Is it hard to write spyware?"

"Don't worry. We'll try it when I come home." Rasmus doesn't sound eager to get off the phone, but he has to go. "We'll track down this lunatic, no problem."

In the café the music has changed from Steely Dan to Gotan Project. Iben has been in touch with people in England and France and is feeling energized. "They all send their regards."

"Thanks."

"And they had loads of ideas about who might've e-mailed us. I borrowed a notepad from the bar and began a list. Here, look." The list already has more than twenty names.

Malene sits down. "I don't know where to begin."

"Let's move to an Internet café."

Malene hasn't finished her wine, but she understands that collecting information is Iben's way of dealing with stress, so she drains her glass quickly.

While they're getting ready to leave, Malene's cell phone rings. It's Lotta from the Swedish Study Program on the Holocaust and Genocide.

"Iben called me earlier. Her phone has been busy so I thought I'd try yours. I wanted you to know that I've phoned around. Nobody seems to have received any e-mails. That's all, really. Except everyone I spoke to came up with people who might have done it. Do you have pen and paper handy?"

Malene adds to Iben's list. "Thanks. That's great."

"You're welcome. Take it as a thank-you for your article. It was great."

"What? Which article?"

" 'A Guitarist from Banja Luka.' About Mirko Zigic. We had it translated and printed it in our weekly paper."

"But Iben wrote it."

"She did? I thought it was you."

"No, I didn't. She did." Iben must have left out her byline in the Word version of the article. Then it hits her what the mistake means. "Christ!"

"What's the matter?"

Malene has to make sure. "Lotta, that article, is it on your Web site now in my name?"

"I think so. I mean, what we publish in print instantly goes onto our Web site as well. Automatically. Not that I—"

Iben interrupts. "Tell me. What's happened?"

Malene needs to sit down, but somewhere else, where they aren't visible from the street. Holding the phone, she puts her arm around Iben.

"Iben, I'm so very sorry. In Sweden your article about Zigic was put on the Internet under my name."

Iben backs away. "I see. Now we know. It couldn't be anyone else, could it?"

Malene doesn't like the tone of her voice. "No."

"Mirko Zigic is the only one we've both written about."

A GUITARIST FROM BANJA LUKA

Old friends of Serb war criminal Mirko Zigic
still cannot grasp that their schoolmate is wanted by
the International War Crimes Tribunal at The Hague.

■

BY IBEN HØJGAARD

"Mirko was a guitarist in the band and composed most of their music," says Ljiljana Peric, who was at secondary school in the same class as Mirko Zigic.

"No question about it, he had something special. He believed he could make a living as a rock musician after leaving school. His band played a kind of intense, poetic guitar rock that only became the 'in' thing a few years later. He was good, and we all wished him well, but no one really believed that he'd make it apart from the boys in his band and a handful of groupies."

Ljiljana Peric is a political scientist from Serbia who attended the Oslo conference "Strengthening Democratic Media in the Aftermath of War." Our hotel rooms were on the same floor, and, chatting in the elevator one afternoon, Peric touched on her early friendship with Mirko Zigic. Zigic has been charged with war crimes and is wanted by the International War Crimes Tribunal at The Hague.

We agreed to meet in the hotel bar that evening, and that I would bring my tape recorder.

THE GOOD YEARS: UNTIL 1990

That evening, Peric began by describing the high school in Banja Luka, the town where she and Zigic grew up.

"It was a large school, with more than a thousand pupils, and was built in the 1970s. Mirko was good-looking, and had a mane of blond hair and a thin face that made him look like a rock star. He arranged gigs in cafés and bars, not only for his own band but for others too. He might have made it if the fashion for U.S. grunge music had arrived a few years earlier and not when the war started.

"I used to gossip about him with my girlfriends. Some of them were crazy about him. And I have such a clear image of Mirko putting up posters for concerts that he had arranged himself. He was so passionate about music, always insisting that everyone should subscribe to his favorite music and not waste time on dumbed-down pop.

"We were a mixed school—Serbs, Muslims, Croats—but we never paid much attention to ethnic divisions. After the economic crisis of the eighties the future looked bright for young people. The Yugoslav economy was buoyant and the country politically independent of both the Eastern and Western Blocs. Lots of people went shopping for clothes in Italy and traveled to places like Budapest for concerts or theater. The recent Communist past meant that tickets were much cheaper.

"In 1990, one year after we had left school, there were occasional TV reports about small paramilitary groups stopping cars at roadblocks to check identity papers. It seemed to be happening only in the countryside, so we figured it must be gangs of peasant blockheads who had nothing better to do than play soldier. Nobody I knew even imagined it might be a precursor to war.

"But only a few months later, the war began. Suddenly, these stupid peasants morphed into real soldiers. The TV news was full of massacres, one after the other. The broadcasters would advise viewers several times a day to send children and old people out of the room because they were about to show Serb bodies that were decapitated or half decomposed, floating down rivers—that sort of thing."

THE PROPAGANDA

"These images made us very sad and angry, of course. We all shared a desperate wish to help, to do something.

"This was Serb-controlled TV, and just when the viewers were at their most upset and vulnerable, the screens would fill with war propaganda. We were told that Muslims and Croats were on the rampage, killing Serb civilians, reminding us that this was a repetition of what happened during World War Two when 'they' murdered four hundred thousand of 'us.' We watched this kind of thing day in and day out.

"Naturally we discussed what was going on, but the Serb government had a tight grip on all information. Then one day a Muslim friend of mine said: 'Ljiljana, listen to yourself. Do you realize what you're saying? How do you know? Who says that this is what's really going on?'

"I had to admit that the propaganda had affected me. I, who had felt so sure of seeing through their lies! I decided to avoid the official spokesmen from that day on and stopped watching TV, listening to the radio, or reading the newspapers—but it's hard to do when your country is at war.

"Not everyone had friends who could help them hold on to the truth. Anyway, before long, our generation was scattered all over the world. People escaped to Britain, Scandinavia, Italy, the United States. Not just Muslims and Croats, but young male Serbs who wanted to avoid military service. Many of our young men were called up and others volunteered. The majority of us could not understand what went on in the heads of those who went willingly to war. Still, Mirko wasn't the only one who did—far from it."

IT MUST BE A MISTAKE

"The war went on and on. Tens of thousands died, neighbor turned against neighbor, and old friends informed on each other, leading to imprisonment or execution. It was incomprehensible. We couldn't trust the radio or the television, yet endless stories made the rounds.

"We heard about Mirko by word of mouth. What was said about him was different . . . well, even worse. As a squad leader he had turned up with his men at the home of his Muslim second cousin and raped her. He killed her afterward. And he'd cut the ears and the tongue off a young Serb soldier who had talked about deserting.

"None of this was reported in the papers, of course, but the stories kept coming. They'd always begin with something like 'Have you heard what they're saying about Mirko? That he . . . ?' Even then the talk was about the kind of crimes he's now being charged with at The Hague. He was said to have asked for camp duty purely for entertainment. He would make prisoners rape and murder each other and he would watch, with that big, bold grin of his.

"A friend of mine has another female friend who knew Mirko well. Her boyfriend, a Muslim, had been sent to the Omarska camp. One day a man phoned her—she's sure it was Mirko. The voice on the phone asked how she was. Then he told her he held a hammer in his hand, that her boyfriend was with him in the room, and, because she was going out with a Muslim, she should stay on the line and listen hard. She listened as her boyfriend was beaten to death. He was screaming. She felt sure that she recognized the voice. It was impossible, she said, to put the receiver down.

"We heard these things and couldn't make sense of them.

"Mirko was still only twenty-one years old. We, the women who had stayed behind, discussed the rumors. I argued that the more frightening he came across in these stories, the more people would want to back out of the war. Maybe he was inventing lies, sacrificing his reputation in order to save innocent people.

"We all wanted this to be true. Wanted it so much."

DO YOU EVER SEE ANY OF THEM?

"One day, some two years after the beginning of the war, I met him in Banja Luka, on the pedestrian street called Gospodska Ulica.

"It was a bright, sunny day. Everything looked so peaceful. One of the cafés on the other side of the street was playing dance music. The air smelled of cement dust from the restoration work at the Serbian Orthodox church. Trucks were rumbling to and from the site.

"Mirko was still slim but more muscular. He was wearing stonewashed jeans and his hair was as long as ever. He stepped out of the door of a shoe store. No escort of soldiers or military insignia in sight.

"He looked pleased to see me. I felt I shouldn't let him hug me, but he did. I told him what I'd been doing, speaking quickly. I didn't want any gaps where I'd have to ask what he had been doing.

"There were no telltale signs in his face—he might have had a job in insurance or sales or something completely ordinary like that. Then he asked: 'Do you ever see any of them—people from the past?'

"The saliva seemed to dry inside my mouth. A chill ran down my spine. I looked away. These few words were worse than anything I'd ever heard.

"I'm a Serb. I wasn't in any danger, but I had to leave at once. Even today I cannot understand how, from that moment on, I knew that everything they said about him was true. I spent the rest of the day crying and several more phoning old friends telling them I'd seen Mirko. I had to find release for the pressure inside me. It was like the strain you feel when a friend suddenly dies."

OTHER SOLDIERS

Ten years after these events, Peric was still deeply affected. We sat in silence for a while.

She asked me about my work at the DCIG. I found it impossible to resist trying to put her account into a theoretical context. Several researchers connected to the DCIG are currently working on studies of men who have engaged in genocide.

Christopher Browning has carried out one of the major classical investigations into this type of behavior. We have described his work in an earlier *Genocide News* article called "The Psychology of Evil." Browning based his observations on a study of five hundred ordinary German men who had been sent to Poland during World War II and, once there, had been ordered to kill Jews. These are his findings:

- 10–20 percent applied for other tasks and were transferred, usually without any problems;
- 50–80 percent did not apply for other tasks. They carried out the killings they were ordered to do, but stopped afterward;
- 20–30 percent started killing more Jews than ordered, and carried on murdering when off-duty.

This last group of men might go straight from pubs or cinemas to the Jewish ghettos, where they'd use the inhabitants as targets for shooting practice. Often they'd go on a spree of torture, rape, and murder.

But statistical data do not capture what drives an individual. What are the men like who manage to avoid such tasks? And what about the men who seem prepared to take the killing farther than they were commanded? We spoke for a while about the mystery of cruelty.

Peric told me about another boy from their year at school who had volunteered together with Mirko Zigic.

"Predrag wanted to be an engineer, but that's out of the question now. At school he probably looked up to Mirko. After volunteering, they were placed in the same paramilitary unit, but no Predrag stories ever circulated in Banja Luka. When he was sent home nine months later, his head was shaking as if he had Parkinson's disease.

"Predrag never spoke much after that, and refused point-blank to say anything about Mirko or their wartime experiences together. Friends made him see a doctor, but his tremor was incurable. Of course, we all knew what the cause was. Many of the returning soldiers suffered from strange medical conditions."

AFTER THE WAR

Before meeting Ljiljana Peric, I had read about what happened to Mirko Zigic just before the Dayton Peace Accord. He had been dismissed from his paramilitary unit and emigrated to Russia, where he linked up with Slav extremists, possibly with the Mafia as well.

Until recently, it was generally thought that active participants in genocide do not have any trouble distinguishing between the time for killing and the time for peace. This assumption is based on studies of German perpetrators, which show that after the end of World War II these men had no higher rates of criminal convictions than other men. In other words, although in wartime some men will shoot a civilian in the street for not greeting them properly, in peacetime they are as capable as anyone of controlling their behavior. Among German war criminals the notable aftereffects included nightmares, concentration deficits, reduced work capacity, and high incidence of suicide—but not increased criminality.

However, it's now clear that one should not generalize on the basis of the post-Holocaust findings. Presently, war criminals in the former Yugoslav states show a significantly higher rate of violence and criminal acts, and many have joined the Mafia.

Banja Luka, the biggest town in the recently declared Republic Srpska, was only approximately fifty kilometers from the Prijedor concentration camps. Peric had tried to avoid meeting Mirko Zigic after the war, but saw him about from time to time.

"Mirko's skin had changed. It had cleared up since his teenage days, but it looked oddly rubbery, almost as if it were coated with wax. His teeth used to be in poor shape, but now they were white and regular. I assumed that he wore dentures, even though he was not yet twenty-four. He tied his long blond hair back in a ponytail and had a full, traditional Serb-Orthodox beard.

"I would turn down a side street the moment I spotted his tall figure, but I knew sooner or later I wouldn't be able to escape his company. Some of our mutual friends would invite him to parties without warning the rest of us."

IN THE COMPANY OF FRIENDS

"You must take into account that before the war we all went to the same parties—would-be victims as well as would-be executioners. We tried again after the war, but the atmosphere was so strange. For instance, radio stations played music from the seventies and the eighties only. And in many other ways we behaved as if the nineties hadn't happened. The parties were part of that: trying to avoid the past.

"I realize, of course, that we have to look forward and rely on old friendships in order to build a new nation. It's just that people have very different limits of how far they'll go to maintain an acceptable social atmosphere. I mean, you might be hanging out in the kitchen at three o'clock in the morning, chatting away to some men, and then, suddenly, you realize that they were in the White Eagles or one of the other notorious paramilitary units.

"The first time I found myself face-to-face with Mirko in a crowded room was shortly after a new rumor had started making the rounds. Apparently he had killed two Croatian journalists after the war. A friend and I left the party to go and sit in a garden a few houses away. Unlike many others at school, I was never in love with Mirko, but the woman I was with had once been his girlfriend.

"One thing I asked her was 'Do you remember how we would quiz girls about the boys they were going out with—how could they stand this one or that one? And they'd say that the boy was different when they were alone together: he'd be relaxed and was so sweet and kind that we wouldn't recognize him. Was it the other way around with you and Mirko? We all thought he was a sweet, poetic kind of guy, and only cared about his music. We took for granted that you two had a wonderful time together. Did he change when you were alone? Show a completely unexpected side?'

"She said that he didn't."

THE NEXT MORNING

Peric had something to add when we met the following morning.

"I've listened to those who say they always knew what Mirko was really like. It's what they want to believe now that they know the truth. I used to go on bicycle rides into the woods alone with him. Now that I know he's a rapist I would like to think that I had sensed a deep flaw in him, but the fact is, I didn't."

anne-lise

It's Monday morning. Anne-Lise arrives at the DCIG and steps into the Winter Garden. She tries to clear her head and sound cheerful and friendly.

"Good morning."

Camilla is the only one in. Her eyes are fixed on her monitor. "Good morning."

With her coat over her arm, Anne-Lise stops and looks about her. The library door is closed as usual. The only sound is the faint hum from Camilla's computer.

Camilla keeps staring at the screen, and Anne-Lise walks off to the library. She hangs up her coat and checks her hair in a small mirror she keeps inside a cupboard. It looks all right, but she goes over it with the brush all the same. It is dark and carefully cut in a pageboy style, which covers the sides of her broad jaw, but her face still looks too square. She bends closer to the mirror. The skin under her eyes hasn't aged more than you'd expect in someone almost forty.

She picks a few hairs off her black turtleneck sweater and has a quick look to make sure that there are none on her camel-colored skirt. She's ready to start work.

From the beginning one of her main tasks has been to scan the keyword lists at the back of every volume in the library and use a text-recognition program to turn them into Word files. After editing the lists, she enters the keywords into the library database. She is deep into her work when she hears Malene arrive. A few minutes later she hears Iben's voice.

Anne-Lise knows from the talk last Friday that Malene and Iben were invited to a party. She walks into the Winter Garden. "Hello. How was the party?"

Malene replies, but looks at Iben. "It was okay."

Anne-Lise sees that the others have little plates, each with a fresh buttered roll. There's also a tray with an extra roll, butter, plate, and a knife.

"Oh, look, fresh rolls! Did you bring them, Camilla?"

"Yes."

"Is today special?"

"No."

"Thanks. I'll bring some next Monday."

Anne-Lise butters one half of the spare roll. Holding her plate, she takes a few steps toward Iben's desk, but Iben is engrossed in something on her computer.

Anne-Lise stands motionless for a few seconds. Nobody takes any notice of her, so she walks away, back to the library.

She tries to put her mind to the next keyword editing job. There is a neat stack of reports to the right of her on the desk, and each one has to be checked to make sure that the keywords are relevant. She starts with a report describing the massacre of at least two thousand Muslims in India.

She can hear the others chatting now and, sure enough, they're discussing the party. It's hard to follow what they're saying from behind her closed door. Anne-Lise concentrates on the screen to block out their voices. The computer lists the keywords "electric," "food," and "sex." Far too general. She quickly looks through the pages of the report, corrects the keywords, and extends them to enable searches on specifics such as "electrical shocks to the sexual organs," "rotten food," and "sexual violation."

Iben's voice is louder now, and what she is saying sounds important. Anne-Lise hurries to the door. She must become familiar with what they're talking about or else she'll be lost when they chat later over lunch.

The Winter Garden is full of animated talk. They're joking about one of the journalists who interviewed Iben when she came back home from Kenya. Iben says that she kept asking her about what they were fed in captivity.

When the others have said their piece, Anne-Lise tries to join in. "Was it because she was doing a feature on food?"

"No, not at all. No matter what I said, she wouldn't let go. Back she'd come with another question about the food."

Iben looks impatient, but Anne-Lise carries on. "And did she write about it for the paper?"

"Yes."

Iben turns back to her computer.

Anne-Lise glances at Malene. Is she looking this way? No. One more try. "I suppose you felt differently about reading interviews after your own experience?"

Iben clicks again and again, scrolling through a file. Anne-Lise still does not want to leave. After all, Iben often keeps working while she speaks to other people.

But Iben turns to Camilla instead. "Camilla, do you remember that e-mail they sent us, with the new French links? Do you have it?"

"I do."

"Could you mail it to me, please?"

"Sure. You'll have it in just a moment."

All three of them stare at their screens. Anne-Lise fiddles with things she finds on a shelf next to the fax machine.

"I shouldn't ask you any more questions, should I?"

Iben looks up and smiles for a fraction of a moment. "Of course you should. It's fine, Anne-Lise—but later, when I've got time to explain. Right now my head is full of things I have to do."

Back in the library, Anne-Lise hears them laugh. Malene has said something funny.

Anne-Lise has mentioned quite a few times that she'd like to be in the Winter Garden too. In the beginning Paul used to tell her that he thought it was a good idea, but after a while he backed off. It would be impractical, he said, blaming lack of space and problems with telephone lines and computer connections. He added that it would be better if her workplace was close to the main book collection.

She thought that the real reason was that the others had conspired to keep their cozy threesome. Presumably Paul had asked for their opinion.

Anne-Lise's first day at the DCIG was just a few days after the death of Malene's aunt, and it had seemed natural enough that they shut her out back then. She had assumed that it would get easier the longer they worked together. Now it seems that the barriers will never come down.

Paul had emphasized that Anne-Lise should go into the Winter Garden whenever she liked. He repeats this every so often and she takes him at his word, even when it makes her feel awkward.

During the lunch break, Camilla echoes Anne-Lise's question and asks Iben if she feels differently about reading interviews after having been interviewed herself. Iben responds at length.

Some days, usually after a holiday or a nice weekend, Anne-Lise steps into the office naively hoping that things will soon change for the better. As recently as yesterday evening she told Henrik that she felt much more able to cope, and that she would try to have a proper conversation with everyone. But most of the lunch break is spent discussing Swedish dentists. Three hours into the workweek and already Anne-Lise feels limp and dull. Still, she steels herself, making one more effort to join in.

She picks up on something Camilla has just said. "Isn't it expensive to drive to Malmö? The bridge tolls, I mean. You know, something happened to me when . . ."

She turns to Malene, and just as she is about to continue, Malene interrupts and talks past Anne-Lise to Iben and Camilla. There is no opportunity in their three-way exchange.

Anne-Lise can't take any more.

Lunch is over and she walks down one of the remote passages behind the library's East European collection. At these times she always brings her compact; her face must not show that she has been crying.

Twenty minutes later she returns to her desk. Once again, Anne-Lise makes up her mind to ignore them for the rest of the day.

Obviously, an individual can't ostracize a group. Most likely, they won't even notice, but that's not the point. She has to protect herself, especially today. After work she has to prepare a special birthday dinner for Henrik and she must have enough energy left for their guests.

She throws herself into her work. There are reports waiting to be scanned, Word files to be transferred into the database, and keywords to be checked.

She makes her own coffee in the kitchen to avoid using the thermos in the Winter Garden. After a while she phones Henrik, wishes him a happy birthday, and talks to him for a little longer, using a tone of voice that betrays a hint of what she's going through. It helps her to think that he understands her situation.

Since Malene is the Center's contact person for everyone using the DCIG facilities, including all library borrowers, Anne-Lise works alone and almost exclusively with archival tasks. Boxes full of documentation pour in steadily, and there are few chances to talk to anyone during an ordinary working day.

Anne-Lise phones a colleague in the Strasbourg genocide library, whom she met during a course about the HURIDOCS cataloging system. She tells him that she has come across a reference to an article in a UN report that would interest him. She mentions other reports and keeps talking, spinning the conversation out.

He listens to her. She hopes that he won't notice that she's drinking in his every word. Talking to him will keep her going for a few more hours. She needs a friendly voice to mask her colleagues' silence.

Afterward Anne-Lise turns her attention to proofreading. The German, Spanish, and English observers have reported the torching of Nigerian villages, and the perpetrators' names must be checked and cross-referenced. The text-recognition program has recorded their names, but just one small slip could lead to confusion later.

Malene comes in to collect some volumes, carrying a growing pile of books around with her. Still buoyed from her conversation with her Strasbourg colleague, Anne-Lise smiles at Malene, but Malene leaves the room without saying a word.

Anne-Lise stops working. For the umpteenth time she starts filling out another job application. As she types, she realizes that she's losing control.

I shouldn't be feeling like this, she thinks. They're turning me into a different Anne-Lise. This could've been the perfect job. She imagines each tap on the keyboard as if it were a knife plunging into Malene's body. Or Iben's.

Malene! Anne-Lise screams inwardly as she hits the keys as hard as she can.

But this is not the real me.

· · ·

Toward the end of the afternoon the Winter Garden is alive with laughter. One of the computers is running *Chris and the Chocolate Factory* audio files.

True, Anne-Lise had decided to stay away from them for the rest of the day, but the last time they listened to *Chris*, all four of them had had so much fun together. Anne-Lise had joined in their jokes and laughed along as if it were all perfectly normal.

The familiarity did not last, but that evening she had met Henrik in the driveway.

"We had a really good laugh together today!" She went on to say that it looked as if the others were coming around at last. Wasn't it good that she had stuck it out despite everything?

Later Henrik copied a CD with *Chris* episodes that a colleague of his had recorded from a morning radio show. Anne-Lise had put the CD in her handbag and it was still there. There had been no opportune moment to tell the women about it.

Chris's voice is coming from Camilla's computer.

Iben and Malene stand at Camilla's desk. Anne-Lise joins them, trying to act natural. When Malene does her Paul imitation, Anne-Lise laughs. Then she turns to the others. "I have a CD with *Chris* episodes that aren't on the Internet. Would you like to hear it?"

"Sure! Why don't you go and get it?"

"Great idea."

She goes to the library and when she returns with the CD seconds later, Iben and Malene are already back at their desks.

Anne-Lise stops. "Oh, you're busy now. We should listen to it another time?"

Malene looks up. "No, no. Put it on, by all means."

"But are you still in the mood?"

"Of course we are. Put it on."

Anne-Lise loads the CD onto Camilla's computer. Camilla has pushed her chair away to leaf through a document folder. Anne-Lise turns to look at the others. The atmosphere has changed. She should never have gone ahead—not now when they're all back at work.

Camilla is looking up at her expectantly.

Anne-Lise selects track eight, an episode that she thinks is the funniest. She presses Play. "I hope you'll like this one."

It's a brilliant sketch, but no one comes over to listen and no one laughs. Now and then Camilla looks up from the documents. Malene and Iben are studying their computer screens.

Anne-Lise keeps standing at Camilla's desk. After another thirty seconds, she speaks. "I'll stop it now. You're not listening."

"No, don't. Leave it."

"But you're not enjoying it."

Malene swings around to face Anne-Lise. "I always work while I'm listening to something."

Now Iben looks up. "This is where we work, you know. We're meant to get things done. It can't all be fun and games."

Anne-Lise lets the CD run. She remembers listening to some of these episodes at home and how she and Henrik were practically crying with laughter. In an attempt to work and listen as the others are doing, she turns the pages of an American journal, but she's unable to absorb a single word. When the episode ends, she presses Stop.

Camilla puts down her folder. "Why did you do that?"

"I'm taking the CD out. You're all too busy just now."

"Don't. Leave it."

"But you aren't listening."

"How would you know? I was."

"But . . . not properly . . . you're all . . ."

Iben punches hard on the Enter key. "I was listening too. You said you wanted us to hear it. Why are you changing your mind?"

Malene looks up and sighs. "Anne-Lise, please. Do stop whining."

The next track starts. Once again they are deep in their work. Nobody utters a sound.

they've chosen to invite only their immediate family and a couple who
are old friends. Anything grander to celebrate Henrik's birthday
is not practical—not on a weekday night. Even so it should still
be quite a party, with a total of eight grown-ups and seven children. It's such a challenge to serve a good dinner that suits
everyone.

Once home from work, Anne-Lise went straight to the
kitchen and now, with the guests due to arrive in three quarters
of an hour, Henrik has joined her. They send the children off to
play in the garden, but Ulrik and Clara are too excited and keep
running back into the kitchen. To keep them occupied, Anne-
Lise gives them a game of garden ring toss so she and Henrik
have time to prepare the food.

Their idea is to stick to an autumn menu. Anne-Lise cuts up
root vegetables for the soup while pieces of bacon for the gar-
nish are frying in a pan. Henrik washes the mushrooms for a
casserole, one of his famous signature dishes, which will go
nicely with the venison steaks. He's bending low over the sink,
and his thin six-and-a-half-foot frame makes him look out of
place. They have talked about getting another sink that is higher,
but it's pointless, since he is seldom in the kitchen.

It would help Henrik more if he could change the way he

sits at work. Spending sixty hours a week in the bank has meant that his posture has grown steadily worse.

While he chops the mushrooms, Henrik natters on. "I've often fantasized that I'm a guest at a dinner party and find that Malene and several of her family and friends have been invited too. When the hostess tells me that I'm seated next to Malene, I reply that I don't want to sit anywhere near her. I say calmly, but loudly enough for everyone to hear it, 'I'm so sorry—anyone but Malene Jensen.' And the hostess will wonder why. What's wrong with dear Malene, so young and talented and pretty? And in such a fascinating job as well."

Anne-Lise looks up from her work. Henrik is still wearing his office clothes: white shirt and neatly pressed trousers. There's a concerned frown on his face.

"I'd have to explain and I would. I'd say, 'It's offensive, I know, but I simply could not bear having Malene next to me at the table. If I can't sit away from her, I shall have to leave.' In my fantasy, the other guests become anxious and stare, but I'm not bothered. In front of these people, who all think they know her, I continue: 'Every day at work Malene torments my wife, Anne-Lise. My wife is developing problems with stress as a direct result of Malene's behavior. I would rather sit beside a drug-addled gangster. She's so mean and selfish. She may appear to be well educated and privileged, but she clearly couldn't care less that her behavior is making our entire family suffer.' "

Anne-Lise tips the chopped vegetables into the blender. "You don't think I'm a bad mother, do you?"

"No, no. Not at all! You know that. But what if Malene is really making you physically ill?"

She pulls his face down close to kiss his cheek quickly before she adds the celery to the blender. "Do you think you would truly do all that . . . what you just said?"

"Certainly."

"Something tells me that the guests would still believe that Malene is a wonderful person. And you'd never be invited back."

"They wouldn't take kindly to it, of course. At dinner parties you're meant to behave yourself and make polite conversation. It's at home and at work that people show their true colors. I suppose people must think she is a fine woman."

Clara has come in, complaining that Ulrik has hit her.

Anne-Lise takes the sizzling pan off the burner. "Did he hit you? Show me where it hurts and I'll blow on it."

Clara sobs, but it doesn't sound that bad.

Anne-Lise and Henrik have lived together for nearly twenty years, but waited longer than most before starting a family. Anne-Lise wanted to give Henrik space and time to satisfy his youthful ambitions and capacity for hard work. If they waited, she'd thought, they would both have more time to enjoy their children and their home life. Many years passed before she realized that Henrik would never change. It was a stark choice for her: would she take on the whole burden of raising the children or resign herself to being childless? She made her decision and has coped well, feeling that she has grown as a person. Henrik is working at least as hard as she does. He has had a meteoric career as an economist with a major Danish bank. It is thanks to his income that they were able to buy a large house and turn it into the home they had always wanted.

"But even if I were never invited back, they would have something to think about. Afterward, they might see Malene differently, and maybe it would occur to them to wonder about her now and then. 'What does go on inside her head when she's not having a good time? When she's not dressed up and smiling at us? God knows. Is she really a witch, as that man claims?' I'd do the same to Iben and Camilla. They all deserve it."

"I had no idea that you've been dreaming about revenge on my behalf."

"I haven't. I only want to tell the truth. They're ganging up against my lovely wife."

Clara is allowed some of the berries set aside for the dessert and runs out to Ulrik again. Anne-Lise returns the frying pan to the stove.

"Henrik, what can I say? You paint quite a picture!"

A knock on the door. Children's voices in the driveway.

Anne-Lise calls from the bedroom. "You open it. I'm not quite ready."

She throws herself on the bed. She hasn't had a minute's peace since she closed the DCIG door behind her this afternoon. She looks up at the white ceiling. Such a large, smooth surface, like a glacier. She stretches out her arms. The white bedspread follows her movement and the folds form a pattern. It's like making angel's wings in the snow.

As if I were dead, she thinks. The thought is meaningless.

Ulrik rushes into the room. Her fragment of peace shatters. She gets up and helps him find a plastic lizard that he wants to show the other children. Then she walks downstairs.

"Lovely to see you!"

"Many happy returns! Thank you for asking us!"

"Of course. We're so pleased you could come."

Their cheeks are glowing as they step from the cold autumn evening into the golden lamplight of the hall.

"What a tempting smell!"

"I do hope you'll like it."

The children are jostling to get their coats off in the small hall. Mette bends to hand her son two little parcels. "Now, off you go to find Ulrik and Clara, and give them their presents."

The adults, still trying to deal with their own coats, keep bumping into each other.

"Sorry!"

"Don't worry. Here, have a hanger."

"Oh, Henrik, hello! Happy birthday!"

"Thank you. We wanted to wait and have a big party, but when neither Lotte and Michael nor Rikke and Morten could make it for the next two weekends, we thought . . ."

"Happy birthday! And, for you, a small token . . ."

"Thank you! That's very nice of you."

Henrik leads the way into the living room, where he offers everyone a glass of white wine.

Anne-Lise stands in front of the hall mirror. Her body is still tense. This is how she feels each morning when the alarm clock cuts into the middle of a dream. Even in her sleep, she can sense that something is wrong. Soon everything will fall apart.

But she is at home, and she's awake. She must force herself to believe that the Center isn't the only reality. Her anxiety stays with her, however, as she joins the others.

Henrik raises his glass.

"Cheers—and welcome!"

Upstairs the alarm clock ticks away on the small gray bedside table. The dream will end, and soon she will be walking through the dark morning to face another day.

Training to become a librarian was something that had appealed to Anne-Lise partly because she had so many happy memories of going to the library as a child. Every evening, when her parents closed their grocery store, she would go to bed in her room over the shop and read long, difficult novels. She'd always dreamed of a job working with books.

After school, she used to help out in the shop. She was embarrassed that their items were more expensive and of worse quality than those in the supermarkets. The customers were mostly old folk or neighbors picking up a last-minute ingredient just before supper, or her schoolmates wanting cigarettes and sweets.

Many of her school friends came from well-to-do homes, and most of them went on to study law, economics, or business, in line with the family ambitions. Anne-Lise didn't want to decide her future that way.

Not until Henrik's banking career took off had she experienced wealth. Now old friends would make remarks such as "It must be such fun to have a lot of money." And it was fun; but Henrik's success also led to arguments, especially because Anne-Lise never cared for the lifestyle that many of Henrik's colleagues considered appropriate for the wives.

The soup has turned out well. It's just the right consistency, thanks to her last-minute addition of Jerusalem artichokes. The venison steaks are perhaps a little too well done, but they still taste good with the mushroom casserole. And Henrik's special selection of red wine suits the main course to perfection. The children have wolfed down fish cakes and fried potatoes at a separate table and are already off to play. Anne-Lise's mother leaves the table to find out what they are up to. The adults propose toasts, drink, talk, and laugh.

Anne-Lise goes to the bathroom. She takes three cotton-wool pads from a clear plastic bag hanging on the side of the cupboard, pulls the pads apart, and rolls the woolly fluff into small, hard balls.

The dessert is a Spanish-style custard layered on top of forest berries.

Mette, who is married to Henrik's brother, leans forward to speak to Anne-Lise across the corner of the table. "How's work?"

"Fine. I'm busy, but it's good to know that what you do matters. This week alone we've had requests from Buenos Aires and Rome, as well as from New York and Brussels, though that's not unusual. Lots of other inquiries too. And the project leader who takes most of the calls was away lecturing on a couple of occasions, and so I was the one who—"

"Henrik said the other women don't always . . . you know, treat you right."

"He said what?"

"Well, that it could be hard at times."

"What exactly did he say?"

"Please . . . nothing special. Just that sometimes you were fed up when things didn't go well."

"I see. And was that all?"

Mette glances apologetically at Henrik, who's looking alarmed.

"It was like this," she says, speaking more rapidly than before. "I was telling Henrik about one of my superiors who is being difficult. He's out to get me, you know. And Henrik said that it's normal to have problems with people at work. At some point when we were talking about how common it is, he said that, to him, your colleagues seem extremely unpleasant. He also said that you're very, very good at your work and have always treated them as pleasantly as you can, but they don't talk to you."

"It isn't that bad, you know."

Anne-Lise looks at Mette, and then at Henrik. She's unable to organize her thoughts enough to let her sister-in-law know that she hasn't said anything wrong. Instead she stays very quiet. She smiles at Mette but can feel the corners of her mouth start to stiffen into a grimace.

She knows what has happened. It is the office atmosphere—its sheer nastiness; she has dragged it home and is inflicting it on these innocent people.

She has to get away.

Henrik hurries after her and catches up with her at the top of the stairs. She pulls him into the bedroom and slams the door.

"Everyone judges each other by how well they do in their jobs. And they believe it's your own fault if you're doing badly. I don't need my friends to think that I can't get on with my colleagues."

"Of course they don't think that."

"No? I'll tell you, they do! Right now some of them are wondering if it isn't Anne-Lise who is being difficult, Anne-Lise who is trouble. She's an oddball."

"I'm sure you're wrong."

"And I'm sure I'm right. I trusted you and confided in you and now you've betrayed that trust. Why don't you tell everyone your own secrets instead?"

"Anne-Lise . . ."

She throws herself on the bed and buries her head in her pillow, though no tears come. "All I want is just one place where I'm free to be myself, where I'm not marked down as a lousy, boring librarian."

"Nobody ever called you anything of the sort."

"If people don't respect you they start treating you like dirt."

She feels Henrik stroking the back of her head and neck.

"Darling, calm down. Please forgive me for mentioning it. I'll never, ever look down on you. Neither will our children, nor our friends. That just won't ever happen."

two policemen stop Anne-Lise when she steps into the lobby of the DCIG building the following morning.

"Where are you headed, madam?"

The policemen seem so serious, she thinks someone in the building has died. Their manner affects her.

"I work in the Danish Center for Information on Genocide."

"Do you have any identification?"

"Of course. But could you tell me what this is about?"

The men speak without emotion: there have been threats against the employees of the Center.

"Is anybody hurt?"

"Nothing like that. But you'd better speak to our colleagues. They're in your office right now."

They let Anne-Lise pass. She hurries along to the elevator and phones Henrik on the way up, but he's not in his office.

No policemen on the landing. No guard at the door to the Center. Anne-Lise steps into the Winter Garden. Camilla is just coming out of Paul's office, and when she sees Anne-Lise her face lights up as if she were about to hug her colleague out of sheer relief.

"Oh, Anne-Lise! There you are! We had no idea where you were."

"I only—"

"Come in here! We're all in Paul's room."

The others are seated around Paul's conference table. Two police officers are at the head. One of them has a sensitive face that reminds her of a teacher in Clara's nursery school, and the other one looks older and is presumably more senior. Iben makes room for Anne-Lise by shifting a pile of folders with data on East Timor.

"We tried to get in touch with you last night. We phoned several times, but you weren't in and you hadn't turned your answering machine on. And then when you didn't turn up at your usual time . . ."

"I was just a little delayed. I'm so sorry, I had no idea."

Now Paul takes the lead. "You see, we were quite worried about you, afraid that something might have happened. Listen, did you get one of the e-mails?"

Anne-Lise's colleagues are all staring at her with interest. That's new.

"E-mails? No. What do you mean? Anyway, I was at home last night."

"You were?"

"Yes. It was Henrik's birthday."

Anne-Lise sits down. Iben flips through her address book and realizes that she has the wrong number for Anne-Lise.

Iben turns to the policemen. "Well, so far it looks like only Malene and I have received these messages."

Anne-Lise pours herself a cup of coffee while Paul explains what happened and Iben elaborates.

"It was only when we found out that the e-mails had probably been sent by Mirko Zigic that the police—"

The older of the two officers interrupts. "Interpol is looking for Zigic. We hope there might be a chance of picking him up here in Denmark."

Apparently Iben and Malene spent hours in an Internet café last night but found nothing to lead them to Zigic. The e-mails were sent via an anonymizer site and are impossible to trace. The two look exhausted, especially Iben, who has deep shadows under her eyes. Even so, they appear to be bursting with energy—on an adrenaline high. Their eyes seem to be urging everyone, even Anne-Lise, to stick together.

The police have given the office a preliminary once-over and have checked Iben's and Malene's apartments, but so far they have found no clues. They ask general questions about the women's work at the DCIG.

About half an hour later the older policeman begins to tap on the table. "That's it for now. We can't do much more at present. The investigation will be handed over to the computer crime unit here in Copenhagen."

Iben shoves away a pile of photocopies. "I see. So you're leaving?"

"That's right."

"And what if Zigic turns up here?"

"Two of our men are downstairs, guarding the door. They know the score. Don't worry."

They stare at him.

"I can assure you that it is highly unlikely—extremely unlikely—that Zigic would come here. If he does, he'll be doing us all a good turn, because then we can put him away."

Iben refuses to be reassured. "Are you telling me that the two guards downstairs know all about arresting an experienced mercenary? A mass murderer who's personally killed and tortured hundreds of victims?"

The younger officer nods calmly. "You're obviously upset, but please remember that men like Zigic don't bother to e-mail their victims first before assassinating them."

"Sure. He'll just sneak up behind his victim in the street without warning . . . like Olof Palme's killer, right?" Malene interjects.

The older policeman looks at Malene and pushes his mug of coffee out of the way. "That was a problem handled by the Swedish police. Bloody tragic. But a Swedish case."

He begins to pack his briefcase. "We're all busy people. My colleague and I have to get back to the station. If there are any new developments, call the computer crime unit."

The door closes behind them.

The five employees stay on in the conference room to talk about the situation.

Iben speaks without her usual composure and repeats herself several times. "Of course the cops are right. This isn't serious."

But something has changed.

Anne-Lise scans the others for signs of fear. What about Camilla, Paul, and Malene? Are they really scared? Or are they playacting as well?

They talk about the risks and about who, apart from Mirko Zigic, could have sent the e-mails. For much of the time they are simply making the same points again and again, and after about an hour, Paul gets up.

"You all stay here. I understand that there's a lot for you to talk about. The trouble is, I simply have to go. I have an appointment at the Foreign Affairs Ministry. Fill me in later if you come up with something."

Camilla looks up with disbelief. "Paul! You're not leaving?"

"That's the idea. Is there a problem?"

"But think of the danger!"

"Come on, I don't think anything bad will happen."

Iben interrupts. "It seems to me that we should regard this as a very serious matter."

Paul's face looks grave and he sits back down on the edge of his chair. "You must believe me, I am taking it seriously. Honestly. Very much so."

He studies each face in turn. Anne-Lise enjoys the attention.

"However, what that police officer said must be true," Paul continues. "No experienced soldier would bother e-mailing his victims before murdering them. The sender's aim is only to scare us. Maybe to distract us from our work here, which seems to me to be the real danger. We can't let it happen."

He stands up. "Anyway, continue talking. I don't expect you to do much more than that today. Later this week, we'll get up to speed again."

They stay seated around the table and discuss options for protecting themselves and catching Zigic, aware that there is something faintly insulting about Paul's manner. It was all very well for him to say, "I understand that there's a lot for you to talk about," but then he made it obvious that he personally hadn't the slightest need to talk. Does he think that they need to sit about empathizing all day just because they're women?

They decide to try to concentrate on work.

Back in the library, Anne-Lise phones Henrik. "They actually looked at me!" She can't get over it. "And spoke to me as if I were really there. No barriers!"

Henrik is pleased. "Heartfelt thanks to whoever sent those e-mails."

She twists the phone cord around her finger. "Shush."

Everyone in the office knows that the one thing that can disturb Paul's unruffled demeanor is the prospect of another meeting at the Ministry for Foreign Affairs, since the outcome of such visits determines the DCIG's ability to grow and its future existence. Although the Ministry for Science,

Technology, and Development pays its running costs, the Center is an independent organization and has to raise money for its projects, publications, and conferences by applying for grants from private and state foundations. One way or another, a substantial proportion of its finances can be traced back to the Ministry for Foreign Affairs.

Paul carries a heavy responsibility. To avoid layoffs, each year he must convince the Foreign Affairs Ministry that the Center is effective enough to justify their approval for new project funding. As he has told his staff, that isn't his only problem. The men from the ministry might well decide that the DCIG is *too* effective. It could occur to them that it would be desirable, all things considered, to shift the DCIG maintenance grant to their ministry. True, at first glance it might not seem to matter which arm of the government supports the Center, but Paul knows better.

The working briefs of the DCIG and the Danish Institute for Human Rights are very similar. The DIHR is an independent organization too, but its fixed costs are paid by the Ministry for Foreign Affairs. The day may come when some young, inexperienced civil service advisor sees the advantages of making the DCIG part of the DIHR, with its hundred or so staff members. The upshot for Paul would be the loss of his special claim to give television interviews. And according to Paul, the DCIG's duty to inform the public about genocide issues would be undermined.

Yet as far as anyone knows, today's meeting at the ministry is not particularly important. Apparently Paul is out just to make a good impression.

Anne-Lise spends the rest of the morning unpacking parcels of printed matter from abroad and recording their contents.

By lunchtime Paul still isn't back. The women have their usual lunch in the small meeting room, except the bread is stale because no one could face breaking the police cordon to buy fresh rolls.

Camilla hardly eats a thing. She looks defeated, her arms hanging limply by her sides. "But what if it isn't Zigic? It could be one of so many people, couldn't it?"

Iben replies energetically, quickly swallowing the last bite: "You're right. The other day I tried to arrive at a figure for how many men known to have participated actively in genocides are still alive. Fifteen million, at least! More than three times the number of men alive in Denmark today. If you count people who've backed a killer at some point, the number is much, much larger—maybe several hundred million. That's like the entire population of Europe. Or the U.S., for that matter. So, Zigic or no Zigic, there's no telling who else might have been provoked by what's on our Web site."

Malene gives her a puzzled look.

Iben answers her question before she's even asked it. "I calculated a ballpark figure like this: one million in Rwanda, and about the same number in Sudan and Cambodia. At least five million in China, and three million in Russia. Then pool all the rest."

Iben turns to Camilla. "Something happens, changes, inside most men in wartime. Did you read the three reports on genocide in Bosnia by Stjernfelt that appeared in the *Week* a few years ago?"

"No. I didn't."

"Basically, it was the same story over and over again. A woman meets a nice man, her family likes him, and she feels safe with him. She has no inkling about the dark side to his character; neither has he. Probably. Anyway, no one would have guessed what he was capable of. Then the war begins."

Anne-Lise has often thought that Iben, rather than Malene, should be the one who does lecture tours. Iben always becomes so absorbed in what she is saying.

"Then, one morning, his wife gets out of bed only to find him gone. Maybe there's a note telling her that he has gone to join some obscure military unit or other. If she's lucky, he will return to her and the children. It could take a few years, or just a few months. By then she will have heard that he has been shooting at civilians or herding people in front of execution squads or torturing prisoners. He might well have raped women and then killed them, or robbed houses and burned them down. But there he is, back home, ready to pick up his normal life where he left off."

"Then what happens?"

"I've written about it many times. For instance, in the Zigic article. Some men simply shrug the whole experience off. 'That was during the war,' they'll say, and settle into peacetime life as if rape and murder couldn't be farther from their minds. Others never let go of the past. They've changed."

"Are you saying that all men have a kind of war button? Like, you press it and they start murdering?"

"Put that way—yes, I am. Not all, but most men. It's a fact. If you don't believe me, just check out our library. Isn't that so, Malene?"

"Yes, it is."

Camilla is silent, but looks distressed at the turn their conversation is taking.

Iben is still fired up. She takes a slice of chorizo from one of the boxes and squeezes the plastic lid back on.

"I'll tell you a story. When I was little, we had this dog, a German shepherd called Max. All the children in the street liked playing with Max, and at times it couldn't have been much fun for him. We'd pull his tail or poke him in the eye by mistake, or stick our fingers into his mouth, but he put up with it. Max had been with us for years when we took him for a long walk one day. We let him off the lead because we knew he always came when we called." She hesitates.

"Anyway, that day we set out to walk in a nearby stretch of woodland. Suddenly Max was off. Calling him had no effect. When my father finally found him it was in the much larger adjacent wood. Max had killed a young deer and was wild with excitement. There was blood all over his head. He had never seen a deer before in his life, but he knew what to do. He had run the animal down and leapt straight for its throat."

Camilla listens, her mouth hanging open.

"We spoke to the vet about what had happened and he said that Max was dangerous now that he had experienced bloodlust. Hunting and killing had changed him. In a way, he had become another dog. We realized that we were more to blame than he was, but there was nothing else we could do. My mom and dad had to ask the vet to put Max down. All the kids in the street cried."

Iben and Malene exchange a quick glance. Anne-Lise realizes that Malene has heard all this before. After the break she and Iben will go into the kitchen or the copier room to talk privately.

Camilla has pushed her plate away. She looks at Iben. "So what you're saying is that men are like the dog in your story?"

Malene leans forward over the table. "Iben thinks that we're all a little like animals, don't you, Iben?"

"In some ways, yes, I think we are. We should have known better and not let Max run free in the woods. It was instinct—he couldn't help himself."

There is something about all this that appears to make Camilla more excited than Anne-Lise has ever seen her before. She has dropped the charming voice she uses on the telephone. "So you think Mirko Zigic is one of these men. We're to feel sorry for him, because he's got this instinct for . . . say, hanging people upside down from branches?"

"He's a frightening man, regardless of his motivation. Just like Max became a frightening dog, particularly around children."

Anne-Lise enters the exchange for the first time. "If there's something in men that makes them all potential murderers, then is it present in women too?"

Iben replies: "It might be . . . but you never read about all-female militias rampaging through the countryside, killing and looting and burning everything to the ground."

Camilla grasps a fork in her hands as if she's trying to bend it. "In a way it sounds to me as if you are defending the man who has threatened to kill you. Or all of us."

"All I'm saying is that these men are victims of war as well. War reveals something inside them that normally would have gone undiscovered. When the war ends, they're probably just as shaken as the survivors. In shock, if you like, wondering 'What happened? What did I do?' "

Camilla quickly looks around the group. "Well, it doesn't make sense to me to compare the suffering of the executioner with the suffering of the people he has killed."

Malene sighs demonstratively. "Here we go. Back to the familiar old debate: 'How much of human behavior is due to instinct and how much to free will?' "

Iben snaps at Malene: "Old debate it might be, but I can't recall us ever talking about it."

Malene seems confused.

"From a purely ethical point of view it's important to hang on to what the victims have a right to demand . . . Oh, forget it; I don't know where this is going."

All three have a new edginess to their voices. Is it fear of Mirko Zigic that has caused this tension? Whatever it is, they are different. Wilder.

Anne-Lise feels like retreating to the library. She senses that in a moment one of them could lose control and every chance of reconciliation between them would be lost.

Camilla puts the fork down. "What I'm hearing, Iben, is that you feel that everyone is a victim—rapists, the lot."

"I suppose I do."

"And a man who rapes in peacetime—what about him? His basic instincts are getting the better of him too, right?"

"All I'm saying is that I've been surprised by how many men seem to have this built-in tendency—something that's normally suppressed."

"And that means that we should pity them, does it? Be supportive and offer them therapy sessions because they've nobody to talk to about the women they've raped?" Camilla's usually gentle voice is tinged with anger. "We're talking about men who might kill us!"

"Let's not talk about them then."

Malene speaks quietly. "Iben wants to understand every point of view, regardless of whose it is."

Silence.

"Iben thinks that Zigic has gone underground someplace, maybe here in Copenhagen, and is agonizing away. You know, like . . . 'I've raped my friends' wives and daughters. I've painted the Serbian eagle on the walls of their houses using body parts dipped in their blood as my brush—but hey! Does that make me a bad human being?' "

Malene starts to laugh at her own irony, but nobody is smiling. "He would be utterly . . . disoriented."

"Yes, of course."

Malene glances at Iben sympathetically, then she looks at Camilla. "If we think he is in any way 'normal,' then imagine what it must be like to live with all that and have no one to talk to about it."

Anne-Lise suddenly senses that something is being aimed at her. She wants to get up and leave, but being included by them is what she has always wanted.

Camilla interrupts Malene. "No way would I let him talk to me, that's for sure! I'm prepared to try to understand lots of people and make allowances, but that kind of thing—no, that's where I draw the line."

Iben is more direct. "I wonder, is his loneliness getting hold of him? Maybe he's simply writing these e-mails because he's so isolated? Maybe we could make use of that?"

Anne-Lise pushes back her chair. As she stands up, Malene's words reach her. Softly.

"Perhaps it's only people like us who have this need to talk. Someone like him might not feel the same way."

Malene's eyes rest calmly, almost amiably, on Anne-Lise.

Anne-Lise turns to go but remembers that she should do her part in clearing the table. She reaches for one of the dishes and watches Malene smile blandly.

"But then, we're clearly different from some people. Speaking for myself, I could never bear to work the way you do, Anne-Lise. You know, alone all day long, year in and year out."

malene, Iben, and Camilla sit together in silence. They're waiting, their hands lying on the table. How will Anne-Lise reply?

Holding the small dish with cheese and liver pâté, Anne-Lise stops, her eyes glued to the tabletop. She mumbles an answer, so low that it is hard to grasp what she is saying: "I feel the same way as you do. I'd like to have someone to talk to."

The responses come in a rush. "What do you mean?"

"You have us to talk to, anytime you like."

"We're here for you."

She can't see how she can answer them, how she can be friendly and honest at the same time. She cannot allow the smallest crack in the wall of lies she has built to protect herself, or the truth will come flooding in—the real truth full of anger and tears and howls of hatred. She can no longer imagine a constructive way of being truthful.

Anne-Lise remains silent.

Malene apparently takes no notice. She addresses the other two. "We know that Anne-Lise doesn't work closely with anyone else. Not the way we do."

Iben and Camilla join in, their voices confident and confiding.

"She can't chat the way we do when we're sitting at our desks."

"But that's hardly our fault."

"Come on, nobody has said that it's anybody's fault."

"Anne-Lise, you know you can always come and join us. It isn't as if your office is shut off, is it?"

"But somehow it sounded as if we'd done something wrong."

"Oh, no. No."

"Anne-Lise, what do you really mean?"

"Do you think we don't want to talk to you? It sounded a bit like that."

"You don't think that, do you? You know you can always come to see us, don't you?"

All three of them are looking at her. Anne-Lise summons all her courage to speak. She almost spits out the words, enunciating each one crisply: "You three are such good friends. Clearly that is why you speak to each other in a different way from the way you speak to me." She stares at the plate in her hand, then at the lunch table. The smell of the food is getting to her.

Malene smiles. "That's true. Iben and I are old friends and that's—you know—different from being friendly with people you work with."

Again, their words pour out almost in unison.

"Naturally."

"People who work together should treat each other well—that goes without saying. But that's quite different from being close friends."

"I've come to the library loads of times to ask if you wanted something, like when I was going the bakery or the supermarket."

"And when we take a break we always tell you."

Iben leans forward and her face has an earnest expression. "We don't always remember to go to the library and tell Anne-Lise if we're having an interesting discussion. We probably could do better, couldn't we?"

Anne-Lise's throat tightens. The conversation isn't over yet.

Malene looks at her and raises her voice just enough to be heard above the other two. "Now, you must admit it's understandable if anyone talks more with a close friend than with a colleague?"

Camilla won't let go either. "There's no way we can work out how much it means to you if you don't tell us. Many people really do prefer to keep to themselves."

Malene nods pleasantly at Camilla. "I'd like to hear what Anne-Lise has to say."

Anne-Lise realizes that she needs to pee. Her voice is faint. "Yes . . ."

Malene is staring straight at her with genuine interest. Anne-Lise finally tries to say something, more to herself: "Yes, of course I understand."

She knows when she tells Henrik about this he will be irritated with her for backing down.

The others continue to protest their innocence to each other.

After a while Anne-Lise tries to add something else. "Maybe I'd rather not be so . . ." She thinks of Henrik and tries to finish her sentence with conviction. "Well, it matters to me that I'm supposed to keep my door shut."

Camilla suddenly stands. With both hands on the table, she leans toward Anne-Lise. "What's this? We've been through it before, Anne-Lise." Camilla takes a deep breath and looks at Malene and Iben for support. "We agreed! And I don't want to go over it again!"

Iben makes a small gesture for Camilla to sit down, but Camilla hasn't finished.

"I won't put my health on the line just so the door can be left open. I simply won't!"

Iben gently replies. "But Anne-Lise didn't say that the door has to be open. She's only saying it makes a difference to her that it's shut."

Anger is bringing out red spots on Camilla's neck. "I've read all about it. It's the drafts you don't notice that are the most dangerous. Drafts can make you an invalid! Force you into early retirement!"

They all pause, waiting for Anne-Lise to speak. It's too much. Outside the sun breaks through the clouds, suddenly brightening the room.

She opens her mouth, but the words don't come. Suddenly she's aware of pressure behind her eyes. She manages to keep the tears back, but her hands and arms begin to tremble. This will not do. She can't just sit here, speechless and shaking.

The others are exchanging looks.

Oh, they'll be able to use this against her, all right. From now on they'll say she is mentally unstable. She has never trembled like this before, as if she were an alcoholic or a drug addict.

Her words come too quickly: "And then there's the whole thing about the library users, the fact that I'm not allowed to talk to them. If I could, it would make a difference. In other libraries, researchers contact the librarian. I thought I'd be the Center's librarian and people would come to me. I didn't think I'd just be doing archival work. That's what they told me when I was interviewed . . ."

Malene interrupts. Her voice sounds truly caring, warm and reassuring. "Anne-Lise, if you feel like an outsider here, it's good that you've told us. We can do something about it now. I must say that I don't believe it's the only reason you feel so unhappy, but even if this place isn't as bad as you think, we still need to work something out. You mustn't feel so bad. You can be absolutely certain that we all want to help you."

Anne-Lise raises her head and sees Malene look quickly at the other two, who are nodding nervously.

"I think you've made such a good start by telling us about how you've been feeling. Maybe the next thing to do is to arrange a meeting with Paul and decide on some changes together. How do you think that sounds?"

"It sounds like a good idea."

"Great! We'll do everything we can to turn this office into a good place to work."

"Okay." Anne-Lise can't hold on any longer. She is crying quietly now. The sudden kindness has overwhelmed her.

Malene has more to say. "But the changes mustn't be at the expense of the people who use the Center."

"No, of course not."

"It's what you said about having contact with the users that's so problematic. There must be plenty of other things that we could do to make you happier. The users like having one person who handles all their needs, you know, from appointments to events and research projects. And that includes book requests."

Anne-Lise hears her own voice. High-pitched, almost a shriek. "But they don't always like it! They often want me to help them."

"No, Anne-Lise. That's not right. If someone said they preferred to speak to you, they would be passed on to you at once. No question about it."

"But you told Camilla off because she transferred Stephan Colwitz's call from Geneva to my phone."

"No, I did not."

"When you were ill, I spoke to him. I dealt with his question and then after you came back, he phoned again and asked Camilla to put him through to me. It was about some books he was interested in. And then I heard you reprimand Camilla. You said she mustn't do that again."

"Anne-Lise, maybe you should go home. You're not well. It's like some kind of breakdown. What you're saying simply isn't true."

Anne-Lise's skin feels damp all over. She turns to Camilla. "Camilla, didn't Malene tell you off for putting Stephan Colwitz through to me?"

Camilla has been on the edge of her chair all this time. Now she leaps up and lashes out at Anne-Lise. "You can't turn this place upside down just to suit you. It isn't your office. You have to consider the rest of us as well."

"But Malene has told you that you mustn't transfer people to me when they ask for the librarian, hasn't she?"

Camilla looks at Malene. "I can't take any more of this. I've had enough."

Malene almost throws herself off her chair and walks away. In the doorway, she stops, turns to Anne-Lise, and sneers: "I could reel off hundreds of examples when we've paid particular attention to what you wanted. You couldn't have found a place where your colleagues treated you better; it simply doesn't exist! When I think of all the time I spent explaining your tasks to you and the research problems and—"

"But they weren't part of my training! Why do you always give me jobs that you know I haven't been trained for? It took me four years to become a qualified librarian. Can't you just let me get on and do what I'm supposed to do?"

Iben cuts in: "Many people are only too pleased to have a variety of tasks at work."

"But . . . I'm knowledgeable about books. Here, all I'm doing is filing, as if I were a secretary."

Malene makes a point of glancing apologetically at Camilla before turning to Anne-Lise. "That wasn't a very clever thing to say."

Iben backs her up. "Secretaries are important too."

"I know. Why do you keep telling me?"

"Because you said . . ."

"But . . . you knew what I meant . . ."

Suddenly Camilla runs off. She has heard the phone ring.

The others follow her more slowly. Halfway out of the room they pause, as if to add something. But they don't.

Anne-Lise sits still, breathing heavily, her arms resting on the table. She looks at her arms and blinks several times. This lunch break will come back to haunt her. Everything. Her shaking—they will use that against her as well.

malene

malene remembers the times when she was little and came running home after playing with one of her friends. She would rush straight into the living room where her mother, Jytte, would be seated. Her mother's friend, Susan, would be there too, always in the same place on their plush brown velvet sofa. Her mom would tell Malene to go off and play somewhere else, upstairs or in the garden. Malene remembers glimpsing her mother's wet cheeks as her mother would stare past her friend.

When Malene mentioned this years later, her mother explained that to protect her daughter she would normally cry about her work in the bathroom or in the bedroom. She only wept in the living room when Susan was there.

Malene's mother was a secretary in a large accounting firm, and her father was an insurance man. Both of them worked in Kolding. Malene was the only one in the family to go to university.

Her mother had been with the firm for about ten years when the office came under a new administrative head. Malene's mother had been responsible for staff schedules, but he took that away from her. He allocated lower-grade secretarial work to her and managed to find fault with everything she did.

After a few weeks the boss started to tell jokes at her expense, even when she was present. He also made it clear that people who didn't laugh along irritated him, hinting that soon one of them would become the butt of his jokes.

Gradually people became anxious when she was around. They began to avoid eye contact with her, and her very presence in the office seemed to create tension and make the whole atmosphere unpleasant. Not long after that, several people took her to task, regardless of whether the boss was there or not.

Then came the news that the boss had been promoted. He had moved to another branch office. Once more, Malene's mother wept, but this time with joy. There were celebrations at home and Malene's father opened a bottle of port that had been in a cupboard since the previous Christmas.

Jytte's work life, however, did not change. Everyone still felt awkward the moment she came through the door. They all hoped that she would leave quietly and find another job. It soon became clear to her, and to others as well, that she had lost her old easy manner.

Her doctor referred her to a psychologist, but she never worked again. Young Malene felt dreadfully ashamed when her mother spoke self-pityingly about it in public, even in front of people she barely knew.

"At my old job, they used to behave as if they wanted me dead. How can people behave like that?"

Camilla is sitting at her desk. Iben and Malene are standing close together so that they can't be overheard in the library. The lunch break is over. None of them had expected to be attacked by Anne-Lise in the middle of such a stressful situation.

Malene plays with Camilla's stapler, snapping out flattened, useless staples.

"It's fair, isn't it, that I show more affection toward my best friend than toward a colleague? Isn't that the point of having a close friend? What does she expect?"

Iben strokes Malene's arm comfortingly.

"Instead of offering us something we can base a friendship on, she simply demands favors. It's so immature, like a spoiled child."

Malene keeps glancing back and forth between Iben and Camilla. Both appear as worn out as she feels. She can hear how tired her voice sounds.

"I don't think I've ever met a person who's so incapable of giving a little of herself."

"It's typical of her attitude. It's like this thing she has about not working in the library. I mean, is she a trained librarian, or isn't she? What did she think she was supposed to be doing here? Doesn't she want to work with books and have her desk where the books are?"

Malene sighs. She sweeps up the flattened staples and throws them into Camilla's wastepaper basket. "Anne-Lise simply has no idea what it's like when your colleagues are really out to get you. That much is obvious."

Malene tells Camilla a little of what happened to her mother. "You see, that's why I find Anne-Lise so especially hard to take. She has accidentally hit on something that really hurts me."

Iben interrupts her. "But, Malene, it's not because you're more vulnerable than most. Anyone would be upset to have to listen to that kind of thing."

"Yes, you're right."

"And it's even more infuriating when it comes from someone we've all struggled to keep happy."

The door to the corridor opens. Anne-Lise announces that she is going home. She has a headache. Malene is so annoyed with her that she can't even make herself look up. No one speaks.

Then Malene decides to say something. "Get better soon."

From the landing they hear the faint whining noise as the elevator goes down. Iben begins to pick her words slowly.

"Now we know . . . why she always comes across as devious. And why all of us have found it difficult to get along with her. It's because, in her warped view, we're nothing but a band of bullies who want to bring her down."

"It's unbelievable. How long do you think she has hated us beneath all those smiles, always pretending everything's fine?"

Camilla looks up at the others. "How did she keep it up . . . lying to us every single day? I can't imagine being that insincere month in and month out."

Suddenly Iben sounds more collected and serious. "But maybe that's exactly what she didn't do."

"What do you mean?"

"Maybe she couldn't stand lying to us forever. Maybe she has been burning up inside and felt she had to find an outlet."

The other two are silent.

"An outlet, for instance, of sending us e-mails?" Iben suggests.

The others see her point at once.

"If Anne-Lise sent the e-mails last night, she might have felt guilty today. To deal with that, one obvious strategy would be to prove to herself that we're all nasty—worse than her. Which could explain why she lost control just now at lunch."

Camilla adds a thought. "She didn't seem the slightest bit nervous this morning when she heard about the e-mails for the first time."

The idea makes sense to Malene too. "It's obvious that she hates Iben and me the most. It would also explain why Paul hasn't had one."

Of course, it's only hypothetical. Still, it doesn't *have* to be Mirko Zigic or some other mass murderer who sent the e-mails.

Malene realizes that she isn't furious with Anne-Lise, although she ought to be. The others feel the same way—she can see it in their faces. More than anything, they are relieved. Iben doesn't have to crash at Grith's apartment again tonight. Malene won't find it as difficult to fall asleep as she did the night before. A confrontation with trained killers—now that would be a life-or-death matter. But an office conflict, that can be sorted out.

The front door opens. The doorway frames a man with a muscular neck, wearing a safari jacket. The women freeze. But then they realize he's not threatening them.

Malene smiles. "Hello! How did you get past the police downstairs?"

"Police? What police?"

"Didn't two guards stop you in the downstairs lobby?"

"No one stopped me. I came here because your Web site shows that you've got Ben Kiernan's book about Cambodia, *The Pol Pot Regime.* I'd like to borrow it, if possible. And I'd be grateful if you could recommend more reading about the Cambodian genocide."

They look at each other.

He explains: "I need it for senior-year teaching."

Another moment of silence.

"So, if you have any introductory teaching material, I'd like to have a look at that as well."

The Center's users mustn't be worried by internal problems. Malene walks toward the visitor.

"Please come in. Let's see what we can find. We have a great deal on your subject. You know about the book by Marcher and Frederiksen, don't you?"

"Yes. Do you have it?"

"Of course. And we have quite a few files of unpublished teaching material. I've read it all and it's very good. Let's go to the library and have a look around."

Malene is ready to lead the way.

Iben gets up. "I think I'd better go downstairs and find out what's happened."

The teacher is curious and well read. Malene speaks about Cambodia, trying to sound relaxed. She tells him about the lectures that DCIG staff offer free of charge. She could come to his school.

While they talk, her mind strays. She tries to understand Anne-Lise, but can't recall ever having been hard on her. On the contrary, she has always been friendly and professional. Right? They have always told Anne-Lise when they are taking a break, even though she can be such a wet blanket. Everyone has tried to be pleasant to her, but, after all, other people should have a good time too. And there's work to be done.

She goes on to speak about a recent DCIG seminar on Cambodia with Chandra Lor as the lead speaker. Lor, a genocide survivor, was the first head of the Tuol Sleng Genocide Museum in Phnom Penh. His story is miraculous. In the 1970s, government troops and guerrilla forces killed almost 3.3 million of the country's 7.1 million population. The Pol Pot regime exterminated practically everybody who had either a family relationship with the previous government or simply an education. Chandra Lor was the son of a deposed senator and a university student. The video of the seminar shows Lor speaking about his daily fight to escape death. The teacher could show it to his pupils.

Malene hears Iben return and excuses herself for a moment.

Iben confirms that there are no policemen at the door. She intends to call the number the two officers gave them and ask what's going on.

Malene goes back to the teacher. They start chatting about Western European communism. In the 1950s, Pol Pot and some of the top men in his government were students in Paris, and their views were strongly influenced by the French Communist Party. Should the French Communists accept a share of the guilt for the Cambodian tragedy? She pulls out a book of photographs from the Tuol Sleng Museum collection. The building was once a notorious prison. The photos show the primitive instruments of torture and the prison cells. Many of the cells were windowless and so small that the prisoners could neither lie down nor stand.

Iben interrupts them, apologizing to the teacher. "I've spoken to the woman who's in charge of the investigation, and her attitude is totally different. She said that 'the evidence pointing to Zigic is absurdly vague and, as it is, the police have spent far too much time over two e-mails.' She is in charge of the case now, but she won't allocate any more time to it."

"What did you say?"

"Well, of course I tried to argue that our safety should be paramount and because of our work we're a special case, but I got nowhere. She wouldn't even listen."

Maybe Iben wasn't all that persuasive. How can you convince someone that you are in mortal danger if you actually feel enormously relieved because you're pretty certain that a timid librarian sent the e-mails?

The idea that the e-mails might be harmless is not disputed by the phone calls they receive from helpful colleagues abroad during the afternoon. The war criminals they suggest only add to their already unmanageably long list.

After the tense, anxious morning, not even a call from Lotta in Sweden about Zigic seems important. There are rumors that Zigic has gone underground somewhere inside the Scandinavian Customs Union, possibly in Sweden.

f Anne-Lise sent the e-mails she obviously must be emotionally disturbed, perhaps even borderline psychotic. If so, she has so far been able to hide her state of mind from her colleagues.

That is why Iben thought Malene should come along with her to see her friend Grith, the clinical psychologist. Malene is mildly skeptical, but she has only met Grith a few times and hasn't a clue what insight she might provide. Besides, Malene does agree that it's sensible to get a professional evaluation of Anne-Lise's behavior.

Grith is a tall, thin woman with large, slightly droopy breasts. She has the kind of body that's supposed to drive men wild. Watching her, Malene thinks that Grith's erotic pull must be limited to when she sits down or stands still. When her long limbs are moving she looks like an awkward fourteen-year-old. The suspicion that she is likely to fall over any minute makes Malene, for one, feel rather nervous.

Grith practices her clinical skills at the Copenhagen National Hospital. They sit on the large square cushions of Grith's gray sofa.

"The first thing to do is to make the client's experience your starting point. The idea is always to support whatever the client believes. It is his or her reality, after all, regardless of how the rest of the world sees it. Clients often feel insecure, so we don't move on until we've understood how they perceive what has happened."

She leans forward from her seat on the sofa. It strikes Malene that there's something unfeminine about her, despite her large dark eyes.

Grith turns to Malene. "Anyway, why don't you tell me about your problem?"

"I don't have one! We're here because one of our colleagues has a problem."

"Okay. How do you see *her* problem?"

"But, look, even before we sat down we told you . . ."

Malene stops and starts again, trying to adopt the slightly learned tone that Grith and Iben seem to assume when they're together.

"Anne-Lise gives me the impression of being terribly angry. She might have sent us threatening e-mails."

Malene pauses to pick a piece of dried mango from a bowl of tropical mix. "Iben, you've got to help me with this."

"Grith, I told you."

"Sure, but I need to get a sense of the situation. Try to describe why this woman is feeling so angry."

Malene won't say anything. Instead she catches Grith's eye and then Iben's.

It doesn't take long before Iben speaks up. "Anne-Lise believes that being colleagues means being friends. And because we don't treat her as a close friend, she has jumped to the conclusion that we are all bad people and that we're bullying her."

"You're giving me the view from the outside. Can't you—?"

Iben won't let Grith interrupt her and runs on: "Being viewed in this way is incredibly unpleasant for all of us. Her hostility is palpable . . . even if she never sent the e-mails."

"Iben, let's stay with her perception of being shut out from a community. Now that's a very unpleasant feeling too."

"We can't think how to make her understand that we're just following the ordinary rules of the workplace and that no one is persecuting her or anything."

"And remember, feeling excluded is awful. Being cast as the outsider would make anyone angry."

"Sure, but—"

"What if we choose to believe her perception? Some part of her story is probably true. When does she feel angry, do you think? Any particular time, or times?"

"She might've been angry last night, when the e-mails were sent. But listen, no one is trying to exclude her."

Grith's voice, always calm, grows even slower and deeper. "Hold on, let's stay with her for a while. Last night, you said. Did anything special take place in the office yesterday?"

"We had quite a nice day together. Chatted a great deal. I remember talking about that journalist, the woman who wouldn't stop asking me about how we were fed in Africa. Later in the afternoon we listened to *Chris and the Chocolate Factory*." She looks at Malene. "It was fun, wasn't it?"

"Yes, it was."

Grith's large eyes are fixed on Iben. "And as far as you know, no one in the office has been hard on this woman?"

"People have been irritated with her, but that's normal. We all have our ups and downs, but there's certainly nothing unusual about that?"

"Not at all. Quite normal."

"So, she might misinterpret mood swings that the rest of us think nothing of, if she's another personality type. It's the kind of thing I thought we might talk about."

Grith leans back, stretching one arm out on the back of the sofa. Her flexibility makes her thin, elongated limb seem to flow along the cushion.

"Iben, you've never seen anyone have a go at this woman?"

"I can't think of anything. We try to be helpful and kind. Don't we, Malene?"

"Yes, we do."

Iben is quiet for a moment. "Still, it's difficult to know what goes on inside her head because she withdraws into her shell a lot. She can seem quite odd. That's what we wanted to talk to you about . . ."

Grith uses both hands to lift the mug of tea to her lips, the way Malene sometimes needs to do. Not that Grith has arthritis, of course. She listens and blows on her drink before interrupting Iben.

"You said that the door to her workplace is always closed?"

"Yes, Camilla likes the library door to be closed, to keep out drafts. It's debatable . . ."

"And we do debate it," Malene points out.

"True. But Camilla has worked in that office longer than she has. And that door has always been shut. It's a bit much."

Grith asks more questions, especially about Camilla. Would she harass Anne-Lise when the others are out of earshot?

It's still Iben who fields the questions. "She wouldn't . . . Look, Camilla is okay, isn't she?"

Iben's question puts a stop to Malene's discreet finger-exercise session. It's the time in the evening when she usually massages her knuckles.

She nods. "Yes. Camilla is easy to work with."

Grith pushes a fine strand of hair away from her cheek.

"It could be just a little thing," she says. "You two might not notice. You're committed to creating a good working atmosphere for the whole office, and that's great. You talk with this woman and invite her to join your group, even though you're not that keen about her. What do other people do? Someone in your office is giving her a hard time. And if you don't demonstratively take her side, she might well feel that you're all bullies. That's enough to make anyone unhappy and very angry . . ."

Iben tries to interrupt, but Grith continues. "It explains why she's reserved and insecure in your company. It's quite understandable."

"Grith, it's not—"

"Try to see things her way and the pieces fall into place. Don't ignore her angle."

Iben has been so eager to get in a word that she has to draw a breath. She says quickly, "Grith, listen. Apart from the head of the Center—and he's almost always out—there are no other people. Just Camilla and us!"

"Is that so?"

Malene leans forward to get a little closer to Iben. She looks at Grith. "Grith, only us. You see? No one is harassing her."

By now Grith's measured approach has become even more deliberate. "Is that so? I assumed there were more . . . that there was a large staff."

"There isn't. We're it."

Silence. Grith's eyes flit around the room, scanning the bookshelf, the bare walls, the small table with the telephone, the dining table made from heavy wooden beams.

Then she looks calmly at her visitors and smiles.

"Aha . . ."

. . .

They talk about the possibility that Anne-Lise is envious of them, maybe because of their friendship, or because their jobs are more exciting, or their relationship with Paul is better than hers; any envy she feels that might remind her of other disturbing situations in her past, when she felt undervalued and excluded. Maybe she didn't dare allow herself to show anger then.

At last, they've arrived at the point where psychological expertise might help them understand.

Malene sums up: "Something about Anne-Lise's personality makes her reactions unpredictable. We wondered if that 'something' means it's essential that we treat her with special care? Could she cope if we confronted her and told her that we think she has sent the e-mails?"

Malene waits for Grith to say something illuminating.

She doesn't.

Malene tries again. "Of course, we've also come to you because we want to help Anne-Lise. Do you think she needs psychological counseling?"

Grith says that they mustn't expect yes-or-no answers and doles out psychological tidbits straight from an advice column.

Malene starts checking out the furniture. The large brass standard lamp behind Iben is elegant and casts a pretty light. The cachepot on the windowsill is stylish too and would be perfect for her own place.

What a disappointing session. Or it would've been if she had come here expecting something special.

Malene realizes that her main reaction is relief. If you're close to someone, you can easily develop all kinds of funny ideas about that person's relationships with others. Now that she has seen Iben with her "other friend," she can be reassured that Iben is much closer to her than to Grith.

Malene warms her hands on her mug. God knows what Grith has observed tonight and what she thinks about the whole episode.

Grith sets out bags of potato chips and they devour them instantly. Malene thinks that they should leave soon.

Grith starts to speak about one of her patients: "She's a woman with what people used to call a split or multiple personality."

"Christ! One of your patients?"

Malene has always been fascinated by stories of people with split personalities but has never met anyone who has actually known someone with them. Her interest makes Grith warm to her subject.

"Yes. Only the new classification for psychiatric conditions calls it dissociative identity disorder, or DID for short. My patient has at least two personalities, in addition to her dominant one. One of them is a little girl. That's very common."

At last Grith is coming alive. It's impossible to tell what has held her back, but she is completely animated now; her eyes seem even larger, and as she talks, her thin arms flail about.

"In psychiatry we've come to take a much greater interest in DID than we did before. All those Hollywood films packed with clichés about split personalities were distracting, I suppose. Somehow they made psychologists and psychiatrists take their cases less seriously than they should. Most people in the trade thought it was embarrassing and dull to write up DID case histories in professional journals, but it's not like that anymore—things are moving fast. During the last twenty years or so, the number of recorded cases in the U.S. has risen sharply, and so have the much more common borderline cases."

"How many people do you think suffer from DID, including the minor cases?"

"Just over six billion, give or take."

"But that's the entire—"

"Think about it. We've all done things that we would hardly have believed we were capable of. It's especially common in young people, while the personality is still in transition, to a certain extent. You do things and then you forget all about them."

Grith looks at Iben and then over at Malene. "Can either of you recall having done anything like that?"

They both try hard to remember. Neither speaks.

After a while, Grith continues: "See what I mean about forgetting? Keep trying. Can you recall ever experiencing a deep feeling of regret?"

"I suppose so . . ."

"Maybe I can . . ."

"There, you see! Behaving badly is dramatic, so it ought to be something you remember. But sitting alone in your kitchen and repenting over a glass of milk is sad and dull, so in theory it should be more difficult to remember. In practice, though, we recall these dreary moments of regret quite easily. You know that and I do too. It's because we're all split—a little anyway. But in the kitchen, with that glass of milk, we are who we know ourselves to be."

Malene's voice sounds faint at first. "Grith, you describe it so well—the whole scene, that glass of milk, everything."

"Thanks. Everyone knows that when you're depressed you can only remember sad things and it's difficult to think of something cheerful. It's as if the happy experiences have vanished. The important thing to remember is that the divide between one aspect of a personality and another needn't be anywhere near as extreme as with the characters you see in films. The sides to dissociated personality are usually much less starkly differentiated, but even so, the split can be enough for a patient to forget what he or she was up to ten minutes earlier. Or it can make days or months or even whole years of a life disappear into the shadows."

Malene has a question: "So, just as an example, is it conceivable that Anne-Lise might have sent the e-mails but can't remember having done it?"

"It certainly is. She might not have a complete alternative identity, with a name and so on; but even so, she could have sent them and forgotten about it."

Malene had taken off her shoes earlier. She gently rubs the sole of one foot over Grith's rug, registering the rough surface with her toes.

"We could never be frightened of Anne-Lise," she says. "At least, the Anne-Lise we know—that's why we wouldn't take her threat to kill us seriously. But how different might her other personality be?"

"If I've understood you correctly, no one knows if Anne-Lise wrote the e-mails. They could have been sent by anyone at all. Right?"

"Right. Absolutely anyone. I was just wondering, you know, 'If . . . then what?' "

"If she did, then she could be like the other cases I've come across. Each identity can have any combination of characteristics, and other identities are entirely independent of the person you think you know. The 'other' could be the complete opposite."

Iben stares at the tropical fruit slices. She raises her hand a little but doesn't actually reach out for the bowl. "What you're saying is that hypothetically we all could have many sides to our personality that we don't know of. And these 'others' might be out of control, doing all kinds of things, while we have no memory of it?"

"That's right."

"Logically, then, it's impossible for a person to know if there are any 'others.' "

"Yes . . . well, no. People often seem to have an idea that something is going on, if they dare to pick up the signs. The possibility of fluid identity boundaries is one of the new areas of research. So are the implications of discovering that splitting is relatively common. Even if you're one of the rare cases of zero awareness of other identities, looking for physical traces usually works: objects in your home in unexpected places, something as simple as a shopping bag in the wrong room—that sort of thing."

Malene accidentally kicks out with one foot and her toes hit a table leg. It hurts, but not too much. The others don't notice. She bends over a little to examine her foot and massages a tender arthritic toe.

She hears Iben laugh. "But, Grith, if we stick to just these two e-mails . . . then what? Could they have been sent by anyone? Apart from ourselves, that is?"

Grith appears to flounder momentarily. "What I'm about to say isn't that . . . Of course, they can't . . . but in purely theoretical terms . . ."

At last she finds a way of saying what she really means.

"Look, if I didn't know you, I would have guessed that the likeliest possibility would be that a split personality would send messages to herself. We aren't talking about two sides of the same personality, but two separate individuals, even though they inhabit the same body. One of them might remember everything from the other's life, but not vice versa. It's usual for one identity to hate the other, accusing it of being 'evil' or 'self-righteous.' " She pauses for a moment and stares at Malene.

Dropping her professional manner, she becomes more relaxed. "But why should it be one of you? Why should the e-mails have anything to do with a split personality? People who develop deeper than normal splitting usually have other psychological problems, like a traumatic childhood."

The atmosphere in the room has changed. It seems so strange to be in this place, sitting on this sofa, watching each other and wondering. Twenty years of science have proven that strange things could be hiding inside their minds. Absolutely anything. Or anybody. And at the same time, they are looking at you and wondering about you.

For a while no one speaks.

This atmosphere—did Grith plan to create it?

Malene can't help but remember how often Iben told everyone that she was "someone else" in Nairobi. And though the police were positive that no one had broken into her apartment, Iben had insisted that the door was open and a stack of papers had been arranged more neatly than she had left it. Iben is so knowing about aspects of her personality and uses scientific terminology when she discusses her own psychology with Malene and Grith. But perhaps there is another hidden self, one she couldn't know of "logically," to use her own word.

Malene makes a pact with herself not even to think about this, regardless of what Iben's other best friend and her science might say.

It's late when Malene phones Iben.

"Are you in bed?"

"Yeah."

"Sorry. Did I wake you?"

"No, don't worry. I was reading."

"I can't stop thinking about how it could've been anybody."

"I shouldn't have brought you along?"

"Of course you should! It was good. Fascinating."

"That's what I thought. Grith often says something unexpected."

When Malene steps into the office the following morning, she notes that the library door is closed, as usual.

She tries to catch Camilla's attention. "Is she in?"

Camilla nods.

Malene checks the corridor. Sure enough, the door from the hallway to the library is open, so Anne-Lise did come in today.

She whispers to Camilla: "What happened?"

"Nothing special."

"Did she say anything?"

"No. Just 'Good morning.' "

Camilla is always curt in the mornings. Malene sits down at her desk. Something is wrong, but she can't quite put her finger on it. As her computer goes through its start-up routine, she ponders the odd atmosphere in the office. What might have caused it? Nothing seems out of the ordinary. Is it she who has changed?

After a good night's sleep Malene has decided that they all overreacted yesterday. If you're attacked, that's what you do: go on the defensive. They should be able to rise above their anger, though. Working here brings certain obligations. They spend every day compiling and passing on information about the tragedies that follow when anger overrules common sense. So, if not even Malene, Iben, and Camilla can show self-control, who can?

Obviously Anne-Lise is in bad shape just now. Maybe her home life isn't that great and, if so, her colleagues should support her. Malene considers dropping in on Anne-Lise in the library and asking her how she is, but feels that would be overdoing it. Instead she stays where she is, dealing with a few jobs she didn't complete yesterday afternoon. She's waiting for Iben.

Iben turns up at a quarter past nine. She and Malene talk in low voices, leaning across their desks. It's hard to know how much Anne-Lise can hear through the closed door. To catch what they're saying, Camilla has to walk over to them.

Malene explains what she's figured out: "When someone behaves like Anne-Lise, the normal response is for her coworkers to crucify her. We didn't and that's good. But it isn't good enough."

The others are listening attentively.

"We could carry on as if nothing happened, or be more distant than before, because she behaved so aggressively. That sort of treatment would make anyone resign, sooner or later."

Malene says, while she looks at Iben: "It would be so easy to do: just let things take their natural course. We'd get everything we wanted: peace and quiet, and a new colleague who might be an asset to the Center. Great, but it would be the same as deliberately shutting her out, and we must try to do better than that."

"What, then?"

"We should learn from the conflict-resolution projects we write about. The first, crucial step is to get the opposing sides to sit down together and talk about their problems. And we know that an independent adjudicator must be present at the meetings."

Camilla is taken aback. "It's a bit heavy, don't you think?"

But Iben agrees. "I'd like to have a meeting with her."

"I'm sure she'd like the idea," Malene says. "Usually it's the stronger party that has the most reservations about a reconciliation process. In this situation, we are the strong ones. And we should tell Paul. We'll need a neutral adjudicator, someone with authority."

Camilla looks skeptical. "But the projects deal with international conflict resolution. And you're suggesting Paul is to be our judge and peacekeeping force all rolled into one?"

Malene gives a little laugh.

When Paul arrives, they chat about this and that; then he disappears into his office. Malene stares at the closed door and hesitates. The presentation of their case could wait until lunchtime.

Her working day is taken up mainly with phone calls to foundations in Germany on behalf of a research team at the Institute of History at Copenhagen University. The team is arranging a conference focused on the crimes against humanity at the end of World War II when Germany was defeated. Fifteen million Germans were expelled from Eastern and Central Europe and some two million women were raped. The researchers turned to the DCIG for help in raising funds, and Malene suggested that they should appeal to German as well as Danish sources of grant money. Her first lead was a human rights institute called Schutzgemeinschaft für Menschenrechte, Humanität, und Toleranz.

Her hands feel tender. She hopes it doesn't mean that another attack of arthritis is on its way. It would be so irritating now, when it's important to be in the office. Besides, tonight Rasmus comes back from Cologne.

The whole morning passes without Paul emerging from his room. Anne-Lise is also lying low. Nobody has spotted her outside the library.

At eleven-thirty Paul puts a call through to Camilla—despite the fact that she's only a few steps away—to say that he's going out for lunch. Camilla passes this on to the others, and they all exchange glances. In the end Malene responds with an "Oh, I'll do it" shrug.

She walks slowly toward Paul's office and knocks on the door.

"Yes?"

She mumbles about the German human rights conference, but after a few minutes she gets to the point: "I'm not sure if you heard, but . . . did you know that Anne-Lise had a kind of breakdown yesterday, here in the office?"

"No, I did not!"

Malene tells him what happened. She adds that it's time they all sat down together, so that everyone can express her views.

Paul sits up. "You're right, Malene. Good of you to tell me."

"When do you think we should meet?"

"Now. We need to nip this in the bud straight away."

Malene goes to tell the others. On her way to the library she reflects that to behave in the way she has must be a part of being mature. A colleague has thrown wild accusations in your face and, as likely as not, sent you threatening hate mail. You overcome your dislike and invite her to talk about moving on and working together. Could anything be more constructive?

Anne-Lise sits behind piles of books stacked on her desk. In here, the books absorb the light and it always seems darker than the Winter Garden, even though there are the same number of lamps and windows in both rooms.

"Anne-Lise, Paul would like to see us all in his room, right now."

Malene doesn't smile; neither does Anne-Lise.

"I'm coming."

Seated at the small conference table in Paul's room, they begin their meeting. It is orderly, without the emotional undercurrents of the day before. Soberly they go through what has happened and what they ought to do in the future. Everyone is very accommodating. Iben even apologizes to Anne-Lise.

"Anne-Lise, we may not have paid enough attention to you. We'll do our best to make it up to you, now that we know that you don't like working alone as much as you've been doing."

"It upsets me to think that you've been feeling miserable all this time," Camilla adds. "You should've told us ages ago. Nobody has to put up with feeling like that. We should all enjoy coming to work here."

Anne-Lise looks, wide-eyed, from one to the other.

Paul seems pleased. After a surprisingly short time, he sums up: "It's so easy to misjudge one another, isn't it? I'm afraid I have to accept my share of the responsibility. We ought to talk together more often about how we work as a team, like we're doing now."

He turns to Anne-Lise. "Do you think that the others were harassing you?"

When she speaks, her voice sounds thick and she keeps clearing her throat. "No . . . no, I don't."

"So you were simply thrown off-balance? It was all a misunderstanding?"

"Yes."

"Good. Then it's settled!"

Paul's voice sounds as if he's been dealt a winning hand at cards. Slowly, he looks around the table, making eye contact with each of the women. Then he speaks directly to Anne-Lise again: "But you do feel you're on your own too much in the library?"

"Yes."

"And you'd like more contact with the library users?"

"Yes."

He takes a large sip of coffee.

"What about the rest of you? Now that we're talking about what we want from each other—what do you want from Anne-Lise?"

Iben replies first. "Anne-Lise, you must make it clear what your needs are. More than you have done so far." She looks around at the others. "If Anne-Lise doesn't tell us, we have nothing to go by."

"Obviously. Anne-Lise, will you do that?"

"Yes."

Paul smiles delightedly at everybody. "Good! I'm sure we've all learned something today. Let's shake hands on it, and promise that we'll do whatever we can to create a better working atmosphere."

Awkwardly, hands reach out between the coffee mugs on the table.

Paul continues to speak as he gets up to go: "From now on the door between the large office and the library will always be left open. And all user inquiries about books and other library matters will immediately be passed on to Anne-Lise. There, we've done it. Fantastic!"

"*Hold it!*"

"Paul, we haven't agreed to anything of the sort!"

"It's impossible to carve up user contacts like that!"

"I won't sit in a draft!"

"You can't decide just like that!"

Paul is forced to sit down again. He tries to smile, but he is impatient.

Iben has been pushing her coffee cup around with small circular movements. Then she sits up and looks over at Camilla.

"Camilla, I've thought of a solution, but it's up to you to say if you think it will work. Of course you mustn't sit somewhere that might make you ill. But what if we moved your desk so that it wasn't in the path of any drafts from the door?"

"I suppose . . ."

Malene takes over now—in fact, she and Iben had worked this out earlier, when they were alone in the copier room: "It is more practical for you to sit close to Paul's door, but it won't make a huge difference if you don't. Besides, he isn't in a lot of the time."

"No . . ." Camilla sounds vague, looks distant.

Malene tries to sweeten the pill: "What if we moved your desk closer to ours? After all, you speak to us more than to Paul. It would be nice." Malene glances anxiously at Iben. They haven't discussed this.

Iben appears to agree but doesn't like it. The exchange is so quick that no one else notices.

Iben smiles. "Sure, it would be great if you sat closer to us. And we've never felt any drafts over where we are."

Camilla now looks quite pleased, if somewhat confused. The matter is resolved. Camilla's desk will be moved next to Iben and Malene's, and the library door will be kept open.

Once more Paul is ready to end the meeting.

Malene speaks up quickly. "Paul, one more thing. About the user contacts and the library!"

He looks mildly irritated. "What about it?"

"It's critical that the DCIG provides the best possible service. We must organize our office with that goal in mind. After all, we're here to adjust to the users' needs, not the other way around."

Paul mutters approvingly and Malene continues: "Clients don't like being shunted around to a different member of staff every time they want to ask another question."

"But it happens."

"Ideally, it shouldn't, unless the established contact can't provide an answer. Think of a financial institution. The bank or firm sees to it that the same person always deals with the same clients. The experts aren't consulted unless the assigned advisor can't deal with whatever the question is."

Malene stops for a moment and looks around the table. "We need to give our clients the best possible service we can. Besides, one of Anne-Lise's demands has already been met."

Iben backs her up. "I agree with Malene."

Camilla follows her lead. "So do I."

One of Malene's hands feels itchy and she scratches it. "Think about it," she says. "If Anne-Lise suddenly takes over part of my work, everyone outside the Center will think that somehow I've failed to cope. It's the only conclusion they could possibly draw."

Paul takes the initiative. "Malene, nobody is in any doubt that you're good at your job. Of course you're able to handle library queries perfectly well. Truly, you're a real asset to the Center and we all value your work here. That was never an issue."

Anne-Lise says nothing.

Malene steals a glance at Anne-Lise's hands. Are they trembling, like yesterday? No, they're not. She tries to establish eye contact with Anne-Lise.

"Anne-Lise, leaving the door open to your place will certainly make a huge difference, don't you think?"

Anne-Lise hesitates for what seems a long time. "I suppose so," she says, her voice still husky.

Paul hesitates too. "Malene, let me think about this."

They are back at their desks, except for Anne-Lise. Paul has asked her to stay behind. Perhaps he wants to discuss the e-mails and who the sender might be? The others work away, trying to seem indifferent to what is going on behind Paul's door.

One of the windows on Malene's screen shows the arrival time for Rasmus's flight. She has already been to the airport site to check for delays, but it's still too early.

Paul's door opens and Anne-Lise comes out first. Both she and Paul seem fine, which must mean that she hasn't admitted to sending the e-mails. Or could it be that she confessed, in return for him not letting on to the others?

Paul is on his way out. "Have a good lunch, everyone! And Malene, I've decided that you keep all user contacts except for book queries. Anything about books goes straight to Anne-Lise."

Malene reaches the elevator just in time to get in with him. Paul has to raise his voice above the whining of the elevator. "Anne-Lise feels there have been quite a few issues: airing out the copier room; lack of recognition for her work. It's time we accommodated some of her requests. Hopefully things will pan out better in the future."

When Malene comes back, Iben and Camilla look up inquiringly. Malene's impulse is to slam the desktop hard with her fist, but she can't because of her sore fingers. What is she to say to the people who are used to calling her all day long? By now they expect her to field all their questions. Should she tell them something such as "So sorry, but I'm not allowed to help you with books anymore because Paul has forbidden it"? Or maybe a brisk "I'm not allowed to deal with these questions anymore"?

Malene is the only one in the office who is familiar with every current research project; she knows the personalities involved and their requirements. Her wealth of knowledge has been built up carefully over three years. Now that Anne-Lise has got her hooks into Paul, he has ruined everything in less time than it has taken the elevator to reach the ground floor.

Malene forces herself to smile at Iben and Camilla, knowing that they can easily see how upset she is. Then she smiles again, more genuinely, because there is something funny about her inability to hide what she feels.

She knows she must look through her article for *Genocide News*, but she can't concentrate. If only she could speak with Iben right now without having Camilla around and without Anne-Lise lurking behind the door that, ironically, is still closed.

She has a new e-mail, a brief message: "Meet you in the kitchen?"

Malene nods. She puts down the article, "Europe's Forgotten Genocide," grabs her mug, and walks over to the coffee thermos. She gives it a little shake and pretends it's empty, then heads toward the kitchen, ostensibly to refill it. In a while Iben joins her.

It's a tiny, rather shabby kitchen, but there is one quality item: a gleaming coffeemaker. Malene fills the thermos to the top—might as well, now that she's here.

"It wouldn't bother me so much if it weren't Anne-Lise who's taking over. I've put lots of energy and time into looking after the users."

"I know, I know. It doesn't make any sense."

"She'll ruin everything in just a couple of weeks. I can't bear it."

"I understand, I really do . . ."

"The whole place will become so dull and dead! Humorless, just like Anne-Lise herself. I mean, just look at her. She'll be the one representing the Center to the outside world—is that what we need? I don't think so!"

"I'm sure Paul hasn't thought it through properly."

"If Paul himself took over, the knowledge I've built up would still be lost, but at least he'd do it with style. But Anne-Lise! I ask you! It's pointless."

"And did you notice the way no one wanted to talk about how we go about providing the best possible service?"

"Oh, I did. Obviously, they just don't care! There is one reason and one reason alone for what happened: Paul is a man. What does he do when he finds out that Anne-Lise has blubbered her way through an entire lunch break? He makes an instant decision in her favor. I'd better start weeping crocodile tears as well. Christ! Just imagine the changes we could make."

So far Malene has had only a single operation to treat one of her hands, but it is impossible to predict what the future might bring. The condition of arthritic joints can deteriorate suddenly, and irreversibly, or it can remain stable for long periods. The illness can move to new parts of the body and begin its crippling process there. Malene's arthritis has remained at its present level, which is relatively mild, for several years now. Her hands and feet have caused her the most agony, but one of her knees has been troublesome too. Her sore feet make running and many sports impossible.

Besides having to face an unpredictable future, Malene's worst problem is the sudden attacks when her illness becomes acute. There are days when she cannot work and no painkillers are powerful enough to enable her to walk. Every two or three months—so far—Rasmus has had to carry her to a taxi that then takes her to the rheumatology clinic at the National Hospital, where she gets injections straight into the affected joints. After a day or so the worst pain has passed.

She knows that some arthritic patients define their identity in terms of their illness. Arthritis dictates the books they read, the friends they want to be with, and the meetings they attend. Malene resists this. She tries to avoid drawing attention to the differences between herself and healthy people. One way is to turn up at work, even when the pain is severe, and to rely on office aids like her ergonomic computer mouse and chair. She speaks about her illness as little as possible and never complains to anyone except Rasmus and Iben.

It is hard for Malene to get up from a chair unless she can roll it away from the table, shift her weight to her feet, and then push herself upright. In the office everyone has a chair with wheels, but in her apartment the wheeled chair at the dining table looks a little out of place. Usually no one remarks on it, though.

Malene's kitchen knives have upright handles that she can grip like a saw, so she won't have to bend her wrist when using them, and she owns a selection of kitchen implements with thick, soft handles that make them easier to hold. With a little goodwill the chubby, colorful shapes could be taken for smart designer ware. Some guests have actually asked where she bought them, because they'd like to get them too. But deep down there is always the persistent underlying fear that another attack could strike at any time, the dreadful possibility that tomorrow she might fall ill again.

You are always hoping, trying to convince yourself: I'm doing really well. I've hardly felt a twinge for the last five weeks. Maybe it's gone away.

During the good days Malene remembers what it was like to be free and physically independent of others. Sometimes, perhaps most often in the spring, she even indulges in an expensive whim, like buying shoes that are not made by an orthopedic shoe maker. And then, always, your hopes are crushed. It seems so arbitrary that you can't help yourself, and you start looking for explanations. Should I stop eating chocolate? Or bread made with yeast? Am I sleeping enough? Or maybe too much? Are the attacks stress-related? Am I being punished? What have I done?

And so it goes, year after year. Malene cannot see any discernible order. The only pattern is that what happens always seems random.

When the attack begins it brings not only the crippling pain but also psychological malaise and disappointment. So, three weeks on a no-sugar diet had no effect, and neither did avoiding stress. It didn't help to meditate or attend sessions with a healer. The disappointment mingles with the pain, the helplessness, and the humiliation of having to be carried down the stairs once again.

All this doesn't suit Malene—she who has fought for an academic career, who now lives in a city despite the provincial life that was charted for her; she who has traveled alone in Africa and Latin America and Asia. Some people advise her to give up, to stop fantasizing about better days. But she's not like that—she can't simply resign herself to this. She *needs* to beat the system. But with every new setback she succumbs to a bitter rage at having it rammed down her throat that she is not in control of her own body.

Rasmus's plane from Cologne is due to land just before eight in the evening. His firm is paying for a taxi from the airport, so with a bit of luck he should arrive around nine o'clock. After he has stayed in all those smart German hotels, Malene wants to make him feel that coming home is still special. But how to plan a festive evening for someone who has spent ten days stuffing himself with food and drink in elegant restaurants?

Her idea is a meal that's light and easy, something they can enjoy in the bedroom. She decides to serve prosciutto, olives, organic tomatoes with olive oil, goat cheese, and slow-risen spelt bread from Emmery's. Rasmus loves good bread and happily eats slice after slice with just butter and salt on top.

To make up for the simple menu, she puts effort into the drinks, recreating the blends of fresh-squeezed fruit juices that they both loved on their holiday in Vietnam. She has bought four kinds of fruit: lime, orange, peach, and melon. They'll mix the juice with the golden tequila from another of Rasmus's trips. As an extra, she has also got the coming month's Cinematek program—the film house is showing a John Cassavetes retrospective. Malene hasn't mentioned this when they've spoken on the phone. She wants it to be a surprise.

The moment Rasmus steps in through the door, one look is enough to tell her. It's not food and drink that he's been missing. He realizes that she is in no mood for foreplay on the hall floor and instead they go straight to the bedroom.

She lies with her head on his chest, sniffing his scent. The hotel's unfamiliar shower gel adds a new note.

He is truly fired up tonight. It seems easy to keep her mind off DCIG, and for a while her body tells her that she is succeeding. But then she finds herself looking at a cupboard door that hasn't closed properly. It juts out from the wall at the same angle as that of the open window. And from the bed it's difficult to make out the image on Rasmus's film poster by the door. It looks like a dark rectangle with patches of reflected light from the lamp in the ceiling.

She tries to concentrate on what they are doing, but it's a challenge.

"Rasmus, no, I'm not with you. Let's wait awhile."

He rolls away from her. A muscle in his face twitches irritably, but when he speaks his voice is kind. "Malene, what's wrong?"

"I don't know. It's . . . nothing. I just don't seem to be in the mood."

He sighs, but is gentle with her. "Let me fix you a drink. A bit more lime and no melon—what do you say?"

She sits up. "I'm sorry, forgive me. Somehow it doesn't seem . . ."

She sits level with his belly, looking down over his handsome body.

"Let me help you."

"I'm not a cow that needs milking," he snaps.

"I didn't mean that."

They go to the kitchen and set out the food. Malene speaks about events in the office, but Rasmus has already heard most of it because she called him on his cell phone at Cologne airport.

Rasmus is the only one from the film studies course who has gone into IT. Two years ago, when Malene met Rasmus for the first time, he was still a member of his film group and they were all out shooting an interview in Lake Peblinge, with both interviewer and interviewee up to their chests in water. Malene walked past while Rasmus was shouting directions from the lakeside path. Curiosity made her stop and look, and it didn't take Rasmus long to chat her up. One year has passed since he moved into her apartment.

Listening to her speaking about her day, he seems rather gloomy. She asks him why and after hesitating for a moment, he tells her: "Malene, I'll happily support you—it's just that it's all the time, it never stops. There's always *something* on your mind. Don't you ever relax?"

Malene feels fed up with the way Anne-Lise and the whole office situation has spoiled her evening. It's been eating away at her. "Rasmus! It's not my fault that someone sent me a death threat. And it's not my fault that I lost a whole area of my work today."

"True. Sure."

"But you sound as if you're blaming me. Anyone would be angry if he or she were told to hand over important work to a colleague who's useless."

"I said it's true. Look, I know it's not your fault and it's really serious.

And still you took all this trouble to make great food. And fantastic drinks." He starts slicing the tomatoes as he speaks. "But you know what I mean. You always have to worry about something."

"There you go. You still think I'm to blame."

"No, listen. I had a good time in Cologne. I enjoyed it there, just as I enjoyed my sales trips to Norway and Austria and Portugal. Every time I'm away I have to convince myself that I'll enjoy returning home to you just as much."

"Rasmus, don't start. Not now, with all this happening in my life."

He puts down the knife. "The last time I came home it was the same. You were unhappy because your best friend had disappointed you by not writing while she was in Kenya. It mattered to you, I understand that. The time before that you were in the middle of one of your attacks . . . but that's okay. It's not the arthritis that bothers me. But then there was the time you were miserable because you were just back from the trip to your friend Charlotte."

His expression softens. "It would be wonderful if I could just look forward to coming home and being with you." He must have seen that his blows had hit home. "Malene, I'm trying to tell you that all this makes what we've got together seem so fragile."

She has not the slightest wish to cooperate. If he feels he has to talk about how "fragile" their relationship is, then it's up to him. But she starts to question him all the same, and then she can't stop the tears from coming.

Rasmus backs down, saying that he simply meant that their relationship is worth fighting for and they should do everything they can to strengthen it. Slowly, he comforts her, gently caressing her sore fingers. Sometimes she feels as if he too gains some peace by soothing her poor joints. They are both reclining on the new sofa. He massages her shoulders, her head resting in his lap. A little later they laugh about getting so emotional and joke about the way her tears made patterns on the surface of her melon juice cocktail.

Malene wonders about Anne-Lise and her husband—if they are ever like this. In a suburban villa, shared with their two children, everything must be different. Are Anne-Lise and Henrik happy tonight? Now that Paul has handed Anne-Lise the responsibility for book inquiries, might they be toasting her success with champagne? Malene finds this scene hard to visualize. Besides, she has never seen Anne-Lise truly happy and at ease. Why should getting the book inquiries change her?

Rasmus's massage is making her relax. Her thoughts drift. She thinks about Iben. Imagine: Iben has no lover to be with. How empty the evenings must be for her, alone with her microwaved food. How she must long for someone to love.

Rasmus has moved on to rub her scalp. The tickly feeling is wonderful. She has filled the room with candles. Rasmus and she don't speak.

Maybe Gunnar and Iben wouldn't be such a crazy match. Iben was obviously attracted to Gunnar, but it hadn't seemed such a good fit at first. Not that Malene would ever have tried to stop it, naturally.

She has a glimpse of Gunnar and Iben's future. They live in Gunnar's apartment, sharing it with his pieces of African furniture, their baby, and visits from his two daughters from his first marriage. Without Malene wanting to be, she is suddenly part of this setup. Rasmus has left her and she, like an unmarried, sickly aunt, comes to see her friends often. She shakes the image off almost before it has even formed in her mind.

A little later she and Rasmus are in bed together, and now Malene takes the initiative. She notes the odd scent of hotel toiletries again and does everything she can to make it special for him. His weight on her is just right, and she enjoys his strong, healthy hands. She has an orgasm this time, though a small one.

Rasmus wants to get up and have something more to eat. He is content now, easier to talk to. She is less sure about her own feelings.

Back in bed they lie and talk. She shows him the printout of the e-mail from revenge_is_near. He says she mustn't be afraid, she'll be all right. She tells him about the evening they spent with Grith and about the mental disorder that causes a person's identity to split and dissociate. This interests him. He is sitting up, eating prosciutto with leftover pieces of melon. There's a slice of bread with butter and salt on the side.

"What Grith says is, the e-mailer might behave like a perfectly normal person—not someone obviously violent, that is. It could be anyone who knows us. And whoever it is also knows a great deal about genocides."

"So how would you go about finding out who it is?" Rasmus asks.

"Well, it could be someone who is connected to the Center and whose personality has split to separate out his or her anger—someone we meet often, perhaps every day."

Later, when Malene has started her evening finger exercises, using her blue ball, Rasmus still ponders what she has said. His mouth glistens with melon juice.

"Did Grith explain how to find out if a person has parceled off anger and so on into a separate personality?"

"No, she didn't."

"So you might think Anne-Lise did it, but you can't prove it? You have to treat her as if she were innocent?"

Malene smiles to let him know that he has hit the nail on the head. "You're so right."

They lie close, comfortable together, and fantasize about how they could trap the sender of the e-mails. Malene's head rests on Rasmus's chest, and her arms are around him. She looks out through the window.

She thinks about Iben and how it has only been forty-eight hours since Iben was too scared to come here and stay the night because she really believed that someone might break in and kill her while she slept. What has changed since then?

Sometimes you feel deeply sad on the first truly lovely day in spring. Sometimes you feel fresh and alert after a stupidly late night. Now Malene feels exactly the opposite of what she expected: she feels safe. She loves holding her tentative lover close and thinks that she would do anything at all to make him happier about being with her.

EUROPE'S FORGOTTEN GENOCIDE

In May a conference arranged by the Danish Center for Information on Genocide will examine the expulsion of 15 million Germans from their homes in Eastern Europe. It is one of the world's largest ethnic-cleansing operations, but until recently it was more frequently discussed among Holocaust deniers than among serious researchers.

∎

BY MALENE JENSEN

The Second World War was almost over, and the Soviet Red Army was pushing into Germany. The Russian soldiers had fought for two years in German-occupied Russia and Poland, marching through landscapes scarred by the Nazi attempt to conquer the Slav race.

Even before the declaration of war, Hitler had instructed German army leaders to kill "all men, women, and children of Polish origin, showing neither mercy nor compassion." Apart from acts of war, German soldiers took part in this genocide by shooting, executing, and enforcing planned mass death by starvation on at least ten million Russians and Poles. Now the situation was reversed. The Soviet soldiers found the German countryside and its villages empty of able-bodied men. German aggression had cost practically every Russian soldier the life of a loved one—a family member, an old friend, a comrade-in-arms—and for four years they had all been hungry, frozen, and without women.

The men went berserk. There are endless eyewitness accounts of how all women, from ten to eighty, were raped. Some died after multiple rapes. Not all the women were shot afterward, but the Russian officer Aleksandr Solzhenitsyn, later a Nobel Prize–winning author, wrote about what he had seen in the long epic poem *Prussian Nights:* "Virgins were made women, and soon the women would be dead bodies, as, sick of mind and with bloodshot eyes, they begged: 'Kill me, soldier!' "

THE RAPES NO ONE WANTS TO REMEMBER

Afterward all those involved tried to suppress awareness of these violations. The subject was taboo until a German book about it was finally published in 1992, *Befreier und Befreite* (*Liberators and the Liberated*), a collection of papers edited by Helke Sander and Barbara Johr. In his contribution, the statistician Gerhard Reichling estimates that 1.9 million German women were raped during the months of the invasion. The number of actual rapes is many times greater, since it was rare for a woman to be raped only once. A major proportion of the forty thousand written witness accounts held in the German Bundesarchiv-Ostdokumentation (a state archive for documentation about the Eastern Front, housed in the city of Bayreuth) describes how groups of women were kept captive in cellars to be used by soldiers in any way the men wanted, at any time.

There are several eyewitness accounts describing what took place in the East Prussian country town of Nemmersdorf, where naked women were crucified on the doors, nails hammered through their hands and feet. Children, wounded soldiers from the German army, and old men who had never been called up were shot in the back of the head or transported to Russian concentration camps or clubbed to death.

Ilya Ehrenburg, the Stalinist writer, wrote in a leaflet distributed to the

Russian soldiers: "Count not the days, nor the kilometers traveled. Count only the number of Germans you have killed. Kill Germans—this is your mother's prayer. Kill Germans—this is the cry from the land of Russia. Do not hesitate. Do not stop. Kill."

The soldiery was not only Russian, but included Mongolian cavalry and contingents from the other 150, mainly Asiatic, nationalities under Soviet rule. All were let loose to do anything and everything they wanted, except show mercy. Gang rapes were rewarded as if they were heroic acts. *Not* participating in the killing of German civilians could lead to court-martial and was punished by either imprisonment (as in the case of Solzhenitsyn) or execution.

The winter of 1945 was harsh. The exodus of Germans from East Prussia took place at temperatures of eighteen to twenty-five degrees below zero. The Soviet air force, and later its tank divisions, shot at and bombed the refugees. In a flanking maneuver the infantry cut off escape routes to West Germany and many of the refugees chose to walk toward the coast instead, where they tried to board ships. One of these ships, the *Wilhelm Gustloff*, designed to carry 1,460 passengers, was sunk by a Soviet submarine. Of the 11,000 civilians on board, 9,000 died in that one attack—roughly six times as many as drowned in the sinking of the *Titanic*.

KÖNIGSBERG BECOMES KALININGRAD

Many fugitives were stranded in Königsberg, the besieged East Prussian capital. The harbor city of Königsberg was once one of Germany's finest, cultured and elegant and full of beautiful old buildings, including a famous cathedral, museums, and theaters. Before Hitler's rise to power, the university in Königsberg was internationally acclaimed. The city boasted seven newspapers and Germany's biggest bookshop, which catered to—among others—its many scientists and artists. In July 1944 a group of Königsberg officers carried out a failed attempt to kill Hitler.

Over the seven hundred years of its existence, Königsberg's population had grown to 380,000, but after it surrendered to the Nazis only about 100,000 remained: many of them were refugees who had fled from the countryside east of the city and others were families on the run from the bombing raids on Berlin who now harbored the hope of returning to the German capital.

The American diplomat and historian George Frost Kennan flew over the

deserted East Prussian land. He wrote in his memoirs: "The Russian invasion is a catastrophe for this region that has no counterpart in contemporary Europe. In many areas the original population has been decimated so
that hardly a man, woman, or child remains alive; it is impossible to believe
that they all managed to escape to the West."

After the defeat of Germany this part of the old Prussian territory came
under Soviet rule. This meant that three quarters of the remaining population of Königsberg died from sickness and starvation. The 25,000 survivors
were deported in 1947 to what was to become the newly designated DDR.
Some ended up in Nazi-built concentration camps, which were now used by
both the Polish and the Soviets. Here, about 75 percent of the prisoners
died, mainly from starvation, typhus, and torture.

EXPULSIONS IN THE POSTWAR YEARS

The forced displacement of civilians from the old German provinces of East
Prussia, Silesia, and Pomerania continued during the postwar years. Stalin,
at his meetings with Churchill and Roosevelt, insisted on holding on to the
parts of Poland that the Soviet Union had annexed after Stalin's pact with
Hitler in 1939. Poland therefore had to be compensated. At the Teheran
conference in December 1943, Churchill used three matches to demonstrate how this could be done: he put down two matches first, removed the
right one, and added a new match to the left of the remaining one.

In the real world, this shift in Polish territory led to the removal of 3 million Germans from their old homeland, which now belonged to Poland, and
the relocation of the displaced people. They were left to fend for themselves
and make a living as best they could. The emptied rural areas and towns
were then to be repopulated by the 3 million Poles deported from the new
Soviet territory.

With callous brutality, Germans were also driven out of German-
speaking regions in Czechoslovakia, Hungary, Yugoslavia, and other European countries. They lost their homes and all property that they could not
carry.

EUROPE'S LARGEST ETHNIC-CLEANSING OPERATION

More than 15 million Germans were expelled from their native regions. Also,
more than 2 million German civilians either were murdered or died from
starvation, cold, or the terrible ordeals they endured during 1945 and the

first five years after peace was declared. Sheer numbers make this one of Europe's largest genocides, and it wiped out East German culture.

No one doubts the correctness of the figures, which are based on documentation in German archives. Despite this, international research has paid relatively little attention to this mass extermination.

In the *Encyclopedia of Genocide,* the deportation of Germans is referred to in a table listing the greatest genocides of the twentieth century, but there is no separate article describing it. This work of reference does, however, include long articles about other numerically smaller genocides.

Similar weaknesses are found in other standard works, such as *Century of Genocide* and *The History and Sociology of Genocide.* Nobody contradicts that the postwar forced displacement of Germans was one of the largest Europe has ever seen, but it is also true that nobody has chosen to write about it at any length. It is not difficult to understand why this should be.

"The Germans started it." No serious researcher would like to be associated with changing the emphasis placed on the German slaughter of Jews, Slavs, gypsies, and homosexuals. It was indeed the Germans who systematized genocide and constructed machinery that made killing people more efficient than ever before.

It follows that the question of guilt is critical. Can German children be held responsible for unimaginable crimes against humanity committed by their older male relatives? The Nazis themselves would have argued that this is the case: according to their principles, whole populations are rightly punished for the crimes of individuals.

But do we still think this way today?

AN INFORMATION GAP

Even though academic interest in the ethnic cleansing of Germans has increased a great deal during recent years—both inside and outside Germany—it can still be difficult to find precise and objective information. For instance, if one tries to look up the greatest shipping disaster in the world—the sinking of the *Wilhelm Gustloff*—there is no entry in the *Danish National Encyclopedia, Encyclopaedia Britannica*, or the large German encyclopedia *Brockhaus.*

Web searches on the German words *Vertreibung* ("expulsion"), *deutsche* ("German"), and "1945" produce many thousands of links, mostly to the large societies supporting German displaced persons. The objectivity of such societies is obviously questionable. A search on the corresponding English words results in a much more compact collection of links.

However, many of these sites display distorted narratives of the history of the Second World War and especially of the Holocaust. Although they claim to provide neutral, academically valid research results, much is in fact written by those who deny the reality of the Holocaust. In many cases, Holocaust denial is a symptom of alignment with neo-Nazi organizations.

THE DCIG ARRANGES A CONFERENCE
ABOUT THE GERMAN EXPULSION

In other words, it is still difficult to find reliable information about this particular genocide and especially for those not professionally concerned with genocide research. Highly tendentious books and Web sites are mixed in with more valid sources.

This is why the DCIG will be holding a public conference about the expulsion. The conference will take place on May 15–17. The Center hopes it will help support new research and detach the knowledge of this tragedy from the home pages created by those who aim to falsify history.

Set these dates aside now. Further information about the program and registration will be available in a later issue of Genocide News.

frederik Thorsteinsson is the only man on the DCIG board who is younger than Paul, which might have something to do with Paul's dislike of him.

Frederik's main academic subject was history. His doctoral thesis, "The Origins of the Democratic Tradition in Denmark," was completed at an unusually early age and was awarded Copenhagen University's Gold Medal. After a stint at the Modern History Research Unit at Roskilde University, he landed the post at the Center for Democracy at the Ministry of Foreign Affairs and then the place on the DCIG board.

It was not long before Frederik and Paul had their first skirmish. They disagreed about how to handle an information project in Republika Srpska, the Bosnian Serb republic. During the week of the worst infighting, the DCIG staff held their Christmas party at a chic lakeside restaurant. Late that evening, Paul, Malene, and Iben ended up in a club in Nørrebro full of stragglers from umpteen other Christmas dinners.

In the middle of the noise and music Paul suddenly confided in Malene: "Malene, don't you see that Frederik is only in it for himself? That's why he's always so fucking astute and politically correct. All he thinks about is his own career. I mean, can you point to one single ethical value he'd stick to if it wasn't in his own interest?"

The following Monday, Paul asked Malene to have a word with him in his office. He tried to backtrack on what he had said, but he didn't do too good a job of it.

"Malene, I'm not happy about what I said to you on Friday night. You know what I mean—about Frederik. I have no real reason to suspect him of bad faith, and it was very poor form to pass my doubts on to you. I really regret it. So, could we let it stay between us?"

She said, "Yes, of course."

"I'm probably prejudiced," Paul went on. "To me, he looks just like an SS officer in one of those American war films from the sixties. That is, apart from his hairstyle."

Malene laughed. Actually, Paul's description seemed rather apt: Frederik was easily six inches taller than all the other men on the board and was apparently very pleased with his blond hair, high cheekbones, and small, straight nose.

Women tend to like Frederik, who can be charming in spite of his upper-class mannerisms. Indeed, Malene suspects he could have any one of the four women working in the Center, but no one mentions this when Paul is within earshot. Malene herself has a great relationship with Frederik, with just the right amount of flirtation.

Three weeks after the Christmas party, Paul was offered a seat on the board of the Center for Democracy, and he accepted at once. In one way, even though he isn't the deputy chairman, he is now senior to Frederik.

On Wednesday afternoon Frederik phones Malene. He is researching a book and needs to see proceedings from old Polish court cases.

Of course Malene can arrange for him to have access to the documents, but by now Paul's new rule is in force. She should refer Frederik and his library request to Anne-Lise. She looks quickly across the desk at Iben. Iben has obviously figured out who is on the other end of the line. They raise their eyebrows simultaneously.

Malene pauses briefly and then says, pleasantly, that she will arrange to have the document boxes put in the large meeting room.

Afterward Malene confesses to Iben. "Look, I simply couldn't do it. Not today." She tries to smile. "Not when it was Frederik who asked me."

Iben says nothing, just reaches out for her mug of coffee.

Malene catches on to what was left unsaid. "I know, I know."

She locates the registration code. It's easy, because Anne-Lise has entered the codes in the library catalog. She chats with Iben for a few moments to steady herself before fetching the boxes. As she passes Anne-Lise's desk, she makes an effort to say hello.

The Polish documents are buried at the back of the library, on shelving left from the days when the city council kept its archives there. On the way out, pushing a small trolley with five boxes, Malene feels she must say something.

"How's it going?"

"Fine." Anne-Lise asks no questions.

Malene pushes the trolley along to the large meeting room. The board meets there every other month, but it too has gradually filled up with bookshelves and, despite its name, the room is mainly used by visitors who want to read in peace.

Frederik stops by Iben's and Malene's desks for a chat before going off with Malene to start on the boxes.

After lunch Paul turns up. He checks his mail in his office and then drifts back into the Winter Garden. They see at once his phony nonchalance and know it means trouble.

"Look, Malene, we've got something to discuss, you and I. Why don't you drop in as soon as it suits you?"

Malene gets up. "Now, if you like."

Camilla is at her desk. Malene makes sure to close Paul's door.

"Have a seat, Malene." One of Paul's hands moves toward his chin. "Look, we made a deal yesterday."

"Yes, we did."

"It's now Anne-Lise's responsibility to work directly with users on anything to do with the library."

"That's right."

Paul always speaks carefully when he has to step into his managerial role. "Have you decided . . . not to keep your promise?"

"Not at all. Only, Frederik and I have been working together a lot. I just wanted to help him."

"Only Frederik. Then you have referred everyone else to Anne-Lise?"

"Not yet. We only agreed on this yesterday, but I will do it."

Paul says nothing, just looks at her.

Malene studies the backs of the photo frames on Paul's desk. They cast pale, angular shadows across the piles of paper. Then she looks up. "You must have spoken with Anne-Lise?"

"No. I asked Frederik how the new system was working."

Malene thinks this sounds unlikely.

Then, in a different tone of voice, Paul says, "What you achieved by contacting the Austrian foundations was really impressive."

"Thanks. The embassy made a lot of good suggestions."

Then, without warning, Paul suddenly changes the subject again. "I was under the impression that the door to the library was meant to be kept open. Right?"

"It will be, but we can't open it until Camilla's desk has been moved. And that can't be done until Bjarne fixes the network links and all the plugs."

Paul inhales, a brisk little reverse puff.

Malene speaks quickly. "I'm not the one dealing with it."

"I didn't think so, Malene. But have you told Camilla that the sockets and the rest of it must be done as soon as possible?"

"Actually, yes, I have. I didn't quite put it like that, but I did tell her. And I reminded her it should be soon. She says that it's cheaper if we let Bjarne pick a day when he's not too busy. Presumably he's had a lot to do this week."

Paul starts sifting through some papers. "Okay. I'll speak to Camilla about this."

After the meeting in Paul's office, Malene goes to the kitchen to make fresh coffee. Iben turns up, but so does Frederik: he wants to get hold of more court documents from Poland.

The DCIG archive holds one of the world's largest collections of documents relating to the ethnic cleansing of Germans from the Polish regions. It is the result of Paul's sometimes rather unconventional methods of developing the Center's assets. Some two years ago he persuaded an academic friend of his to offer a year's research fellowship to a Polish sociologist whom Paul had promised to help. In return, the sociologist was charged with driving around the Polish provinces and photocopying all the relevant papers he could obtain, mostly from town halls, courts, and churches.

Malene has met the Pole, a thin, opinionated man whose views put him well to the right of any Danish sociologist she has ever come across. He must have been photocopying for a year nonstop—or made somebody else do it. His collection of material, never before archived in the same place, arrived inside 278 cardboard boxes, filling three containers. Some of the documents looked remarkably like originals.

The Pole obtained a temporary work permit through inscrutable channels, and before it expired he found himself a Danish wife and went to live with her in Odense.

When Frederik announces that he needs additional documentation, Iben and Malene exchange a quick glance.

Iben nods toward Malene, inviting her to tell him what has been decided. Malene explains quietly and precisely—very properly—that, from now on, all requests for books and documents must be presented to Anne-Lise.

Frederik clearly finds the new order strange and says something to that effect.

Malene looks from him to Iben and back again before she speaks up, not minding if her tone is sarcastic. "Well, that's what teamwork is all about: adjusting to what the other person needs or wants." She raises her mug in a kind of toast. The movement is so energetic that some of the coffee slops over. "So, that's how it's going to be."

Frederik leans against the kitchen counter and gives her a quizzical look. "It sounds oddly formal to me."

Malene wipes the dribbles off the mug with her finger. "We aren't that formal, are we, Iben?"

"Guess not."

Malene touches Frederik's arm to steer him toward the door. "Frederik, you go back to your reading. I'll go and tell Anne-Lise what you want and then she'll bring it to you."

"Thanks."

"Not at all. From now on you'll be working together with Anne-Lise. Just as we all try to do."

Later that afternoon Malene and Frederik get together in the meeting room to discuss the English version of the invitation to the conference. They sit side by side at the large table, scribbling changes on Malene's printout. Malene's green marker pen dominates the top of the sheet, while Frederik's additions in blue ballpoint snake around the lines in the last paragraph.

Anne-Lise knocks and enters the room. "Hello there. Am I disturbing you?"

"Not at all."

"Oh, good."

Anne-Lise pauses briefly and looks at Frederik. "Frederik, we have the documents you want from the courts in Gryfice, Lobez, and Nowograd, but not from Koszalin."

Anne-Lise walks toward the table. She looks self-assured enough, but somehow her usually earnest expression seems about to disintegrate.

"Places down there have several names, of course, so when I recorded the items in our Polish collection I took special care to enter automatic links into the database. The cross-referencing should ensure that everything is easy to locate, regardless of whether you search the German or the Polish name. Even so, I did take the precaution of starting a new search using the German name for Koszalin, which is Köslin, with a German 'ö,' and there are no documents under that name either."

Anne-Lise must have prepared this little talk for her first customer since Paul's directive. Malene notices that her eyeliner has been freshened up, probably just before she came in.

With an obvious effort, she turns to Malene. "So, I went on to phone a string of offices in Koszalin. I was told that all the papers in the town had been taken to the German Bundesarchiv's 'Ostdok' division in Bayreuth. I phoned Bayreuth and got them to give me the details of where the Koszalin documents are stored. Look, I've written down the phone number and I have an e-mail address for you as well."

Malene's arms are stretched across the tabletop. One elbow obscures some of the text that she and Frederik have been working on.

She hesitates, then glances at Frederik. "I could've sworn the documents were here. How strange."

Anne-Lise sounds more certain now. "But they're not. I've checked everything carefully. I'm quite sure."

"Right, of course. If you say so."

Anne-Lise puts a sheet of paper on the table. On it she's written a few names, a phone number, and an e-mail address.

"She'll get your documents. I just wanted to keep you informed. I'll phone these people myself."

Frederik has also placed an elbow on the conference printout. He looks up at Anne-Lise and sounds a little confused.

"Did you say 'all the papers in the town' a moment ago? You do know, don't you, that I wasn't looking for papers from the *town* of Koszalin?"

Anne-Lise blinks. "What do you mean?"

"Koszalin is the name of a province as well as a town. It's the documents from the small county courts in the province that I need."

"In the province . . . ?"

Malene picks up the piece of paper with the address written on it. "Oh, Frederik, look! It's Ilona's address!"

Frederik casts an eye on the paper. "Is it? I can't remember."

"Yes, of course it is!"

Before Frederik has time to reply, Anne-Lise speaks up: "Malene! Didn't you tell me to look for the Koszalin court?"

"No, I didn't." Malene looks at her blandly. "I never said that. I know very well that we haven't a single document from a town of that size. What I said was 'the documents from Koszalin and from the courts in Grufice, Lobez, and Nowograd.' "

One of Anne-Lise's heels taps audibly against the linoleum-covered floor.

"Maybe you said—"

"I did say 'the documents from Koszalin.' "

Anne-Lise purses her mouth. Her lips tighten. She seems on the verge of saying something aggressive, but apparently thinks better of it.

The room is filled for a moment by the dull rumble of a bus passing in the street.

Malene breaks the silence. "I'm one hundred percent sure of what I said, you know."

Anne-Lise doesn't answer.

Malene tries a smile. "Anne-Lise, I can understand perfectly well how irritating it must be to have picked up the wrong end of the stick. Maybe I should've expressed myself more clearly, but it seemed much more complicated to say it all. We have documents from five courts in the province of Koszalin. Their names are Bielograd, Darlowo, Swidwin, Zlocieniek, and Kolobrzeg."

In the street outside another large diesel engine follows the bus.

Then Malene continues: "But you're the one who's spent weeks and weeks typing all the information into the database. It simply didn't occur to me that you wouldn't know." Malene breaks off at that point.

Frederik tries to be just as sympathetic. "Don't worry about it. It doesn't matter."

Anne-Lise is no longer looking at either of them. She straightens up and appears determined.

"I'll find what you want at once. Now that I know exactly what to look for, it'll take no time at all."

Malene clutches one of her hands in the other. "Great. You'll manage just fine."

On Wednesday evening one of Rasmus's old friends turns up to talk. Malene fidgets about elsewhere, in the bedroom, the kitchen, the hallway.

She can't help thinking about the office. I did say "the documents from Koszalin," she tells herself bad-temperedly. Then, suddenly, the evening is over. By the time Rasmus's friend leaves, she has already taken a tablet for her headache.

Both Malene and Rasmus are tired. They sit leaning against the sofa cushions, one in each corner, with their feet in each other's lap. Malene does her finger exercises.

She asks Rasmus what Jonas wanted. It seems Jonas has problems at work.

The sound of the clock radio. Toes on the tiled bathroom floor. Toothpaste. Wafts of damp air from the shower. The smell of Rasmus's deodorant. Cotton wool. Low-fat yogurt. Coffee.

When Malene turns up at the Center on Thursday morning, the others are all in the Winter Garden, standing around Camilla's chair. Malene glances quickly at Camilla and sees that she must have been crying.

Even before Malene puts her bag down, Paul explains: "Camilla has received one of the e-mails too."

He hands Malene a printout.

ANYBODY WHO HOSTS OR GIVES HELP TO OUR ENEMIES IS OUR
ENEMY. YOU, CAMILLA BATZ, WILL DISCOVER THAT COLLABORATORS
WHO THINK THEMSELVES INNOCENT OFTEN DIE TOO.

The e-mail was sent yesterday evening, at 9:57 p.m. The sender, as before, is revenge_is_near@imhidden.com.

Malene is outraged. She looks up from the printout and stares at Anne-Lise, who avoids her eyes.

Anne-Lise is leaning against Camilla's filing cabinet and resting one of her hands on top of it, next to the postage machine. She doesn't seem as tense as you would expect. How accomplished a liar is she? A good one, to be sure. Just think of how she managed to hide the fact that she hates her colleagues for months. Besides, she might have blanked out writing the e-mails, like the cases of split personality Grith told them about. Maybe she's dimly aware of having done it, as if it were a dream. Malene cannot bear even to look at Anne-Lise, and turns her back to engage with what the rest of the group is saying.

Camilla points at the bottle of whiskey in front of her. "I've had two shots already."

The bottle was a gift to Paul after a lecture. He has brought it over, together with a few small tumblers. Camilla gives a nervous laugh. It's impossible to tell what she is feeling.

Malene wants to tell Camilla how very fond of her she is, but cannot think of a way to put it. "Have you called Finn?"

Camilla trembles. "I have. He wanted to come over right away, but I told him there was no need."

Once Finn was married to Camilla's best friend. The friend's advanced uterine cancer was diagnosed within days of her giving birth to a baby daughter. During the first two months after the diagnosis, Camilla took a lot of time off work. Later she moved in to help Finn look after both his wife and the new baby.

During the eighteen months that followed, Camilla's friend steadily weakened and finally she died. At first Camilla went back to live in her own place, but now she has a son with Finn and has moved into his home on Amager Island. Finn works as a plumber, mostly on Amager. Camilla brings him to the summer and Christmas office parties. He's a small, bald man, but friendly and always ready to share a joke.

Malene goes over to Camilla and puts her arms around her. It's an impulse; they have never hugged before. Camilla's body is warm and Malene realizes to her surprise that she is close to tears as well. But she doesn't start to cry. Instead she shouts, in an odd voice that seems to rise from somewhere deep inside her: "Camilla, we won't let them get away with it!"

She hears Iben speak behind her. "Malene? You didn't react like this when we were e-mailed."

Malene steps away from Camilla. It's true. She is furious with whoever has done this, but can't think why she's reacting so strongly.

"I know. But it's so . . ."

Iben watches her.

"They shouldn't be sending this stuff to Camilla!" She stops and turns to Camilla. "You haven't done anything. We're the ones who wrote the articles. It isn't fair to pick on you!"

They can hear the elevator stop at their landing. The door opens and Bjarne, the Center's freelance IT advisor and technician, steps out. He has come to move the connections serving Camilla's desk.

Anne-Lise's voice is strident. "We must do everything we can to find out who's writing these e-mails."

They nod, but nobody looks in her direction.

There they stand. Everyone agrees, naturally. But what can they do? Nothing that they haven't done already.

When Bjarne has been told where the desk is meant to go, he wanders off to the small storeroom where the office server is kept, as well as leads and other pieces of equipment he'll need. Paul is the only one sitting down. He asks Camilla if she would prefer to go home and try to recover from the shock. "Thanks, Paul. But no, I wouldn't. There's nobody at home. I'd rather stay here with all of you."

"Camilla, why don't you sit in a meeting room if you want some quiet?" Iben suggests.

"What I'd really like to do is lie down. Just for a bit, on the couch in the library."

Malene squeezes her arm. "You do what feels right for you. I'll deal with any phone calls today."

"You're all so sweet and kind to me." Camilla looks around from one colleague to another. Her expression is still distressed, but in a more familiar way. "I wasn't very pleasant to you when you were sent these e-mails."

Malene comforts her. "But Camilla, things are different now. Our e-mails arrived at the same time. Now it's clear to all of us that it's not just an isolated occurrence. That makes the whole thing more serious. For us too."

Malene glances at Anne-Lise. She doesn't look that frightened. Why not? Now it seems that all the Center's staff are under threat, so shouldn't her body language be more tense?

Camilla worries. "But I should've—"

Malene interrupts her. "Camilla, you mustn't blame yourself. All you have to do now is decide whether you'd rather stay here and let me take the phone calls, or if you'd prefer to rest on the couch. Or whatever else you want to do."

Camilla thanks her but then starts crying again. Paul gets up and says that he must notify the police.

Malene and Iben escort Camilla to the couch, with Anne-Lise trailing behind them. Once they are in the library aisles, Anne-Lise seems to feel that Camilla has entered her area of responsibility and comes closer.

"Shall I take it from here? There's a blanket somewhere and some water, and if there is anything else, I'm sure . . ."

Malene intends to reply, but Iben speaks first: "Camilla, what do you think? Is there anything you'd like?"

But all Camilla wants to do is rest quietly, so Malene and Iben leave her alone.

Bjarne is back in the Winter Garden now, on his knees behind the set of pigeonholes, which he has pushed away from the wall. To check the new connections for Camilla's desk, he wants it moved out of the way. Malene and Iben decide they can do it. To protect the floor they jam wads of junk mail under its legs and together push the desk to its new position, Malene shoving the desk to avoid taking any of the weight directly on her hands.

Then they move a couple of small shelves, the monitor, the plants, and Camilla's other bits and pieces, trying to arrange everything as nicely as possible. Anne-Lise comes in to join them, leaving the door between the Winter Garden and the library open for the first time.

The three of them dawdle restlessly for a while. Iben and Anne-Lise push two large shelving units sideways to give Camilla more light and air around her new workplace. Bjarne curses when he discovers that the networking cables have been laid in a strange way, which means that a new set must be joined up to the server.

All this should satisfy Anne-Lise. They are working together "as a team," and Iben chats to her. Malene ought to join in, but can find nothing to say.

When Anne-Lise returns to her desk, the door is still left open. Everyone will be able to hear what everyone else is saying from now on. At least, Anne-Lise can pick up what the rest of them are talking about. Anne-Lise herself never says anything, of course.

It's almost lunchtime. Iben and Malene still haven't done any proper work. Iben nods to tell Malene they should talk. They meet in the copier room.

Iben stands very close to Malene and speaks in a whisper: "I have the impression that Camilla is scared of a man, someone she knows."

"What do you mean?"

"It's probably nothing . . . I know we shouldn't speculate about every little thing, but didn't it strike you how strongly she reacted to this? Two large shots of whiskey at nine o'clock in the morning? Then resting on the couch or sleeping or whatever, because she won't go home and won't go back to work either?"

Malene hadn't thought of this, but Iben has a point.

Iben has more to say. "When Camilla phoned Finn I overheard her say 'I knew he'd be back.' "

"Anything else?"

"Nothing. Just that."

"What does it mean?"

"No idea. I tried to ask her, but she avoided the question."

The light in the copier room is bleak. Malene backs away a little.

"Couldn't she explain at all? It couldn't be about a friend coming to visit or something like that?"

"No. I have no idea what she was going on about, but it wasn't like that. I could have misheard, of course."

"Well, yes. I mean, Camilla is so sensible. She wouldn't drag us into something dangerous. Did you ask her again?"

"I did, but indirectly. She could be frightened of someone she knows, and that's why she's taking the e-mails even more seriously than we did."

Malene leans on the copier. "I'll ask her too."

Iben's voice is still very quiet. "Do that. But somehow I don't think it will get you anywhere."

Malene takes the phone calls that afternoon, as agreed. When Finn rings to ask how Camilla is doing, Malene goes to the library to find out and wakes her up. Camilla follows Malene back to the Winter Garden, but stops in the doorway.

"Oh, look! Is that how it's going to be from now on?"

Malene glances at Iben before replying. "Yes—well, no; it's up to you to decide. We just moved your desk because Bjarne wanted it closer to the new connections. So that he could check if it all worked."

Iben chimes in. "It's just temporary, Camilla. We'll help you if you want to move the desk somewhere else."

Camilla sits at Malene's place to take Finn's call, since her phone is not connected. When the call has ended, she comes over to consider the new position of her desk.

"I suppose it's all right like that."

Malene has been searching the shelves for a particular copy of *La Lettre de la Fédération Internationale des Ligues des Droits de l'Homme*. She smiles.

"We think so too."

Iben looks up from her screen, concerned. "Try it out for a couple of days. You need to get used to the new setup before you make up your mind."

"The network connection at my old place is gone, isn't it?"

"Yes. Anyway, Bjarne said there was something wrong with it. He's in the server room now."

Anne-Lise comes in through the open door and Camilla stares at her a fraction longer than normal, as if she might not be fully awake yet.

Bjarne eats lunch with them and today Paul joins them as well. All six have a discussion about the extent to which continued economic growth in the West is an essential condition for African development. And, conversely, the way certain economic mechanisms lead to conflicts of interest between the industrialized states and the third world.

After lunch they settle down to work, but are very aware of the open library door. Iben speaks up, distinctly and quite loudly. "How's it going in there?"

Anne-Lise's desk is placed so that she cannot see into the Winter Garden. So her reply comes from just behind the door frame. "I'm fine."

Iben and Camilla converse politely, as if they are strangers attending a reception. Malene tries to think up ideas for a lecture she has agreed to write for Paul. She stares silently at her screen. If this is what it's going to be like from now on, she thinks, I'll have to leave.

She wonders what Iben makes of their new circumstances. There have been times when Iben seems to have found Anne-Lise worthwhile. Could it be that this new, formal tone between her and Malene suits Iben better?

iben

the minute twitching of muscles in Iben's cheeks is enough to drive more drops of sweat from her scalp. She can feel them running down her skin under the white T-shirt she has draped over the top of her head and the back of her neck as protection from the sun. Sweat trickles down behind her large sunglasses, along her nose and the rest of her face, sliding over the thick layer of sun lotion that covers her skin. However hard she squints her eyes, she cannot escape the color, the red glare of the sun as the light pierces her dark glasses and her eyelids.

Their truck stands on the dirt track snaking between the mud huts of the slum. They are almost surrounded by a crowd that is growing all the time. People seem frightened and excited, but no one dares to approach closer than fifty feet or so, for fear of the armed men who are guarding the four hostages. There is shouting and talking from the back of the crowd. When Iben opens her eyes wide again, she sees an ocean of heads, a rippling surface formed by the women's colorful headdresses and the men's shorn black curls.

There was an attack earlier in the day, when the people almost reached the driver's cabin before two of them were shot and the crowd withdrew again. By now the bodies must have been carried away along the open sewers that also serve as paths between the myriad huts. Above the noise of radio stations broadcasting in Arabic and Swahili, Iben can hear crying and shouting from somewhere in there.

Since the shooting, some of the Nubian men have formed a line to stop the teeming mass of people from drifting closer. These men are as co-ordinated as militiamen in civvies. They all wear similar clothes, trousers and garish shirts, possibly European leftovers from the 1970s. They stand as if nailed to the spot, but they are alert. One of them carries a heavy machine gun of the same type as the hostage takers'; the rest are armed only with clubs and long, sharp pangas. They wait.

The boy stands right in front of Iben, clutching his machine gun and intoning long prayers and quotes from the Bible while he scans the sea of people. The crowd is growing larger all the time, and more heavily armed. Like the other hostage takers, the boy belongs to the Luo tribe. Iben observes him as he slowly goes to pieces.

It's impossible to predict what he will do. Iben shifts her thigh a little along the sheet of metal, part of the car's framework that serves as their seat. It is burning hot and she pulls her leg back again.

On the horizon, beyond the tin roofs of the shacks, the skyscrapers in the center of Nairobi rise against the backdrop of pale blue sky. If one of the Nubians surrounding the car has called the police, they should have been here already. The police force is notorious for being corrupt and violent, but what other hope is there?

The line of men in front of the car moves forward a few steps. There are two men with machine guns now, and both are pointed at the driver's cab. In a while, they'll probably have ten.

One of the two Luos in the driver's cabin cries out in fear. The boy shifts to stand right in front of Iben. His mouth is twisting as he takes aim with his gun.

The crowd in front of the truck moves in a little closer, then backs away. The front line of Nubians has gone through this pattern of advance and retreat before. Cathy, who works with Iben, shakes her head every time. Now she whispers, "What does it mean? Why are they doing that?"

No one answers, because there seems to be no point to the movement. Maybe the crowd is reacting to something going on inside the cab.

The two Nubians who were shot did not have an easy death. In films, killings happen quickly, almost cleanly. This was different. The two men in their dated nylon shirts had lain on the baked, cracked mud in front of the truck, thrashing about in spasms, piss stains spreading on their trousers.

Cathy is fidgeting. She seems to want more sunscreen for her sandaled feet, but doesn't dare ask permission to look for the tube in her rucksack. Next to her, Roberto must fear that the kidnappers will kill the leader first. Slightly built and with the kind of Italianate looks that can seem a touch effeminate, he doesn't look like any kind of leader.

The other Luo on the tailgate catches Iben's eye. He has lost a couple of teeth, is taller than the others, and smells more strongly of the slum.

She looks down at once, but not quickly enough.

"You. Yes, you!"

He puts his panga under her chin. It is so wide that she can see its far edge as the sharp blade touches her throat. This is the moment when I should think of my loved ones back home, a voice inside her says. No one comes to mind.

She tries, pushes herself. Everyone I love, everyone who loves me.

Still nobody. Only the thought that I've wasted my life, I'm going to die, and no man will weep for the love and the loss of me. I have no children and no father. My mother will weep, and so will the two women who are my best friends. But that's not enough, not nearly enough.

You deserve to die, murmurs the voice inside her head. You've had twenty-eight years and you've done nothing with them.

Then the voice scolds her. You always think too much, always about yourself, always self-critical. Now you must act.

The tall Luo interrupts her thoughts. "You get out of the truck. Get the driver out. Then you take the wheel."

Iben looks up at him. She does her best to make her every movement calm and controlled. "Get the driver out? Why?"

The tall Luo's black face is contorted and inscrutable, like a corpse preserved in a bog. "You open the door. You carry the driver out. Then you go sit at the wheel."

"How . . . why carry him?"

"He is dead."

Iben senses that the man holding the panga at her throat feels something after all, behind his tense, closed features. It's the broken rhythm of his breathing that gives him away, and the slight quivering of the blade against her skin.

"They got to him. They cut his throat."

That voice inside her head, her thoughts, reminds her of the dead bodies she writes about all the time. They deserved better than just twenty-eight years of life. Everyone does. Everyone deserves to find someone to love, a child to care for. And everyone includes me.

Iben lifts her hand slowly to point at the panga held against her neck. She wills her eyes to look pleading, but has no idea what kind of expression is creeping across her face. The thin cotton of her trousers is soaked with sweat where her body touches the white metal seat.

She realizes that for a moment he feels hesitant about causing any more deaths. But this lasts only for a few seconds, and then his face looks stony again.

His voice is deep. "You open the door. You carry my friend out."

A quick glance at Roberto, Cathy, and Mark convinces her that they too have worked out why, every now and then, the Nubians advance toward the truck and take aim with their guns. The trigger is any move by the hostage taker on the passenger seat. He needs to shove the dead man out of the cab so he can drive the truck away. Every time he tries to do so the Nubians walk forward until he gives up. The man towering over Iben wants her to do something that none of the Luos dares to.

With the panga against her neck, Iben glances down at the ground, the dried crust of mud mixed with excrement and garbage. Could she run more than sixty feet between the truck and the line of Nubians to hide among them? If the hostage takers shoot her dead, retribution will be immediate, so they have nothing to gain by killing her. But then, there's no telling how rationally they think.

Without a word she stands, her eyes fixed on her comrades. Cathy begins to cry.

The Nubians cheer when they see Iben climbing down from the tailgate of the truck. Some of them step forward. One man must be confused, because he drops his large black spear. But still no one dares to move into no-man's-land. Instead most of them jostle to get back into their former positions behind the front line.

In the dust on the road that could have led to freedom, Iben looks around with fresh eyes. Can she avoid carrying out the order for just a little longer?

She wonders if she should shout "Here I come" so that the hostage taker in the cab doesn't shoot her from sheer surprise when he sees her coming up from behind. On the other hand, it would give the Nubians more time to react, and they might well decide it's worth shooting one hostage to stop the other three from being driven away.

She looks at the tall man on the tailgate and speaks to him quietly. "Tell him I'm coming. I mustn't frighten him."

The two Luos talk for a moment. None of the Nubians reacts. It seems that Iben was right in thinking that none of them understands Dhuluo.

The conflict between Nubians and Luos in the slum began when a Luo family refused to pay rent to a Nubian landlord. The landlord summoned a group of men from his tribe to meet him at the family's shack. They wounded six tenants and killed two more. The group went on to challenge other tenants and attacked anyone who couldn't pay. After slaughtering and dismembering another ten victims, well over a thousand men from each tribe clashed in the slums, stealing, raping, and killing within each other's territories. The police separated the two armies using tear gas and rubber bullets, but were also accused of having taken the opportunity to rape and steal themselves.

The original reason for the refusal to pay rent in the slum was that Kenya's president, Daniel arap Moi, had informed the Luos that the rent demands were extortionate, since the state, not the Nubians, owned the land in the Kibera area. It was the British colonial administration that had given the Nubians their management rights.

Iben hesitates. Will the boy on the back of the truck really shoot her if she doesn't move the dead driver?

There's a childishness about him that sets him apart from the other, harder-faced boys here, some of whom are just eight years old.

She tries to see what the two Nubians with machine guns are up to. One of them is out of sight behind the truck. The other is right there, wearing a white shirt, dark green trousers, and a baseball cap. She can't make out his face, his willingness to kill, at this distance.

Smells. Dust. Sunlight.

The Nubian with the gun. The boy on the truck with the gun. The horde of onlookers. A fly, insisting on crawling into her ear.

On the tailgate the hostage takers wave their weapons and shout.

At home in the quiet Copenhagen office, Iben's place opposite Malene stands empty. She has a vision of the pale winter afternoon light falling over her bare desk with its waiting keyboard and curling Post-it notes. The fading light of the office seems to merge with the emptiness of her remembered life.

She grabs the door handle on the driver's side and hears the crowd stir, then shout. Their language is just as incomprehensible to her as Dhuluo. The dead driver has been propped up against the door, and when she opens it the body falls out of the car sideways. Iben has to jump away to avoid being knocked over.

Until today, the only corpse she has ever seen was her father's. It was nine years ago, and the staff at Roskilde District Hospital had washed the body, closed its eyes, and placed it in a small private room with net-curtained windows.

The dead driver is suspended, with his feet jammed under the pedals. His chest and head have swung out and down, hitting the ground just in front of Iben. A swarm of flies rises from his chest, where his blood-soaked shirt and trousers have already stiffened in the heat.

His face is twisted, his mouth open and his skin gray from blood loss.

Iben backs away into the cloud of dust. It is as if she is no longer herself.

She hasn't thought about how the terrified man on the passenger seat might react. It turns out he has an automatic handgun.

Like everyone here he is used to the flies, but there are so many and they swarm around him for a different reason: he was sprayed with his friend's blood inside the hot cab. His arms holding the gun are tired now after battling with the large, insistent insects.

He swings the gun around to point it at Iben. His voice is hoarse. "You shall . . . you shall sit."

Iben feels nauseous. She stares at the ridges on the road. A few seconds—is it minutes?—pass and still she feels as if she is someone else.

She sits down on the driver's seat. The man cannot risk keeping his gun trained on her all the time and has turned to face the wall of Nubians in front of them.

"The police will come," Iben says. "The police will be here soon."

"You drive!"

But she does not start driving. She knows that turning the ignition key will mean the end for both of them.

"Drive!"

Suddenly he leaps up. He must have thought that someone was sneaking up to the door on his side. Someone who would cut his throat, as they did to his friend. He throws the door open and sticks his gun out.

His back is turned. He has given her a fraction of a second. Iben springs out and runs away at an angle to the truck. To aim at her, he has to move over to her seat.

Her feet are pounding, raising clouds of dust. Now, soon, the rattle of the machine gun. The blood, the thump as she hits the ground. But it's all strangely quiet. Iben runs and runs.

At last she reaches the human wall. The people part and close around her like dark water. She runs on, falling into the crowd. Then, though her legs keep kicking out, she can move no further. The dark mass that has saved her now holds her. She recognizes some of the men and women she has met at football matches or training days or reconciliation meetings. They will starve and die if their rent income from the Luos is reduced further, just as the Luos may die if the rents are not lowered.

Her body melts under her, but many hands hold her upright. They give her water, pour it into her mouth and over her head and body. She drinks from their plastic buckets and calabashes, knowing that it will give her diarrhea for a week at least. It doesn't matter.

That ever-alert part of her mind wonders if she shouldn't move into the densest part of the crowd to observe her colleagues in relative safety. But it's impossible: all her strength has gone; she is soaked to the skin and still terrified that the armed men in the truck will catch sight of her. Instead she ends up sitting on the ground, leaning against a hard cow-dung wall and holding on to a toothless elderly woman whom she doesn't recognize, but who behaves as if they were old friends.

Iben has been working in Kenya for an international organization called Stop Ethnic Cleansing, which tries to remain neutral in the tribal conflicts. In the Nairobi slums, humanitarian organizations tend to be nervous about the Kenyan government's Luo-friendly policies, and this sometimes makes SEC look pro-Nubian—and hence, presumably, anti-Luo.

The Nubian crowd is not likely to have gathered here simply to save the lives of four strangers, but they would like the kidnapping to fail. They need to ensure that SEC doesn't withdraw from its reconciliation work in the slums because it fears for the lives of its aid workers. The people have come to fight for their own lives.

Iben's feet stamp in the dust, as if still wanting to run. She hears her own noisy breathing. Her mind is in a whirl, analyzing everything that led up to this.

It was Roberto's secretary who had received the invitation for SEC staff to meet an important tribal leader. When the boy in the Hong Kong T-shirt came along as a guide to show them the way, Roberto's secretary had assured them that this was perfectly in order. Had she known about the plan to ambush them and take them hostage all along?

Iben recalls the expression on the secretary's face (caring), and the tone of her voice (cheerful). No reason to point the finger at her. Except . . . she knew what she was doing. Of course. She is a Luo, and since everyone around her believes in tribal allegiances, so must she. She is bound to ask herself if other people will support her family and their way of life. Or are they out to destroy them? Any talk about impartiality would sound like treachery.

The sound of a car siren causes a scare. At last, the police are coming.

Iben climbs up the wall she has been leaning against, finding footholds on protruding bits of the framework of branches. It is so low that there is only one and a half feet to climb, but in the shade of the overhanging tin roof her white face is less obvious.

An open truck full of policemen pulls up. Another truckload stops on the other side of the crowd. The hostages and their guards remain as they were when she ran off. All sit and stand in exactly the same positions. Even with the police here, the prisoners look cowed.

The howl of the sirens is piercing, but Iben feels relieved—until she realizes what's going on, that is. The police are attacking the crowd with long white truncheons. Several of the beaten Nubians are too badly injured to get up again.

Iben wants to rush to the officer in charge and cry out, "No! Don't! They want to set us free. You've got it wrong! Don't hit them." She wants to stop the beatings before someone is crippled for life.

Her toothless companion clings to her and tries to make Iben follow her into the network of sewer paths between the houses. She speaks all the time, a fast, meaningless babble, but Iben cannot face running away from the crowd that turned up to help her when she and her companions' lives were in danger. The woman throws her arms around Iben and weighs her down, sobbing helplessly.

Already at a distance, Iben shouts at the police that they're hitting the wrong people. But the road has emptied quickly as the crowd flees into the fine-meshed network of alleyways. The police won't chase them there. Only the injured are left behind, scattered here and there on the road. And in the middle of it all, the large white SEC truck stands untouched.

A couple of yards away from the police, Iben begins to think again. She stops shouting and glances quickly over her shoulder. Is the old woman still around? Is there a place to disappear into?

Then two policemen grab hold of her. They don't hit her, just march her off to join her fellow hostages and their captors. She tries to explain what's happened. Several times. Still they escort her back to the seat she managed to get away from.

Cathy buries her face in her hands. She whispers to Roberto, her voice despairing, "It's *you* who should know about the police. They protect these men. You should have known."

She seems to be brimming with a mixture of tears, anger, and something else, something new at least to Iben. Cathy keeps repeating herself, mumbling like the old bag lady who hangs around on the street corner near the DCIG office. "It's your fault. You're in charge. It's your job to protect us."

Iben steals a glance at Roberto's face, but it looks blank.

Two policemen heave the dead driver's body onto the back of the truck.

The way ahead has been cleared, and now the hostage takers can drive on.

O ne evening, at dusk, Iben was walking along the suburban streets. It wasn't long after her father's death. The snow reflected the blue-tinged winter light. She was breathing easily, listening to the snow crystals crunching under her boots. Beneath a fruit tree, its branches covered with snow, two women were calling their cats. There must be others in this quiet town who came to call their cats at nightfall.

"Kitty, kitty, kitty, come to Mommy."

Iben suddenly felt that all these women were calling her dead father. All around town, mothers straightened their backs and got up from their kitchen tables or from the corner of their sofas or from double beds with only a single duvet and a tear-stained pillow. They got up and stood in lit doorways, calling out into Roskilde's still darkness.

"Kitty kitty, come to Mommy. Come inside. Kitty-cat, come to me."

Iben is rooting around in the discount boxes at Company's, looking for blouses. Next to one box are bits of fur that look like the dyed coats of cats.

Could they be?

She has already been to seven shops without finding anything that would do. All this tramping around shops is Gunnar's fault. He doesn't appear to be interested in how people dress, but he fell for Malene and she both knows and cares about clothes.

While Iben examines a cream-colored blouse to see if it's shaped properly at the waist, she tells herself that it doesn't matter in the slightest what she wears.

Why would I start running into him now? Where, anyway? I've never met him by chance before.

She starts looking through the next box, wrestling with her thoughts.

The following morning, Paul, carrying a stack of papers, wanders into the library to say something to Anne-Lise. He sounds annoyed. The new arrangements mean that the entire office can hear them.

"Anne-Lise, there are some mysterious stains on the printouts you just gave me. They're covered in fingerprints and something like toner, but it's brown."

When Iben looks up from her screen Malene is already watching her. They do their best not to smile.

"Oh, no," Anne-Lise replies. "The stuff's all over my hands as well. What could it be?"

Now Paul sounds more confused than irritated. "And there's some on your nose. A long mark. You must have rubbed it with your finger. And there are some stains on your blouse."

"Oh, no!"

There are sounds of Anne-Lise rummaging through papers, and then of drawers being opened and shut. She can't find the source of the color. Paul leaves and walks back to his office. Iben and Malene don't move.

A little later Anne-Lise comes into the Winter Garden to ask the others' opinion. "You know, at first I thought maybe my lipstick had come apart, but it's fine. My handbag is completely clean inside. And now I've no idea."

Iben watches Anne-Lise. Does she suspect them of playing a practical joke? Anne-Lise shows them her hands. The reddish brown material has stuck under her cuticles and in the deep crevices on the backs of her fingers.

Iben asks if it smells of anything.

Anne-Lise holds one of her hands a bit away from her nose and considers the odor.

"I don't know. It smells a bit like food. Slightly sweet, maybe?"

Later, back in the library, Anne-Lise screams. They all jump up and run to her.

She is standing in the middle of the floor, her hands stretched out stiffly in front of her with her fingers spread.

"It came from the shelf . . . and I thought I'd . . ."

It's easy to see what has happened. Anne-Lise had noticed more reddish brown spots on a shelf unit she uses regularly. She pulled out books and box files and found a trail of dried drops that apparently came from a magazine box on the top shelf. When she reached for it, the box slipped from her hand. Anne-Lise leapt backward and the box landed just in front of her, spraying her clothes and face. Fortunately, it wasn't a large amount. Even so, it is now sticking to her hair and face, and her right hand and arm are moist and gluey with blood.

She stands still, gasping for breath, speechless. Nobody is keen on getting too close to her, as that would mean stepping in the pool around her feet.

Iben steels herself to do something. "Anne-Lise, this is awful! I don't . . . look, you lie down. We'll clean up . . ."

Iben gasps and holds her breath in a futile attempt to escape the sweetly nauseating stench of the congealing blood that covers the floor. She would like to help, but has to run to the lavatory. As she hovers over the basin wondering if she'll throw up, Malene joins her. She says she feels just as bad.

By the time they return, Camilla has opened all the windows and found a cloth and a bucket. She is wiping the floor. Anne-Lise is sitting limply in her chair, about to pass out. She has taken off her cardigan, dropped it on the floor, and tried to clean herself up with damp tissues, but she still looks dreadful.

They can't think of what to say. What does this mean? Who could've thought up such a thing?

When Paul finds out, his first reaction is to march over to each window and door, without a word, to check for any signs of a break-in.

"When was it done?" Iben asks Anne-Lise. "I mean, the blood—when could it have been put there?"

Anne-Lise's voice is a whisper: "I don't . . . I don't use that box often. It . . . When was it . . . last week?"

They are all immersed in their own thoughts as they clean up Anne-Lise's books and papers. Each item has to be wiped with a damp cloth.

After a while Anne-Lise pulls herself together and goes off to the restroom to wash. Paul comes back to say that, as far as he can see, no locks have been tampered with. He manages to lower the shelf to the floor so they can clean behind it.

Most likely it was pigs' blood from a butcher's, they tell each other as they work away. They're doing absolutely everything they shouldn't do at the scene of a crime, Iben thinks. Every single clue is being washed away. But they carry on, just the same. It seems that all of them, including Paul, tacitly agree that the police should not be asked to deal with this, which also means they must think that someone connected to the Center is responsible.

Once the worst of the mess has been cleared up and Anne-Lise has returned from the restroom, Paul takes charge. "We need to have a meeting about this. Anne-Lise, is there anything we can do for you? It must've been appalling. I mean, the Center will put up the money to pay for new clothes. But, well, I don't know. Would you like to see a psychologist?"

Anne-Lise looks better—in one piece again. She doesn't want any counseling, she says, but she would like to go home. Now. She is not in the mood for a meeting.

Paul orders a taxi for her. Everyone tries to be supportive and comforting until the taxi takes her away. Then they go into Paul's office to talk.

Paul is calm.

"I know this has been a terrible shock for everyone, especially for Anne-Lise. But looking at it from a broader perspective . . . you know, I think we should allow ourselves to feel slightly relieved. It's clearly not Mirko Zigic or some other experienced killer who's threatening the Center. They wouldn't waste their energy on this kind of prank. It's quite a relief, don't you agree? This looks more like the handiwork of one of those neo-Nazi teenagers. They keep sending me letters, but they've never done anything worse than break three windowpanes at my home. And they shoved a decaying fish through our mail slot. This has been nasty, but, when all is said and done, it has also clarified the situation: we're not being chased by Zigic or any of his kind."

Paul has clearly prepared this little lecture for them, and they listen in silence, unwilling to interrupt him.

"Now, many of us will have come to the conclusion that whoever is bothering us must have a link to the Center. We can't be certain, of course. Our front door isn't locked during working hours, so anybody could slip inside.

"I'll take action immediately. Naturally, the board must be told, and I'll explain that we need a secure front door and a CCTV camera on the stairs. If the camera is wired up to our computers, we will all have access to an on-screen window showing us who is approaching our landing. And we'll be able to lock both our front door and the street door with one keystroke, without moving from our desks. The board has to accept that it's worth spending money on getting our security systems up to speed.

"They will ask me how I can be sure that this isn't an inside job. Now, I cannot imagine that any of you would want to do this kind of thing to Anne-Lise—it's simply unbelievable. But, again, I have to say that we can't be certain at this stage—just that we can choose either to trust each other or not."

Paul looks pleased with himself. "My experience tells me that trust always brings out the best in people. Much more effective than trying to control everyone, which is what I'll tell the board. Unless there's a strong reason for changing my mind, I choose to trust the people I work with."

He pauses, but nobody speaks up.

"Do you agree? Or does anyone want to comment?"

Nobody does.

They all stay on to chat, mostly about the reasons for a private war against DCIG and when the person might have sneaked in. Iben notices that Paul, for all his declared faith in his colleagues, is alert and watching them closely. Will someone give herself away? His casual questions and intent way of listening are quite transparent.

But then, he's not the only one. They all make a point of insisting on their good intentions, each declaring, with slight variations, "The person who did this must be caught!" meaning "It wasn't me!"

"If we all agree that none of us has done this," Malene asks, "shouldn't we call the police?"

Paul smiles. "Yes, of course. You're right. I'll do it at once."

. . .

In the evening Iben visits her mother in Roskilde. It is the ninth anniversary of her father's death and they have met on that day ever since he died. It has become a tradition for them to have a special meal together, with the fine wines and good food that Iben's father liked so much. At the dining table, halfway through the first course, the appetizing smell of sautéed lamb chops is wafting through from the kitchen. As usual, it is very quiet.

Iben's mother wants to talk about the Center and Iben's safety. Iben would prefer to change the topic, but explains patiently: "Mom, it can't have been any of the men you read about in our newsletter. The police checked the locks and said there was no sign of a break-in."

"But someone did get in all the same."

"I don't think Serbian mass murderers can be bothered with sending e-mails or tricks like pouring blood into a magazine box."

Iben could have admitted that, ever since receiving the threatening e-mail, she has taken a combat knife with her everywhere she goes. In fact, she has taped the sheath upside down to her leg, the handle level with the top of her sock, and has practiced drawing the knife in case of a violent attack. Her fastest time so far is three seconds. But she hasn't told anyone about the knife, not even Grith or Malene. Her own nervousness has started to annoy her, but it doesn't abate.

Her mother seems to be concentrating on the remains of her portion of salmon terrine, but looks up quickly when Iben draws in her breath. She doesn't say anything.

"I know it must seem far-fetched to you, but what Grith said about split identities is the only thing that makes sense to me. It's somehow reasonable that one personality needn't know what the other one is up to. And if all that is true, then Anne-Lise might have poured the blood into the box file herself. Maybe some part of her hates her everyday self. I know it sounds odd, but . . . can you think of a better explanation?"

All this is somehow unbearably grim. Iben blinks a few times before starting up again. "Grith says that it's not that unusual. And Anne-Lise seems different . . . I mean, I think she has psychological problems."

Iben's mother slowly eats her last forkful of terrine before coming out with what's on her mind: "By now you've been there long enough, haven't you? It would look all right if you applied for other jobs, I mean."

"I don't want to apply for other jobs."

"There you are . . . well, all I thought was—"

"What we do matters. Someone has to do it. And anyway, Malene works there too."

"Yes, of course."

They take the plates to the kitchen. Iben's mother returns with the meat dish, and Iben follows with the red wine and salad.

Iben's mother is a nurse and her father was a doctor. When Iben reflects on her childhood, she often thinks that she and her father were less than kind to her mother. From the age of six onward, Iben devoured books and loved discussing them with her father. Iben's mother was never a member of their smart little mutual admiration society. Grith has argued more than once that Iben collaborated with her father because she was terrified that he would despise her as he did her mother. Later Iben became a medical student, just like her father. One of the outcomes of Iben's breakdown within a year of his death was that she left medicine and took up literature instead.

They drink a toast to the dead man and speak a little about him, recalling some of the things they did together. Then Iben asks her mother how her week has been.

Still, Iben can't help feeling irritated at her mother's remark about how she should get a new job. Her mother won't leave it alone, hanging on even though she tries to change the subject.

"But it seems such a ghastly place. You wouldn't want to stay on forever, would you?"

"It isn't ghastly at all!"

"Blood pouring from the shelves, and—"

"Mom, that's an exception! I've been there for two years now, for Christ's sake! Other things have happened. Please stop harping on about this."

"But of course . . . I didn't mean . . ."

Iben really wants to be nice, to behave like the sympathetic person she finds it so easy to be when she is with other people. It's strange, but the minute she sets foot in this house, she feels resentful, hemmed in, fighting to break free. Whenever she comes here it doesn't take long before she starts slouching and dragging her feet across the pretty parquet floors. She waves her arms about more than usual when she holds forth at the dining table. This time, in the middle of their conversation, she hears herself allude to her sex life in Copenhagen (she doesn't have one). Besides, true or not, she would never say anything like that even to her friends.

It's a fact: "back home in Roskilde" Iben becomes somebody else. She understands perfectly well why her mother finds it hard to get along with her.

Over the beautifully cooked lamb chops, Iben tries to explain. "Isak Dinesen wrote something to the effect that we take on the identity of the masks we wear. In books about the psychology of social interaction, people are always discussing role-playing and how we pick roles for each other. But that's not what really happens. It's the other way around . . ."

Speaking of "roles" reminds Iben's mother about a previous neighbor, who once joined an amateur dramatic society attached to the open-air stage in the Dyrehaven Park. But Iben won't be distracted by anecdotes.

"We don't just put on a different mask or choose to act out a role. The change isn't external, just as it isn't voluntary. Instead, we are transformed into shifting but fully realized people, or 'identities.' Each of us contains a variety of identities."

Iben's mother has to get up to see to the apple tart in the kitchen. Afterward, Iben can't find a way to return to the subject.

Iben travels back to Copenhagen by train. She sits very still, looking out into the darkness. The lights in Høje Taastrup slip by. It's good that Mom is worried about me, she thinks. I would've been much more upset if she hadn't cared.

Time passes, but she still mulls over the evening with her mother. Did I really give her a chance to understand what I was talking about? That bit about Isak Dinesen and identities—perhaps I was being too cryptic?

The inside of the train car is reflected in the dark windowpane. She has to press her face against the glass and shelter her eyes with her hands in order to see what is outside.

Did I even bother trying to make myself understood? I meant to sound as if I was sharing my thoughts with her, but in reality I was being ruthless. I didn't even give her a chance to understand. It was almost as if I wanted to punish her. Isak Dinesen? Christ, how stupid can you get? There I was, trying to make a detached analysis of identity, and all the time I was caught up in one myself, trapped inside the head of a rebellious teenage girl!

Iben leans back and stops trying to penetrate the blackness outside. Inside the car there isn't much to see. She is almost alone. The only other passenger is a man sitting several seats away. Only the back of his round, bald head is visible.

She thinks about the others at the DCIG. What characters can they turn into?

hen Iben comes into work the next morning, Camilla isn't there. Iben presses Play on the blinking answering machine and hears Camilla's voice saying that she isn't well and won't be in today.

Camilla doesn't answer her phone, but there's a recorded message giving her cell phone number, so Iben dials it.

Camilla is reticent. "It's personal. I'd rather not get any of you mixed up in this." Her voice is as melodious and warm as usual, but a little cagey.

Iben tries to find out what the problem is, but Camilla avoids straight answers. She is scared—that much is obvious; but Iben is curious.

"Where are you?"

"Oh, nowhere special."

"But you don't want to be at home?"

"No, not right now. Better not."

"Look, Camilla, if you have any idea at all about who might be behind the stunt with the blood, then I think you ought to tell the rest of us."

"You're right, I know that. But I'm absolutely certain that the person I'm worrying about isn't after any of you."

"Camilla, listen. We were the ones who received those e-mails. And the blood was on Anne-Lise's shelf."

Camilla doesn't reply. They chat for a while and then she bursts into tears.

"There was a man once . . . it was so silly of me, but I went out with him. A long time ago. I didn't want to tell you. The whole thing is so . . . I just didn't want anyone to know."

"Oh, Camilla, you mustn't worry." Iben feels herself soften. She holds the receiver with both hands, the way Malene sometimes does. "You can trust us! Honestly, all of us—and I mean all—know what it's like to fall for somebody who's not the right one. Don't feel bad. We've all been there!"

Iben gives Camilla time to reply, but the line remains silent. Iben reassures her again. "Nobody will judge you. It doesn't matter who you've been in love with. But are you sure we have nothing to fear from this man—that he isn't after any of us?"

"No! You mustn't think that. Please don't worry."

It's hard to think of what to say next.

"Is Finn there with you?"

"Oh, yes. Well, no—but he will be, when he comes back from work. He can leave early today."

"It would be nice to know where you are."

"I'd rather not say."

"I'm only asking because there might be something one of us can do for you?"

"No, thank you. But the fewer people who know, the better, I think."

Paul turns up in the middle of their conversation and wants to speak to Camilla too. She promises him that she'll be back in a few days, when the new security measures are in place.

Malene arrives next. Iben notes the taxi-borne neatness of her hair and skin; she isn't windswept and red with cold from cycling. Malene's arthritis has probably acted up this morning, but Iben makes no mention of it. They chat about Camilla and who the man she's scared of might be.

According to Malene, Camilla is imagining things. "The e-mails couldn't possibly have come from one of her old boyfriends. Never mind who he is—it doesn't make any sense."

Anne-Lise comes along to talk to them. After what she went through yesterday, she might well have called in sick herself. Paul urged her to take time off, but she must have more steel in her than anyone thought.

Malene holds the fingers of one hand with her other hand. She waits until Anne-Lise has left.

"Iben, did Camilla ever tell you who she went out with before she got together with Finn?"

Later that afternoon Iben is on the phone, talking to yet another unemployed graduate. Practically every week, a few of these forlorn young ex-academics contact the Center and want to know if there might be a position available, or at least a freelance job, or a project assistantship—or a chance to make the coffee, anything. Iben tries to turn them down as gently as possible, but many won't take no for an answer.

While Iben listens to the job seeker's long list of qualifications, Anne-Lise emerges from the library. She looks deeply serious.

"Malene, may I have a word?"

"Of course."

Malene makes no sign of getting up, so Anne-Lise asks again: "Could you join me in the library for a moment?"

Malene's calm seems almost a pose. "Why? Can't you tell me whatever it is in front of Iben?"

"I thought maybe you'd prefer—"

"There's nothing you can say to me that Iben isn't allowed to hear." Malene turns to look at the door to Paul's office. Today, just for once, it's been left wide open, and she smiles faintly, as if he can see her. "And the same goes for Paul. Now that we've got an open-door policy . . ."

Anne-Lise still waits.

Finally Malene gets up. With a quick wink to Iben, she follows Anne-Lise into the library.

Neither of them closes the door, but Anne-Lise leads the way in among the shelving so that Iben can hear only a distant murmur of their voices.

Iben's anxious caller gives up, and she returns to her work on a new article for *Genocide News* on the mass killings in the Sudan. Two million people murdered over the last twenty years. She has never written anything lengthy on Sudan before, and her desk is awash with books and papers.

The voices in the library are raised now. Paul probably can't hear what is being said, but Iben can. Anne-Lise is speaking loudly, but sounds unsure of herself.

". . . say they have never heard of any library search facility here, except what's available online."

Malene crisply enunciates every word—a sign of anger that Iben recognizes. "And who would have liked to know about other search options?"

"That's not important."

"Anne-Lise, I normally tell people what is available. If I have failed to do so, I would like to know who has been given the wrong information. Obviously. How else can I make up for my mistake?"

The answer is inaudible, but Malene's voice cuts through the mumble. "Anne-Lise, please get on with it. I have other things to do."

A short pause. Now Anne-Lise speaks very quickly. "What I've heard, in so many words, is that you've tried to keep customers away from the library."

"So tell me who you're referring to!"

"Certainly that doesn't matter."

Malene sounds even more authoritative now. "I'm sorry, but I disagree. You and I are in this together. Anything you hear about one of your colleagues should be passed on—it's part of being a team. We're meant to work together here—you too! The Center is what matters. And because of that, everyone must be given the chance to make up for her mistakes, so that we can improve our service."

Anne-Lise turns the volume down again, but now her tone is plaintive.

A moment later Malene returns and whispers to Iben: "Anne-Lise has talked with Erik Prins about me."

"About you?"

"That woman is fucking unbelievable."

"I overheard some of your conversation."

"Thought you might."

Erik Prins is a small man with a potbelly and oddly shiny skin. His clothes look as if he's had them for decades. He is probably in his late thirties, but people think of him as much older.

For years Erik has been working on a huge tome about Scandinavian foreign policy after the Second World War. Nobody knows how his years of writing have been financed—possibly a grant or, more likely, some kind of state benefit. No one has wanted to know enough to ask.

Erik often comes to the Center to read or look for new books. When he has been sitting in the large meeting room they usually need to air it afterward. He likes to eat while he reads, and his dull food parcels always carry a powerful smell of liver sausage and damp rye bread. Even so, Malene has always singled Erik out among the users of the Center and gives him the best possible support. She often finds time for a chat as well. They talk about this and that, including Erik's old classmate from his time as a history student, Frederik Thorsteinsson.

Paul has told them that, on several occasions, the DCIG board has noted Erik's praise of the Center's excellent service. Without fail, Frederik passes Erik's opinions on to the board, and his pronouncements have come to be regarded as practically infallible. The members are highly educated researchers, experts in their fields, who feel that the shabby little man speaks for Everyman and is a perfect representative of the Center's typical user.

Iben smiles, but she is concerned. "I must say, I've never heard of anyone who hasn't been happy with your work. And Erik, of all people! That spoiled little man!"

She doesn't give a damn if Anne-Lise can hear what she's saying, but she lowers her voice slightly to keep Paul out of it.

"Maybe he complimented Anne-Lise. You know, like you do when you first collaborate with somebody new—oiling the wheels, kind of thing. He'll have told her something like she's very good at her job and he wishes he had known about her before."

Iben's eyes shift away uneasily, just for a second. Then she continues: "That's the kind of thing a person would say. He could've said it to you. Or to me, or anybody."

Malene leans back in her chair with a weary sigh. "True. Everyone says things like that, just to be friendly. It's too bad that Anne-Lise takes it all so seriously."

But later on, when Malene and Iben get together in the copier room, Malene brings up the subject again. Iben realizes this will take some time and sits down on the table. The copier thumps on and on, copying, sorting, and stapling a large selection of newspaper cuttings that Camilla should have gotten ready for circulation to the board today. Now Iben has taken on the job.

Malene paces restlessly up and down. "I've been thinking about what

Anne-Lise said. How come she says that I've tried to exclude her? She obviously believes it. Maybe she has cross-examined Erik about it."

Iben tucks her hands under her thighs. "Or it could be a bit of everything? He thought that he'd better be kind and she responded by questioning him."

"Yes, and he felt pressured to say something about me and they've ended up discussing me in detail. We mustn't forget that now he depends on her, more than on anyone else here. Being on good terms with her is more important for Erik than getting on with me now. It's Anne-Lise who can give him special treats."

"Yep. Now what?"

"Iben, this is important. If she goes on gossiping behind my back, she might turn lots of people against me. Like Frederik. And Ole. Anyone."

"She could."

"Yes. So I must find out."

Today Paul joins them for lunch. The atmosphere is tense, although nobody mentions Erik Prins or the conversation in the library. Earlier, Malene went down to the supermarket to get fresh rolls. She asked if she could get anything for anyone else. Anne-Lise handed her the money to buy a portion of carpaccio, the kind that comes with olive oil and grated Parmesan. Now she says that everyone must have some, but apart from Paul no one does.

After a while Iben cannot bear the silence, which is broken only by terse exchanges; she decides to tell them about the book she has been reading into the small hours of the morning. Grith lent it to her the other day.

"It's about split personalities. It's a fact that nine out of ten patients are women. And almost all of them have been subjected to violence or other abuse in childhood. The author puts it quite plainly: 'A split personality is a little girl imagining that the abuse is directed toward another person.' Which is why at least one of the personalities is often still a little girl."

Grith's book is called *Dissociative Identity Disorder: Diagnosis, Clinical Features, and Treatment of Multiple Personality.* Maybe this isn't an ideal subject for discussion right now, but Iben tries to speak without hinting at any of the office subtexts.

"It's very hard for anyone to know if she has DID—a split identity, that is. As your 'normal self,' you can't recall having had a bad childhood. Many patients forget altogether and might even remember the man who abused them as a good person."

The others stay focused on their food and don't respond to what she is telling them. They do seem interested, though, so Iben carries on.

"The best indication is that you can't remember what you've done for a period of time, or you feel you've been behaving out of character. But it's not cut and dried. A survey of people with no psychological problems showed that about seventy-five percent of the subjects have had moments when they easily did something that they used to think was difficult. More than fifty percent said that after driving a car for a long time, there were whole stretches of the journey they couldn't remember. And one out of every ten said they'd found themselves wearing clothes they couldn't re-member putting on."

Suddenly Malene laughs, just as she is about to bite into her cheese sandwich.

"Iben, you're such a geek! Come on, what next? A blow-by-blow ac-count of someone's thesis on postcolonial literature?"

Iben stops rattling off the study results.

After the break, Iben senses that Malene again has something to say, for her ears only. The two of them wait for the others to leave the room. Ole, the board chairman, phones and wants to speak to Paul, who hurries off. Anne-Lise does not leave and makes a show of settling down with the daily paper.

Malene and Iben give up and wander back to their desks. While she was out shopping, Malene had called Erik Prins.

"He swore that under no circumstances would he have said anything about not being pleased with my work. It seems that Anne-Lise was fish-ing for something she could use against me. At least, that's the impression Erik got."

Malene has been composed throughout the lunch break. Now she is sputtering with anger. "I'm going to ask Paul to see me. There's no way I can put up with the way Anne-Lise keeps undermining my standing with the users. I have to work with them every day. She's going around looking for chances to bad-mouth me. It's so disloyal and unprofessional, trying to stab me in the back like that." She leans forward. "Paul must understand that we've stood by that woman for long enough. And it's likely that she's the e-mailer. The idea that it's Camilla's ex-boyfriend is just stupid!"

Anne-Lise walks by and Iben and Malene fall silent. With Anne-Lise back in the library they must finish their talk elsewhere.

The coffee thermos is full and they have already spent a long time in the copier room, which means that they have just about used up any legitimate excuse. That's too bad, though. What they were talking about can't wait.

In the kitchen the rickety dishwasher is churning and the smell of the detergent mixes with the ever-present smell of coffee. The air is hot and damp from the steam that escapes from the whirling hot water. Side by side, they perch on the edge of the kitchen table.

Malene puts a hand to her forehead. Then she asks Iben to come along to the talk with Paul. "You know he always takes what you say seriously."

"What about Camilla? Wouldn't it be better to wait until all three of us are here so we can see him together?"

"Yes, I suppose so. Of course—it'd be best." Malene looks vaguely at the dull day beyond the steamy windowpane. "It's just . . . I'm not sure. You know as well as I do that if Paul puts pressure on Camilla she'll probably back down. The two of us are stronger when we act alone—especially if she comes along and then, halfway through, starts to agree with Paul."

Iben knows this is true and nods.

Malene looks sad. "I feel that I've tried everything to get on better with Anne-Lise. But today I've had to face the fact that I've failed."

Iben rubs her thumb against the tabletop. She doesn't say anything and Malene carries on.

"The only thing we can do is regroup and move on."

Iben looks up from the table and meets Malene's eyes. "What about waiting for a few days? You know, to let things cool off a little."

the café is darker than Iben's usual haunts. As far as she can guess, it is a place where journalists, technicians, and musicians hang out, most of them after working in Broadcasting House just opposite.

As always since the e-mail, she chooses to sit with her back against the wall in a place where she can keep an eye on the door, even though it makes her feel like the number one suspect in a police thriller.

It's early evening but already the night has drawn in. The café is lit by a few spotlights that cast thin crescents of light on the roughly plastered walls. Iben scans one of the entertainment magazines that she used to read a few years ago. She tries to remember what Malene said as they cycled home together after the evening at Sophie's.

Was it "As long as you're not taking Gunnar away from me"?

No, that's not quite right. Maybe she said "You and Gunnar would probably get on better than I do with him. I could get worried about that." What exactly did she say?

Malene's words have faded completely from Iben's mind.

When Iben has skimmed through the last magazine and read everything she wants to read from the small collection of daily papers, she leaves the café in a bad mood. A cold wind is scouring the pavement. It has jammed a plastic bag in between the front-wheel spokes of her bicycle. What Malene says she feels about life comes to Iben's mind as she rummages in her pocket for the bicycle key. Malene sees herself as an outsider, isolated from the common experience that she supposes healthy people must share.

But Malene has someone to love, regardless of his being away on business so much. And not only does Malene have someone, she also knows that if her relationship with Rasmus were to break up, she's both pretty and smart enough to catch any one of twenty other interesting and interested men. Gunnar, for instance.

I'm the one who's the true outsider, Iben thinks. I'm the one who has lived alone for the last three years. I don't have anyone chasing me. And when I do finally meet someone, he'll probably be older and already married. I'm the one still waiting for my real life to begin.

What if Malene had said "You mustn't take Gunnar away from me"? But no, she wouldn't have said that, no matter how much her feet were hurting her that evening.

Iben puts reflective straps around the hems of her trousers and then, with chilly fingers, pulls the lamps from her bag and fixes them on the back and front of the bike. The front light works, but the rear one is broken. Still, if the police spot it, it's easier to talk yourself out of a fine if the light is at least in place.

She has barely sat down on the seat when she gives a sudden start and her heart leaps in her chest. Gunnar has emerged from Broadcasting House and is walking toward the café. He is alone. He is wearing a black leather jacket and his shoulders are hunched against the cold.

She gets off her bicycle and goes to meet him. As soon as he sees her, he pulls his shoulders back and straightens up. Already she feels happy.

"Iben! Good to see you! Why don't you come and have a glass of wine with me? That place I told you about, the Metro Bar, is just across the road."

The sticky tape that she's used to fasten the knife to her leg has caught a hair. It prickles sharply with every step she takes.

They sit at the same table she sat at earlier. After nearly two hours of drinking wine on an empty stomach, Iben is feeling giggly, but at the same time calmer than before they met. She looks at Gunnar's hands. They are large and shapely. The wine is really getting to her. Perhaps evenings like this are the reason Malene persists in meeting this man even though Rasmus objects?

Gunnar tops up Iben's glass. "I've met so many people who've turned into madmen, killing friends and family and complete strangers. Hacking them to death with hoes or spades or whatever else was at hand, apparently without thinking twice. But we shouldn't forget that people, possibly the very same people, are also capable of incredible and inexplicable goodness. I've come across that as well. Villagers who have hidden and protected strangers who've emerged out of the jungle, risking their lives for someone they had no reason to help."

When Gunnar speaks, his words flow in unusually long and coherent thoughts. Iben relaxes. She speaks the same way—the very rhythms of their speech mesh.

"It's true. But when the stranger appears after hiding in the jungle, what determines whether he is saved or left to his own devices and an almost certain death? Or whether he's killed or not? Is it just impulse? A reaction that no one can trace to its source?"

The café is invaded by a small but noisy group of classical musicians, fresh from a Broadcasting House orchestra rehearsal. They pick the table next to Gunnar and Iben's and make a racket by trying to park their instrument cases nearby.

Iben continues: "I once watched this TV documentary about lions. Immediately after the kill—it was an antelope, I think—they fought over the flesh. They really went at each other and could easily have caused serious wounds. But afterward they all slept so peacefully, heads resting on each other's bellies. It didn't take long for all their distrust and aggression to vanish. And naturally they weren't haranguing each other about 'evil' or 'treachery.' "

Should she stop talking? She glances at Gunnar, who seems to be listening attentively. She takes a sip of wine and decides to go on.

"That night a flock of hyenas attacked the lions. During the fight several of the lions behaved as if they were deliberately putting their lives on the line in order to protect their mates. And yet these were the very same animals that had been fighting tooth and nail earlier in the day.

"I keep feeling that it's easy to trace the causes of change, from caring to killing and back again, among animals of the same species. If there's a food shortage or an acute need to reproduce, they're prepared to fight to the death. But when that sort of thing is not an issue, they are loving toward each other, like trusting members of a close family. The change is quick as a flash and relatively uncomplicated. They simply leave the past behind them."

Young men have smooth faces, but when Gunnar smiles slight laughter lines form on either side of his mouth. "Not many people construe mankind in terms of lions."

Iben touches the edge of her sleeve. "But then, in some ways we're not like animals. I mean, for people it isn't solely the desire for food or sex that triggers the kind of actions we regard as evil. It's much more complex than that, although it looks simple: press one button and we will fight, maybe kill, press another and we behave like decent human beings. We don't know what these buttons are, or who's pressing them. We don't even know what instinct it is that drives us."

One of Gunnar's hands rests near the center of the tabletop.

"And that's what your work at DCIG is about, isn't it? I mean, research into 'push-buttons'?"

"That's the idea, though I've never heard it described like that. Still, something triggers the impulse to kill in one segment of society, and they begin to murder another. What is the trigger? And what triggers goodness? If only we could learn to understand the mechanisms, then it should be possible to intervene at an early stage and stop the whole process from developing."

"And when that happens the Center will be awarded the Nobel Prize for Peace, Medicine, and Literature all at the same time."

They both laugh.

The noise from the table next to theirs has stopped. One of the musicians has taken her cello from its case and, in the sudden stillness, moves the bow across the strings. One single note rings out, deep and lasting. Doesn't it sound a little like the wail of an animal? Iben thinks. Maybe the cry of a lion cub. But then again, it doesn't. The note is too pure, too cultured.

When the sound has died away the talking starts up again at the musicians' table. The cellist was obviously using her instrument to illustrate a point. Now she lovingly puts it away again.

Under the table Gunnar's leg touches Iben's. She is scared that he will notice the knife and think that she's paranoid, so she pulls her leg away.

Gunnar breaks the silence. "I can't remember when I was last with someone who made talking together feel so . . . natural."

Does he say this kind of thing to Malene too? Suddenly Iben recalls the acute attacks of illness that force Malene to go to the rheumatological clinic. Her memory flashes up an image of Malene's face distorted with pain.

The big, low candle on their table gutters as a new group of people arrives.

Iben looks at Gunnar. He is somehow too large compared to the flimsy café chair. She can see a trace of tension in his face.

"Iben, if you would like to drop in at my place, anytime, you would be very welcome."

The following morning Iben and Malene are in Paul's office, standing together while he swivels irritably back and forth on his chic executive chair. He has seemed annoyed right from the very start of the meeting. Iben was feeling ill at ease even before they went in to see him. Part of the reason is Malene's and her agreement that Iben should present the facts of the situation.

Iben speaks briefly. "All in all, we feel that it would be good for Anne-Lise to take some sick leave. She needs to recover away from the Center. She isn't herself at the moment."

Paul's next swirl on his chair is especially vigorous.

"No way."

Neither Iben nor Malene can think of anything to do or say for a moment.

"Why . . . ?" Malene finally asks.

Paul stares at them. "She isn't sick. Simple as that."

Both Iben and Malene squirm at the thought of having to present an analysis of Anne-Lise's mental state without any proper evidence.

"Let's do some straight talking," Paul says. "To force sick leave on an employee is something you only do when you're desperate for a chance to fire them. It means that the problem is off your desk for a while and hopefully it will go away on its own. It never does, though."

Iben and Malene are falling over themselves to distance themselves from what he is implying.

"No, that's not it at all . . ."

"Oh, no."

Iben winces. "You mustn't take it like that. All we mean is, maybe Anne-Lise should take some time off. Some problem at home might be troubling her. Anyway, she clearly isn't stable right now. You even offered her the chance to see a psychologist."

Malene follows this up. "What we feel is, she might slip into real mental illness unless she gets some peace."

Paul is unusually direct. "Look, you know as well as I do that to send someone home on these terms is to push her down the slippery slope toward dismissal. For Anne-Lise it would be nearly impossible to return to work here. She has a husband and children who will be affected, one way or another. Besides, the work she does here is excellent. We've hardly given the new measures time to work. You should do the decent thing and give Anne-Lise a chance."

Iben feels blood rushing to her cheeks. A pulse is starting to beat in her temple. "We only made the suggestion because we're working so closely, and collaborating with her is very difficult at the moment. We thought that it would be reasonable to give her some time to get on an even keel . . . and we've tried everything else. Malene saw to it that we, and you, had a meeting with Anne-Lise. And we've changed the way we work . . ."

Malene interrupts. She sounds more upset than she probably wants to. "It might also be dangerous to let her carry on. No matter how difficult it is for us to think of her as . . . unbalanced, there is the matter of the death threats."

Paul stops her. "What's this about the situation being dangerous for *you*? She's the only one around here who had blood poured all over her."

"She could easily have set that up herself!"

Malene catches Paul's eye and then looks at Iben. The effect is to shift Paul's attention.

"Iben, tell Paul again about the books you've been reading."

Iben would dearly like this to end soon or, preferably, for it never to have started. She tries to run through some of her psychiatric insights, but her new knowledge sounds quite out of place.

Paul watches her, his eyes clouding with such disappointment that Iben feels she can't bear it much longer. He interrupts her. "I am person-

ally convinced that the e-mails are not sent by anyone on our team. I expect you to trust the others in the same way."

Malene tries to offer a little support for her friend. "But—"

He almost shouts now: "It is out of the question!"

Then Paul stops turning around in his chair and speaks more quietly.
"We do not, any of us, suspect Anne-Lise. Or Camilla. Period! The video
camera is going to be in place over our front door pretty soon. Once we all
feel safe, everything will sort itself out."

Malene opens her mouth, but a quick glance at Paul makes her close it
again.

They all reflect for a moment.

Paul is the first to break the silence. "Look, I hear what you're saying.
Clearly there are problems, but I won't mention anything about this at the
board meeting today. I'm going to forget what I've heard, unless of course
you would feel differently? It's really to protect you. I'm afraid your behavior wouldn't look too good."

ben and Malene are sitting in the coastal line train on their way to
Denmark's Louisiana Museum of Modern Art. The DCIG and
the Institute of Human Rights have joined forces to run a two-
day conference called "The Reestablishment of Democracy and
Civic Trust in the Former Yugoslavia." Many people are expected
to attend, including 140 international delegates.

The train is relatively empty, because at this time of the
morning the commuters travel into Copenhagen. The sharp
November-morning light pours into the car. The sun stands so
low over the horizon that it shines directly into their eyes as they
try to observe the luxurious seaside villas.

During the week after their awkward meeting in Paul's office, Malene suggested to Paul that they should invest in a new
piece of software. Running on a section of the DCIG site with
restricted access, the program would allow researchers to read
and review one another's papers. Subscribers could arrange online meetings and keep chatting round the clock, as well as in-
teract via notices on a bulletin board.

Malene would take on the role of webmaster for this closed
section of the site. Once it was up and running, DCIG would be
on its way to becoming a virtual research center, at comparatively minimal cost. Before Malene took her idea to Paul, she in-

vestigated the running costs and looked into what other organizations felt about virtual meeting places that were similar. She had tabulated advantages and drawbacks, alongside informed comments.

Despite all this, Paul said no.

Malene keeps coming back to Paul's refusal. "All he had to do was check out what I had prepared for him. If the Swedes get there first, we'll be totally sidelined when it comes to research support. I don't understand him."

Iben can't think of anything new to say. They have been over this several times already.

Malene takes a drink from the large coffee she bought at the station, and then starts up again. Her warm coffee breath envelops Iben.

"I can't help wondering if he is planning to take up another post and wants to take my idea with him."

Iben doesn't think so. Malene can probably read it on her face.

"Then what? Do you think he has other work in mind for me, something I haven't even heard about yet?"

The train has passed through a forest and the sunlight hits Iben's eyes.

"It couldn't be something to do with cutting back on our activities, could it? Like working less closely with the researchers?"

That would be idiotic and Iben says so. They both look out at the houses slipping past.

"Malene, there's one more possible reason for his decision," Iben says. "I've been thinking it over for a while."

"What is it?"

"Look, it's only based on a hunch. Nothing solid."

"Go on."

"The way I remember it, when I arrived at the Center, you always had Paul's backing for your ideas, not just for this kind of project. Right?"

Malene nods.

"And Paul wasn't all that alert to what the library might need."

"True."

"It seems to me that, between then and now, something has changed— something that no one has wanted to talk about so far."

Malene has pushed her coffee away, and her eyes are fixed on Iben.

"What occurs to me is that Paul is very anxious about running such a small outfit. He's aware of the risk that someone higher up might look at the DCIG and decide it's time to merge it with another organization, inevitably a bigger one. We'd be absorbed, sooner or later. Until recently, Paul believed that the Center had to grow or die, which is why he used to encourage you to work like crazy on whatever research initiatives you came up with, so that we could secure new areas of expertise and therefore more support from grants."

"Yes, that's exactly how it used to be. And now it's like—"

"What if Paul has picked up on a hint that we're going to be cut off from the Ministry for Science, Technology, and Development? I don't know anything, of course. But what if? In that case we'd almost certainly be transferred to the Foreign Affairs Ministry. And then, in one of their restructuring moves, Human Rights would swallow us up. That's a no-brainer.

"If Paul has heard rumors like that, it would explain why he's always so nervous before going to meetings at the ministry. And, being Paul, he'll already have thought through the next twenty moves in the game and planned ways of winning it.

"Say that he has noticed that state research libraries are small units scattered among the different ministries. Now, there's a possible plank to cling to, because the more vigorously our library expands, the greater Paul's chance of presenting the DCIG as 'a major library with additional research facilities.' That in turn would give him scope to maneuver the DCIG into the arms of another ministry, like Culture, or Justice, or Asylum Seekers, Immigrants, and Integration—whatever takes his fancy. He'd be safe in his director's post then, and nobody would be breathing down his neck, because the system accepts that research libraries are independent units, however small."

Iben can see that none of this has occurred to Malene. At least there are some advantages to lying awake and alone at night, Iben thinks.

"Look, Malene, if this is his rescue plan, then your initiatives could ruin it. He'd prefer to become part of almost any ministry as long as it isn't Foreign Affairs. If avoiding that means scaling down everything you've proposed in support of research, so be it."

"But he was so keen on the Center being associated with this conference and the one about the Germans in 1945. What do you make of that?"

In the aisle next to them an elderly lady fusses about with her little wheeled suitcase. Malene seems not to notice her at all.

Iben speaks quickly now. "Paul is walking a tightrope. Some years from now, he and Frederik will be competing for the same top post. They both already know it. Before then, Paul has to demonstrate that he is capable of building a stronger, better organization than Frederik. But in the current situation he feels that all research initiatives must be one-time events, like conferences and so on. That would mean that from now on, your function in the day-to-day work of the Center would be to support Anne-Lise."

Malene sits back heavily in her seat, staring into the middle distance.

"I haven't heard anybody say this and I don't know anything for sure," Iben says, "but I can't help speculating."

Iben cannot recall having seen such bright sunshine in November. The delegates have gathered in the restaurant and on the outside terrace, enjoying the views over the sculpture park on the slope down to the sea. Iben recognizes quite a few people. Malene, who has managed research assistance practically singlehandedly for three years, is very well informed about who everyone is. Quite a few people comment on the e-mail threats or on articles in the DCIG online magazine. Others who haven't met Iben since her return from Africa tell her how happy they were to learn that the hostage episode had ended in such a satisfactory way. "It's great that you all got out alive," they say, even though it was four months ago.

New delegates are arriving all the time. Malene notices that one of the speakers from Bosnia looks lost and goes off to explain the conference setup to him. Paul is outside in the park with Morten Kjærum, executive director of the Institute of Human Rights, and Birte Weiss, who used to be the minister for research and information technology. Anne-Lise stands by his side and appears to be trying to follow their conversation. This is the first time Paul has invited the Center's librarian to a conference.

At ten o'clock, Morten Kjærum welcomes the delegates in the great hall downstairs and is followed by the first speaker, a young city mayor from Bosnia.

His body is as taut and powerful as a soldier's, even under the layer of fat that the southern European diet has deposited ever since the Dayton Peace Treaty. From where Iben and Malene are sitting, he looks almost boyish. Like the other delegates from the former Yugoslavia, but unlike their Danish hosts, he is wearing a dark suit, white shirt, and wide tie. The style of his dark hair reminds Iben of Russians in old spy films.

The talk deals with the Serb ethnic cleansing in his own locality, but despite this the presentation is unemotional and plainly instructive.

He reads out statistics from the overhead projector:

184 people were killed.
416 houses were burned to the ground.
1,783 persons were expelled.
73 persons were exposed to rape or torture or both.

He sticks to basics for the rest of his talk too. Most of those present know the facts already and no one takes any notes. At the end, many people wonder why in the world he was invited.

Someone asks a question: "How come you survived?"

He replies carefully, in a tone that remains factual and unengaged: "Some of us had feared what would happen before it did. We had gathered together. They told us to hand over our weapons, but we bought new rifles from Serb soldiers. Then the top Serbs ordered that all the men should go to the school in the town. We ran off into the forest. They shot the men in the school later that day. We lived in the forest for several months."

The mayor is standing with his back half turned to the audience, looking up at the bright square with its tabulated numbers. He speaks in a monotone.

"Then the Serbs surrounded the forest. They said they would let us live if we surrendered and kill us if we refused. I was in command of the whole group and I decided that we would not surrender. We learned later that every single one of us would have been killed if I had decided the other way. We ambushed twenty Serbs in the forest and took them prisoner. Then we did a deal. The prisoners would be freed if we were allowed to travel to a Bosnian enclave. We joined the Bosnian army there. I fought and quite soon was made a colonel. I led my men to free my town. Then they made me mayor."

No one can think of how to comment. For a few seconds the entire audience hesitates, and then a few questions are asked based on his talk.

During the coffee break, Iben goes off to look for Paul and finds him on the terrace, deep in conversation with the board chairman, Ole Henningsen. Ole is a heavily built man in his early sixties who sports a large white beard. Before he became interested in genocide research he wrote several historical works about the Soviet Union. He is one of the experts on contemporary history who regularly appears on television. Sometimes he does quiz shows too.

Iben notices Frederik's blond head above the crowd. He is walking away, possibly after having just left the other two. Paul is leaning forward to speak confidingly with Ole, who is known to be happy with the way Paul runs things. As Iben arrives, she hears the last words of what has clearly been a complaint about the way the Danish Institute of Human Rights had tried to exclude the Center from being a co-organizer of this conference.

". . . seems to me that they simply weren't interested in using our expertise."

Paul's eyes are hidden behind his sunglasses, and it is possible that he hasn't yet noticed that Iben has joined them.

"I'm considering taking the issue up with Morten."

Iben knows that the DCIG got in on the act only because Paul heard through some of his contacts that the DIHR was planning the conference. He managed to make sure the Center was involved at the last minute, just before the invitations and press releases were sent out.

One result of this collaboration is that the conference lasts for two days instead of one, which has made it more attractive for delegates from abroad. The DCIG contributed only 15,000 kroner, but added its unrivaled mailing list of European researchers interested in postwar Yugoslavia. Iben also spent several hours on the layout of the conference papers, and Paul wrote a full-page article about the conference for *Information,* describing the speakers' backgrounds and speculating about the likely outcome.

Because the arrangements were made at the last moment, there had been no time to inform the board members—including its deputy chairman, Frederik Thorsteinsson. And because Frederik didn't know of the plans, his Center for Democracy only heard about the conference when it was too late to join in the organizing of it. Paul, in his capacity as a member of the Center for Democracy's board, might have mentioned it to Frederik, but it seems that he didn't. At least, Iben assumes he didn't.

When Iben joins Paul and Ole on the terrace, Ole immediately changes the subject and, in his pleasant voice, asks her how she is. All the board members have been very attentive to Iben ever since she returned from Kenya. Ole goes on to praise her recent articles.

Back in the hall the next speaker is an aging Bosnian journalist and intellectual.

"Now we have to force ourselves to hope again. We want a better future for Bosnia. And we will achieve it, with the help of organizations such as those represented here today."

The speaker's elaborate descriptions of his captivity in a shed outside Sarajevo make Iben feel oddly unfocused, as if her past is trying to return to her.

Omoro stands in the circle. He sings.

She pushes at the carapace of the dead beetle in the mud wall.

But she doesn't want to think about that. Not now.

They break for lunch and Iben sits next to Malene at one of the long communal tables in Louisiana's restaurant. Their table is at a right angle to the huge windows and to the panoramic view of Øresund's glittering water. Beyond the straits, the outline of the Swedish coast is unusually clear.

All the delegates are busy networking in a mixture of languages, mostly English or the Scandinavian ones, and the noise level is terrific.

Malene scatters lots of salt over her food. She's on a conference high.

"I've had a chat with Frederik and slipped a mention of Erik Prins into the conversation. As far as I could make out, Erik hasn't said anything bad about me to Frederik. Naturally I didn't ask him point-blank; he wouldn't have said anyway. It was just that I sensed he acted toward me the same way he always has."

Iben then spots Anne-Lise at one of the tables in the middle of the room and whispers to Malene: "Look. Anne-Lise is talking to Lea."

Lea is a young and successful sociologist who works closely with the only female member of the DCIG board, Tatiana Blumenfeld. Tatiana is held in enormous respect by practically everyone. It would be very bad news if Lea passed on an impression that Malene is a troublemaker in the office.

"I'll talk to Lea during one of the breaks," Iben says reassuringly. "When it seems appropriate, I'll explain the real situation."

"Thank you."

Iben finishes chewing a bite of spinach quiche before she speaks again.

"Brigitte is around, you know. I've seen her. If you have a word with her, Tatiana will hear the truth from two independent sources."

Brigitte is one of Tatiana's Ph.D. students.

Iben leans back to look across the backs of people at their table. She observes that Lea seems amused by something Anne-Lise has said.

The first lecture after the lunch break is "Serbian Intellectuals and the University of Belgrade After Democratization in the Balkans."

At the next break Iben zigzags between the groups in the restaurant. She feels the weight of the knife against her leg. What if it was one of these delegates who hatched the plan to send the e-mails and deposited the blood on the bookshelf?

One of the academics who often comes to study at the DCIG stops Iben. He seems puzzled. "Something about you has changed. What is it?"

"What makes you ask?"

"Nothing I can put my finger on . . . just something."

"Maybe I'm a little tired."

"No, no. That's not it."

He starts speaking about the e-mails, which he heard about when Zigic was at the top of the list of suspects. Now he is keen to tell her the latest news. "The story is that Zigic's group of Serbian Mafia is expanding its network into Russia and the USA. Zigic has been sighted recently in the States and in Germany."

Suddenly Lea turns up at Iben's side. She says that she truly likes everything about the DCIG. "Every few months or so, you seem to improve on some aspect of what you do!"

"Oh, good. Thanks."

"Take what your Anne-Lise just told me about fixing up the library so there is space for readers again—clearing the book stacks off the reading desks and so on."

This is the first Iben has heard of such a plan. She knows Malene will explode when she learns about it. Obviously, she had better go along with Lea for now.

"Yes, it is one of the better ideas we've had."

People are heading back to listen to the last lecture, and Lea joins the movement in the direction of the concert hall, but she makes a final remark: "It's so much better to be able to read with Anne-Lise close at hand. And the books as well. Such an improvement on using the meeting room."

the silence is everywhere—over the desks and between the shelving units. It makes wandering around in the Center feel strange. Bleak strip lighting, stillness. Despite the stacks of paper, the computer screens, and all the usual office clutter, Iben feels as if she's walking in the mist over a dank meadow.

It could be that her mind is somehow more porous because she woke up so early after yet another wakeful night. Everything about the office and herself seems unreal and dreamlike.

Just in case Anne-Lise also turns up at work abnormally early and catches Iben on the library computer, Iben has an excuse ready. Her story is that she wants to add a few new keywords on the articles about Sudan that she is working on. The access codes to the database are kept in Anne-Lise's computer. Iben has never used the program before, but that doesn't matter much.

She sits down on Anne-Lise's chair and can't avoid looking at the photograph of Anne-Lise's husband and children. It is placed right next to a digital clock, which blinks 07:18.

The computer is in standby mode. When Iben presses a key a dialog box pops up. It denies access and asks for a password. She tries pressing Enter, which usually does the trick for most of the office computers, but Anne-Lise has actually installed proper password protection. Iben tries "Anne-Lise," but still the system won't let her log on.

Complete silence.

Iben and Malene need something tangible to show Paul if they are to defend the Center and themselves against Anne-Lise. Without some proof that Anne-Lise sent the e-mails, he will not force her to take sick leave and she will keep wandering about among the bookcases, growing weirder all the time, until her bottled-up rage finally explodes.

Iben doesn't dare try any more passwords, because the computer might block any further attempts to log on, and Anne-Lise mustn't find out that someone has been tampering with it. Iben puts the light out, closes the door, and settles back at her own desk, where she tries to concentrate on what a group of Dutch experts has written about Muslims in the southern Russian states.

The others arrive. She gives Malene a whispered account of what has happened, and later, in midmorning, she goes to the library.

"Anne-Lise, tell me something: if I come across some new keywords that I think should be added to the library database, what should I do?"

"You just tell me. I'll key them in. That's no problem at all."

"Yes, sure. But what if I thought I might as well do it myself? How do I go about it?"

"Iben, it's far easier if you give them to me. I'll see to it."

"Thanks. But I'd like to be able to do it myself."

"Well, now . . . I usually manage the database. I have the necessary overview. Why not just leave it to me?"

"But what if I want to learn?"

Iben is aware that it doesn't sound all that plausible, but she doesn't care. How could Anne-Lise object? They repeat themselves a couple more times, but in the end Anne-Lise shows Iben how new keywords are entered for a title of a book or an article. Then Iben gets to the point.

"If I'm in and you're not here, can I just start your computer and get on with this?"

"How do you mean, if I'm not here? Why shouldn't I be here?"

"Oh, I don't know. If you were ill or had left early or something."

It is obvious that Anne-Lise doesn't like the way this is going, but she doesn't attempt to find out what Iben is really after. "You simply start my computer."

Iben smiles and tries to keep her expression innocent. "Right. You don't have a personal password or anything?"

"No."

Anne-Lise looks as if she's telling the truth. She is good at that and doesn't let on that there's any more to this than a chat about entering new keywords. It's only to be expected. She has proven quite capable of coming in every day for months without giving away how deeply she hates them all.

Iben probes a little further. "What if your computer is on standby?"

"That makes no difference."

"Still no password protection?"

"Not at all. It shouldn't be necessary, should it? Do the rest of you use passwords?"

Iben looks at her. "No, we don't. It's useful to be able to access everybody else's computer if you want to look something up."

"There you are. I agree."

They smile at each other. Irritated, Iben returns to the Winter Garden. Today was the last chance of being alone in the office before nine o'clock. Tomorrow Bjarne will install the new computer-controlled lock and the CCTV camera on the landing. It means Camilla will be back at work, and she always comes in much earlier than everybody else because Paul has allowed her the same working hours as her husband.

It doesn't take Bjarne long to install the camera, but then there's the cable through the Winter Garden to the server and the new piece of software to be installed on everyone's computer. Camilla loads it on first and Iben and Malene line up to test it. Malene goes out onto the landing.

"Hey, can you save my picture?"

Iben fiddles with the new menu options and keyboard commands.

"Yes, I think so . . . There, I've saved you."

Malene hurries along to Camilla's screen. "Oh, no! I look awful!"

Iben has to laugh, because it's true. Malene's face is an enormous bloated mask. Her greasy-looking skin is spotted with white blotches.

"You must be standing too close! Wait."

Iben runs outside. "Now save me too!"

Back at Camilla's computer, they burst out laughing. "I look just like you!"

"I suppose if you stood farther away . . ."

"Except then it's hard to see who it is."

What kind of surveillance camera is this? It makes everyone look the same.

Malene wants Iben to take another picture of her and runs out again. She shouts from the landing: "Imagine the Wanted Persons descriptions! 'Two females, both looking like blobby white frogs, wanted for . . .' "

Malene must be having a good day or she wouldn't be able to run around like this. They can't stop laughing.

Bjarne joins in the merriment. He turns toward the library door. "Hello in there! Anne-Lise, won't you come and have your picture taken too?"

Anne-Lise says that she is busy.

Malene looks quickly at Iben before calling out. "Oh, Anne-Lise! Why not do something for the fun of it? Just this once!"

It seems that Anne-Lise doesn't hear her, though the door is open, of course.

But the break ends. Phones ring. There are e-mails to be sent.

Bjarne is still there at lunchtime and helps divert the tension. He chews happily on a ham and beetroot salad sandwich from his voluminous lunch box and laughs a lot, enjoying the attention the women pay him. Meanwhile, Iben wonders about Anne-Lise's behavior. She has been odd since day one, but this is different. Isn't she being strange in a new way?

Anne-Lise eats a fish paste sandwich. The way she looks down all the time, you see more of her eyebrows than of her eyes. Knowing the kind of thing she's capable of is enough to make you nervous about being alone with her in the office.

Bjarne is talking about his girlfriend, a landscape architect, and how hard it is for her to get commissions. He tells them about some of her recent job applications.

Iben looks at Anne-Lise's mouth, tightly shut when she chews, and her cheeks, bulging as the lump of food is shifted about behind her closed lips. How little sets her apart from other withdrawn people, Iben thinks. If I didn't know what I know about her, would I see what kind of person she is?

That evening Iben cycles home from work in the pouring rain through the dark streets lit only by reflections of car headlights on the wet pavement. Luckily she's dressed for the weather. Inside the downstairs hall-way she pulls off her waterproof clothes. Underneath them she is damp with sweat.

Walking upstairs to her apartment, Iben is glad to know that the knife is there, taped to her leg. Before unlocking her door, she always bends to touch it through her trousers. Images play in her head about how quickly she could draw it. It's not very rational. Knife or no knife, she would be no match for an experienced fighter. Besides, that's neither here nor there now that it's clear Anne-Lise sent the e-mails.

Once more she steps over the pile of junk mail on the doormat; once more she walks around her apartment to make sure nobody is hiding; once more she sticks a square block of frozen cod into the microwave oven. And once more she checks her e-mail—nothing new except spam—and glances at the answering machine, which doesn't blink.

She sits down to eat at the small round dining table, a piece she inherited from her grandmother. Her living room is furnished with casually acquired bits and pieces and looks rather bare. Sometime soon, she tells herself, I must follow Malene's example—buy a sofa at least, just in case I have a guest. But he wouldn't think it looked homey or pretty, like Malene's. Maybe a patterned throw, in hot colors, would help. Then the room wouldn't be so plain—all white walls, bookshelves, and dark wood. She has thought about this kind of thing so often, but now she feels ready to go ahead and do something about it.

She props her book up and reads while she eats her piece of cod with some red peppers and crisp-bread. The book is Raul Hilberg's *The Destruction of the European Jews,* which she bought secondhand on the Internet.

After supper, she washes her hair. Then, her damp hair wrapped in a towel and a cup of tea at hand, she settles down to phone Grith, just to gossip. Nobody answers.

Iben doesn't have Gunnar's number in her address book, but she knows it by heart after having heard it only once. She has never used it and doesn't ring him tonight either. Instead she calls her mother and talks with her, while the television rumbles on in the background. Her mother says that she ran into some old friends recently and they thought it was great to see Iben interviewed on television about her captivity. They send their regards. Iben's mother says that they asked her to tell Iben they're pleased it all ended so well.

hen Iben goes out again later that evening, it is still raining. It's late—half past ten already. She dislikes being outside when it is too dark to see who is walking toward you or crossing the road in your direction. Inwardly she curses the plan she and Malene have made, which keeps her away from her cozy bed and Hilberg's book.

Malene and Rasmus pick her up in a taxi. It takes them to the DCIG building. As Iben peers up at the office windows from under her umbrella, water trickles down the back of her neck.

"No lights on."

They need to spend at least one hour in the office without being disturbed, and her greatest fear is that Paul might come by.

Once inside, Iben's heart beats faster. This isn't a "real" break-in, she tells herself. If we had to face a guard, or the DCIG board, we could talk our way out of it.

Malene's breathing tells Iben that she too feels anxious. She echoes Iben's thoughts. "It's not a real break-in. Why shouldn't we be in our own workplace?"

They listen for sounds. Nothing. After taking the ancient elevator to the top floor, they listen again. Somewhere below them, a person leaves an office. They almost stop breathing. The person calls the elevator, its door bangs, and they hear its customary whine as it descends. Is it a guard perhaps? Or somebody working late? A cleaner? What would Paul do if a security guard phoned him in the middle of the night? Ever since the confrontation about Anne-Lise's mental health, their relationship with him has been somewhat strained. Paul would have to inform Ole and Frederik and the rest of the board.

What is the worst-case scenario? It has to be that Anne-Lise didn't write these e-mails and that somewhere in the darkness Mirko Zigic is waiting for them.

When the person downstairs has left, Malene enters the security code—it's 110795, the date the massacre at Srebenica began.

In the Winter Garden many small points of red or green light glow on computers, phones, and other equipment. Hardly any light from the city penetrates the curtain of rain, but after they have stood about in the dark room for a while, the piles of paper take on a faint glow, like rectangular moons.

They avoid switching on any lamps. Iben and Malene, who know this place well enough to find their way around it blindfolded, walk toward the library. Malene leads, and Rasmus and Iben follow.

The darkness is more opaque in the library, but Iben and Malene have both brought their bicycle lamps. Rasmus sits down on Anne-Lise's chair and the women stand on either side of him. He uses the keyboard with lightning-quick familiarity.

"Yep, it's password protected. I can't get around it, but that's okay. Just checking. Let's go find the server."

They make their way to the small, windowless storage room where the server is kept, close the door, and then turn on the lights.

"I need the administrator's password. Let's look for it." Rasmus has good instincts about where people will write things down that they shouldn't write down. He checks underneath the blotting pad and the keyboard and behind the monitor. While he's at it, he looks over the folders on the shelf. The others help, but in the end they give up.

"Looks like I'll have to switch off the server."

Without waiting for an answer and without closing Windows, Rasmus switches it off at the wall. Iben leans against an unpainted chipboard shelf full of office materials. Safe behind a closed door and with the light on, she takes several deep breaths, almost like sighs.

Rasmus puts a disk into the drive and switches the terminal on again.

After a while, he exclaims: "Just what I hoped! It's programmed to look for a start-up disk in the drive before it begins running its own program from the hard drive. That way, if there's a problem, the administrator can start it up from a disk. I've put in my own start-up program, which will direct the computer to read my copy of Windows. I've got the CD here."

His little black bag holds innumerable homemade CDs. He loads one of them into the computer. It responds and a stream of numbers and letters flows across the screen.

"Good. That worked." Rasmus, like all true enthusiasts, is beginning to forget his surroundings. His whole being focuses happily on the computer. "There! It's running my program. I'll get the administrator's password in no time."

Iben watches him. There's something touching about men and computers—so besotted they are by the mysterious possibilities inside the machine. It's odd: only now can she see clearly what she has sensed before. Rasmus simply isn't right for Malene. It actually saddens her to realize how true this is.

Rasmus is absorbed. ". . . and to do that, I've the perfect hacker's helpmate."

He loads another program from a disk. It triggers another flow of windows and options. Boxes race across the screen, and Rasmus fills them in faster than she can read them.

The women exchange glances.

Iben constantly listens out for any noise on the other side of the closed door, but so far the only sounds are those made by the computer and Rasmus, who keeps saying "Yes!" or swearing.

After more typing, Rasmus says he has cracked it. He removes both his disks, then turns the computer off, and then on again. Start-up brings the usual password request, and Rasmus keys in the code he has just broken. Bjarne has chosen to protect the computer system with the word *superspliff.*

They laugh a little uncertainly. Rasmus looks more alive than Iben has ever seen him.

"There. I'm logged on as the administrator for your entire network. It's set up in a rather outdated way, but it means we can read what's in any of the office computers."

"What? Can Paul and Bjarne read everything on our computers?"

"Everything! There's no hiding place." He doesn't bother to look up at Iben and Malene. "First, I'll search for any file containing that e-mail address 'revenge_is_near.' "

Paul's and Camilla's computers are switched off and can't be searched. Rasmus could turn them on, but there's no point. Several of Iben's and Malene's files turn up, because they have been e-mailing people all over the world to ask about the possible identity of the sender. Anne-Lise, on the other hand, doesn't seem to have written a single e-mail containing the phrase 'revenge_is_near.' Strange. Hasn't she told anybody what happened?

Rasmus starts looking for other revealing phrases.

"Of course, what we're specifically looking for is a trail to any private webmail address she might have on the Net rather than in this computer. That is, apart from Outlook, has she been using Explorer to check e-mail accounts held elsewhere? Like an anonymizer site?"

He makes several searches, but finds nothing. His next move is to go through her computer folders, searching for any interesting files.

"Weird . . . Most people keep personal stuff somewhere on their hard disk." Rasmus stares at the screen, completely transfixed. Suddenly he calls out: "Hey! Look at this!"

"What's that?"

"It's a program that wipes all traces of your Internet activity. She must have downloaded it from the Net. That's why we can't find anything. It means that she knows what she's doing. Did you know that she was good at that kind of thing?"

"No."

"No idea."

"With this, she'd be able to create her own addresses on the Net and cover her tracks afterward—that kind of thing?" Malene asks.

"That's exactly what I'm thinking."

While Rasmus searches Anne-Lise's files, Iben and Malene go to the library to look through her papers.

The corridor is windowless too, so they could put the light on, but they don't need to. Their bodies have memorized the precise layout of the office. Iben remembers a dream she had in which the tight passages between the shelving in the Center merged with images from a film about the sinking of a German submarine. She had watched the film on television a few months earlier. The action mainly took place inside the torpedoed and fatally damaged submarine. In her dream its crew was locked into the narrow aisles between the office bookshelves. Lamps blinking RED ALERT warned them of the Center's slow, silent descent toward the bottom of the sea.

While they wait for Rasmus, Iben and Malene decide to play a game of walking through the dark faster and faster to discover just how well they instinctively know where any obstacles are. Iben starts running and Malene runs after her.

They race through the Winter Garden. Their bodies compute distances and directions precisely. No need to use their head, or their eyes. Malene must be thrilled to be able to move so freely without pain.

Iben catches her breath.

"You know, it's great to be here and say and do whatever one likes. Just for once." Malene speaks loudly enough for Rasmus to hear.

"Isn't it? Look, I can say, for instance, 'Paul, you simply have to relocate Anne-Lise to a fish-filleting factory in Svalbard, because she's ruining everything here.' "

"And I can say, 'Paul, it's time you woke up. If you don't lock her into a phone booth with a year's supply of fish paste sandwiches . . .' "

"And a clock. She'll need a clock."

" '. . . then the Center is going to become such a dump that Frederik will get Kjærum's job at Human Rights, and not you!' "

"Got that, Paul?"

"You have no idea, have you? Always off to your bloody meetings, or whatever."

They spend some time at Anne-Lise's desk, searching her papers for evidence, before returning to see what Rasmus has found. He is busy tracing preserved fragments of Anne-Lise's e-mails, the pieces her clean-up program couldn't delete.

"We should've brought a few beers."

"No problem. There's a bottle of whiskey in Paul's cupboard."

"Do you think it's really safe to have some?"

"Sure. He'll never notice. Camilla had some the other day."

The whiskey is a an exclusive brand of single malt, but over time Paul has been given so many similar bottles that he doesn't mind leaving one in the office. Iben goes to fetch it and three glasses.

"Look, I've brought some water as well. I've read that water 'opens up' a good whiskey. Just a little, to release the aroma."

"Isn't it a shame to dilute it?"

"But it's not diluting it—that really would be a shame. Only a drop or two. I'll put it in my glass and you can keep your drink straight. Then we'll swap to see if we can taste the difference."

When they've all tested the whiskey several times, mixed with different amounts of water, Iben and Malene return to Anne-Lise's desk. This time they put on the overhead lights. No need to be neurotic. It makes their search much quicker and easier, and, anyway, who'd be standing down in the street staring at the top-floor windows?

One of Anne-Lise's desk drawers is locked. They try to shift the lock with a ruler, but it breaks. Iben puts the bits in the back pocket of her jeans. So what if Anne-Lise doesn't find it tomorrow? All anyone can say is that it's lost.

They try inserting a paper knife instead. Neither of them knows a thing about locks, but this time it works. It's a cheap desk and the locks are mainly just for show, but it's fun all the same. They must have an unexpected talent for robbery.

It's as if the normal rules no longer apply. Everything in the office is familiar and at the same time strange and new.

"Now we can close that fucking door at last!" Malene almost shouts.

She slams it shut and they both laugh.

Rasmus comes in and seems surprised at the lights and noise.

"Doesn't matter. Nobody will come here at this hour!" Iben is very loud now.

"Anyway, we're allowed. We work here."

"We work all sorts of hours!"

"See? We're just so motivated!"

Rasmus speaks quietly. "Listen, I've found something."

They turn the light off and he explains as they walk along. "I've loaded a program that searches the whole network for fragments of deleted files."

Back in the server room he shows them a few lines from a file that was probably on Anne-Lise's hard disk. In two lines of apparently random characters the word "Malene" turns up and, a little later on, a sentence: "I no longer know myself. I have never experienced hating anyone the way I hate her . . . I might do anything to her . . . she makes me feel sick through and through."

They stand in silence, staring at the screen.

Malene suddenly needs to sit down. "You see . . . So what's new?"

Iben feels a little groggy owing to lack of sleep. She leans forward over Malene's shoulder. "I don't think it'll be enough for Paul. He certainly won't admit this as evidence, will he?"

"No, he won't. He knows perfectly well that she can't stand me. His only reaction so far has been to hand my responsibilities over to her. Like I said: nothing we don't know already."

Rasmus goes off to have a pee. While he's away, they read Anne-Lise's latest incoming e-mails. Only two are marked as unread. The first one is a request.

"Dear Anne-Lise. I need to know as much as possible about child killings in East Timor. Please collate a list of what is in the library and e-mail it to me as soon as you can. Is tomorrow morning possible? Regards, Tatiana."

Malene quietly deletes it.

The next mail is from Sweden.

"Hi, Anne-Lise. Thanks a million for that list. Brilliant! Best, Lotta."

They delete that one too.

Anne-Lise has read all the other e-mails, so they leave them untouched.

Then they both drink some more whiskey before going back to Anne-Lise's desk. They keep the lights off this time, ambling about in the dark, happy that the Center is theirs for the time being.

Iben misjudges the layout of the rooms only once. She walks straight into the door between the Winter Garden and the library, forgetting that Malene has closed it. She falls and knocks a few magazine folders off a shelf, but doesn't hurt herself. She gets up quickly. Some magazines have landed on the floor, but putting the light on seems too much hassle, so she picks up the ones nearby and puts them back any old way. Time enough to sort them out tomorrow.

Malene is back in the library. Iben hears her rummaging over by the readers' desks. There is a huge crash.

Malene doesn't laugh out loud, but her voice shakes a little. "Oops!"

Iben gets the drift at once. Malene has knocked over one of the very tall stacks of books that Anne-Lise has put on the floor while she sorts them.

Iben goes in to check the damage.

"Look, it doesn't matter. It kind of fell over, all by itself." Malene seems unfazed.

Iben gives another stack a brisk tap. "You mean like this? Oh, look! It fell over too."

Malene gives a third stack a push. "It's like the domino effect!"

Iben is on her way through the Winter Garden to put the bottle of whiskey back in Paul's cupboard when she hears the whining of the elevator. The sound lasts only a moment, then stops. Someone gets out on their floor.

Iben rushes quietly back to the library. She tells Malene in a loud whisper: "Zigic! It's Zigic!"

She walks toward Malene's voice, whispering in the dark.

"No. No . . ."

She reaches out and touches Malene's blouse.

"No, it can't be."

They stand side by side, holding hands, their backs against the shelving on the far side of the open door to the Winter Garden.

Someone is fiddling with the locks on the front door.

Malene's voice is low. "Are all the lights off?"

"Not in the server room. Where Rasmus is."

"I wonder can he hear . . . ?"

There are many hiding places in the maze of shelving at the back of the library, but Iben lacks the courage to go there. Once more, she has a fleeting impression of the Center's network of passages transforming into the torpedoed submarine as it sinks inexorably into the deep ocean trenches with their intolerable pressure.

The main door opens. The lights are switched on. How can they tell if it's Zigic just by listening?

There are two people outside the door. One walks in shoes with hard soles toward Paul's office; the other walks more quietly. The quiet one stops at Malene's desk and rustles through her papers, looking for something.

Iben stands absolutely still, her heart hammering in her chest. The man in the Winter Garden is only a few feet away. She feels the sweat soaking through her top; a drop runs down her leg until it's stopped by the tape that holds the knife in place.

A woman speaks: "You must've had something in mind when you drove her to Århus."

It's Helen's voice, Paul's wife. Iben relaxes.

Helen is a secondary school teacher. Her looks have faded, but her features and her shock of blond curls still hint at how very good-looking she once was. Her manner has changed as well, and with time she's become rather odd. She always excuses herself from Center get-togethers, such as the Christmas lunch, and always at the last minute.

Paul's voice comes from his office. "Just shut up! Stop harping on about it!"

Helen is shouting now. "It's your fault! You make me like this, the way you keep avoiding my questions. It reminds me."

"What utter crap!"

Iben has never heard Paul speak this way—despairing, superior, and angry, like someone telling a disabled child off for pestering them.

Helen's voice is still very loud. Maybe they've been out and she has drunk too much. "But it's true! You always avoid things—that's what you do."

"That's nonsense! I'm telling you the truth. End of story." Paul is closer now, somewhere in the Winter Garden. He must have picked up some papers he needs for tomorrow, since he's due to be away from the Center all day.

Sounding resigned more than anything else, Paul adds: "If I really thought Malene was so gorgeous, I'd have lunch with these people once in a while, wouldn't I?" A bunch of papers lands on a desktop. "Which is what I ought to do. I'm their boss. But I can't face having to listen to all their chitchat. I don't think of Malene in that way, believe me."

Helen doesn't say anything, but seems to be rolling about in one of the office chairs.

Silence.

When Paul speaks again, he's regained his familiar, slightly too controlled office voice.

"Oh, I want to show you something."

"What?"

"The library. Anne-Lise has started to clear the readers' desks. It's going to look really good."

"I'm not in the mood."

"Oh, come on. It's right next door."

Now Paul is on the other side of the library door.

Iben jumps when Helen shouts angrily: "I don't care about your fucking readers' desks. Can't you get that into your thick head!"

Nothing more can be heard for a moment, except the drumming of the rain. Then Paul sighs deeply. Something makes a slapping noise.

The front door opens, the light is turned off, the door slams shut.

They're gone.

Iben's heart is still pounding in her chest. She stays where she is, pressed against the shelf.

Besides, Paul and Helen may well come back. Malene takes Iben's hand and places it over her heart. It beats wildly and she too has been sweating.

Despite the dark, Iben knows that they're smiling tensely at each other. They listen as the elevator descends and stops.

They can't hear anybody walk across the downstairs hallway.

They can't hear the street door open and close and a car start in the rain.

Even so, after several minutes, they have to assume that Paul will not come back.

They're still standing in the same place. Iben feels strange—drunk and queasy. But she didn't drink that much, so it must be the fear that's making her feel sick.

A little later Rasmus comes in. "Holy shit!" he whispers to them.

They laugh from sheer relief.

"Look, girls, I wouldn't mind going home now."

"We're with you!"

"I turned the light off and stayed under the server desk all the time they were here. Now I have to restore everything on the server to the way it was before."

They stay close to him as they leave the library and use the bicycle lights until they get into the server room, where the light is on. It is good to be able to see properly.

Rasmus fixes the computer while Iben and Malene look on distractedly. At one point, the e-mails from Tatiana and Lotta to Anne-Lise pop up on the screen.

"Why did you delete them?"

Malene shrugs.

Rasmus reads the e-mails. "Hmm . . ."

He keys in the right command. "You have to remove them from the system entirely then."

He deletes Anne-Lise's unread mail. And no one says any more about it.

t he telephone wakes Iben the next morning. It's Malene and she's been crying. It doesn't take Iben long to figure out what's wrong. She knows that Malene has been taking painkillers recently but still hasn't been able to get much sleep.

"Iben, I have to go to the clinic."

Iben sits up and pushes a pillow behind her back. "Oh, Malene, you poor thing. But you seemed so well yesterday?"

"I don't know what's happened. It doesn't usually hit me like this."

"Is it very bad?"

"It's awful. It came on during the night. It doesn't usually happen that quickly. I don't know . . . oh, God, I can't trust anything anymore. And it hurts so much, even though I've taken my pills. I can barely think. My knee is huge and the skin feels tight right up my thigh. I've never felt it coming on so quickly."

"Should I come over?"

"Would you mind?"

"Of course not."

"It's just that Rasmus has left for the airport. I've called the ambulatory unit and they'll try to fit me in shortly after nine."

"I'll be at your place in half an hour."

Iben has gone with Malene to the rheumatological clinic

several times before, when her friend was too ill to walk down the stairs by herself. In the hospital Iben would stay by her side while Malene would lie on the paper-covered couch in the doctor's examination room. She would hold her friend's hand while the doctor inserted a wide-bore needle into Malene's knee joint, draining off one syringe of liquid after another.

The last time, they both believed that there would be no more visits for a while, but the doctor had been worried.

"We shouldn't do this too often, you know. Recurrence of inflammatory episodes can erode the joint surfaces. I'll prescribe something that should help."

Malene was put on methotrexate. It helped a great deal. Until today, that is.

"I can't walk . . . I can barely stand. All I can do is sit here."

Faintly, Iben hears Malene cough or sob, or maybe both. She must have put her hand over the receiver.

Then Malene speaks in a voice that is no longer familiar. "I can't do anything. Because it hurts so bad. I can't do anything at all."

"Malene, don't try. Just wait. I'll be with you soon."

Cycling over to Malene's, she thinks, as she did over and over again during the night, that they shouldn't have deleted the e-mail from Tatiana. Regardless of what Anne-Lise has done to us, she tells herself, we must make sure that we're not equally at fault. We mustn't be tempted to do things that are simply wrong, or else we'll be stooping to her level. And then we can't claim that we're simply fighting for what's best for the Center. Iben pulls out her cell phone and dials the DCIG to say that she'll be in late and that Malene is ill.

Anne-Lise answers; Camilla isn't in yet.

Iben tells her about Malene's attack of arthritis.

"That's awful. Is it bad?" If you didn't know her, you wouldn't have a clue that she hated Malene.

Iben overtakes a bicycle pulling a trailer.

"Anne-Lise, one more thing. When I saw Lea at Louisiana, she mentioned that Tatiana is about to start on a major paper. I thought you'd be the right person to suggest books from our library for her research."

"I could do that. What's the subject?"

"Don't know. But why don't you phone her and ask if you can help?"

Anne-Lise pauses briefly before answering. "That's so nice of you. I'll do that. Thank you for the advice."

"Don't thank me. I'm just helping a colleague."

"No, Iben, it's different. I can't tell you how pleased I am."

Anne-Lise sounds unusually happy. Iben loses her concentration a little as she looks over the tops of the parked cars to try to find a gap in the traffic and slip across Østerbro Street.

She unlocks the door to Malene's apartment with the spare key she keeps for times like this. Malene is lying on the sofa. Before he left, Rasmus helped her into a loose-fitting tracksuit, made her some breakfast, and helped her to go to the bathroom. Rasmus is on his way to Glasgow with a group of other salesmen.

Malene is pale, but even without her makeup she looks lovely.

"Malene, what lousy luck."

"Umm."

"What have you taken?"

"Two ibuprofens at five this morning. And then two paracetamols and then two more ibuprofens. I'm not allowed any more."

"And it got this bad in just one night?"

"Yes, it did."

Iben packs an overnight bag. Then, while Malene is still lying down, Iben gently slides on her shoes, lacing them loosely but tying the knots firmly. Iben puts Malene's arm around her own neck, careful not to jolt her friend's hand, and, as effectively as she can, she helps her to stand up. When they reach the hall, Iben eases Malene into her coat.

On the landing, Iben lets Malene lean against the banister while she quickly grabs her jacket and picks up both of their bags. Iben can see that Malene's eyes are full of pain, but also of something else—something that she's certain no one else except Rasmus has seen.

Making their way down the stairs is the hardest part, but together they have mastered it. Iben tells the waiting taxi driver how to help Malene into the cab.

Once they're through door 42 of the hospital, maneuvering is easier, because here the corridors are wide and the elevators roomy. The ambulatory unit at the rheumatological clinic has no proper waiting room, only a selection of chairs and magazines placed in a cul-de-sac in the corridor. Iben helps Malene out of her coat, finds her a chair and another one for her leg, and then goes off to register her arrival.

Now it should take an hour at most until a doctor comes along to drain the fluid out of the inflamed knee joint. If Malene had the energy, she might have felt some relief. As it is, all she can do is endure it.

Iben sits down next to her. "Is there anything I can do for you?"

Malene has put one of her hands lightly on her swollen knee. She stares straight ahead. "No, Iben, not a thing. Thanks."

"You know that all you have to do is say . . ."

"It's okay. You can go off to work now, if you like."

"No way. I'll stay here with you. But I need to go downstairs and make some calls. They won't take long. Is there anything you'd like me to get you from the kiosk?"

Malene doesn't move. "No, thanks."

Iben walks with long, swift steps, aware of the ease with which she can move. Dear God, thank you, she thinks, and then feels ashamed.

But she has nothing to be ashamed of. After all, she is doing everything she can to help Malene. She has no reason whatsoever to feel bad.

And besides, she was also being helpful to Anne-Lise.

The air is chilly and still damp after the night's rain. A handful of people are wandering around between the parked cars, smoking or talking into their cell phones. Iben phones Nisa at the Danish Institute for International Studies to ask for current statistics on the ongoing genocide of Amazonian Indians. Nisa asks her how things are going at the DCIG.

Iben has a shrewd idea of what she's angling for. "Good. We're just preparing the Chechnya issue."

Sure enough, Nisa soon gets to the point. "Somebody told me you're having problems with Anne-Lise?"

Iben has to smile at how quickly gossip spreads. She's glad that she and Malene have managed to defend themselves, but she knows she must be discreet. "Really? Who told you that?"

"Just something Erling said."

That's all right. Erling sits on the same research committee as Ole Henningsen. It wouldn't be bad if the information filtered through that way.

"Erling? What did he tell you?"

"He told me that Anne-Lise has an alcohol problem."

"Nisa, I'm not sure. But now that you say it . . . well, it would explain a lot."

Nisa tries to find out more, but Iben's brief responses demonstrate that at the DCIG they intend to keep Anne-Lise's problems internal.

After the Louisiana conference a week and a half ago, Iben and Malene had gotten together in Malene's apartment to plan a defense strategy. If Anne-Lise keeps criticizing them behind their backs, they could end up being fired, and then they'd never be able to get a job in human rights again. With all the changes going on at the moment, they knew they didn't have much time. They needed to establish that Anne-Lise's perceptions of her colleagues were grossly distorted. Iben then swung into action. The following day she called Lea to "chat about the conference." She mentioned how she and Malene viewed recent events in the DCIG office. This was when Lea, who once had to share an office with an alcoholic, asked if Anne-Lise drank too much.

Iben hadn't given this a moment's thought before, but now things suddenly fell into place. So much would make perfect sense if Anne-Lise were hitting the bottle because of problems at home.

Lea must have passed the story on, because there were other vague inquiries from contacts at the university. Iben and Malene both realized that to hint at their misgivings about Anne-Lise's possible alcohol problem was the wisest way to make people realize what a difficult and unstable person she was to work with. Throughout this whole unpleasant business, Iben has urged that they should not aim to harm Anne-Lise more than they absolutely have to. It is important to her that she behaves as a "good" person would, given the circumstances. So Iben has tried to stick to this approach in spite of Anne-Lise's ingratiating herself with Lea, Brigitte, and others in the network, and despite the way Anne-Lise seems unaffected by the unpleasant atmosphere in the office that weighs so heavily on Iben and Malene. Anne-Lise seems prepared to fight on forever, as if she's in her element on the field of battle.

When Iben returns to the rheumatology clinic, Malene is still waiting to see the doctor. Her eyes are fixed on the wall in front of her, and her breathing is shallow and troubled. She keeps her arms tight to her body.

The needle that the doctor will soon use is a massive affair, a small tube with a sharply pointed tip, designed to allow viscous fluid to flow in. Iben knows that she should go into the examination room with Malene and hold her hand during the procedure.

She begins to tell Malene about the phone calls but soon gives up: Malene is too distracted to respond. They sit there for almost another hour before the doctor calls Malene. He's new, but comes across as trustworthy. His neatly trimmed white beard and relaxed movements remind Iben of Ole, only he's younger and some twenty pounds lighter.

Iben and the doctor help Malene onto the couch. He palpates her knee to assess the extent of the swelling. The pressure inside the joint is so great that a bulge, distended with fluid, has pushed its way between two tendons at the back of her knee. He seems puzzled.

"And you tell me everything was fine last night?"

"Yes."

He slides his hand along her leg below the knee. "I see. Well, it's most unusual for the swelling to reach this state so quickly."

"I know. It's never been like this before."

"What did you do yesterday? Any sudden or odd movements?"

Iben watches the many little twitches of pain that come and go on Malene's face. She wishes she could do something to help her.

Malene tries to sound pleasant, but her voice is dry and squeaky. "Well, I did."

The doctor focuses his entire attention on her knee.

Malene tries to explain. "I ran around. Moved faster than I normally do. But I felt fine at the time."

At last he looks up, gazing at her calmly. "You certainly managed to damage your knee."

Even though he is addressing Malene, he looks across to Iben, almost as if he thinks she is her friend's partner.

"What you must always keep in mind is that your joints are no longer what they once were. The bone surfaces are both softer and rougher, and that's why it's easier to injure them. Also, because the bone is more exposed, it's more prone to cracking. Fragments can come off inside the joint. Your pain may well be due to one of these small local fractures. Which means that I'll have to send you off to X-ray before I aspirate the joint."

"But . . . how long will that take?"

"I'll phone them right away and find out when they can see you. Schedules are tight here, but let's hope they'll be able to fit you in."

He has already lifted the receiver when Malene bursts into tears. "Can't you drain my knee now? Just a little?"

"I'm afraid not. It could cause damage."

"Please, can't you do something? Take some out. Just a little."

From where she lies on the couch her head is turned toward the doctor. He leans forward across the desk. "When I tell you I can't, it's not because I want to make you miserable, but because I'm doing what's best for you—for your knee."

He arranges with the X-ray receptionist that, if all goes well, Malene will be seen in about an hour's time.

"I'll phone the porters. They'll send someone to take you across."

Tears are streaming down Malene's face, but she makes no sound.

Iben's voice is shrill. "Can't you give her something for the pain? You can't leave her in this state!"

"Of course. Tell me, Malene, what have you taken so far?"

When he hears the quantities of painkillers that Malene has swallowed this morning, he says it is essential that she wait before taking any more. He promises that by the time she's allowed any more medication, he will already have drained her knee joint.

As Iben helps Malene out of the room, the doctor assures them that he'll contact the X-ray department again and try to get Malene in earlier. A porter has come along with a wheelchair and pushes her along the dilapidated corridors. Iben accompanies them, carrying their coats.

Then they wait. Again. The X-ray waiting area is a long, narrow passage where patients, attached to their drips, sleep in their beds. It's hard to think of anything to chat about. Iben feels it's not right to rattle on about any old thing, but there's not much else to say. It hurts and that's it.

After half an hour Malene finally speaks. "Rasmus will be landing soon."

"Of course. It's annoying that you're not allowed to keep your cell phone on."

There are drops of sweat on Malene's rigid upper lip. She says nothing, so Iben carries on talking.

"He would have phoned. No question about that."

Iben hears Malene's deliberate breathing. In. Pause. Out. Pause. In. Pause. It's maddening not to be able to do something.

"Malene, would you like me to pop outside with your cell phone to see if there's a message from Rasmus?"

A stranger slowly turns her face toward Iben and nods. Iben's smile feels artificial.

"Good. I'll do that."

She takes Malene's cell phone from her coat pocket, still smiling, and heads outside.

There's a message from Rasmus. Against the background noise of the airport, his low voice is like a caress.

"Hello, Squidgy Bum. I have to board soon. Two seconds. Peter is okay again, just like you thought. 'Let's make that a dozen USB connections.' That's it, not another word. You're so smart! I'll be home before you know it and then I'll suck and lick you until you drive the people downstairs crazy and they start banging on the ceiling and the windows crack. But we'll carry on anyway, without windowpanes, and then the next-door neighbors will give us grief too. But we won't give a fuck, will we? Sweet Malene. Kiss."

Iben presses the key to save the message for Malene. Then she stands still, the cold piercing her. No one has ever spoken to her like that. No one has ever used that kind of voice, a sweet, sexy voice.

So what?

She thinks of Gunnar. Malene keeps him on hold "just in case." Gunnar. Right now, he's presumably sitting in his editor's chair in his office at *Development*. Lord alone knows what he thinks. How much he envies Rasmus, perhaps. Rasmus, who is allowed to leave such messages for Malene.

When Malene met Rasmus three years ago, she thought he'd be nothing more than a fling. For weeks she told stories about him, giving away the most intimate details, the weird or selfish things he did, his lopsided cock—everything. Then, all of a sudden, Malene stopped handing out these tidbits. Iben has a pretty good idea that it is now Rasmus who is learning amazingly personal things about her. There's no telling what kind of image he has of his beloved's best friend.

When Rasmus is not away on sales trips, Malene often complains that they don't see enough of each other. Most evenings he isn't back from work much before bedtime. She sometimes seems happier when he's away on business because then she can look forward to seeing him again and is able to forget how late he works when he's back home.

Once Malene told her delightedly that she and Rasmus had been talking about having a baby. For a while afterward Iben asked about their plans, but now it's been at least a year since Malene mentioned it.

The days when she is most down, Iben thinks about her friend's situation and suspects that Rasmus will be off the moment he finds the right woman. Even when she isn't feeling pessimistic, Iben still believes that Malene and Rasmus's relationship has lasted only because of Rasmus's constant travels. Yet Iben hardly dares to think of how bitter Malene would be if Rasmus were to leave her.

Iben punches in Gunnar's work number on her cell phone but then deletes each number, one by one. Next, she phones Tatiana's secretary in the RTC office and asks for some pictures from their archive for the next DCIG newsletter.

Iben knows the secretary well and casually slips in mention of their problems at work. "I'm not positive that she drinks too much. Or else, it could be that some of her problems are caused by trying to stop. I have seen her shaking like a leaf once . . . Yes, in the office."

Iben returns to the long passage crowded with semiconscious patients waiting to be X-rayed.

"Malene, Rasmus left a message for you. It's a great message."

Malene doesn't respond.

"He says . . . he's crazy about you and you're going to have a fantastic time when he gets back."

Still no response. It's clear that Malene has lost touch with her surroundings; there are beads of sweat all over her pale face, and she radiates discomfort.

Iben leans back in her chair, looking around for the usual supply of torn magazines. There are none. She checks her bag but seems to have forgotten to put in the thin volume of lectures by Christopher Browning that she is currently reading. All she can do is sit in silence by Malene's side.

They wait until Malene is called in. Then they wait for Malene's X-rays to be developed. And then they wait for the porter to turn up with the wheelchair.

Back in the rheumatology clinic, the doctor immediately sees how poorly Malene is doing by now and brings them into the consulting room at once.

Malene sits quietly as he examines the X-rays. He phones Medical Imaging to consult with a radiologist. The X-rays show a small, dark line across one of the bones in the knee joint.

When he has finished the call, he is still uncertain. "The X-rays don't show anything unusual. I want to examine your knee again more thoroughly, to look for injured tendons and such."

Iben can tell by Malene's face that this is not the time to hold her aching hand.

After more probing, it doesn't take long before five large syringes are lined up on the little table next to the couch, each one filled with turgid yellow fluid.

At last Malene feels better. She sits up, but cautiously.

"Ouch! Fuck . . . oh, no!" She sighs deeply, many times, and looks around the room as if she hasn't seen it before. "Oh, God. It still hurts so badly. But at least I can feel the rest of me." She blinks and turns her head, first to one side, and then to the other. "Thank you." And then, "Iben . . . thank you."

Iben feels tearful as she looks at her friend, but doesn't cry. It's over for now. Malene is gradually becoming her old self.

"Oh, man! Practically everything still hurts. Especially my feet and hands. That came on overnight as well."

The doctor is bending over one of her hands. "Aha. Now, that would explain it!"

"What explains what?"

"Look, you didn't take your tablets yesterday. Perhaps not the day before either."

"Of course I did."

He looks skeptical. "I've checked your notes. Last time you were here, about six weeks ago, Niels put you on methotrexate, once a week."

"Yes."

"And until the methotrexate started to work, you were to take cortisone daily."

"Yes, I know."

"But as long as you're taking these things, you shouldn't be having any unprovoked attacks."

"But I have taken my medication."

"Then this shouldn't have happened. Inflammation in every joint . . ." Obviously the doctor does not believe her; he simply can't be bothered arguing. He mutters something and starts writing up his notes.

Then something occurs to him: "Your medication. Have you got it here?"

Iben finds Malene's medicine in her handbag. The tablets are kept in an art nouveau silver cigarette case, which Malene had bought secondhand and had lined with velvet.

The doctor leans across the table. He takes one of the tablets and holds it up. "There you are. This isn't cortisone."

"But . . . I put them in there myself."

The doctor's thick finger pushes the small white tablets around on the velvety surface. He leans back in his chair, completely sure of himself.

When he speaks, his lips curl a little. "The proper pills are notched in a different way from these. But you must have been taking them until the day before yesterday, at least, or you would have had one of these attacks earlier."

"What are you saying? That yesterday someone exchanged my proper medication for . . . ?" Malene's voice cracks.

Iben makes a sudden noise, as if someone has hit her hard in the solar plexus.

Suddenly they both know that someone has been tampering with Malene's tablets.

Malene keeps her medicine in her bag, which she always puts on the floor next to her desk. Yesterday, only a very few people would have had access to it.

Malene throws her head back and screams. "How could she do this? She's sick!"

Then she starts crying: "I can't . . . Oh, I couldn't . . ."

Something flashes across Iben's mind. Anne-Lise couldn't be that evil! Could she?

It must be someone else.

But then her common sense tells her that her instinct must be wrong. Anne-Lise is capable of all kinds of things. And despite her outward calm, they know that, deep down, Anne-Lise is enraged.

anne-lise

It must be said that for a long time now we've had a sneaking suspicion that you might decide to leave us and go on to greater things. And of course we realized that you would prefer to work on something meaningful, somewhere that would offer you the opportunity to make the world a better place. This is precisely why we're all sad that you're leaving us, and so soon too."

Everyone on the staff of Lyngby Central Library had gathered for the farewell party on Anne-Lise's last day. They stood about in the large lobby, holding their glasses of white wine and plates of canapés. The large windows offered panoramic views of Lake Mølle and its landscaped surroundings.

The head librarian's words seemed entirely genuine. "We will miss your warmth and your ability to share in our lives as if we were all your close friends. We will miss your sense of fun. Naturally, whoever succeeds you will find you a hard act to follow. I believe that there's not one of us who, when faced with a troublesome database—indeed, any computer problem—has not instinctively thought of consulting you first. Of course it did occur to us, on occasion, that it wasn't fair to rely on your goodwill all the time!"

Anne-Lise's colleagues beamed at this.

"So then we'd try asking each other instead. But sooner or

later we'd always end up coming back to you. And you'd have the answer, of course!"

By now they were all laughing. Anne-Lise looked around the circle of faces. It had been a difficult decision to leave after all the years of working in this place. But she had taken a leap into the unknown and hoped that her new job at the Danish Center for Information on Genocide would bring new, interesting responsibilities and would also give her the opportunity to meet a whole range of fascinating people.

She took the whole scene in: the lake's oddly dark green water glinting outside, the ducks swimming right beneath the library windows, her colleagues standing around chatting—and the hand-colored engraving of old Lyngby, her farewell gift.

The head librarian raised her glass and looked at Anne-Lise. "I believe—no, I know—that you will have a great time in your new job. But maybe you will, from time to time, think about us and remember us fondly? I'd like to believe that too. I feel we have created a special atmosphere here and we've shared many good years together. In any case, you can be certain that we will always think fondly of you."

On her first day at the DCIG, Anne-Lise came in to work full of hope, but also a little apprehensive about not being able to meet the expectations of her academically qualified new colleagues, who were younger than she was. Still, she had decided to change her job precisely because she wanted new challenges. She put on a new cashmere twinset, and she had asked her hairdresser to freshen up her hair color.

The first three days went well enough. Malene taught her the cataloging system and set her up recording the new books and documents that had come in while the library was understaffed. The previous librarian had followed her husband to his new job in Finland about a month earlier.

Cataloging meant that Anne-Lise worked in the library on her own. It seemed such a dark place, as if the crowded shelves somehow absorbed all the light. It would be good to join the others sometime soon, she thought. More lamps in the library would help in the meantime, but Anne-Lise realized that she should wait awhile before asking for anything. Her priority at this point was to ensure that her relationship with her new colleagues got off to a good start.

There was another problem, though. A door next to her desk led to a small room housing a copier and a printer. When it was left open, the fumes made it difficult to breathe. She kept closing the door, but the others left it open every time they used the machines. Anne-Lise resigned herself to this for the time being.

Malene's aunt had died a few days before Anne-Lise started work. It was heartening that they felt able to discuss family issues and it was, of course, perfectly understandable that some of the others' conversations were conducted in whispers. As the days went by, however, Anne-Lise felt no less excluded. She sat alone in the library working on the catalog from morning till night, except during breaks.

Anne-Lise tried to tell them things about herself so that they might get to know her better. She wanted to show them that she could be fun, but somehow her jokes didn't seem to go over well with them. They seemed to have their own brand of humor.

After more than a week had passed, Anne-Lise felt that she could finally raise the matter of the copier room door. She was in the Winter Garden. Malene and Iben were sitting at their desks and were obviously keen to get back to work. She felt quite awkward, standing in middle of the floor with nothing to do with her hands.

Malene smiled at her and explained that they had always kept the door open because if they didn't, the air in the copier room became unbearable.

"I see, of course. But certainly the best thing would be to leave the window open in there. Otherwise the awful smell permeates the library."

No one responded.

Anne-Lise went on. "And of course the fumes spread to you as well."

"We've tried leaving the window open, but it gets too cold if you have a lot of copying to do. Your predecessor didn't have any problem with it."

For a few days Anne-Lise agreed to what the others wanted and left the door open. Only when the big copier had been running nonstop for more than an hour and the chemical smell became so suffocating that she couldn't breathe did she open the window. Although nothing was said, she noticed later that the window had been closed again.

One day, Paul overheard them discussing the matter and suggested that they should alternate between keeping the window and the door open. The others apparently thought Anne-Lise had spoken about the problem within Paul's earshot on purpose. For the rest of the afternoon the women fell silent every time she passed through, punishing her for the unpardonable sin of "squealing to the boss."

In bed with Henrik that evening, Anne-Lise wept for the first time, longing for her old job. It was hard for her to admit that she didn't much care for Malene and Iben. They had a way of giggling together and talking about people she didn't know that seemed to exclude everyone else. Camilla, on the other hand, seemed very nice. She was married and had children and was about the same age as she was. Maybe they would get on well once they got to know each other better.

The next morning she pulled herself together. She had to believe that all this was just a minor setback. She put on more makeup than usual; then she wiped it off again just before leaving home.

They still didn't speak to her. While she ruminated on how best to handle the situation, she tried not to feel scared. It takes time to adjust to a new place of work, she thought. If I'm determined and stay calm, it will be all right in the end.

During the lunch break she again tried her best to pretend that everything was fine. She listened to Iben's and Malene's girlish anecdotes and watched Camilla to see when she should smile or laugh.

A couple of days later Anne-Lise picked a time when Paul was away to ask the others right out if there was something she had done to annoy them. They said no, not at all, but Anne-Lise didn't give up. She did everything she could to convince them that they must let her know. In the end, Iben admitted that they thought Anne-Lise had been rather inconsiderate about the copier room window.

This little exchange of views did some good. Despite Paul's suggestion that the window stay open after every second use, Anne-Lise emphasized that as far as she was concerned, it was all right if they always shut it.

They became nicer to her after that. For a while.

But then Iben and Malene were sending faxes and there seemed to be a private joke going between them. On her first day, Anne-Lise had sent a fax to the chairman of the board by mistake. She hadn't known that his number was on Speed Dial and the fax went off the second Anne-Lise keyed in the first digit. Now Iben's and Malene's voices were loud enough to ensure that Anne-Lise could hear them.

"I mustn't make a mistake when I send this fax!"

Iben laughed. "Who is it for?"

"It's for Ole."

"Oh, but it's so-o easy to do!"

They didn't say anything else, but the sneering tone of their voices made it clear that they were making fun of her.

Camilla also made it clear that she wanted to keep her distance from Anne-Lise, even though they had had a few good conversations when the others were not around.

Barely five months into her new job, Anne-Lise was so wound up that she cried almost every evening. She cried in the car on the way home. She cried in the kitchen when she cooked supper and the children watched television. Later on, in bed with Henrik, she sobbed in his arms. Less than half a year ago, she had been happy and her worst problem at work had been boredom.

Henrik tried to comfort her by saying that she could easily get another job, but all that did was make Anne-Lise sob even harder.

"But don't you see? There are no other jobs. Everybody is cutting back. And if a place does have a vacancy, they'll pick someone younger!"

Anne-Lise clung to Henrik. She went over what she had done in the office and regretted everything. "If only I'd kept quiet about that window! If only I'd let it be!"

Henrik held her close to calm her. "Come on, that's neither here nor there. It's such a little thing."

"Yes, I know. Such a stupid little thing! I couldn't know, could I? How was I to know that just mentioning the smell was so frowned upon? The others get their way, always—with everything! And all I wanted was to close the stupid door!"

The next morning Anne-Lise went to an Internet site where she could download a program that traced and recovered files that had been deleted from her hard disk. While the others assumed that she was silently at work, plugging away at her deadly dull cataloging job, she ran the newly installed program. It turned out that quite a few fascinating things were hidden inside her computer.

Anne-Lise's predecessor might never have protested to her colleagues about her working conditions, but she certainly e-mailed both her husband and her friends to tell them how intensely she detested every hour she had to spend at the Center. She had written to a friend to say what fantastic luck it was that her husband had got the Finnish job, because it was damn near impossible to find another job as a librarian in Denmark.

Anne-Lise also found evidence of wide-ranging communications with the Center's users. Clearly, the previous librarian had escaped being corralled into only scanning files and updating the catalog. Malene had taken over the entire external relations side of the librarian's job during the three weeks before Anne-Lise's appointment. Anne-Lise could not imagine what her situation would be like if she tried to reclaim the position. All hell would break loose.

almost a year has passed since Anne-Lise started working at the DCIG. It is late in the afternoon when she steps into the old elevator to leave the office. Through the closed main door to the Center she can still faintly hear Malene laughing. Then the sound of amusement fades as the elevator's whining seals her in.

Soon she'll be outside the building, the moment she has been looking forward to all day; she even fell asleep last night comforting herself with the thought of it, its never-ending cycle: a few pleasant hours with her family before the dread of the next day at work overwhelms her and then the consoling thought that that day too will eventually end.

She breathes in deeply several times.

Near the top edge of one of the elevator's wooden panels someone has scratched three filthy little drawings. Anne-Lise stares at the drawings as the trembling descent of the elevator slowly transports her down and away from the DCIG.

Today Henrik is collecting the children. He will take them to soccer practice and dance class and wait for them, doing some of his paperwork in the car. This way Anne-Lise will have at least an hour and a half to herself before she has to prepare dinner. She decided a few days ago that it was about time she had her old friend Nicola over. They haven't had a real opportunity to chat, just the two of them, in more than a year.

Anne-Lise stops to buy cakes for their afternoon tea and is on her way home when, suddenly, she finds herself east of Lyngby, driving on the northbound motorway toward Helsingør. How odd. She must have been in the wrong lane when the motorway divided. She finds a slip road and soon picks up the direction back to the Lyngby bypass.

Anne-Lise and Henrik live in an old-style house with red-limed walls, near the nature reserve at Holte. It stands just a few rows away from the wildly expensive homes with views over Lake Fure, and has a larger garden than most of the neighboring villas. The area is the perfect place to raise children, which is the main reason Anne-Lise and Henrik chose it over the wealthier districts along the Øresund coast.

When Anne-Lise eventually pulls up in front of her home, Nicola is waiting for her on the porch. She looks warm in her short, obviously expensive fur jacket, tight dark brown trousers, and leather boots. Must be Prada boots, Anne-Lise thinks. Nicola loves Prada.

Nicola is beaming with pleasure. She gives Anne-Lise a big hug, and their friendship immediately picks up where it left off a year ago.

"I've told everybody that dinner will be late tonight, because I want a chance to see Henrik and the kids as well. And I'm so looking forward to seeing what you two have done to the house since last time."

Over the years Anne-Lise and Henrik have made quite a few changes. They've had three walls taken down to enlarge some of the rooms. Together they built a stone table and a huge cupboard in the old scullery at the back of the house, and they've decorated several rooms with stucco ornaments brought back from Italy. When they were more or less happy with the house, they'd started on the garden.

Anne-Lise unlocks the front door and explains that they haven't really done anything special since the last time.

Nicola steps inside. "Oh, come on. I don't believe it. I know you two. There's no stopping you!"

As she fills the electric kettle, Anne-Lise asks Nicola how her son is. Anne-Lise is very fond of Nicola; it's strange that it's taken her so long to invite her over.

They met each other many years ago through Jutta, a mutual friend they rarely see now. Jutta's boyfriend had studied business management and both Anne-Lise and Nicola met their husbands through him. Since then Nicola's husband has become a managing director in Maersk Oil. Although living on one of the most elegant streets in Hellerup has changed Nicola to a certain degree, she has kept her nursing job and remains the kind of person whom Anne-Lise feels she can trust to say exactly what she thinks.

They have their tea and cakes. Afterward, Nicola insists that they do a tour of the house. They end up in the garden, looking at the group of rhododendrons the previous owner planted at least forty years ago. The foliage on the lilac trees is turning an autumnal brown, and the leaves from the dogwood bush near the apple tree lie scattered on the ground, so that the tree's deep-red branches are almost bare.

Anne-Lise remembers how, just a few years ago, she and Henrik would get up early and spend their Saturdays and Sundays working on their home. At the end of each day, they would stand together and admire their achievements. But apathy has set in, and now she's finding it difficult to whip up enough interest to do anything at all.

The two women go back inside and sit in front of the fireplace. They chat about their families and old friends.

Anne-Lise thinks that Nicola won't notice any change in her, but as she's describing Clara's new dance outfit, Nicola interrupts her: "Anne-Lise?"

"Yes?"

"You must tell me what's wrong."

Anne-Lise stares at her.

"It's something to do with your new job, isn't it? Is it the same old problem?"

Soon after Anne-Lise started work at the DCIG, she told Nicola a little about how the others behaved, but she kept the worst to herself.

Nicola is concerned. "You've changed so much. I hardly recognize you."

"I haven't changed!"

"Anne-Lise, listen. You're not yourself. Don't you remember what you used to be like?" Nicola looks Anne-Lise in the eye and reaches out a hand to console her. A gold bracelet slips out from under the thin white shirt-sleeve. "Why don't you give your old boss a ring? She really liked you. Maybe they could take you back."

Anne-Lise is speechless. She feels so defeated. Does Nicola really believe it would be that easy to get her old job back? The room becomes blurred; her eyes are filling with tears.

Nicola takes her hand. "You must tell someone about what your colleagues are doing to you. If you don't, they'll ruin your life away from work as well."

Anne-Lise is sniffing back the tears. She clears her throat and Nicola runs off to fetch a roll of paper towels.

Soon everything comes pouring out. For the first time Anne-Lise tells someone apart from Henrik what it is really like.

"I can't understand how they can be so callous! And yet they think of themselves as such good, idealistic people . . ."

Nicola is rubbing her arm gently. It's so different from the way Anne-Lise is treated at work.

"It doesn't matter one iota to them if I lose my job, or my husband divorces me, or my children get into trouble, but I still have to work with them. I have to smile and talk to them. Every single day, I'm forced to look them in the eye and pretend I don't hate them."

"Anne-Lise, you must stop working there."

"But I can't!"

"Yes, you can. Just stop. You'll find another job soon enough."

Anne-Lise tears herself away. "But I'll become . . . like Jutta!"

"Nonsense. You won't."

"Yes, I will! I don't want to be like her. I'd *hate* to be like her!"

Nicola's voice is calm and gentle. "Anne-Lise, you will never be like Jutta. I'm sure of that. Whatever happens, you won't."

When Nicola and Anne-Lise were friends with Jutta, Jutta was working for a marketing company. She and the company director had a falling out and Jutta couldn't stand working there any longer. Afterward she landed another job, but then got into trouble with her colleagues. Meanwhile, her husband became a self-employed investment broker and did very well, earning far more than either Anne-Lise's or Nicola's husband. Although Jutta didn't need to work financially, she disliked staying at home all day and decided to open a small shop selling exclusive Italian and French kitchenware. Her husband put up the cash to help her get started, but in the end she couldn't cope with managing a store either.

Now Jutta is better dressed than ever. She has turned the house into an amazing display of Oregon pine, all the floors and the paneling. The furniture has been designed by a Swedish architect, with whom Jutta got in touch after seeing a long article about his ideas in an interior design magazine. When she meets working women, she always asks how they are getting along and invariably says something like "How wonderful for you!"—but her interest is only superficial. She apparently believes the mantra preached by all her magazines: buy all these things and they will make you a better person.

A few years ago Jutta would occasionally phone Anne-Lise or Nicola when she was drunk. They never found out how often she drank alone at home, but the phone calls prompted them to talk about trying to help her. She not only rejected their help but also managed to do it in a condescending way. Worst of all, her children were said to have become aggressive and problematic. Could it be that Jutta has abandoned her responsibility for her children as well?

Anne-Lise and Nicola hear Henrik's car in the driveway. Her family has arrived home.

For a moment Anne-Lise is confused. Then she makes a dash for the door, calling out to Nicola: "Tell them I'm in the bathroom!" In the hall, she suddenly turns back and pops her head around the door. "Nicola, thank you! I just have to . . ."

She runs into the bathroom to fix her face. Outside, the children's voices call, "Mommy! Mommy!" as they run to the living room. It feels so bad to hide from them. Henrik comes in and slams the front door.

Anne-Lise washes off the smeared mascara and lipstick and rinses her eyes with cold water. As she goes through the motions quickly, she listens to Ulrik running around from room to room, looking for her. Before the Center, Anne-Lise could not have imagined ever being tempted just to let go, to follow in the footsteps of Jutta. But then, maybe she's already on that downward slope? Maybe everyone else thinks so but Nicola is the only one who dared say anything. Whatever happens, her problems must not affect Clara and Ulrik. She can't let them pay the price for her troubles at the DCIG.

A few weeks after Nicola's visit, Iben and Malene both receive an anonymous e-mail from someone who is threatening to kill them. The office is unsettled by this turn of events, and for the first time Anne-Lise dares to mention that the others don't always treat her well.

Malene, Iben, and Camilla instantly jump down her throat. Either they are extremely accomplished liars or they are so dishonest with themselves that they aren't even aware of what they are doing. To them, "the librarian" is a dull, colorless creature with poor social skills because that's exactly what they expect her to be and they won't let Anne-Lise change their minds.

The day after their attack Paul asks her to join a staff meeting in his office. At the meeting the others claim that the door between the Winter Garden and the library has always been closed. Anne-Lise knows differently—the door was always open when she started and it was only a month later that Camilla began to complain that she would get arthritis from the draft.

Paul doesn't agree with them and makes his first-ever decision in Anne-Lise's favor. After having been patient for a whole year, at last she will be allowed contact with the Center's users, as she was promised in her interview. Also, the door to the library will not be closed anymore.

It takes less than a week for the others to get their revenge, in an act crueler than Anne-Lise could have imagined. One morning she discovers a brown powder all over her hands. She has managed to stain her blouse with it, and smudge her face with brownish red streaks.

Anne-Lise observes Malene's face. That woman knows something; it feels just like the time when Malene humiliated her in front of Frederik Thorsteinsson a few days earlier. But Anne-Lise still can't figure out what the substance is. She searches her office area. When she knocks over a box file on the top shelf, the fluid inside it splashes out. She closes her eyes instantly, leaps backward, and hears the box crash to the floor.

She screams and opens her eyes. Thick, viscous fluid is spattered everywhere. Her clothes are covered in spots and stains. It is blood. Her skin is sticky with blood. It is so awful that her mind blanks out. All she can do is look at Malene, who has appeared in the doorway. Malene acts as if she is truly shocked, but she's not convincing enough. There's a smug little smile lurking behind her frown.

Anne-Lise wants to leave and go home, and accepts Paul's offer of a taxi even though her car is parked right outside.

Only when she's home and has taken a shower does she call Henrik. While she talks to him, she wanders from room to room in her white dressing gown with her damp hair wrapped in a white towel. Something significant happened today. She feels deeply uneasy, but after the hot bath it all seems rather remote.

Henrik is shouting into the phone. "That's it! You've got to stop working there! They'll kill you next!"

"But, you know, when they saw me covered in blood, they were so upset. They felt genuinely sorry for me. At least, Iben and Camilla did."

Anne-Lise is on her way to the kitchen. "I think they regretted it. Maybe they've got their anger out of their system now. Maybe this will be the end of it."

"Anne-Lise, it will *not* be the end."

"But they helped me clean up, you know. I think they felt shocked at what they'd done."

"Anne-Lise—try to get it into your head. They. Will. Not. Stop."

Anne-Lise doesn't answer him.

Henrik takes a deep breath. For a moment he can't think of what to say. Then he makes up his mind. "I'm coming home now. I'll tell everyone that I'm not feeling well. I'll be with you in twenty minutes."

In the kitchen, Anne-Lise makes a cheese roll. She drifts about, bare feet on the parquet, while she eats.

Maybe it is not just the others who have rid themselves of their anger. She too has purged herself of something—only she doesn't yet know what it is.

anne-Lise hears the engine of Henrik's Audi outside. He storms into the hall.

"Anne-Lise, you're coming with me. I've told Yngve what you've had to put up with and he says he can see you right away. Let's go." Henrik would have liked to drag Anne-Lise to the car at once, but she has to get dressed and tidy herself up.

Yngve is their family doctor. They have been with him for years, long before they moved to Holte. When Henrik had trouble with his knee after a car accident, Yngve was more help-ful than the orthopedic consultant. Later, when they were trying for a baby and Anne-Lise initially failed to get pregnant, Yngve again impressed them more than the gynecologist she had been referred to.

Yngve is now in his fifties, but people still seem to find him exceptionally attractive. He wears his dark hair cut short and keeps his powerful, square chin clean-shaven. His voice is deep and melodious.

Somehow Anne-Lise always has the impression that he is a lonely man. She wonders if he is gay. There's definitely some-thing different about him.

The receptionist shows them into his consultation room. It smells faintly of soap and the medicinal scents of bandages and antiseptics. Henrik and Anne-Lise settle into the two cheap black plastic chairs. Yngve has never bothered to refurbish his offices.

He comes into the room, sits down, and puts his large hands on the desk, palms down. Then he turns to Anne-Lise and asks her why she has come today.

She doesn't get very far before he interrupts her. "Sorry, Anne-Lise. I want to make it clear from the start that any kind of systematic bullying is deadly—more dangerous than drinking or smoking. The victims sometimes think they can hold out and deal with the situation, but it's impossible."

"Yes."

"I see quite a few people who have been bullied in my practice. Sometimes they commit suicide, or they contract illnesses. Some die. Some become unemployable; others start drinking or doing drugs. One way or another, being bullied does enormous damage."

Henrik straightens up and turns to Anne-Lise. For the moment he thinks that he and Yngve are of one mind. "You see. You have to go on sick leave. Tell them tomorrow and resign. Not one more day in that place."

Yngve taps a small notebook on the desktop. "Right. That certainly is one solution. But I'm afraid I believe it's the wrong one."

Anne-Lise casts a sidelong glance at Henrik. His only reaction is to stay perched on his flimsy chair, smiling and waiting, curious to hear why the doctor thinks that he's wrong.

Anne-Lise wants to have her say. "I've installed a program on my office computer that deletes any evidence of Internet searches. Now I can spend time at work checking job seekers' sites and sending off applications."

Yngve smiles at her. "Good idea. Have you applied anywhere yet?"

"Over the last six months I've applied twenty-two times, but I wasn't called for an interview even once. I've followed up each one and I phoned to ask what was wrong, as you should. But they get so many applications and always seem to pick someone younger."

Henrik adds, "Which is why we've stopped applying for a bit."

"Yes. Just for a bit. I needed a break. For now."

Yngve puts his hands together. "Anne-Lise, you have three options. One, you allow yourself to be pushed out of your job and, the way the market operates now, you might never work again. Two, you stay and let the others carry on bullying you. But you have a third option: stay on and make the others stop persecuting you."

Henrik is surprised. "I thought that the experts agreed that when you're being bullied, the best thing to do is get out as quickly as possible? Because it's a battle you can't win?"

"That's what they say."

Conventional wisdom doesn't influence Yngve. As he speaks, it's clear that he is indifferent to "the experts." His calm brown eyes rest first on Anne-Lise, then on Henrik.

"Anne-Lise, if you resign, you will spend the rest of your life thinking of yourself as a loser, and of the world as an evil place. It's destructive. But if you let them work you over, they will destroy you. My advice is to confront them. Can you do that?"

At first Anne-Lise couldn't see the point of Henrik's insistence on seeing their doctor. Now she feels it was a very good idea.

"Yes."

"Are you sure?"

"Yes."

"Excellent. I'm glad to hear you say that. Having gotten to know you over all these years, I'm sure you can. And I'm convinced you'll be able to change your working conditions."

There is something about the doctor's manner, the way he speaks in his deep voice, that makes Anne-Lise trust him implicitly. Now he's smiling at her.

"Do you believe me when I say you can change things at work?"

"Yes . . . yes, I do."

"Good."

Anne-Lise observes Yngve's large hands. He is leaning forward in his chair, poised to go on to the next item on the agenda.

"I want you to know that no one has been able to demonstrate any common personality traits in people who have been subjected to bullying at work. It has been studied, of course. The usual theory is that bullies go for people who are socially maladjusted in some way—introverts or slackers or incompetents or whatever. None of this turns out to be true. On the contrary, it's often the more able members of staff who are picked on. But there does seem to be one recurring aspect in the victim's personality, which is that they, to a greater extent than their colleagues, dislike being confrontational. They are rather passive, hoping that their tormentors will stop. Which doesn't happen, of course. So, there you are, Anne-Lise. Are you afraid of standing up to your colleagues?"

Anne-Lise thinks about what a special person the doctor is. Coming from someone else, his paternal tone would be almost offensive, but from Yngve it seems completely desirable and convincing.

"I wasn't scared in my previous job. But what is important to me right now is being included in their group, so naturally I avoid making waves. There's something else: I always feel that something dreadful will happen if I do express my opinion about anything at all."

There's a crash outside the office—a tray or something—but Yngve's face doesn't register a thing.

"Yes, I see. It makes it easier to push you around. Listen."

"Yes?"

"These characters will become more and more aggressive as time goes by. The essential thing is to make them realize there are limits. This far and no farther."

Yngve seems more pensive than usual. Could it be that he was once bullied too, perhaps long ago? She cannot ask him.

"Bullying is very common among children, both at school and in afterschool clubs and so forth. Teachers spend hours telling the kids not to be bullies and devising punishments for them if they are found out. Political initiatives are aimed solely at putting an end to bullying, all doomed to fail, or so it seems. Now and then bullied children have been brought to see me. Almost invariably they suffer from serious illnesses or psychological trauma, rooted in their victimization."

He picks up a pen, balances it on the palm of his hand, and stares at it for a moment. Then he looks up at them. "Adult bullying is less well recognized, but it is also common. Maybe you think I'm being melodramatic, but I take bullying as seriously as heart disease or cancer. I do and I should."

Anne-Lise wonders whether Yngve has a lover. If he really is gay, that is.

"The fact is, people kill each other. Regardless of whatever action is taken and whatever we are taught, victimizing others is part of human nature."

What Yngve says is quite different from the views of the genocide researchers Anne-Lise is familiar with. At the DCIG she has read articles about ordinary people killing other ordinary people, but the investigators always argue that the circumstances were exceptional, and start with the premise that, for human beings, cooperation and kindness are the norm. None of these research papers has ever said that murder is an unavoidable outcome of "human nature," yet Yngve's view has resonance.

"We eat, we reproduce, we protect those closest to us. And we reject those who are different from us and kill our rivals. Human beings try, more or less effectively, to exert control over our instincts. We are different from animals in that we have exceptional willpower. For instance, in no other species is there an entire community where no one has sex. Just think of the Vatican.

"But most people give in to temptation at some point. Your concentration slips for just a moment and there you are: being unfaithful, eating fattening foods, or slowly torturing a colleague to death. The latter, of course, is forbidden, so a person may prefer not to be conscious of what they're doing—like a form of self-deception.

"Consider your colleagues' states of mind, Anne-Lise. They feel a little like you would if you were alone one evening, watching television and feeling hungry with a large bowl of chips sitting in front of you. You're determined not to eat them and stick to your resolve, but if the program captures your attention, you forget and start reaching for the chips. Before you realize it, they're gone. You may not even be able to recall having eaten them.

"That's what you are to your colleagues: a temptation. At the outset they may well have decided to be pleasant toward you. Or maybe they never did. Either way, they still see you as a rival and, without their planning to, there will be times when they can't resist going after you. The reaction is so instinctive that afterward they'll hardly remember."

Yngve is very persuasive, but his arguments upset Anne-Lise. Still, something about the man makes her sit calmly and listen. Henrik has also been very quiet. She can hear Yngve's receptionist rummaging about on the other side of the door, no doubt cleaning up whatever was spilled. Anne-Lise considers how she has always thought of Yngve as being lonely, even though she knows absolutely nothing about his private life. Does it have something to do with his intelligence, or was she responding intuitively to the faintly depressed tone that never quite leaves his voice?

They agree that Anne-Lise shouldn't accuse the others of having rigged the blood trap. Without proof, she would be fighting a losing battle, and it would expose her even more to her colleagues' anger.

"Anne-Lise, can you think of something they've done that was clearly wrong? Or an argument you're certain to win if there's a confrontation?"

"I'm not sure. I make wrong decisions all the time and I do stupid things. My head is bursting with how horrible it all is. I'm not my normal self."

"Of course, that's understandable. But things will change. Look forward to that, even though it's hard for you now."

The receptionist comes in to say the next patient is waiting. She speaks quickly, as if she is scared of Yngve. He answers pleasantly enough and turns back to Anne-Lise.

"Haven't you witnessed anything they've done that goes against the Center's interests?"

Anne-Lise reflects carefully. "One of the users, a man called Erik Prins, told me that Malene had given him false information about library searches, just to keep him away from me. That could be—"

"Would you have put up with that in your previous job?"

"Not for a moment."

"There you are! Be confident. It's unacceptable now as well." He flattens his hands on the tabletop again. "This is a battle you can win, isn't it?"

"Yes."

"Do you really believe that?"

"Yes, I do."

"Excellent." He gets up and shakes their hands, first Henrik's and then Anne-Lise's. "I want to see you again. It's my job to deal with any issue that's seriously threatening your well-being, whether it be physical or psychological. You are not going to let your colleagues push you into unemployment. You will fight them."

"Yes. Yes, I will."

"Very good. Now let's decide when you should come back and tell me how things have progressed. Maybe in about three weeks' time?"

"Yes."

"Good. Just ask for an appointment at reception."

When Anne-Lise and Henrik step outside, they're both surprised that it is still bright. It feels as if it should be evening by now, but the incident at the DCIG was only a few hours ago. They have several hours before they need to collect the children.

Anne-Lise keeps her promise to Yngve, but afterward her life at work doesn't get any better. It has done her no good to confront Malene about Erik Prins. Malene simply shifts the blame and demands to know who the user is. Anne-Lise is more at fault than ever.

The Winter Garden seems quieter now that the door is always open. They speak in low voices, or e-mail each other, or wander off to talk in the kitchen or the meeting rooms. A few times Anne-Lise has surprised them while they are using a made-up sign language and giggling a lot.

During lunch Iben gives little lectures, often based on the books she reads when she can't sleep. These days she seems to be sticking to psychiatry textbooks. While Iben goes on about mental health problems, she watches Anne-Lise. It's plain for all to see that Iben thinks Anne-Lise must be suffering from dissociative identity disorder.

One evening after yet another hostile day of pointed remarks and hints that she's somehow deranged, Anne-Lise is reading *Little House in the Big Woods* to her children. Ulrik and Clara are both in Ulrik's room. Clara is lying on her back in the lower bunk, balancing her Barbie doll on her tummy. Sometimes her lips form soundless words; sometimes she mumbles. She seems not to be listening, but the next day she will remember everything that happened in the story.

Ulrik is in the upper bunk. He has pushed the duvet away and rests his head on the edge of the bed.

Clara's mumbling is getting louder.

Ulrik leans forward. "Shut up! Stop making that noise!"

Clara carries on playing with her doll and seems not to notice.

The bedroom air is warm and smells slightly of toothpaste. Anne-Lise can pick up sounds from Henrik's study. He is trying to do something new with his two computers.

Ulrik shouts at Clara more crossly than before. "Shut up! Shut up!"

Anne-Lise reads on about Laura's father, who is walking in the forest and sees a doe with its fawn. Clara's voice fades and becomes inaudible again. Without warning, tears well up in Anne-Lise's eyes. The fawn

doesn't run away. It stands quite still, looking wide-eyed at Laura's father.
The tears are running quietly down Anne-Lise's cheeks. They keep coming
even though there is nothing sad about the story.

After a while, Ulrik notices. "Mommy? What's the matter?"

Laura's father promises that he won't go hunting until the baby animals have grown up. Now Anne-Lise has to look up at her son. She smiles.
She has no idea what is happening to her. "I must have caught a cold."

Clara puts away her doll. "Are you crying?"

"No, no. It's just a cold."

"Does it hurt?"

"No. Not a bit."

"Why are you crying then?"

Ulrik shouts at his sister, "Mommy's not crying! She's got a cold."

Anne-Lise realizes that she is on the verge of falling apart. Her children
must not witness this. She has to get away.

Panic grips her. "There. That's it for tonight."

"No-o-o!"

Anne-Lise fights to suppress her sobbing. "Yes, it's time to go to sleep.
No more reading tonight."

"No-o-o. Please. Read some more. Just a little."

"HENRIK! HENRIK! Please come here!"

She runs out. Henrik comes toward her. Her sobbing is out of control.

"Go to the children. Read them a story."

She stumbles into their bedroom, shuts the door, and throws herself
on their bed, covering her head with a pillow to muffle the sounds she is
making.

Once the children are asleep, Henrik returns to Anne-Lise, walks quietly over to the bed, and sits down close to her. She doesn't open her eyes,
but senses his body weighing down the mattress next to her head. She is
glad that he is there and blindly reaches out her hand to him. He takes it
and strokes her temple with his other hand. They do not speak.

Crying has left Anne-Lise feeling hot and completely empty. The sensation of her body dissolving washes over her. She feels as if she is seeping
away, through the mattress, draining down through the boards and beams
of the house, through the spaces of brick and cement.

Henrik is asking her to please tell him what's the matter. She mutters in response, pressing her nose in between his thigh and the mattress. It's good to feel the warmth of him. Her hand rests between his legs. He asks her again. She doesn't answer, only begins to move her hand.

"Anne-Lise, is this a good idea?"

She looks up at him.

He gets up, closes the door, and dims the light. One of the good things about their solidly built old house is that sounds do not travel. Once the door is closed, there is no need to worry about the children.

His chest is against hers. Every pore in her skin is wide open. She's sweating.

"What's happening?" Henrik asks. She's never been like this before. "I love it," he says, and "I didn't think you felt this way."

And then they are both silent.

A pillow falls to the floor with a faint thump, then the duvet follows, absorbing its own sound as it falls.

This is how I want to die, she thinks. To disappear like this, happy, because in reality, I'm already gone.

Every time he thrusts into her, words form silently inside her. Kill me, she thinks. She must not say it aloud. He would stop at once.

Now she's nearly reduced to nothingness. Softly, she dreams on.

Kill me! Kill me! Kill me!

Anne-Lise has never experienced anything like this. Not with anyone. She registers his smell.

Something has given way inside the mattress. The springs groan like a giant struggling for breath. Anne-Lise finally slips away while her mind whispers on inaudibly.

Kill me! Kill me! Kill me!

all day long Anne-Lise imagines that everything will change now.

True, she knows that she pays far too much attention to what Malene and Iben do, even to the expressions on their faces. All the interpretation and forecasting exhausts her. Still, today something radically new has happened.

In the morning Iben had phoned from National Hospital's rheumatology clinic. She was there with Malene, who was ill. Iben had said that Tatiana planned to write an important article and suggested that Anne-Lise should call Tatiana and offer to help.

None of her new colleagues had ever done anything like this. Anne-Lise phoned Henrik right away.

"There, you see. Maybe we'll collaborate from now on."

He said yes and was so nice to her. She knows well that he doesn't take any of her "fantasies," as he calls them, seriously.

A small part of her is aware that real change isn't very likely. It makes her more vulnerable. Every time they turn on the kindness she can't help thinking that all the tension might be due to her own misunderstanding, or pileup of misunderstandings.

The day at the DCIG is over and Anne-Lise is about to pick Clara up from her nursery class. As she walks into the small yellow-brick school, she meets other parents and children she knows. A good day at the office means that she is not her usual worn-out self, and a cheerful tune she heard on the car radio is playing in her head. This afternoon she almost feels as she used to feel before the DCIG.

She walks through the first, then the second set of doors to the main room. It's quiet in there. After saying hello to a father who is leaving with his two children, she spots Clara at a table, cutting shapes from shiny pieces of colored paper. Anne-Lise sits down and helps her stick the shapes onto a plain white sheet.

Almost at once a teacher comes along to tell her that Clara has been involved in fights twice that day. The second time she fought with a boy and hit him on the head with a branch. The teachers had to bandage the wound.

Anne-Lise's cell phone rings. It's Paul. She interrupts the teacher. "I'm sorry, but it's my boss. Do you mind if I take the call?"

Paul sounds as if it's urgent. "Hello, Anne-Lise. All right for us to talk?"

"Yes, fine."

"That's good. Listen, I've just had a call from Iben. She's in the hospital."

"Yes?"

"She has taken Malene to the rheumatology clinic. They've been there all day."

"I know. Iben called me earlier."

"And she told me, and I'm afraid they are in complete agreement . . ."

Anne-Lise realizes that he's about to say something bad. Paul is being unusually hesitant. Anne-Lise withdraws into a corner and turns her back to the room.

"They believe someone has tampered with Malene's tablets and exchanged her medicine for something that has no effect on . . . on her arthritis. And that's why it has flared up so badly."

"That's terrible."

"And it was extremely painful."

"Yes, I see. Of course. Such a . . ." Anne-Lise stops. She grasps what Paul is actually trying to say. "They think that 'someone' removed her proper medicine?"

"That's what they believe. I'm really not sure how to say this, but . . . they don't want to confront you themselves."

Paul takes a quick breath and speaks again. "They say you are the only one who could have exchanged the tablets."

Anne-Lise suddenly deflates. She stares straight ahead at a world in colored crayons, where smoke whirls from the chimneys of square houses and people have matchstick legs and big round eyes. She sees the pins sticking each drawing to the bulletin board. She sinks down to sit on a child's chair; its back is barely knee height.

She can't think of anything to say. Paul is kind enough not to continue.

Turning to look at Clara, she takes in the scene: the teacher, the other children, and their parents. The teacher tries to look as if she isn't listening.

Anne-Lise whispers: "But Paul, it can't be . . . Paul, you must see that this is crazy! I could never do something like that!"

"I agree, naturally. I don't believe that you did."

Anne-Lise perches on the tiny chair, hunched over. "I didn't! We've worked together for a year, Paul. You must know me by now."

Clara comes along. Her fingers are still stuck in the handles of her blunt child's scissors. Anne-Lise persuades her to go back to the table with the shiny paper. Then she remembers Iben's chatter about how a person can have several different personalities and not be aware of them. Paul will have heard it too, of course.

Is that why Iben has been harping on about these theories? Is it part of a plan to force Paul into firing her?

Behind her a child is screaming. Anne-Lise gets up. The movement is too quick and she feels faint. She bends over to get some blood back to her head. Paul is still speaking, but she can't catch what he's saying. She hurries out of the room to the women's room to finish their talk.

When she returns, the teacher is waiting for her. She insists on going over Clara's fight. Anne-Lise still feels unsteady.

The teacher's tone of voice has acquired a sharp edge. "We had to tell Aleksander to sit still for a quarter of an hour, to make sure he didn't have concussion. Luckily, the bandage did the trick. He was able to play for the rest of the day, but Liselotte was quite worried when she came and noticed the swelling on his head."

The teacher drones on and on. Anne-Lise leans against a wall. This will take some time.

"And I feel I should let you know that Clara has been in a lot of fights recently."

Anne-Lise feels like shouting at her: "It's all my fault! Blame me!

Everything is falling to pieces around me. It's because I can't remember anything. And I cry all the time and my colleagues think I'm impossible." But she manages to keep her composure. They probably think she seems rather distant anyway.

When the subject of fighting has been exhausted, Anne-Lise asks if Clara can stay a little longer. She has to make another phone call and it will be much easier if she doesn't have Clara with her.

"Clara, darling, I have to make a phone call. You go on playing for a while and then I'll come and get you. All right?"

Clara doesn't reply, but tears herself away and runs off with the others.

Back in the restroom, Anne-Lise realizes that it is far from private. Anyone can hear what she's saying, especially if voices are raised. She decides to sit in the car instead.

When she gets into the car, parents are still coming and going. She decides to drive a few blocks away.

Anne-Lise parks on a little side road leading into the Vaserne nature reserve. Certainly no one from the nursery school will come this way. She turns off the engine and sits back to collect her thoughts. The trees outside are bare—winter is approaching. Steeling herself, she dials Iben's home number.

Paul was right. Iben is convinced that Anne-Lise is the one who sent the anonymous e-mails and exchanged Malene's medicine. Anne-Lise tries to defend herself, but nothing she says can persuade Iben. It doesn't take long before Anne-Lise's voice has risen to a shout, as she desperately swears that she didn't do any of it. She swears by everything she believes in—her husband, her health, even her children. This last oath brings stinging regret—she should never, never have sworn by her children, especially to someone as hostile as Iben.

Of course she knows that she hasn't touched the pills. But if there is any truth in the theories about dissociated personalities, then Iben might herself be capable of absolutely anything.

Anne-Lise and Henrik's peaceful time together begins after ten-thirty. The house is quiet and the television is turned off. Henrik sits on their black sofa, going through various papers he has brought home from work.

Some evenings, Anne-Lise reads *Information*. She has convinced Henrik that they should subscribe, hoping it might help her to join in the DCIG chatter. At other times, she lies on the sofa with a throw over her legs and her head resting on Henrik's thigh. This is when she is able to clear her head and recharge her batteries to help her face the next day. It is the quiet evenings with Henrik that have given her the strength to endure the year at the DCIG.

She is resting on the sofa now, sensing the warmth of his leg against her cheek. Now and then his large hand strokes the back of her head and, when he turns a page, his sleeve sometimes touches her cheek.

They have talked about Malene's medication and agree that Malene and Iben are likely to have cooled down by the following day. It could be Malene herself, after all, who mistook one batch of pills for another. Even if Malene and Iben won't buy that theory, it's obvious that someone else could have done it and not just Anne-Lise.

Anne-Lise looks past the stack of books on the coffee table at the engraving of the Lyngby Central Library, speculating what the next day might bring. She thinks about Henrik—how incredibly good he is, and how protective of her.

Once, halfway through a skiing holiday in Austria, Henrik took a phone message saying that Anne-Lise's aunt had fallen seriously ill. He made sure that several members of Anne-Lise's family knew his cell phone number so they could get hold of him if the aunt's condition worsened. But he didn't mention anything about it to her. They enjoyed the week and then, afterward, he told her and added that there had been no point in ruining the holiday for her if the illness wasn't as bad as it had at first seemed.

"Henrik?"

"What is it?"

"About the e-mails . . . ?" She tries to sound as gentle as she can. He mustn't take this the wrong way. She puts her hand on his thigh where it's still warm from her cheek. "Look, I think it was sweet of you to send them. You did it to help me, I know that. And things really did get better. Well, for a while."

"I didn't send the e-mails."

"I think it was sweet of you. Honestly."

"Listen, I did not send them." He puts down his papers.

She peers into his face, trying to read any sign that, yet again, he is protecting her. If he is, he is fantastically good at hiding it.

"If you look at the text of the e-mails, they say different things. Iben is called 'self-righteous,' Malene is told she is 'evil,' and Camilla that she is a 'collaborator' who believes she's innocent. Who, apart from you and I, knows that they really are like that?"

"I've no idea."

"No, neither do I."

She smiles, wanting to persuade him to share his secret with her.

"Come on, you can tell me. I love you for it."

His expression is growing colder. "And do you believe that I exchanged the pills as well?"

She is taken aback. "No. Of course not."

He sees through her. She hadn't foreseen this. The last thing she wants is to sour the air between them.

"Only you've said so often that you truly hate them. And of course I'd understand if you *had* done it."

"But . . . ?"

The muscles around his mouth and eyes have tensed up. It's such a small change, but Anne-Lise cannot bear seeing it.

He puts his hands on her shoulders and speaks slowly. "Anne-Lise, I did not do those things. Neither one nor the other."

"No, I see. I believe you. It's just . . . you know how you can be."

"What if there is some truth in the idea about dissociated identities?" Anne-Lise and Henrik are brushing their teeth together.

"I agree that it looks as if it was an inside job. It's unbelievable, but who else could have done it? Everyone knows Malene's bag. No one could have thought it was my bag or that it was my tablets they were swapping."

"There's Camilla. She's the only one who could have sent the e-mails and exchanged Malene's tablets."

"But that doesn't fit at all. I didn't think she was like that." Anne-Lise drops the toothpaste tube. A line of white paste ends up on the tiled floor. She picks up the tube. "But, it could be why she stayed at home for so long after receiving an e-mail herself. Everything had become too much for her. The story about her ex-partner could just be a cover-up. Oh, I don't know. It still doesn't make any sense. She just isn't like that!"

"Did Iben say anything about how you find out if someone has a split personality?"

"Well, sort of. Camilla could be hiding a bitter hatred toward Iben and Malene. That I would find easy to believe. They don't behave well toward her, but you don't notice it so much compared to the way they treat me. There would be times in her life that she can't or won't remember. But then, that's true of most people."

The top of the toothpaste tube won't screw back on properly. Anne-Lise stops trying and puts it down.

"Dissociated personality is a very serious mental illness, and Iben says that the patient has usually had a terrible childhood, with abuse, physical or sexual. That's something they seem to have in common."

"Okay. What was Camilla's childhood like?"

Anne-Lise takes her time before replying. "I can't remember if she ever said anything about it. She's not like Iben or Malene—they won't stop telling us about that kind of thing."

"I thought she talked a lot during your lunch breaks."

"Oh, she does. She speaks about her choir and how much she enjoys singing. And going to Norway and Sweden on family camping trips. And how much they save at the Metro Hypermarket . . ." When Anne-Lise thinks about it, there hasn't been one single instance of Camilla saying anything more revealing about her past. "Not a word about where or how she grew up. I have simply no idea."

"Four women having lunch together every day and you don't know anything about her childhood? What next? There's something very odd about that!"

He cackles away at his silly joke, but Anne-Lise can't be bothered with it.

"I can't recall Malene or Iben ever saying anything about having the kind of childhood that would cause them serious mental problems now. But judging by the way they've been behaving, they must have had a terrible time." Anne-Lise sits down next to Henrik on the edge of the tub. "But then, probably no worse than most people."

When they are finished in the bathroom, Henrik wanders off to his study to enter a few notes on his personal organizer. Anne-Lise looks out the bedroom window. Apart from a few trees close to the street lamps, the garden is almost invisible in the darkness.

When they are in bed together Henrik continues to speculate: "If the others have got it into their heads that you're the one who sent the e-mails and interfered with the medicine, then it's only a matter of time before they make Paul and the board believe it too. You don't have much time to find proof that Malene mixed up the tablets by mistake. Or that Camilla did it on purpose. If you don't, you'll be out on your ear."

Anne-Lise knows Henrik is right.

Some nights, in the dark quiet of the bedroom, Henrik's familiar smell wafts across from his side of the bed. Anne-Lise remembers it from way back, when she was at college and they lived together in her small student room. It isn't a strong scent, but it makes her feel comfortable and safe.

Henrik is thinking aloud. "Now, her husband is in the plumbing business, isn't he? Maybe I should ask him to fix something for us and make him talk while he's working?"

"Henrik! That's out of the question."

"Okay, okay. We're brainstorming, aren't we? What about finding out who their friends are and getting them to talk?"

Neither Henrik nor Anne-Lise can figure out a way to do this. The only hope is that Anne-Lise can persuade Camilla to open up about herself during work.

Anne-Lise is doubtful. "She doesn't speak openly with anyone, and tomorrow they'll be furious with me."

"They will. But remember, they'll be frightened of you as well. If they really believe you have a split personality and that you're a psychotic basket case, they'll be at a loss about how to handle you. In situations like that, people cope by sticking to routine. You'll see. I suspect that a stranger entering the office tomorrow wouldn't notice a thing out of the ordinary."

"I hope you're right."

But Anne-Lise still thinks that the so-called plan is absurd. Does Henrik truly believe that with such a terrible atmosphere at the DCIG, she can say, out of the blue, "Listen, Camilla, we've never had a proper heart-to-heart, have we? Why not start today? Tell me a bit more about yourself."

chapter 28

t he following morning Malene phones the office to say that she is still ill and won't be coming in to work—this is something Anne-Lise has not foreseen.

Paul is out of the office again as well. He's at a conference in Odense and will be there all day. Anne-Lise is alone with Iben and Camilla, who behave exactly as Henrik predicted. They may well be on edge, but they aren't letting it show. Nobody can prove anything. Anne-Lise thinks that the Winter Garden is a little quieter than usual, but Malene is away, of course.

Like the other two, Anne-Lise throws herself into her work. Her next task is to extract the best database keywords for a collection of eyewitness accounts from the 1971 genocide in what was then East Pakistan. The killing started up suddenly—and unexpectedly—in the aftermath of Pakistan's 1970 parliamentary election, which was won by the oppressed Bengali majority. The ruling minority, drawn from the Punjabi and Pathan tribes, rejected the election result and took over after a military coup. The Bengali population protested by staging a nonviolent general strike, but the army crushed it. Its orders were to kill, loot, and rape. Punjabis and Pashtuns traditionally believed Bengalis to be an inferior race.

The Pakistani soldiers drove about forty million of their

countrymen into exile, flattened several provincial towns every day, raped some 250,000 women of all ages, and killed, in total, about three million people.

Anne-Lise has read piles of witness reports from those nine terrible months. At the moment she is reading about a twenty-five-year-old Bengali woman, married to an officer and the mother of three children. The soldiers took her husband away despite her pleas. She threw herself on the ground in front of their house, begging for his freedom. They brought him back to her later, disfigured by torture and close to death. Another group of soldiers broke into the family house the following morning and raped the woman in front of her husband and children. They tied the husband down and beat the children when they cried. In the afternoon, the soldiers took her to a cellar, where they locked her in and raped her night after night until she lost consciousness. Three months later she returned home. She was pregnant.

Bengali families often rejected sexually abused women on their return because they regarded them as a dishonor to their relatives. This woman was fortunate; although her husband refused to take her back, her neighbors showed her some compassion. When they pressured the husband to accept her back as his wife, he hanged himself.

After reading this account, Anne-Lise goes through it again to find the best descriptive words for the library database, but she grinds to a halt after a few paragraphs. She tries to start from the beginning, but it's no use. I need a break, she thinks after the fourth attempt.

As Anne-Lise steps into the brightly lit Winter Garden, Camilla is on the phone, saying that she must cancel her rehearsal session with the choir tonight because she has to attend a parent-teacher meeting at her daughter's school. The fluorescent light above the shelf of Dutch publications is on the blink. Camilla puts the receiver down and now Anne-Lise can talk to both of them.

"I'm off to the kitchen to make myself a mug of tea. Does anybody else want one?"

To her surprise Iben says that she wouldn't mind some tea, thank you. And her face seems more relaxed than usual; she even looks friendly. But then, Malene is away. Anne-Lise still has serious doubts about her desperate plan of getting to know Camilla better. Anne-Lise's chances here would be so much easier if Iben has resolved that they should all get along, in spite of her accusations yesterday.

Anne-Lise pours water into the electric kettle and waits for it to boil.

Obviously, Camilla is worried about her figure. Her colleagues try not to comment on the rather odd things she has for lunch. Currently, she's eating almost nothing but cucumbers. During the past year Camilla has tried three contradictory diets, all of which have failed to produce a result. At Lyngby, two of Anne-Lise's colleagues also ate erratically, but they would joke about their fad diets. Camilla's problem is that she takes her weight issues far too seriously, even though she is nowhere near as large as Anne-Lise's former colleagues. Camilla is small and on the plump side, but no more than one might expect of a forty-year-old woman with children. Couldn't Camilla's obsessive relationship with her body fit with the kind of upbringing that might also cause DID?

Despite being about the same age as Camilla, Anne-Lise feels she looks younger than her colleague. One reason is Camilla's hairdo, an outdated perm that has dried out her ash-blond hair. The overall effect is dull and matronly.

Anne-Lise recalls the dramatic story of Camilla's friend who died from uterine cancer, and the way Camilla stepped into her friend's life to live with her husband and care for her daughter. Apart from that, all Anne-Lise has to go on is her observations of Camilla's behavior.

The day after Iben and Malene received the e-mails, Iben had been speaking about what made people commit war crimes. She had argued that, in one sense at least, they too were victims of forces they could not control. Anne-Lise had never seen Camilla so upset. Was that significant? And if so, what did it mean? Why couldn't she discuss forgiveness for such crimes? Then there was her strong reaction to receiving one of the e-mailed threats herself. All she had wanted was to lie down and be alone. Was that a typical reaction, or was it a sign of a disturbed person?

The water is about to boil when Iben turns up in the kitchen and leans against the fridge. "I'm aware," Iben begins hesitantly, "that my tirade on the phone yesterday was unreasonable."

It sounds closer to an apology than anything Anne-Lise has ever dared hope for.

"I had no good grounds for being so convinced that you were the one who'd exchanged the pills," Iben continues, looking away timidly.

Anne-Lise realizes that she should try to be receptive to Iben's attempts at conversation or she'll never be able to persuade Camilla to give away her secrets. She must control her anger. "You were very upset, naturally. You weren't yourself. I understand it must have been terrible for you."

"It really was."

Anne-Lise thanks Iben once more for her suggestion about phoning Tatiana. The call went very well—so well, in fact, that she almost got the impression that Tatiana had been expecting it.

"It was so good of you. Let's see if Tatiana will use our library more after this."

Anne-Lise has an impulse to phone Henrik, but discreet conversations are impossible now that the door is open all the time. It wouldn't look right if she were to shut it again, even for a short while.

Over lunch they discuss the changes in the lives of university students in East Pakistan after 1971. The Indian army had intervened in support of the Bengalis to stop the genocide and establish East Pakistan as the independent state of Bangladesh. Part of the contempt felt by the Pashtuns and Punjabis for the Bengalis was related to the fact that they were not a warrior race; indeed, they were regarded as unfit for military service. However, the genocide wrought many changes and the effects were perhaps especially marked in the universities.

One of the top priorities of the Pakistani soldiery had been to kill off university staff, students, and other intellectuals to stop them from becoming leaders. In 1971 the universities became slaughterhouses and, after the secession, the students were so used to carrying arms that conflicts between opposing student factions were frequently settled with shoot-outs. This made universities among the most dangerous places to be in Bangladesh. The extreme violence of the students undermined the whole academic system.

Anne-Lise cannot concentrate. She thinks about the change in Iben's behavior. The peaceful morning has been like a breath of fresh air. She watches Camilla pause before covering her fourth slice of crisp-bread with fat-free cottage cheese and slices of cucumber. The three of them seem quite at ease with each other. Perhaps she can persuade Camilla to reveal something that would show her emotional volatility and prove that she is the one who should be under suspicion.

As Anne-Lise tries to muster the courage to ask Camilla a question, Iben interrupts: "Isn't it amazing how little we know about each other, even though we work so closely together?"

"It is."

Iben has always been pale, but recently she's had dark rings beneath her eyes from lack of sleep. She looks at Anne-Lise and smiles.

"So I was thinking, Anne-Lise, now that we're just sitting here: why don't you tell us a bit more about yourself."

I t's raining hard when Anne-Lise parks in a dark street, well away
from the post office building. She walks quickly. Under the golf
umbrella, which she always keeps in the trunk of the car, not
even her shoes get wet. When she has passed the entrance to the
Tivoli Concert Hall, she turns left at the Central Station.

Anne-Lise is scared. She has never done anything like this
before and it goes against her nature, but her back is against the
wall. If she is fired, she may never work again.

She has to find out more about Camilla.

The edifice in front of her is not so much a single building
as a mass of concrete blocks all joined together: Copenhagen's
Central Post Office.

Outside one of its doors waits a group of women, mostly in
their fifties. Anne-Lise introduces herself: "I'm Brigitte."

They seem pleased that she is joining them this evening.
One of the women unlocks the door with a magnetized ID card
and leads the way down a steep metal staircase.

A woman in a long black dress explains where they are going: "The room we use is actually next to the reception area, but
in the evenings so many of the alarms on the doors have been
set that we have to go via the basement."

They negotiate a maze of corridors lined with doors, almost

all of them closed. The walls have a fresh coat of white paint, and a great many doors are closed. They walk up another metal staircase and into a large plain room that looks like some kind of conference hall. Three of its walls are painted white and the fourth is made of glass. Behind the glass you can see the reception area. The whole place seems designed with space in mind: there is plenty of standing room and just a few pieces of colorful designer furniture. Near the door, about twenty women of all ages are talking and laughing. The air smells of damp coats.

A handful of mature-looking men have settled down with their cans of beer in a group of scarlet egg-shaped chairs. There is an electric keyboard by the glass wall, and a young woman seems to be testing it. She must be the conductor. Anne-Lise feels almost queasy watching her, because she looks like Malene, only not as pretty.

Anne-Lise checked the home page of the Copenhagen Postal Choir and one of the things she found out was that the conductor recently completed a university degree in music. Before last year Anne-Lise used to enjoy being in the company of artistic young women, but now they just annoy her.

The conductor welcomes her. "It's great to see a new face. How did you find out about us?"

"I found you on the Internet."

"Oh, good, our Web site must be doing its job." She turns to the rest of the group and speaks to them in the beautifully controlled voice of a singer, not unlike Camilla's. "Listen, everybody. This is Brigitte; she's going to sing with us tonight. Try not to scare her away! Hopefully she'll come back next Wednesday."

The women laugh and begin to introduce themselves. Talking across each other, they tell Anne-Lise about the choir, its performances in churches and elsewhere, and the various excursions they go on.

"We sing every year at the Summer Festival here in Copenhagen."

"But the main thing is, we always have such a good time together. Great parties, don't you think, ladies?"

Several exclaim at the same time.

The home page had informed Anne-Lise that although most of the singers worked within the post office, the choir has been open to outsiders for a long time.

"Have you sung in a choir before?" one woman asks.

"You'll get the hang of it quickly, don't worry."

The conductor addresses Anne-Lise. "Brigitte, do you know what part you sing?"

"I'm not sure."

"You sound like an alto. Why don't you join the altos for now."

A woman in her early sixties with very black hair holds up her case of sheet music. "Brigitte, my name is Tess. Come and stand next to me. You can sing from my music until you have your own set."

So far, so good. The knot in Anne-Lise's stomach is loosening. When people around you are as kind as this, it is impossible to stay scared for long. She had been so worried that someone would recognize her and instantly see she was lying. Or, almost as bad, that she'd have one of her sudden fits of weeping.

The conductor claps her hands. The men drag themselves away from their chairs at the far end of the room and join the women.

Suddenly Camilla's name is mentioned. "Camilla Batz called me from work this afternoon. She can't come tonight—it's the parent-teacher evening at her daughter's school." The woman has mahogany-colored hair that is pulled back in a knot, and she's wearing a navy scarf.

Anne-Lise whispers to Tess, trying to sound surprised: "Camilla Batz! Does she have curly blond hair?"

"That's right. Do you know her?"

"Yes. How extraordinary. We were childhood friends. How is she? What is she doing now?"

Tess has no time to answer, because the warm-up has begun. Anne-Lise is new to the exercises but follows them as well as she can and keeps her voice low. All the singers practice breathing with their diaphragm and are told to stand with their feet planted evenly on the floor. Shoulders and neck must be relaxed. They launch into "Tears in Heaven" by Eric Clapton.

During the first break Anne-Lise returns to her questioning. "What about Camilla—what does she do now?"

"She works in an office that gives out information about . . . oh, about something—I'm not sure. But she'll be here next Wednesday, so you can see her then. Some of us get together for a beer afterward, so if you join us the two of you will have a chance to catch up."

It surprises Anne-Lise to realize how easy it is to lie.

Tess has a lovely voice, but it's weak. One of the tenors' voices rises above the rest as they sing.

Anne-Lise feels exhilarated, almost intoxicated by the combination of her own adrenaline and the sheer warmth of these people who have welcomed her so readily.

Tess leans over to whisper to her: "I think it's a great song too!"

They must be able to see something of what she feels in her face. The women who are standing near Anne-Lise believe that it is the music that has moved her so much. When the conductor stops to explain a few changes in the rhythm to the male singers, Pernille, an alto in the front row, turns to whisper to Anne-Lise: "Brigitte, does that mean you'll come back?"

Anne-Lise realizes these complete strangers are more sensitive to what she's feeling than the people she has worked with for a whole year.

The singing starts up again. Anne-Lise thinks of Yngve's bleak view of human nature. She refuses to believe him. People aren't like that. She promises herself to find out more about research into the human capacity for evil.

It's a paradox, she thinks, that—in Danish at least—the best brief introduction to the subject is probably two articles written by Iben and published a year ago in two consecutive issues of *Genocide News* under the title "The Psychology of Evil." Anne-Lise makes up her mind to read the articles again when she is back home.

They stop for a break. There are cans of beer and fizzy drinks with a box to collect the money. Anne-Lise pays for a can of fizzy orange. A large woman called Ruth, another alto, expounds on the need to hold notes for different lengths of time in their rendering of "When I'm Sixty-Four."

"The basses have long ones and the tenors short ones. Imagine that!"

Everyone laughs. Normally Anne-Lise wouldn't find this kind of innuendo amusing, but she has been on edge all day and now she shakes with laughter and the fizzy orange drink goes up her nose. She can't swallow, but tries to keep her mouth closed. It doesn't work. The drink sprays all over Ruth's blouse and the table, dribbling down Anne-Lise's chin and onto her own blouse.

"Oh, God, I'm so sorry, Ruth. I'm such an idiot . . ." If only she could run away from the whole scene. But she stays, words tumbling out of her mouth. "I'll clean it up. Is there a rag anywhere? Let me buy you a new blouse . . ." One of the singers has already found a sponge.

The woman with the navy scarf smiles, deepening the laughter lines at the corners of her eyes. "Ruth is too funny for her own good. I can see you agree!"

Ruth is kind as well. "Brigitte, don't apologize. And don't even think of buying me a new blouse. This one can be dry-cleaned just fine."

Anne-Lise stares at the floor. One thought keeps running through her head: It never ends. It never, ever ends! Where can I be the old Anne-Lise?

After a short silence Tess turns to a woman in a black skirt. "Do you remember when I managed to spray you with a mouthful of Coke?"

The woman looks at her, mystified.

"You must remember—I was laughing so hard I couldn't help it."

Anne-Lise raises her head in time to see the woman realize what she is supposed to say.

"Oh, yes, of course! I'd almost forgotten . . ."

Between them, they manage to cheer Anne-Lise up. Her mood has improved when she goes off to the ladies' room. The Eric Clapton song is playing in her head.

Several women are standing in front of the mirror. A soprano called Vibeke speaks to Anne-Lise. "You will enjoy having Camilla here next week. Especially since you know her so well."

"I did, once. We were in the same class up to fourth form, but I haven't seen her in years. How is she now?"

Silence.

"What is it? Have I said something wrong?"

Vibeke backs away from the mirror. "I was under the impression that she had no friends in her class."

"Well, it was quite a long time ago . . . I have no idea what she's doing now."

"Were you really in her class?"

"Yes, why?"

"What did you think about what went on?"

"What do you mean?"

"Where were you when your class gathered around Camilla every single break time and picked on her? When they forced the weakest kids to touch her so that they would scream because everyone said she was dirty and smelly?"

The others try to calm Vibeke down. "Vibeke! Take it easy!"

But Vibeke is on a roll. "What did you think when a pupil in another class tried to kill herself because she was so badly bullied? And the rest of you simply carried on as if nothing had happened? Would anyone have cared if Camilla had tried to kill herself too? What were you thinking?" Vibeke has worked herself up into such a state that Anne-Lise hasn't had a chance to answer before she storms away, slamming the door behind her.

The others start apologizing at once. They tell Anne-Lise that Vibeke has her own problems and that she is prone to outbursts. She had one just before a performance in Malmö. They assure Anne-Lise that if she joins the choir she'll find that there's a much nicer side to Vibeke. Most likely Vibeke will tell her she's sorry.

But no one says anything about the truth of Vibeke's accusations.

As the women walk back to the rehearsal room, no one speaks. Tess comes to meet them. "You're in luck, Brigitte!" She beams.

"Really? Why?"

"It seems Camilla's parent-teacher meeting was over sooner than she'd expected. She's decided to come tonight after all."

Anne-Lise freezes. She hopes the others won't notice.

"She's just taking off her wet things. I told her about you and she thought she could place you right away."

Anne-Lise can barely swallow. "Ahaaa . . ."

She turns away from them and tries to pull herself together. "Oh, damn, I've left my eyeliner in the bathroom. You go ahead and start. I'll be right back."

"Don't worry, Brigitte. We'll wait for you."

At least there is nobody in the bathroom now. Anne-Lise knows that she must get out of there. But how?

She needs to find a different staircase that will take her down into the network of basement corridors that lead to the exit. Then Anne-Lise remembers that her coat and umbrella are still in the rehearsal room. At least she had the foresight to bring a coat that Camilla has never seen her wear, in case the others start describing Brigitte to her. But her wallet, with her driver's license and credit card, is in her coat pocket. How can she grab it without Camilla spotting her?

Why didn't I put the wallet in my handbag? I was just about to. Now it's there, right under Camilla's nose.

When Anne-Lise no longer hears voices in the corridor, she sneaks out of the bathroom and slips away. After turning a few corners and passing through two sets of fire doors, she reaches the top of a staircase that leads down to the basement.

Below, the hallways seem even more confusing. She has no idea where she is in the maze. The lighting is uniform and everywhere looks the same. She searches her memory for markers: a fire hose wound up in a drum, anything, but there's not the smallest piece of graffiti, not a single discarded mailbag. Nothing at all to go by.

After turning several corners, she spots a darkish trail on the light floor. It looks like a skid mark. She can't recall having seen it before. Next, she comes across one of the metal staircases. She runs up it and finds a large door.

If she pushes it, will the alarm go off?

Somewhere down here they keep money and valuables worth millions; security guards must patrol these corridors around the clock. What if she's arrested and dragged away in front of the choir, including Camilla?

She stands still and listens. The door looks heavy. Presumably sounds wouldn't penetrate it easily? She listens but can't hear a thing. No barking of guard dogs. No voices.

She reaches for the handle and pushes it down.

No alarm, but the door is locked. She feels like hitting something, anything, but orders herself to calm down.

Walking noiselessly, she retraces her way along the corridor. Is it the same one? Impossible to be sure.

If only she could make her way to the reception area. Then she could spy on the choir through the glass wall and see when Camilla leaves. And once she's gone, Anne-Lise could run back through the corridors, praying that she won't meet Camilla on the way, and retrieve her coat before anyone starts going through its pockets and discovers she's not Brigitte. Anne-Lise knows that she will have to be improbably lucky to succeed. Still, what other option does she have? She could try finding the route the postal vans take into the complex—there must be vehicle access somewhere—but that wouldn't solve the problem of her wallet.

She comes to another metal staircase and the door at the top is not locked. It leads to a small anteroom with three doors—two of them locked, the third with a large triangular sign saying ALARM pinned above it. She doesn't dare try it and returns to the basement.

How long has she been down here? Twenty-five minutes, according to her watch, but that doesn't feel right. It must be longer.

She hears breathing somewhere nearby. Panting. Possibly the sound made by one—no, two—dogs, excited at picking up a scent and pulling impatiently on their leads.

Anne-Lise stops and takes off her shoes. Then, after turning a corner, she spots a half-used roll of paper towels on the floor. She recognizes it. It tells her that she is not far from the staircase leading up to the entrance door.

She hurries again now, trying all the doors to find one that isn't locked. All the time she hears the panting noises coming from somewhere behind her. At last, one of the doors opens. Behind it is a cupboard full of boxes, bottles, and cleaning equipment. It's dark but she wouldn't dare put the light on even if she could find the switch.

A little later she hears two men walk past. She holds her breath and sits perfectly still on the floor, hugging a vacuum cleaner. The men are speaking an unrecognizable foreign language. Could it be Serbian? Bizarre conspiracy theories flash through her head. It occurs to her, when their voices have died away, that one of them could easily have been Paul's, but that doesn't make sense. Everything is so unfamiliar, almost otherworldly down here in the darkness.

She picks up the strong smell of ammonium chloride.

Then she hears a voice outside calling. "Brigitte! Brigitte!" It's the woman with the navy scarf. "Maybe she got lost on the way back from the restroom?"

Another voice replies: "You know as well as I do that it's Vibeke's fault. I don't know why she has to be like that. Remember when we were with that Swedish choir in Malmö and she . . ."

Their voices gradually fade away.

Anne-Lise persuades herself that the panting is probably not dogs but a defective pump somewhere in the ventilation system. She listens for people talking. Not a sound.

After stealing back out into the corridor, Anne-Lise follows it for a few more turns. Another metal staircase and, at the top of it, a small anteroom. She pulls at one of the door handles, but this one has an alarm and a siren goes off. The sound is like the piercing noise of a giant dog whistle.

Anne-Lise looks around her. She is in the reception area. The choir is staring at her from behind the glass wall.

This is the end.

How can she tell Henrik that she has been fired? Now he'll have to put up with her languishing at home for years: another drunken, useless Jutta. And the children will suffer as their mother slowly falls apart.

Pernille opens the door leading into the rehearsal room. It doesn't matter, now that the alarm has been set off.

"Oh, good. There you are!"

Anne-Lise can't answer. She tries to muster the courage to stand in front of them, exposed as a liar.

Someone calls out. "Hey, Camilla! Your old classmate has found her way back!"

Tess has joined Pernille. "We've been quite worried about you, Brigitte."

Anne-Lise scans the room for Camilla. She can't see her anywhere.

Another voice from the back of the group.

"Camilla?"

Others join in.

"Goodness, where did she go? We keep losing people today."

"Camilla? Camilla, where are you?"

"Look, her bag is gone! It was here a moment ago."

Anne-Lise quietly collects her coat and umbrella. She smiles vaguely at no one in particular.

She hears someone mention how Camilla reacted when she heard about "Brigitte." Even after all these years, Camilla was so upset that she sneaked away without anyone noticing.

Anne-Lise excuses herself. "I'd better leave too."

The women look sympathetically at her.

THE PSYCHOLOGY OF EVIL I

*Interest in the psychology of perpetrators is growing rapidly. Past research
in this area is summarized in this and the next issue of* Genocide News.

■

BY IBEN HØJGAARD

In the Old Testament whole populations are described as being "wiped off
the face of the earth" on twenty-seven separate occasions. The phenomenon
of genocide is integral to not only Western but also non-Western cultures.

For thousands of years genocides have been known to take place in just
about every location on earth, and we know that during recent centuries the
number of killings has been increasing steadily. In the course of the twentieth century, more than 100 million people have died in genocides and
wars. This is more than five times the number killed in this way during the
nineteenth century, and more than ten times the corresponding number in
the eighteenth century. At present there are no signs to suggest that the
rate will level off without active intervention.

Genocide is always committed by the group holding power at the time.
The first time psychologists were able to do research into the mechanisms
driving those who plan and carry out mass murder came after the defeat of
the Nazis at the end of the Second World War.

THE NUREMBERG MILITARY TRIBUNAL

After the defeat of the Nazi regime in Germany, an Allied military tribunal
was set up in Nuremberg to examine the legal cases brought against
twenty-two high-ranking Nazis accused of "crimes against humanity."

During the war, Allied propaganda portrayed the top Nazis as sadistic
madmen and, later, documentary films from the German concentration
camps demonstrated to the rest of Europe and the United States that those
running the system had to be among the sickest, most inhumane people
the world had ever seen.

A sizable group of psychologists and psychiatrists, led by Douglas M.
Kelley and Gustave Gilbert, was given access to the twenty-two prisoners
for the purpose of examining their mental state. The brief was to find out

what was wrong with the Nazi leadership. There was no question in the minds of the experts that the accused were deranged. The task was seen as diagnostic: what conditions afflicted the perpetrators and how mentally unstable were they?

The main diagnostic tools used were IQ and Rorschach tests. The media gave comparatively little publicity to the results of the intelligence testing because the Nazi prisoners turned out to be exceptionally intelligent, an observation that the world definitely did not want to hear. None of the accused had an average IQ—100—or less, and all fell within the range of 106–143, with a mean of 128. This figure is substantially higher than the mean of American college graduates (118), and several high-ranking Nazis were borderline geniuses. In other words, if they were mentally ill, they were remarkably brilliant madmen.

The Rorschach test is a method used to determine personality traits, not intelligence. The psychologist shows the subject a standardized series of cards with symmetrical ink-blot patterns and asks the subject what each image might be. The patterns are meant to stimulate the imagination, but are strictly meaningless, in the sense that no answer is correct. The psychologist takes note of what the examinee says, but also records variables such as the time taken before an answer, any emotional reactions, spontaneous comments, and other responses to the images. The session is intended to chart the subject's personality, thought patterns, and capacity for imaginative expression. The method was developed in the 1920s and is still in use.

The hostility between Douglas M. Kelley and Gustave Gilbert grew in the course of the investigation, and finally it reached the point at which they refused to work together. Kelley, a psychiatrist, was experienced in the use of the Rorschach cards and, after having examined seven of the accused, he found no evidence of mental illness. Even though Gustave Gilbert, a psychologist, was unfamiliar with Rorschach tests, he went on to examine sixteen of the prisoners.

Gilbert wrote several books and articles about his experiences among the Nuremberg war criminals. He described the Nazi leadership as psychopaths and "murderous robots" lacking in conscience and empathy. However, he presented very few analyses of his test results. Instead, his books mostly quoted notes from his informal conversations with the accused. These talks were conducted during a period when several of the prisoners were trying to use the widespread conviction that they were psychotic to their own advantage. Among others, Hitler's deputy Rudolf Hess later admitted that he had simulated mental illness, hoping for less severe punishment and a better opportunity to escape.

Gilbert's unfamiliarity with the analysis of Rorschach test results was the reason that his notes were later handed over to ten experienced Rorschach specialists, who were asked to reevaluate the Nazi leaders. Not one of the ten experts ever delivered his or her interpretation. Presumably, they feared being blamed for the outcome. Feelings would have run high in Europe and the USA if their results had shown that the Nazis were not mentally ill. The general public would simply have concluded that the Rorschach method, on which the investigators' claims to expertise were based, must be flawed. Almost thirty years passed before Gilbert's records were reexamined.

In 1975 the records were published in book form, which meant that for the first time they were subject to scrutiny by interested psychologists. The wide-ranging discussions that followed showed how divided opinions still were. Many found clear evidence of psychopathic, depressive, and violent personalities, while others contested this, pointing to the results of blind tests. In these, Rorschach analysts were unable to distinguish between Nazi responses and those made by non-Nazi and presumably normal subjects.

However, in later years, the Rorschach method was refined still further and given a more systematic, scientific basis. In 1985 the group of researchers who made the best use of the improved methodology (Eric A. Zillmer, Molly Harrower, Barry A. Retzler, and Robert P. Archer) published their conclusion that mental illness was not rife among the Nazi leadership.

Generally, the Nazis were found to have had normal, functional, and individually distinctive personalities—with just two exceptions. Traits shared by them were a marked tendency to overvalue their own abilities and a willingness to adjust their behavior to whoever was construed as the group leader. In other words, these men were unable or unwilling to follow the directions of their "internal compass."

Despite the shared traits, the researchers emphasized that the differences between the top Nazi individuals were much greater than the similarities. There is, they concluded, no uniform "Nazi personality type."

THE ADMINISTRATION OF THE THIRD REICH

For the first fifteen years following the end of World War II, attempts to understand what motivated perpetrators of the Holocaust concentrated on psychological aberrations. The leaders attracted all the attention and the Nuremberg court documentation was the primary source of information.

Another line of investigation attempted to define the so-called authoritarian personality. People with this personality type were thought to do exactly as they were told, even when the orders contradicted common sense or decency. Many believed this personality type to be particularly prevalent in Germanic culture.

The early 1960s brought a shift in emphasis. Three circumstances were crucial:

1. The publication in 1961 of Raul Hilberg's *The Destruction of the European Jews*, a pioneering book in which Hilberg analyzed, for the first time and in great detail, the bureaucratic structure that underpinned the Nazi regime. He showed that Nazi rule was not directed by a united hierarchy that ruled from the top down, as had been generally believed. Instead, the Reich depended on the rivalry for power between several distinct organizations, each one striving to outdo the others. This system expanded into a colossal killing machine, which employed people from every sector of German society.

   Hilberg also realized the necessity of setting up an extensive administrative structure to manage the extermination of millions. Administration meant, as always, rules, documentation, and set procedures. Staff selected either for certain mental disorders or for a specifically Germanic personality type (or types) could not possibly have followed complex operational directives on such a scale.

   Hilberg's book interested many and stimulated further studies of the bureaucracy of the Third Reich and of the middle-ranking managers who were in charge of running the system according to the guidelines laid down by the leadership.

2. Hannah Arendt, the famous American philosopher and intellectual, wrote a book entitled *Eichmann in Jerusalem: A Report on the Banality of Evil*, which came out in 1963. Its core material consisted of her report from the trial of Adolf Eichmann. Israeli intelligence agents had captured him in Argentina and delivered him to stand trial in Jerusalem. The court case took several months. Eichmann had been the head of the Gestapo's Section for Jewish Affairs, and in that position he had carried the ultimate responsibility for organizing the Jew-

ish transports across war-torn Europe to the network of concentration camps.

Arendt argued that the most terrifying thing about Eichmann was precisely that he was not a crazed demon, driven by his obsession to exterminate Jews; instead he was a dull bureaucrat devoid of any note-worthy personal traits. He was, in her view, bereft of any will of his own and followed orders without engagement or any consideration of the consequences. The face of evil was not one of frenzied hatred but of a mediocrity who, above all, cared about advancing his career within the organization.

Hannah Arendt's book portrayed evil in a new light. Her image of it has had immense influence on our attitudes to Nazi Germany and, more generally, to the phenomenon of evil, as well as to large rule-ridden organizations. Her influence persists, even though most con-temporary historians agree that she was wrong in her judgment. She had uncritically accepted Eichmann's own story of his contribution to the Holocaust, distorted by him in order to support his defense.

It appears that Eichmann did in fact defy orders from above, if these interfered with the efficiency of his section's management of Jewish transports. His energetic performance of his work went far be-yond the call of duty. Indeed, his passion for his task was such that he was prepared to weaken the German war effort at times if this allowed more Jewish transports to be completed.

3. The year 1963 also saw the publication of experimental results from the laboratories of the social psychologist Stanley Milgram. His data demonstrate the extent to which ordinary people will obey a perceived authority, even if those in charge have no means of either rewarding or punishing those who serve their purposes.

Originally, Milgram had intended to compare American and German subservience to authority in order to illustrate a presumed trait in the German national character. He never started the German part of his experiment, however, because the first set of results from the USA were more sensational than anyone had imagined.

THE WORLD'S MOST FAMOUS EXPERIMENT IN SOCIAL PSYCHOLOGY
Milgram's experimental paradigm has become internationally recognized through dissemination in school and university textbooks, newspapers,

magazines, films, and television programs. Recently, it was even referred to in a TV commercial.

Two experimental subjects are told that they are participating in an experiment designed to test the effects of punishment on learning. They draw lots to determine who is going to be respectively "teacher" and "pupil." The lottery is fixed beforehand. The true subject is unaware that his companion is an experimental assistant who is predestined to be the pupil. Consequently, the true subject will always be the teacher.

The pupil is strapped into a chair wired up to deliver electrical shocks. The subject/teacher is then led away to another room, where his only contact with the pupil is via a microphone and the text on a display screen showing the pupil's responses. If the pupil answers incorrectly, the teacher is instructed to deliver a punishment shock by pressing a button.

The shocks are mild at first. Another display shows the voltage and grades the severity—as in *15 volts: mild shock*. With each wrong answer, the teacher must gradually increase the voltage in fifteen-volt steps. The scale reaches *420 volts: Danger—severe shock*, and then, finally, *450 volts: XXX*.

To facilitate international comparisons there are precise rules for how the leader of the experiment and his assistant must behave. The pupil is never actually shocked, but when the subject believes that he is delivering 300 volts, the pupil will protest by banging hard on the wall that separates him from the subject. He bangs again at 315 volts and then does or says nothing at all. The implication is that the pupil might be unconscious by this stage.

The teacher is told that any failure to answer a question must be regarded as an incorrect answer, and hence, despite the pupil's silence, the voltage must be increased another step each time.

If the subject protests, the experimental leader has four command options. The first is "Please continue"; then, "The experiment requires that you continue"; and next, "It is absolutely essential that you continue." The last option is "You have no other choice. You must continue." If the subject still refuses to carry on, the experiment is stopped.

The most common response by far is that the subject/teacher protests repeatedly and, as the experiment proceeds, starts to sweat, shake, stutter, groan, and bite his lip.

When the subjects arrive in the lab they are typically relaxed and self-assured, but in the course of the first twenty minutes they usually come close to having a complete breakdown. Twitching nervously, they pace about the room, as if trying to make up their mind whether to leave or not. Often, they keep talking aloud about how they cannot stand this anymore. The subjects know they are free to leave at any time and that a decision to end the experiment will not have any repercussions. All they have to say is that they don't want to do this anymore and then actually stop.

Despite this, two thirds of the subjects in the original experiment continued, obeying the leader to the end. In other words, they increased the shock voltages up to the highest setting, at which point the leader would call a halt.

Stanley Milgram's own view of his results was that they confirmed Hannah Arendt's perception of "the banality of evil." The subject, who in the role of teacher believed that he had used shock strengths that were lethal, was not a deranged monster, but one of a majority, two thirds of a group drawn from the population at large. The behavior of this subgroup was not defined by psychosis, racism, or hatred, but by obedience.

Milgram's experiment was thoroughly tested by several other groups in the USA and elsewhere, and later Milgram, as well as many others, repeated the general idea with various modifications. It is now known that the percentage of wholly obedient subjects is relatively constant, regardless of gender, nationality, and year of testing (early 1960s–the present).

The proportion of obedient subjects decreases by only a few percent if the screams and wails of the pupil are relayed via an intercom system, but falls from about 65 percent to about 40 percent if teacher and pupil are in the same room. Social psychologists also obtained results demonstrating that, if the subject is in a work situation and someone of higher rank gives the destructive orders, the "obedient" percentage increases considerably.

Over the decades these experiments have been both praised and condemned. The criticism focuses on the potentially crucial difference between giving someone electric shocks for a fixed time and carrying on killing people over months or years.

One interesting angle is that many war criminals in postwar trials defended themselves by declaring that they "had to obey orders," but nobody acting for the defense was able to produce a single example of a German soldier being punished for his refusal to serve in concentration camps or in other settings where civilians were murdered.

Milgram's experiments changed the perception of this crucial issue by shifting the attention from enforced obedience to spontaneous acceptance of authority.

ORDINARY MEN

Studies on perpetrators of genocide took a new turn in the 1990s. The trigger was the publication in 1992 of a book entitled *Ordinary Men* by the American professor Christopher Browning, which drew a great deal of attention to the participation of German private soldiers in the Holocaust. This led others to focus on the same issue. For example, in 1995 a Hamburg museum exhibited documentation showing that the German army had executed prisoners of war, as well as Jews and other civilians. Daniel J. Goldhagen's much discussed book *Hitler's Willing Executioners: Ordinary Germans and the Holocaust* came out in 1996.

In his book Christopher Browning describes how, in 1942, a battalion of approximately five hundred reserve policemen from Hamburg was dispatched to Poland for guard duty—or so they thought. By then almost all the younger or more aggressive men were fighting on the front line, and most of the reservists were middle-aged men who had not joined the Nazi Party. Their average age was thirty-nine, which meant that they had grown up and formed their attitudes in a Germany that was not under Nazi rule. The majority came from the Hamburg working class and were likely to have been Communists or Socialist Democrats before Hitler came to power.

Several years after the end of the war the survivors from this battalion were thoroughly questioned by staff in the public prosecutor's office in Hamburg. Browning had found and analyzed the extensive notes from these interrogations.

Early one morning, after three weeks of routine service in Poland, the entire battalion was ordered to get on board trucks. They were driven to the country town of Jozefow. On arrival they received their orders: kill the city's 1,800 Jewish inhabitants.

The commanding officer, a major, wept as he told his men what Berlin demanded of them. He repeatedly made it clear that those who came to him and requested transfer to other duties would be accommodated, but only ten (possibly thirteen) men out of five hundred did so.

The task was new to both officers and men, but an army doctor instructed them in what should have been an effective procedure: they were to put the tip of the rifle bayonet on the back of the victim's neck at the point where his cranium joined the vertebral column and then pull the trigger.

The first batch of victims, children as well as young and old people, were marched along to a forest clearing and told to lie belly down. The soldiers started shooting but were so shaken that many missed, despite the unusually close range. They tended to aim their rifles at the victims' skulls, which exploded when hit by the large-caliber bullets. The men were sprayed with brain matter again and again. In the course of the day many broke down, vomited, and generally became physically incapable of continuing, and an increasing number requested leave to stop participating in the killings. Others hid, or took implausibly long times to search houses that they knew to be empty, or deliberately missed when shooting at Jews who were running away.

When the sun set on Jozefow, between 10 and 20 percent of the men had asked to be allowed off-duty for either physical or psychological reasons. The rest had obeyed orders. But this was only the beginning. Following their initiation in Jozefow, the men adapted and obeyed orders more willingly as, during the months to come, they surrounded one small Polish town after another to round up Jews. Their job was either to send the captives off to extermination camps or to execute them on the spot. In the course of the next ten months the battalion caused the deaths of at least 83,000 Jews. The men had learned to live with their consciences.

The efficiency of the entire German killing machine improved by leaps and bounds. To the huge relief of the soldiery, slaughtering the Jews personally soon became a thing of the past. Instead most of the victims could be crammed into trains and sent off to Treblinka, the main regional extermination camp. Herding Jewish civilians into trains and sending them off to a certain death seemed easy compared to having to kill them one by one. To help the policemen relax in the evenings, their spirit rations were increased and singers and actors were sent from Berlin to entertain them. Also, prisoners of war from the Eastern Front could now be detailed to deal with the more repulsive aspects of their task.

The battalion's past experience had led them to adopt much more effective ways of killing Jews, which were also less emotionally disturbing. The men realized that there was no point in making the victims lie down before shooting them and instead herded them along to line up on the edge of a waiting pit. The double advantage was that they could be shot from a greater distance and that the dead fell straight into their grave.

However, this method meant that many were only wounded as they fell, and it became the task of the East European POWs to go down into the grave and shoot anyone who moved or moaned. The prisoners were given very large vodka rations and were out of their minds with alcohol before descending into the pits, where they had to wade through a knee-high mixture of blood and groundwater. They shot wildly, bullets crisscrossing the bunker dangerously as they aimed at the floating bodies.

Most of the policemen became accustomed to the slaughter as an everyday occurrence and grew hardened to the task. They had learned to cope.

Browning describes some of the men and their lives: There is the normally "strict and unapproachable" SS officer who becomes bedridden with diarrhea and stomach cramps every time another "Jewish action" is announced. We learn of how he attempts to hide his weakness from his superiors.

There is the talented, self-assured officer who enjoys driving his car standing up, like a general. He brings his young bride on a honeymoon trip to Poland and invites her along to a ghetto operation, but his men strongly object to a woman being allowed to watch what they do.

There is the group of entertainers from Berlin, whose members beg to be allowed to join a Jewish action and do some of the killing. The battalion officers permit this.

There is the stench, carried in the wind blowing in over the town of Lublin as thousands of Jewish bodies are burned on the outskirts.

There is the care taken by some of the soldiers when they receive orders to kill their own "kitchen Jews." They avoid raising any suspicion and go to quite a lot of trouble to shoot their servants suddenly from behind and at close range, so they won't suffer or experience the dread to which other Jews were exposed.

RESPONSIBILITY TOWARD COLLEAGUES

Before the publication of Browning's book, obedience to authority was regarded as the primary mechanism that allowed ordinary Germans to turn into mass murderers, a conclusion based partly on the experimental results of Stanley Milgram and others.

Browning's account changes this view. His research indicates that by far the stronger influence is a sense of responsibility to comrades, which made the men carry on regardless. More than anything, the members of the

"Jewish action" battalion wanted to avoid being regarded as weaklings. Also, the killings were widely detested, which meant that backing out marked you as selfish, someone who lacked team spirit—after all, you were handing your share of the killings over to your colleagues.

"EAGER KILLERS"
As time went on, some of the men became so intensely engaged in the killing sessions that they "overreacted" to new orders. They would beat up their victims for no reason at all, or amuse themselves after a drunken evening by driving into a town to shoot at live, moving targets. In the phrase used within this area of research, they developed into "eager killers," Browning's term for "excessive perpetrators."

One example is the forty-eight-year-old officer who, in the early stages, would always see to it that his men got out of harm's way when another Jew-killing excursion was due. Later his behavior changed dramatically. During the "Jewish actions" he often drank as heavily as the Eastern POWs did before they were sent down into the mass graves. He became even more brutal than the battalion's two young SS captains and forced his men to carry out acts of degrading cruelty, such as commanding old Jews from a town ghetto to undress and crawl naked across the forest floor, or telling his men to beat their elderly victims with sticks cut from the trees.

Internationally there is still insufficient data to state with any certainty what proportion of perpetrators is prone to excess. But Browning's calculations do coincide with the results of a social psychology experiment known as the Stanford Prison Experiment. Also, confirmation of the cited figures will be part of the argument in a forthcoming book by the Danish researcher and DCIG user Torben Jørgensen:

- 10–20 percent of perpetrators try to obtain transfer to other duties;
- 50–80 percent do as they are told;
- 10–30 percent develop into eager killers and run riot, intoxicated by torture, rape, and murder.

THE FUTURE
The research into the nature and behavior of the perpetrators of genocide is still hampered by the lack of hard information. There is little statistical justification for extrapolating conclusions based on data from twenty-two

senior party members and one battalion of reservists to the analysis of mechanisms driving millions of human beings.

The Holocaust is, undoubtedly, the genocide that has been most thoroughly investigated. Even so, the gaps in our understanding are huge and the unexplored archival material is vast. Many of the 7,500 guards at Auschwitz were interrogated, but the records have not yet been examined.

Recent research has continued along the lines suggested by Christopher Browning. One approach is that of regional studies, i.e., a precise analysis of a selected region. This opens up opportunities to investigate interactions between the Nazi Party and local police, military, local administration, and business.

To date, very little work has been carried out on the collaboration between the Nazis and the populations of often strongly anti-Semitic Eastern European countries under German occupation. Now that the archives of the former Soviet Union are available to researchers, many new investigations are under way.

It may seem odd to prioritize work on the behavior of individual Germans in the context of exterminations carried out sixty years ago when other genocides, for instance in the Soviet Union and in China, have cost more lives yet remain virtually unexamined. However, there is no other genocide in known history that is as thoroughly recorded, with archival material that is both extensive and accessible. The expectation is that continued research will provide insight well beyond Germany in the 1930s and 1940s, and can be applied to other, less documented genocides.

Above all, such heightened understanding could and should be used to prevent similar catastrophes in the future, events that mankind has been enduring for too long and would prefer to forget.

This article is based on several sources. The most important are the following:
Becoming Evil. How Ordinary People Commit Genocide and Mass Killing *by James Waller (Oxford University Press, 2002).*
Ordinary Men: Reserve Police Battalion 101 and the Final Solution in Poland *by Christopher R. Browning (HarperCollins, 1992).*

A second and final article on the subject "The Psychology of Evil" will appear in the next issue of Genocide News. *It will present a selection of investigations by social psychologists into the minds of genocide perpetrators.*

didn't want to burden you with this before. It's my job to do the worrying, after all."

Paul looks serious. He stands in front of the low bookshelf with back issues of *Genocide News*, his arms crossed over his chest, his feet solidly planted well apart—the posture of a commanding officer demonstrating the serious nature of his speech to the troops. He has asked Anne-Lise to join the others in the Winter Garden.

"I need to bring you up to speed. The lawyers in the Ministry of Finance have started work on a new bill that's going to make our Center part of the Danish Institute for Human Rights."

He pauses deliberately.

Anne-Lise has no idea how the others will react, but secretly she feels that the news of a merger with the DIHR is like divine intervention on her behalf. The move could be her prize for holding out in this inferno. She could keep the vital aspects of her job and be in daily contact with a whole new set of colleagues who might turn out to be as congenial as her former ones at Lyngby Central Library.

But she knows she mustn't show any signs of relief.

Paul's forehead is wrinkled with concern. "It explains why I've been to so many meetings recently." He sighs and appears sheepish. "You've of course wondered what's been keeping me away so often. But then, you must know that I won't let them ruin our Center. I'll fight them with everything I've got."

Malene is there, her first day back since being ill. She's applied an excessive amount of makeup, at least too much for daytime. "Paul! It's such dreadful news!" she whines.

Iben and Camilla follow her lead.

"What can we do to keep the Center as it is?"

"How long have you known this?"

Ever since Anne-Lise found out how badly Camilla was traumatized by bullying at school, she has kept an eye on her colleague to see if she can somehow divine the truth. But Camilla is motionless and her face does not reveal anything. It never does.

"I must admit I thought something was up. You've been away so often."

"Well, we've met other challenges head-on before. But this time it's different: it's one of our own who is undermining our fight for survival."

Anne-Lise stiffens. Has Paul somehow guessed her feelings? She hasn't let on. Perhaps he has discovered something about one of the others? Anne-Lise glances around the small circle. Camilla, Iben, Malene—all look shocked. Or is it guilty? She looks at Paul.

He seems unaware of the effect of his words and carries on regardless.

"Frederik Thorsteinsson has accepted the post as DIHR research coordinator. In other words, he will become one of Morten Kjærum's immediate subordinates, starting five months from now. But Frederik isn't the one who told me. I was informed by a friend who sits on the board of the institute—someone totally reliable."

Paul takes a breath. "Frederik's new position means that it is in his interest to have our Center controlled from within the DIHR. Never mind that he's a member of our board. He's been completely duplicitous."

Malene asks several questions that demonstrate that she, like Paul, is aware of who the decision makers are, and who's who in the ministries and among the NGO administrators.

"To protect our Center we need to get Frederik off our board," Paul continues. "He's not declared that he is compromised when it comes to dealing with this challenge to our independence, so I have no option but to make Ole aware of Frederik's deception. But neither Ole nor I can fire a board member. Only someone from the ministry can do that."

Anne-Lise is excluded from this world of high-level politics, but it obviously fascinates Iben and Malene. They readily agree with everything Paul says, but it occurs to Anne-Lise that Malene is closer to Frederik than anyone else at the Center. If by next year they are part of the DIHR, then at a stroke Malene will have become the boss's favorite, displacing Iben and her strong links with Paul. Anne-Lise feels that she has hit on something worth thinking about, but at the moment cannot figure out what it means.

"You might as well know that I have already found a good replacement for Frederik. There's one clear candidate, and I have total confidence in him. I don't know if any of you know of him . . . Maybe you're too young. He used to be all over the media and even a couple of years ago he was still writing brilliant articles for *Information*. I'm talking about the journalist and Africa expert Gunnar Hartvig Nielsen."

Malene looks up with a pleased expression. "Oh, yes! I know of Gunnar! Of course."

Iben says nothing, but her expression has changed. Again, something is happening but Anne-Lise can't quite tell what it is.

"Gunnar is highly respected for his outstanding writing on South Africa, Rwanda, Uganda, and many other places. With him on board, our profile would be greatly enhanced. People take him seriously. I can't think why he isn't already on dozens of committees, but he isn't. Gunnar doesn't sell himself the way Frederik does. Anyway, I've asked him to come and meet us here so that we can show him what we do."

Anne-Lise watches Iben as Paul speaks. She is picking at one of the springs on her desk lamp. The spring suddenly works itself free and hits the metal arm of the lamp with a loud *ping!* Iben jumps. The lamp is too heavy for just one spring and slumps slowly down toward the desktop.

Anne-Lise has seen Gunnar in the flesh once before. A few years ago she and Nicola went to the Danish National Gallery and he was there. At the time, he was a regular guest on *TV News* as the expert on links between tribal culture and corruption in Africa. Both of them had recognized him even though he looked quite different in real life.

They had walked slowly by as he explained to the lovely, much younger woman at his side what he felt about Abildgaard's painting *The Wounded Philoctetes*. Nicola hadn't read a line of Gunnar's writings about Africa or anything else, but she too had thought he was special. They discreetly passed close behind him several times while he shared his experiences of other paintings with his companion.

The next day Anne-Lise stole a little time off work and got out a volume of Gunnar's articles. She actually took the book home with her and read it in bed.

Paul interrupts her reverie. "You know, I'm positive he'll be interested. His career has gone off-course for some reason. The DCIG board will be just the thing to put him back on track. I had this vision of him cracking open a bottle after I phoned him last night."

That evening, after listening to Anne-Lise talking about the new developments, Henrik responds. "Your boss can't simply fire a member of his board. I realize he usually gets what he wants, but that's . . ."

"What can Paul do to get rid of Frederik?"

"He'd have to rig up some kind of trap or invent a mistake that Frederik has made. That might do the trick."

"Like what?"

Henrik laughs. "How about the deputy chairman sending threatening e-mails to Paul's staff?"

Anne-Lise is so relieved that the Center might come under the DIHR that she laughs too. Later that evening, as soon as the children are asleep, Henrik pulls her along to the black sofa. She lies down on her back, resting her head on his lap.

"I've done something I shouldn't have," he says.

She detects a hint of a smile and realizes there is nothing to be worried about.

"It's quite inappropriate and I could be fired, but if you can assume a false identity and pretend you're a singer in a choir and I don't know what else . . . The thing is, I printed out a copy of Camilla's account statement. I can't see anything out of the ordinary, but maybe you can. I've brought it home with me."

They exchange a grin. Henrik has more to confess.

"As it happens, Malene and Iben also have accounts with us. I have printouts of their statements as well."

Anne-Lise sits up and gives him a big kiss. Henrik produces the documents and they study them together, starting with Camilla's.

Predictably, there are withdrawals to cover credit cards, child-care fees, cell phone bills, and purchases of food at a low-price supermarket chain, clothes at H&M, and toys at Toys R Us. There are also small payments to B&Bs and cheap restaurants in Sweden, membership fees to the Danish Camping Union and to the Copenhagen Postal Choir.

They take their time and examine every entry. After a while they spot something surprising. Camilla gives money to the middle-of-the-road Centrum Democrats. During the last few years she must have taken an interest in the party's publications and meetings. She might even have gone to the meetings straight from work. If she did, she has kept it to herself, undoubtedly because she felt that her political views would not go down well with Iben and Malene—which would have been true, of course.

In itself, there is nothing suspicious about contributing to the Centrum Democrats, but it proves that Camilla thinks seriously about things other than cheap fridges and trips to adventure playgrounds with the kids. If nothing else, Anne-Lise now knows that Camilla can keep a secret.

Once Henrik and Anne-Lise have finished looking through Camilla's account, they go to the kitchen to make a pitcher of hot elderberry cordial. They got into the habit of drinking cordials in the evening when Anne-Lise still took the time to make her own juice, extracting the liquid from berries from the garden. Now they continue the custom with store-bought juice.

Anne-Lise is feeling content. Her thoughts constantly return to how much better things are going to be once she has new colleagues.

They return to the sofa and pick up Iben's statement. The most obvious thing about it is that she is well in the black, to the tune of 183,000 kroner. There was a credit of 120,000 three months ago. They guess it was compensation from the organization she worked for in Kenya. The rest seems to be the result of saving steadily over several months.

Even though Henrik has already spent some time that afternoon skimming the statements, he is too much of a career banker not to become irritated once more at Iben's financial advisor. "This is stupid! Someone should tell her to pay off her student loans. And if she doesn't want to do that, she should invest her cash in premium bonds or a savings account."

This evening, Anne-Lise is in a good enough mood to find her husband's banking instincts funny. She doesn't think Iben's fiscal choices are that significant.

"Won't Iben be taxed on the Kenya compensation? Maybe she keeps the cash accessible because she doesn't know how much she'll have to pay."

"But the bank staff should have told her. It's unacceptable. Her advisor is giving us all a bad name. What's he doing? She clearly hasn't had any advice whatsoever."

Just like Camilla, Iben is paid less than Anne-Lise, but the difference is smaller. They are all paid according to public service scales and, even though Iben and Malene earn good money in recognition of their educational qualifications, Anne-Lise is ahead owing to her seniority.

Iben buys her food mainly at the Nørrebro branch of upmarket Føtex and her books at Athenaeum, the university booksellers. She is a member of both Greenpeace and Amnesty International and subscribes to *Information* and the *Week*. Apart from these debits, she hardly ever spends any money. She has paid seven café bills at a place called the Metro Bar and once bought something unspecified from the kiosk at Roskilde Station. There is just one irregularity: a string of transfers to accounts in the United States, United Kingdom, and Germany.

"Can you figure out who is receiving the money?" Anne-Lise asks.

"Not from the statement, but there are ways. Leave it to me."

In the last three months alone she has made thirteen transfers to seven separate accounts.

"She buys books about genocide and psychiatry on the Internet, but there is no obvious reason why she would use seven different booksellers. So what can it be?"

They're both aware that foreign anonymizer sites charge their users. The person who sent the threatening e-mails would have had to pay fees. Henrik and Anne-Lise don't need to remind each other of this. If it's not that, then what else could she have been buying on the Internet that often?

A smile flits over Henrik's face. "I get sent spam all the time trying to sell me pornography. Maybe she's into that kind of thing?"

Anne-Lise giggles at the thought of earnest Iben surfing the Net in search of erotic sites. It's so out of character.

"But it could be payments for access to things like chat rooms or dating sites."

Anne-Lise associates looking for company on the Internet with loneliness. Seeing Iben and Malene behaving like a couple of teenage girls, she has never thought of either of them as lonely. But what's it like for Iben outside work? She doesn't have a man. She rarely speaks of other female friends.

Henrik and Anne-Lise move on to Malene's statement. She has overdraft protection but exceeds the limit just about every other month. It goes without saying that she too is a member of Amnesty International and Greenpeace, subscribes to *Information* and the *Week*, and is paying off her student loans. She draws heavily on her interest-free account at the very chic furniture store Illums and has made several payments for designer clothes, mostly bought in the small, fashionable shops clustered along the lanes off Strøget. Malene rarely uses supermarkets, presumably because she favors delis and ethnic greengrocers. She has paid restaurant bills a few times, and visited a nightclub once. That evening she withdrew cash four times.

Malene's debits are understandable enough, but one of her sources of income is mysterious. Now and then, three to four thousand kroner is transferred into her account from an unspecified private source—just the backup she needs to cover her spending. Anne-Lise takes note.

"*Ha!*"

Henrik puts down his cordial. "What?"

"Come on! Isn't it obvious?"

Henrik hesitates. "Anne-Lise, I checked these transfers. They are made from an account in Kolding that belongs to a woman called Jytte Jensen."

"Oh. I see." Anne-Lise knows it's unreasonable to feel disappointed. "Jytte Jensen is probably Malene's mother. I must say, I had the impression that Malene's mother was just a secretary who retired early and wasn't well off. Malene says she grew up poor."

"So what was it you thought was so obvious just now?"

"It's . . . I don't know." She's reluctant to say it, but Henrik insists.

"I thought Malene . . . was seeing someone. A rich man. And he paid her for it."

Henrik dislikes Malene too but thinks Anne-Lise has gone a bit overboard. He leans back on the sofa, irritated. "Anne-Lise, really . . . just because she dresses the way she does?"

Anne-Lise reaches out to him. "No, no. Of course not. And the money comes from her mother. So there." She strokes his upper arm. "That is, from her impoverished mother, who is always broke . . ."

few days after the business with Malene's medicine, a policeman phones the Center to let them know that there has been a new development in the e-mail case.

Camilla takes the call, switches it through to Paul at once, and then tells the others. Iben and Malene get up from their desks and walk over to stand by Paul's door. Anne-Lise joins them from the library and they wait anxiously.

When Paul finally emerges, he tells them that the CIA has been casting around Chicago's large Serbian community and has arrested two former private soldiers who have a record of war crimes. Interrogated, one of the men admitted to having sent e-mails to the DCIG.

Paul is deluged with questions.

"Did he do it on his own?"

"Are they keeping him in prison?"

"Did he really want to kill us?"

"Does he know Mirko Zigic?"

"Why send the threats just to us? He didn't write to other people, did he?"

Paul says that he doesn't have any answers. He has told them everything he knows. There are powerful forces at work out there, chasing Mirko Zigic and his associates. The three brief e-mails to the DCIG have somehow taken on international importance.

Malene phones the police herself but gets no more information. Iben meanwhile makes a call to the U.S. embassy, but they don't have anything to add either. The women then ring various institutions in the United States and, finally, their contacts in other genocide centers worldwide. Despite their efforts, they get nowhere.

While the others get more and more worked up, Anne-Lise withdraws to the library and sits looking at the photo of Henrik and the children on her desk. The e-mails never caused her to feel afraid. But she simply doesn't believe the alleged statement by that war criminal. Without a doubt, his "confession" was the result of a fair amount of pressure. In her own mind, she's certain that whoever wrote the e-mails had inside knowledge of the Center, and as far as she's concerned nothing has changed.

She listens as the others discuss the ways that an unknown war criminal living in Chicago could possibly have had access to Malene's tablets, and whether it could have been him who rigged up the blood trap in the library. Their conversation is suitably polite because the library door is of course still open. They discuss the blood on Anne-Lise's bookshelf, sounding as if they had had nothing to do with putting it there.

Anne-Lise notes the line they take when they go on to tell lies about Malene's medicine. Obviously, the likeliest explanation by far is that Malene herself mixed up the pills by accident, but she's making a great show of being persecuted. It reminds Anne-Lise of someone who has lost, say, a wallet and fusses endlessly about who could have stolen it and why—until it turns up in the person's jacket pocket. Camilla and Iben must notice this too, but no one argues with Malene.

In the weeks that follow the admission by the Serb soldier, Malene, Iben, and Camilla change their attitude toward Anne-Lise.

Before, their hostility at times was confusing. One of them would suddenly be so friendly to her that Anne-Lise wondered if she hadn't misjudged them somehow. Maybe, she told herself, it was all just an enormous misunderstanding and the aggression was just a figment of her imagination.

Not now. They don't need to be frightened of what Iben might have called "Anne-Lise's dissociated murderous identity" anymore. They're free to destroy her, and the knives are clearly out. Their goal is to make her leave. Long-term sick leave would suit them. Too bad if it damages her and makes it impossible for her to work again.

One afternoon, weeks after Malene mixed up her pills, she is waiting in the corridor when Anne-Lise comes out from the bathroom. Malene starts to hum a few lines of a song louder than necessary, and at first it seems pointless.

But then it becomes obvious that it's a signal.

Anne-Lise hears somebody in the library react. It's easy to recognize Iben's footsteps as she hurriedly leaves the library through the door into the Winter Garden. When Anne-Lise passes Malene in the corridor, Malene meets her eyes and smiles broadly, as if Anne-Lise would think their snooping was just good clean fun. As if they were all simply playing a game together.

The moment Anne-Lise gets to her desk she spots what Iben has been up to. This morning Anne-Lise brought in a few cuttings from her garden and put the twigs in a tall glass of water to liven the place up. The vase is leaning now, because Iben has put a pad of Post-it notes and a pen underneath it. If Anne-Lise accidentally gives the desk even the tiniest shove, the container will topple.

She advances gingerly and repositions the vase. A pile of valuable papers has been saved.

There's no point in complaining to Paul: she realizes that she has already been to see him too often. Also, it's clear to her that it would make things easier for him if she simply went away and didn't come back. So far he has had enough integrity not to tell her this to her face, but he doesn't openly support her in the way he used to.

All she can do is put up with the situation and keep quiet until the day comes when they merge with Human Rights. Or she must do what Yngve advised: confront them.

Anne-Lise takes in a deep breath and, still standing, blinks so slowly that her eyes close for several seconds. There are no tears. She has a sensation of her skin becoming very thick. She feels as heavy and armored as a rhinoceros.

She steps through the doorway into the Winter Garden. Standing there, she looks down at the two women sitting at their desks. Iben glances at Malene. The look in her eyes says "We've got her now," and she doesn't give a damn if Anne-Lise notices.

Anne-Lise begins to say her piece, resigned, knowing that she has been here before. "Can't we just behave like professionals? You know: I don't interfere with you and you don't interfere with me. Then we could concentrate on our work without wasting our energy on . . . other things."

Malene's inviting smile doesn't change. "Anne-Lise, that would make for such a cold atmosphere, and we wouldn't want that. We are colleagues, after all."

"Just stop doing these things. You know what I mean."

"No, I don't."

Iben backs her up. "What are you talking about?"

"You know well enough."

"No."

"Yes. You do. Don't go into other people's rooms just to cause trouble."

"Why should we . . . ?"

"Anne-Lise, I don't understand what you mean. Please explain."

They manage to make her describe what she thought they had done, step by step. They listen, ready to reply in unison.

"No. No, we'd never do that. Whatever makes you think we would?"

Their voices and body language bubble with laughter, giving their game away. They are enjoying this. They'd just as soon slit my throat if they thought they could get away with it, Anne-Lise thinks. It's even better fun for them now that I'm on to them.

Every night this last week Anne-Lise has had the same nightmares. She is thrown into the crater of a volcano, or strapped down on a table and tortured with red-hot iron bars driven through her flesh, or impaled and hung up in a tree. All the time Iben's and Malene's huge mouths, twisted and grinning, open wider and wider in anticipation of Anne-Lise's demise.

She has woken up and wandered about, trying to shake off the dreams. She has stroked the heads of her sleeping children. She has gone downstairs to the living room and stared at the trees outside the window. Gradually, the lingering sensations of the hot iron touching her, or her body sinking into the lava inside the volcano, evaporate.

Later, when she falls asleep from sheer exhaustion, the nightmares return and she awakes abruptly as she sees again the rows of teeth between their pulled-back lips.

"Your Post-it pad must've slipped under the glass," Malene reasons, "and you were too busy to notice. How annoying! I mean, you could've slopped water over everything."

Iben is shuffling her feet, searching for something like a lost shoe. Next she starts looking under the table, sending an unmistakable signal that the whole thing is beginning to bore her.

Malene becomes distracted too. She looks across the desk at Iben. "What's under the table? What are you looking for?"

Anne-Lise glances at Camilla, who appears to be completely absorbed in her work.

Camilla behaves as if she weren't there at all. Anne-Lise feels like crossing the floor and shouting in her ear: "Are you aware of what's going on? Do you even care? Would you be pleased if I died too?" But Anne-Lise doesn't dare provoke her.

Maybe Camilla's inertia is a survival strategy that she learned to save herself. Maybe Camilla would have a breakdown if someone were to force her to take notice of what is going on in the office right under her very nose. Maybe her unstable mind would give way to lethal rage—awaken a personality capable of e-mail death threats.

Camilla and the others look away from Anne-Lise, and she returns to the library.

Later that afternoon, the DCIG board member Tatiana Blumenfeld has arranged to come and pick up some reference material Anne-Lise has found for her. Tatiana knows everyone in human rights research in Denmark. It matters if she takes you seriously, regardless of which organization you work for. She is also one of the few academics who make use of Anne-Lise's expertise.

Tatiana is a tiny woman in her sixties with jet black hair. She arrives at the board meetings wearing tight black trousers and vivid, unique sweaters. She dashes along the corridors with remarkably long strides for such a small person. The machine-gun clatter of her smart, extremely high-heeled shoes can be heard from afar. Although Anne-Lise has never seen Tatiana with a cigarette, her skin is that of a lifelong chain-smoker.

When Tatiana was a student of psychoanalysis, she laid the foundations for a theory about the therapeutic management of children who had been imprisoned in concentration camps and subjected to torture or forced to watch their close relatives being tortured or murdered. Tatiana developed her theory from her analyses of camp children's drawings and her research led first to a doctorate and then to a tenured post in the Department of Psychology at Copenhagen University. She has also become an associate of the International Rehabilitation Council for Torture Victims, or IRCTV, a highly regarded organization.

Anne-Lise still doesn't feel close to Tatiana. What she knows about her she learned mostly through Tatiana's friend and assistant, Lea. Anne-Lise and Lea met at the Bosnia conference and, during a lunch together, Lea spoke glowingly about her boss.

The doorbell rings. The image on their computer screens shows Tatiana waiting outside on the landing. Anne-Lise keys in the security code and goes to meet her visitor; she wants to usher her to the library before the others have a chance to descend upon her. But no sooner does Tatiana step into the Winter Garden than Malene and Iben are by her side.

"You must come and see the new photos we've put up," Iben says, smiling.

They turn and lead the way to the notice board, Tatiana between them. She steps forward, catches sight of Anne-Lise, and calls out: "Anne-Lise! I'm just going to have a peek at their crazy pictures!"

Of all the people she has met in this place, Anne-Lise has found Tatiana to be the nicest. Her impulse is to protect Tatiana from her venomous colleagues, but then, she knows that Malene and Iben won't want to show their ill will in front of the esteemed guest.

Tatiana exclaims at one of the new pictures. "Oh, look! It's your old librarian! How sweet of you! Do you miss her?"

She is looking at a photograph of the woman whose e-mails showed just how intensely she detested working at the DCIG. Sometime last week, Iben had scanned an old photograph of their ex-librarian and printed an enlarged version to pin up on the wall.

"We do. But have a closer look. We have lots of pictures of our favorite people."

Tatiana takes Malene's prompt and moves closer to the board. She puts on her reading glasses. "No . . . it's me! I look so odd. It's Rome, isn't it?"

"That's right. Ole gave it to us. He was there too."

Tatiana is amused. She puts her coat on Malene's chair and leans forward to examine the picture.

"It was at the conference. God, I look completely sozzled."

At this, she glances quickly at Anne-Lise, apparently alarmed, but with a hint of compassion. Anne-Lise doesn't understand what her expression means.

Iben comes closer to Tatiana. "Never! You wouldn't drink too much at work!"

She smiles at Anne-Lise now, but continues to address Tatiana. "No one would ever think that about you. It's just the heat and the bright light. You look a bit flushed, that's all. And your smile is great. Everyone can see you're happy."

Anne-Lise tries to get a word in with Tatiana too. She finds it hard to sound relaxed and friendly, sensing Iben and Malene's intense desire for her to disappear.

Iben is very good at entertaining visitors and Malene is excellent. A quarter of an hour later, the little group is still chatting in front of the notice board.

Iben mentions the plan to merge the DCIG and DIHR, sounding troubled as she explains.

Tatiana is sympathetic. "Yes, I see. Such a shame. Are you really worried about it?"

"Yes, we are."

Tatiana nods with concern. "I understand, believe me. This is such an efficient office and so very pleasant too. It's a great pity. But don't worry, you're sure to keep your present jobs inside the new organization too." She goes on to talk about her experience of other institutional mergers. "I suspect Paul will be the most put out. After all, he'll have someone else as his boss."

Iben keeps stepping from one foot to the other. "We were wondering about Frederik's role on the board once his senior post in Human Rights is announced. Now that it's no longer in his interest to keep this place independent, it could be problematic, couldn't it?"

Anne-Lise doesn't think they should be discussing this with another member of the board, but Iben is so much more knowledgeable about the rules and what's acceptable in terms of the politics of the organization.

Tatiana, however, sounds surprised. "Iben, it's not problematic in the slightest. Frederik can easily put on different hats at different times. We all do, you know. And he's very professional."

Malene looks intently at Tatiana and edges forward until she is in front of Anne-Lise. "So you don't think there will be a conflict of interests?"

"No, I don't. Absolutely not." Tatiana picks up her coat, ready to get on with library business. "I wouldn't worry about that. Truly. Trust me. But have you spoken to Paul about it?"

Anne-Lise can't think what the correct way of dealing with this straight question about the Center's director might be.

But Malene doesn't hesitate. "No, we haven't raised it with him. You're right, we should."

"Yes, you really ought to. Paul attends the board meetings and can tell you how everything works. I'm sure he will confirm that there's no problem."

Then, at last, Anne-Lise gets to escort Tatiana into the library. She shows her the results of her search, a collection of reports from the Portuguese Foreign Office staff, written in Portuguese and full of details about the Indonesian genocide of 200,000 civilians, roughly a third of the population of occupied East Timor.

Looking through books with someone else brings a special sense of intimacy, like having your hair washed by the hairdresser.

Later Anne-Lise and Tatiana sit at Anne-Lise's computer and search for references to East Timor in international online magazines. The library also holds French investigations that are not yet entered into the database and Tatiana wanders off in search of archive material. Anne-Lise sends an overview of the articles they have selected to the small printer in the Winter Garden.

When she goes to collect the printouts, Iben and Malene are talking. They clearly know that Tatiana can no longer hear them, and Iben's voice is low and relaxed.

"Malene, we simply haven't had time to finalize the texts you need for the exhibition posters. So much has been going on these last few weeks, since Anne-Lise sent us those e-mails." Her tone is so matter-of-fact.

Anne-Lise would prefer to say nothing and retreat to her own space, but she realizes that the remark will be left hanging in the air, ready to hurt her later. Once more they have forced her to join their little game.

She sighs, because she knows what will come next, and speaks quietly. "I didn't send the e-mails."

The anticipation of the hunt makes their eyes shine. Malene takes over. "Oh, yes, you did."

"You know it wasn't me. It was that Serb. The one the CIA arrested."

Iben sounds amused. "You've sent lots of e-mails, to us and other people."

Anne-Lise tries to be firm. "Of course I've sent e-mails, but not threatening ones."

"But I wasn't talking about them."

Malene sides with Iben. "That's not the point at all. We didn't even mention any threats."

She pauses and looks at Anne-Lise, her expression now registering amazement. "Why on earth would you assume that we were talking about those e-mails?"

Anne-Lise feels her insides cramp up. "That's ridiculous! What was I supposed to think? Which e-mails do you mean?"

"Different ones."

"Which ones?"

Malene's voice changes, as if it had all been a playful chat but now Anne-Lise has crossed the line. "Just drop it, Anne-Lise. And do try to stay calm."

Iben chips in: "You mustn't be so paranoid."

Anne-Lise is about to say that she isn't paranoid. But the situation is simply impossible. Every single day something like this occurs. What's the point of protesting yet again? Every day she loses another point in the game.

Anne-Lise goes to the restroom to pull herself together. She checks her face in the mirror. Nothing shows. No tears moistening her face. Have her features become harsher over the last few weeks?

What was the meaning of Tatiana's glance earlier? She seemed concerned. Why? And hadn't they mentioned being drunk at work? How should she interpret that? Could it be that the others are spreading rumors that Anne-Lise drinks during working hours? It would explain Tatiana's reaction.

She feels calmer now and walks back to the library. While she and Tatiana work together, Tatiana asks Anne-Lise about her reaction to the e-mails. Does she feel safer now that the sender has been arrested?

Anne-Lise is pleased at the thought that she could easily have given away more than she does. And if she had, Tatiana would have listened.

It takes them almost an hour to finish their work in the library. Afterward Tatiana has to get back to the Council for Torture Victims. Anne-Lise escorts her through the Winter Garden to the front door. Malene gets up to say goodbye and in no time at all makes Tatiana laugh. Once more, Tatiana lingers in the central room.

Then Iben exclaims, her voice still full of laughter, "Oh, Tatiana, we haven't had time to talk for ages! It's a shame, but there's been so much going on ever since we all—sorry, everyone except Anne-Lise—were sent those threats."

Tatiana doesn't quite understand the tone of Iben's remark. Her mouth opens in surprise. "How do you . . . ?"

Malene helps her out. "Oh, sorry! You couldn't have known! It's a running office gag that Anne-Lise sent those e-mails."

Tatiana looks around and speaks slowly, searching for words. "Oka-ay."

In that instant Anne-Lise feels she has spotted a new side to Tatiana. The older woman is always trying to make an effort to act "young" in front of Malene and Iben. After all, she is more than thirty years older than they are, yet she tries hard to sound just as youthful and energetic.

"Aha! Of course Anne-Lise must've sent the e-mails!"

They are all supposed to laugh or smile now, but the irony sounds awkward coming from Tatiana, and somehow the comment seems out of place.

THE PSYCHOLOGY OF EVIL II

Social psychology contributes a myriad of surprising and uncomfortable insights into studies of perpetrator behavior.

■

BY IBEN HØJGAARD

In his book *On Killing*, Lieutenant Colonel Dave Grossman states that, in a war situation, men and women who kill at a sufficiently great distance from the victims are, to the best of his personal knowledge, not traumatized later in life. The closer the soldier gets to the victim, the harder it is to kill. Yet no government has ever had to cancel plans for genocide for lack of people willing to carry out their orders.

How to resolve this contradiction?

In the previous issue of *Genocide News*, the article "The Psychology of Evil I" referred to Stanley Milgram's experimental work on the parameters of "obedience to authority." There are dozens of other approaches in social psychology that also illuminate the psychology of the perpetrator. This article presents a small selection.

ACTIONS SHAPE ATTITUDES

Generally we believe that it is our attitudes that determine our behavior. However, the reverse is also true: what we do affects our way of thinking, our feelings, and our opinions.

It is unsettling for us when we realize that our actions are in conflict with our beliefs. To distance ourselves from this, we unconsciously tend to adjust our attitudes and feelings rather than change our behavior. Social psychologists have carried out hundreds of experiments, attempting to pin down exactly how this change in attitude is accomplished.

Festinger and Carlsmith devised an experiment in which the subjects were given tedious tasks taking many hours to complete, such as moving tiny four-sided sticks about, forward and back and from side to side. When the leader of the experiment finally told the subjects that the experiment was finished, they were also told that the leader's assistant, who was to instruct the next subject in line and stress how exciting the task was, would be arriving late. The current subjects were then asked if they could possibly take over the assistant's role, meet the new subjects, and tell them about the procedure. One group was asked to lie about what a joy it had been to participate in the experiment. The other group was not asked to feign enthusiasm.

The first group was divided into two sections and offered either one dollar or twenty dollars for their trouble. It is worth noting that in 1959 the value of the dollar was relatively much higher than it is today.

The results showed that those who had been paid one dollar and had lied to the new subjects felt that the experiment had actually been a good experience. Both those who had been paid twenty dollars and those who weren't asked to lie admitted afterward that they had found the experience dull. The larger sum of money provided a strong external incentive to lie to the new subjects, and hence they felt no subconscious need to change their original opinion of the experiment in order to explain their action to themselves. Only those who had received a small reward needed to change their views in order to establish a link between their thoughts and their action. This instinct is driven by lack of internal cogency, an uncomfortable state that is a key concept in social psychology and described by the term *cognitive dissonance.*

There are real-life decisions that lead to cognitive dissonance, and thus to a switch in attitude. Consider a research officer with moral, liberal views who is offered a job with an advertising agency and accepts it. This means that she will begin to suffer from a discrepancy between her ideals and her actions, and unless she rejects the job offer she must try to readjust her convictions to justify her new situation. After a few months she might argue, with genuine passion, that advertising is an essential aspect of democratic societies with a free-market economy. Also, she will probably maintain this opinion for the rest of her life, even if she spends only a relatively brief period in advertising.

Another example is the Jehovah's Witnesses who soon learn that handing out pamphlets in the street serves a dual purpose. It will help to recruit new adherents to the faith, but it will also reinforce the bonds between the faithful and the sect. The first time they might well have been hesitant about going out pamphleteering, but afterward they will come home with a stronger light of faith in their eyes.

The process can lead to increasingly charitable—or increasingly maleficent—behavior. It can also create profound changes in outlook, much more so than would have been possible through words alone.

The Nazis relied heavily on this mechanism to ensure conformity among German citizens. The incalculable risks of refusing to make symbolic signs of support for the regime, e.g., the "Heil Hitler" greeting, must have led individuals to ask themselves: "What's the harm in just lifting my right arm?" But every time someone conforms, his or her way of thinking will have changed.

The conclusion must be that simple acts, which in themselves appear to cause only limited damage, can lead to psychological changes that in turn make possible even greater and more destructive acts.

ROLES SHAPE PEOPLE
In 1971 the social psychologist Phillip G. Zimbardo and some of his colleagues at Stanford University decided to investigate the psychological consequences of the relationship between a prisoner and a prison guard.

They advertised for student subjects, stating that they needed twenty-one males, who would be paid for the two-week experiment. All applicants were interviewed, but only those who seemed reasonably stable, mature, and responsible were picked. They were then randomly divided into two groups: prisoners and guards.

On day one, real policemen came to the homes of ten of the participants and "arrested" them "on suspicion" of break-ins and armed robbery. They were taken to a university basement corridor that had been made to look like a prison and were ordered to undress, be deloused, and put on prison overalls. The designated "guards" were dressed in uniforms, complete with mirrored sunglasses and truncheons.

The guards were called to a meeting and told to keep the prisoners under surveillance but not to hurt them physically. The prisoners stayed in the prison round the clock, while the guards went home to their normal lives after an eight-hour working day.

In the beginning of what became known as the Stanford Prison Experiment, there were no significant personality differences between randomly picked guards and prisoners. Later, both groups were to change remarkably quickly.

The absolute power given to the guards made the prisoners helpless and submissive, enabling the guards to extend their powers still further. This mutual interaction was the start of a self-reinforcing, damaging process.

A third of the guards behaved with increasing callousness and in an arbitrary manner, initiating punishments for no reason and devising inventive means of humiliating the prisoners. In their ordinary lives they had shown no tendencies toward aggressive or tyrannical behavior.

Two of the guards went out of their way to support the prisoners, but never came close to publicly confronting the hostile guards. The rest of the guards were tough, but they did not initiate any unofficial punishments.

The prisoners became depressed, despairing, and passive. Three of them had to be "freed" only four days into the experiment because they wept hysterically, lost the ability to think coherently, and became deeply depressed. A fourth prisoner was released after getting a rash that covered his entire body.

All but three of the prisoners were willing to forgo payment for the days they had spent on the experiment if they could be let out. When they were told that their pleas for "parole" had been turned down, they passively and obediently plodded along back to their cells.

The Stanford Prison Experiment demonstrates that prisoners and guards acted according to the roles given to them by an external agent, gradually changing their thought patterns, values, and emotional responses to fit in. Most of the participants seemed unable to make a distinction between their real selves and their role in the experiment. Prison brutality escalated with each successive day. Ordinary moral values vanished, despite the fact that each group was determined indiscriminately.

The experiment had to be interrupted after six days, mainly because the remaining prisoners were unacceptably close to mental breakdown.

There are of course many other contexts in which the role and the self become contiguous. As James Waller says in his book entitled *Becoming Evil* (parts of this account are based on his analysis of the existing evidence): "Evil acts not only reflect the self, they shape the self."

GROUPS FORMED FOR ALMOST NO REASON

The English social psychologist Henri Tajfel and a few of his colleagues set out to study how many features people must have in common in order to see themselves as part of a group and, as a next step, set up a system of prejudices against other groups.

His first plan was to recruit people without any regard to common features, allocate them at random to groups, and then gradually introduce similarities, negative prejudices, and conflicts between the groups. He expected that this process would allow him to observe how and when group identity is formed.

In his best-known "minimal group" experiment, he asked the subjects to express their opinions of a few abstract paintings and separated them afterward into two groups. One lot were told that they had all expressed a preference for paintings similar to those by Paul Klee, while the others preferred the style of Wassily Kandinsky. None of this was true, as group allocation was entirely random.

The subjects did not know one another and had had no prior contact. Given the opportunity to evaluate photographs of all the subjects, participants ranked those in their own group as better at their jobs and more pleasant to be with. When individuals were asked to distribute money, group members were always favored.

In a similar experiment, some of the subjects were so biased against the other group that they were happier for their own people to receive two dollars rather than three, on condition that the others received one dollar instead of four. In other words, they were more interested in "beating the others" than getting the highest possible payment for their own members.

Until this series of experiments, most social psychologists had assumed that group identity was created gradually in response to shared experiences. Nobody expected prejudice and hostility to emerge between people without any knowledge of their own group or of the others.

Relationships within a group, or between groups, constitute classical fields of research in social psychology. Many different experiments show that our thoughts operate according to an "Us-and-Them" model. The basis for this is straightforward. Everyone is forced to work out how to deal with a world that is endlessly complex. In order to simplify existence and sort out irrelevant information quickly, we divide ourselves into categories.

Categorization is a human way of thinking, as essential as it is unavoidable. Types of category vary between individuals and cultures, but the process is common to us all. It shapes how we understand our environment and our relationship to it.

Social psychology has demonstrated some of the consistent distortions caused by the Us-and-Them model. We tend to exaggerate the similarities of those who belong to our group, just as we exaggerate the homogeneity in other groups and the differences among them. And normally we care more for members of our own group than for others.

In crises or open conflicts, these attitudes become extreme. All mankind has the potential for believing the propaganda machine when it repeats endlessly: "Kill, or be killed!"

THE VICTIM ASKS FOR IT
We are all aware that good people are not immune to bad experiences, but a large majority of us nonetheless try to hold on to the hope of a fundamentally just world, a good place to bring your children into.

As numerous studies demonstrate, this hope, combined with the barely conscious human need for meaning and for coherence in the information we receive, makes us twist reality until it fits into our vision of order.

It is not only those who carry out terrible acts who are deluded by their distorted thought patterns, memories, and sensory input into believing that their world is still just and meaningful. Those who witness the tragedies and, indeed, the victims themselves also collaborate in this fiction.

People struck down by a serious illness, as well as those close to the patient, are often determined to find the cause. They feel a strong need to establish exactly what they have done wrong to deserve the affliction. Again, it is common for victims of violence to wonder about the root cause. "Maybe I asked for it; maybe I shouldn't have walked down that lane so late at night; maybe I shouldn't have worn that dress." Such anxieties become the focus of their thoughts, regardless of the fact that they have the right to walk down any lane and wear any kind of clothes.

Sometimes it seems that victims actively prefer to carry the burden of blame rather than recognize that mere chance can intervene to ruin a life. A wealth of experimental data supports this in every detail.

In one such experiment, Melvin Lerner and Carolyn Simmons asked seventy-two students to watch the punishment, in the form of severe electrical shocks, given every time a victim gave a wrong answer to a question. The victim was an actress, mimicking the pain.

Some of the observers were told that they would be allowed to stop the shocks later in the process. Asked to describe how they felt about the victim, those who believed she would continue to be in pain viewed her more negatively than those who thought that they would be able to control the shocks.

This way of construing the position of the victim is sharpened when we ourselves are inflicting the suffering. Cognitive dissonance makes us like those whom we have helped and dislike those we have hurt.

In the context of his experiment on obedience to authority, Stanley Milgram noted that many of the subjects later said things like: "He (the 'pupil') was so stupid that he really deserved to be shocked." Another, similar argument was that since the pupil had agreed to join the experiment he was asking for trouble. This was despite the fact that those who expressed such a view had also joined the experiment and it had apparently been the luck of the draw that decided who was "teacher" and who was "pupil."

It seems that powerful psychological impulses drive perpetrators to think and feel that their victims deserve what's happening to them. The more appallingly brutal the acts a perpetrator commits, the more strongly he comes to believe that they are only right and proper.

We all have a tendency to construe reality in the same way as the German civilian who commented, when forced by British soldiers to walk through a newly liberated concentration camp: "What awful crimes these people must have committed to be condemned to this kind of punishment."

If you want to read about genocide in the context of social psychology, there are three major works: *Becoming Evil,* James Waller's highly recommended 2002 overview; the classic *The Roots of Evil* by Ervin Staub; and *Understanding Genocide,* a compilation of articles edited by Leonard S. Newman and Ralph Erber.

chapter 32

t is late and Iben trudges heavily to her apartment on the sixth floor. She has spent the evening in Malene's place, discussing Anne-Lise. She feels worn out, and the only thing on her mind is sleep.

At the last turn of the stair she senses someone on the landing outside her door. She looks up. The man is tall, with a mass of tightly curled black hair, graying at the temples. She takes in his black leather jacket and the dead look in his eyes. In an instant she knows that he has been waiting for her, and why.

She flies down the stairs. He goes after her with long strides and soon catches up. He grabs her throat before she has time to scream—or, at least, that is how Anne-Lise usually imagines it. Then he grips her around her waist. Iben's legs, much shorter than his, kick out wildly. She knows what will happen next. So does Anne-Lise.

The reel runs and reruns inside Anne-Lise's head, showing every detail as Iben's face changes. The bleak lamplight picks out the shadows under her eyes. Anne-Lise watches as Iben's expression becomes remorseful. At last she has insight into what she has done, how she lied to herself and convinced herself that she was good—oh, so good—at the same time that she did all she could to ruin another human being.

In Anne-Lise's imagination the knife is large, with broad

teeth cut deep into the steel. Iben will die now. Soon, reflex spasms will make her body twitch. She will weaken fast as life drains from her.

Anne-Lise's tired mind steers in and around the fantasies that coalesce and then fade in her mind, while she tries to concentrate on other things. The familiar images, the rapist in the red tracksuit murdering Malene, the man lying in wait for Iben, can start up even when she is in the Winter Garden, talking with one of the other women.

She would like to make an appointment to see Yngve and be reassured by him. On the other hand, she knows he will insist that she confront Iben and Malene. Anne-Lise would also like to tell Nicola what the last few weeks have been like, yet can't bring herself to answer when her phone indicates that Nicola is on the line. She will keep insisting that Anne-Lise should hand in her notice.

Instead Anne-Lise tries to suppress her fantasies and think about something peaceful. Driving along the motorway in the morning, she speculates about the merger. She is still thinking about it when she turns left onto the Jagt Road exit and when she parks her car and when she rides up in the groaning old elevator with the three pornographic cartoons scratched in the corner. Everything will change when the DCIG becomes part of the DIHR. New colleagues and a new boss.

Anne-Lise thinks about the takeover while she fills her mug with coffee until it spills over the sides. She is still thinking about it later on, when she sends off an e-mail to the wrong address.

Her first task is to assign keywords to classified reports on the genocide carried out by the Soviet Union in Afghanistan. She compares scans from three different books to look for patterns and possible correlations.

She reads about the Soviet occupation of Afghanistan in 1979 and the attempts to change the ethnic composition of Afghan tribes. The army chiefs were especially keen to reduce the number of Pashtuns in the northern Afghan provinces, because it would facilitate their incorporation into the Soviet Union. Reliable figures are scarce, but the UN estimates that between 1978 and 1992, 1.5 to 2 million Afghans were killed. They were subjected to bombs and chemical weapons, but also to air drops of children's toys filled with deadly toxins, massacres, and destruction of crops and wells.

Approximately 6 million inhabitants fled. To prevent them from ever returning, the occupying army destroyed the irrigation systems on which Afghan agriculture depended, turning the refugees' homeland into a desert.

The space bar on Anne-Lise's keyboard isn't working properly; sometimes it adds two or three spaces, sometimes none. Unless she proofreads everything with particular care, the users won't find what they are looking for. She is checking the phrase "torture and murder of foreign journalists, doctors, and aid workers" when Paul steps into the Winter Garden to make an announcement.

"Gunnar is going to drop in sometime this afternoon. I have promised him a tour of the Center and a talk about the funding of our operations. He insists he wants an idea about these things before he agrees to join the board."

Anne-Lise listens through the open door. She can't see the others but senses that the atmosphere has changed. The keyboards have fallen silent and now drawers are being opened and there is the sound of paper being shuffled.

When Iben speaks to Malene, does her voice somehow have an edge?

Anne-Lise's desk is awash with papers, but they're in order. In case the many Post-it notes make it look as if she's behind with a lot of jobs, she puts some of them away. She also decides to get rid of three large sacks of waste paper piled up close to her desk. The sacks, which are stuffed with wrappings of foreign books and magazine packages, actually demonstrate how efficient she is. All the same, they look too messy. She knows the spots the cleaners miss, especially with all the electrical equipment and the leads and sockets, so she does a quick spring clean.

She is almost ready when she hears the others calling out to one another.

"What am I supposed to do with this?"

"Don't know. But what about this, then?"

Anne-Lise can't hear the reply, but they start laughing. Then Iben comes running into the library, holding an empty bottle of rum. Anne-Lise has no idea where the bottle has come from but assumes that Iben brought it to drop it in the glass-recycling bin. It's the kind of thing she would do.

Iben is still laughing. "You've got plenty of room for this kind of thing!" She puts the bottle in one of Anne-Lise's cupboards and turns the key.

Anne-Lise can't see the point, but notices Malene watching in the doorway.

Exasperated, Anne-Lise slaps her hand on the desktop. "Why do you . . . ?" She has no idea how to follow up and mumbles the first thing that comes to mind. "I don't have a drinking problem."

Iben is on her way out. She replies with her back to Anne-Lise: "No. Sure."

"We never said anything of the sort."

"Of course not!"

Malene pops her head around the door to deliver an exit line. "You shouldn't be so uptight. Unless we've hit a sore spot."

Camilla puts a call through to Anne-Lise from one of the library users who is looking for books on aspects of Nazi collaboration in occupied France. As she talks, Anne-Lise thinks about the empty bottle and how she must get rid of it quickly, before Gunnar's visit. They mustn't have a chance to come dashing in and open the cupboard door while Gunnar is here.

When the phone call is over, she wraps the empty bottle in a blue plastic bag, sticks it inside a cardboard box and into another cupboard farther away from her desk. She makes sure that no one sees her hiding the bottle.

That done, she hurriedly opens all her cupboards and drawers, just in case Iben and Malene have planted more false clues to suggest that she's an alcoholic. Having examined every possible hiding place three times, she tries to settle down again, but feels at a loss. Finally she catches sight of Gunnar standing on the landing.

She gets up quickly so she too can be in the Winter Garden when he walks in. He looks as she remembers him: large, tanned, but not conventionally handsome like that pretty boy Frederik.

Her excuse for being there is the roll of labels in the cupboard next to Camilla's desk. She makes a show of needing to count up a large number and separating them. She smiles at Gunnar and he smiles back pleasantly enough.

"I'm here for a meeting with Paul Elkjær."

Anne-Lise has never been unfaithful to Henrik and isn't inclined to be. However, she feels hot and her hands are prickly.

Gunnar's shirt is open at the neck and looks very white against his tanned skin. On top, he wears a black jacket of very soft leather.

He looks at Malene. Malene looks at him. They know each other—it's unmistakable! Neither has spoken yet, but they are clearly more than acquaintances.

Malene gets up. Imagine him knowing her. Liking her. How have they met? How can he bring himself to like her? True, Malene did say that she knew him, but Anne-Lise thought that she meant through his writings, not personally.

Have they been to bed together? Maybe Anne-Lise has him all wrong; maybe he isn't the man she thought.

Anne-Lise also notices Iben's reaction. Iben is using both hands to fiddle with a gray stapler. Gunnar smiles at her and seems to know her too. Or does he smile at every young woman? Maybe he doesn't know Malene after all? Anne-Lise looks back at Malene. Yes, they know each other, all right.

Iben looks paler than usual. She gets up now, but her stance is different. She looks as if she wants to disappear.

It can't be more than a couple of seconds before Camilla addresses Gunnar. "Oh yes. He's waiting for you."

She goes to knock on Paul's door. Maybe ten seconds have passed since Gunnar came in. Maybe five.

Paul opens the door. For a fraction of a moment, the sight of his guest against the backdrop of four women, who seem to be positioned around the room like sculptures, surprises him. He welcomes Gunnar and ushers him inside.

Anne-Lise quickly goes back to the library. Is Gunnar, like so many other men, indifferent to ethical standards? Anne-Lise sits at her desk. She has no idea how to explain to anyone how bad this is. She will simply sound like a hysterical teenager if she says that her heart feels horribly empty just because of that quick glance between Malene and Gunnar.

She had truly believed that there were people who wouldn't be taken in by Iben's and Malene's superficial charms, by their youthful attractiveness. And that, beyond the walls of the DCIG, there were places that functioned on different principles.

Obviously, she got it all wrong. The entire world operates according to Malene's law. There is no place for vindication.

The door to Paul's office opens. With a degree of ceremony Paul escorts Gunnar from desk to desk, introducing the Center's staff to him. All four of them stay in their seats and pretend to be absorbed in their work.

Anne-Lise hears Gunnar say that he already knows Iben and Malene.

Indeed, Malene and he are "old friends" and he has met Iben. He says it so casually, but they must be more than mere acquaintances to him. For one thing, Malene and Iben are less talkative and charming than they usually are in the company of a new, powerful man.

Paul leads the way to the back of the library collection. While the two men discuss the archive, Anne-Lise hears the voice of Ole, the chairman of the board, coming from the Winter Garden.

Camilla sounds pleased. "Hi, Ole! Paul is in the library with Gunnar Hartvig Nielsen."

"No problem. I didn't come for anything important—just the week's cuttings. I wanted to take the folder home tonight."

Everyone in the Center likes Ole. His short white beard reminds Anne-Lise of a couple of other older professors she has met. Like them, he is on the heavy side and dresses more informally than the younger academics who come and go. Perhaps it's a throwback to 1970s university fashion.

Ole often comes by to chat to Paul about policy or matters arising at the next board meeting. Now and then he joins them for Christmas lunch or a summer dinner. Until about six months ago Anne-Lise didn't give a thought to Ole's private life. She knew that he was divorced and had two sons, but that was about it. Then her sister-in-law phoned one Sunday morning to tell her that Ole had been interviewed for the series "My Demons" in the Sunday issue of *Politiken*.

Anne-Lise shot off to the newsstand and bought a paper. Amazingly, like the other famous or almost famous men and women interviewed for the series, Ole had been remarkably frank and told *Politiken*'s star interviewer some deeply personal things.

The interview got a double-page spread and was illustrated with a splendid photograph showing Ole in all his potbellied glory, looking very full of himself; he was standing upright in one of the small fishing boats that were used to smuggle Jews across the straits to Sweden during the Second World War.

Ole had confided to the journalist that he suffered from unipolar affective disorder, or depression, as it used to be called. His bouts of illness had put intolerable stress on his family and often made him act irrationally. Ten years ago, several years after his sons had moved out, his wife left him because she felt unable to help. After the divorce, she went to live in Moscow with a new partner, a Danish diplomat eight years younger than herself. Ole moved into a small but elegant apartment on one of the narrow streets behind the Royal Theater, where he has lived ever since.

He added a professional touch to the interview by mentioning the DCIG:

"In the course of the last century, 40 million human beings were killed in wars. But in the course of the same century approximately 60 million human beings were killed in genocidal purges organized by their own governments. So, how important is it to understand and prevent genocide? Well, if we go by the number of those killed, it is the most important problem of our time."

There seemed to be no limit to what the interviewer from *Politiken* could pry out of his subject. Ole spoke freely about the way modern psychopharmacology had completely changed his life and added that he couldn't stop speculating about what his life might have been like if antidepressants had been available a couple of decades earlier.

He admitted that the pills made him impotent, but thought it a minor drawback compared to relief from the black months of depression. Besides, after a period of getting used to it, he was proud to say that he had taken on the challenge and turned it into something positive. His sex life had become enriched by a number of new "approaches" that, in his experience, pleased women enormously.

Anne-Lise read the interview over and over again. Afterward she discussed it with Henrik. She would never have thought of Ole as depressed. It struck her then how little she knew about her coworkers. Over the last few weeks, she has thought about it even more.

On the Monday after the interview was published, Iben was off and running with a lecture about psychopharmaceuticals, stressing that tiny chemical shifts can cause emotional imbalances and that no amount of therapy would help. This was one of her classic arguments, like her "human beings are like animals" speech.

Inevitably, everyone joked about the things Ole revealed.

When Ole turned up in the office a few days later, he was the center of attention, much more so than usual. Everyone praised him for being so open and honest. Iben spoke of one of her aunts, who had suffered badly from depression. Malene had a story about friends whose marriage had been destroyed by the illness. Ole in turn behaved as if he had expected their response. He took it for granted to such an extent that he glowed at their praise even before they offered it. His acknowledgment of any unspoken awkwardness put them at ease immediately.

Today, smiling broadly and with the folder stuck under his arm, Ole moves toward Paul and Gunnar as they come out of the library.

"Hello, Gunnar. Good to know that we've got something here you can use for *Development*."

Gunnar, who is a head taller than both the other men, looks radiant. The board membership is recognition he should have had long ago.

"Hi, Ole. Of course there's plenty here. But today I'm just looking the place over. Learning a bit more before accepting the offer." He turns to Paul and smiles. "I'm pretty likely to say yes, you know!"

Ole seems to be at a loss, so Gunnar continues: "Sorry, the offer to join your board . . . to replace Frederik Thorsteinsson."

Finally Ole speaks. "I see. Well, that's good news." He leaves it at that.

There is a short pause in the conversation, and suddenly everyone who knows Ole realizes that he had no idea about Paul's offer to Gunnar. Ole doesn't confront Paul, allowing him to retain some dignity. Instead he says that he must hurry off. Maybe Gunnar guesses the truth as well. The joy is wiped from his face, but Paul keeps his cool. "That was good. Now you've had a chance to say hello to our chairman as well. This office is always busy—lots of unpredictable traffic." He leads the way back to his office. "But you will find that out soon enough, once you get to know us all."

The men leave. Silence falls in the Winter Garden. Anne-Lise desperately wants to phone Henrik but the open door makes it impossible. Sometimes she wishes she could simply close the damned thing again, so that she could be herself for a few moments. No doubt they'd all complain if she did.

She can't concentrate on the Afghanistan reports. Instead she opens newly arrived boxes from the International Criminal Tribunal at The Hague and starts sorting the documents. She listens to the talk outside.

Iben is speaking: "Gunnar won't have anything to do with the DCIG now. He won't want to be mixed up in Paul's games."

Malene doesn't seem to agree. "I think he'll say yes to the board membership."

After a brief pause, she adds an explanation: "I mean, they must be discussing it right now."

"He won't do it!"

For once—maybe for the first time—Anne-Lise hears Iben becoming more and more shrill. Her voice has risen to a near scream.

"You can't think that about him!"

Malene sounds different, controlled and rather patronizing. "Iben, I don't know how long he's been waiting for a chance like this. You know he needs to get back in the running."

"But not at the expense of someone else, and in such an underhanded way. He's not like that!"

"You have to take into account that Gunnar has lived in Africa, where corruption is the order of the day."

"So what? I've lived in Africa too."

At this point they fall silent. This is their first open disagreement. It seems to have materialized out of nowhere. Maybe an outsider wouldn't see how furious they are with each other, but for Anne-Lise their fight is a revelation. She's gratified to see them finally direct their meanness at each other.

Somewhere in passing Malene manages to stick in a reference to her illness. Iben does not respond.

A little later, Malene's inquiry is almost gentle. "You know so much about him? Must be magic. I mean, you only spoke to him once, right? At Sophie's?"

Iben has regained control and now sounds self-assured. "We did have a very good talk that evening. Absolutely. Like Rasmus says, some of the best conversations are with people you meet only once."

Malene deflates a little. "I see. Now you have to drag Rasmus into this."

"Why, shouldn't I?"

After a few more minutes of this Iben decamps to the kitchen to cool down.

Anne-Lise stacks magazines on a shelf. She has a view of the Winter Garden from where she is standing.

Iben is back at her desk when at last the door to Paul's office opens. Gunnar steps out, and he isn't smiling. He walks quickly toward the front door and, as he opens it, turns around to face them all and politely says, "Goodbye."

Had it not been for Anne-Lise's feeling of exhaustion, his angry frown would have made her utterly delighted.

Soon after the front door slams behind Gunnar, Paul comes out of his office.

Iben asks him at once: "How did it go?"

"Oh, not so good. Such fucking bad luck that Ole turned up just then." Paul looks irritated. "Well, anyway, let's see how it pans out. Christ, all we're trying to do is save this Center. That's all."

He backs into his office and is about to close the door behind him. "I need to phone Ole."

They all exchange looks. So apparently Paul isn't feeling bad about anything or worried about how Ole will react. What does that mean in terms of the Center's future?

Anne-Lise looks around the Winter Garden, taking in every familiar and tedious detail: the decorous orderliness of the Post-it notes on Camilla's desk, the little plastic troll perched on Malene's desk, the broken spring on Iben's lamp.

In a few months everything might be different.

Ole can't have answered his phone, because Paul joins them again a minute later. He's holding a croissant, presumably left over from Gunnar's visit, and settles into the spare chair next to Malene's desk.

"Well, anyway, the show must go on. Listen to this. Yesterday

I had lunch with a friend of mine. He's friendly with someone on the Conservative Party's foreign policy working committee. That's how I know that in two months' time everyone who's anyone in Brussels will be debating the EU's relationship with Turkey, especially in the light of Turkey's repudiation of the Armenian genocide."

Does Paul intend to make them work as if nothing has happened?

Anne-Lise looks around. Aren't the others finding Paul's manner hard to take as well? She sees that everyone is pretending that it's all quite normal.

"It follows that the Armenians will be on the agenda of the Danish Parliament. Both our own media and the EU's will be falling over each other to run the story. That is why we must be the source for all the most vital and up-to-date information on the subject. In print and on the Internet. In English as well as Danish."

He turns to Iben. "This should be our top priority. Drop Chechnya for now. An issue packed with information on Turkey should be ready to go to the printers in a month's time. We must present the best data, the best background briefings and interviews—in Europe!" When Paul is fired up about something, his enthusiasm is impressive.

"Our Web site must offer the best set of links. When you get to work, keep thinking: What's hidden in this region that no one else has thought of? Think history! We need to be ten times smarter than the press."

He relaxes for a moment. "Over to you, Anne-Lise. Any books we should know about in order to write this up? Any magazines that have already featured the subject?"

This is new. Neither Paul nor any of the others has ever turned to her in this way, she thinks. This is it. I've waited a whole year and now it's happened. At last they're letting me in.

She starts to speak. "There's definitely . . ."

Then she dries up.

"I'm sure . . ." She can't think of anything else to say.

The others glance knowingly at one another. It's totally infuriating. But it's her own fault. She is the one who isn't behaving professionally.

Paul turns to Iben. "Iben, do you have any ideas?"

Of course she has. Iben smiles. There is no hint in her manner that only fifteen minutes ago Ole proved Paul to be deceitful.

"If we approach the foreign freelance journalists, the guys on the spot, we'll get information well beyond our usual range. And there is no problem about compiling an overview of the responses from each of the larger EU states to genocides in Turkey and elsewhere."

Anne-Lise doesn't take in the rest of what she says, because she is preoccupied by the image of Iben running into the library, holding an empty bottle of rum and hiding it in the cupboard. It is beyond Anne-Lise's understanding how this cool-headed, persuasive academic is the same as that manipulative, childish person.

Iben is reaching the end of her suggestions: ". . .would give our clients a better chance of informing themselves not only about the subject itself, but also about the basis for joint European decision making."

Paul swallows the last of his croissant as he listens to Iben. "Great! Well done, Iben! Anne-Lise, we need you to be in on this too."

Somewhere inside Anne-Lise a fuse has blown. The fantasy of Iben feeling the war criminal's knife against her throat in the harsh light of the stairway plays over and over. It is only through a haze that Anne-Lise sees Paul wiping crumbs off his mouth. His lips keep moving, talking to her.

"It's important that you don't just trace lots of articles and review papers but that you also work with Iben to select the most useful ones. You two will have to work as a team. What do you think?"

Iben's clawed hand grips the war criminal's leather jacket. She tugs violently at it. He doesn't react at all. His movements are so assured, so experienced. The big man has done this many times before.

Anne-Lise shakes herself. Is this what Yngve warned me against? she wonders. Am I burned out? Is that why I can't concentrate?

She looks quickly around the circle of her colleagues. Paul has seen it. Now he has to admit that the others were right all along. I'm incompetent. I'll be fired and they will have succeeded.

Her head clears enough to tune back in as Paul is finishing his speech.

"The themed issue of *Genocide News* will also serve to legitimize our existence in the eyes of the politicians. The thing is to be on the offensive. If we can produce the best printed and Web site info on this subject, it will be harder to close us down. So—Iben, Anne-Lise—next month you're working for the Center's survival as well."

Anne-Lise's head is spinning. Has he asked me to do something else? Yes, he must have. I've no idea what it is. Is it true that I'm impossible to work with? Yes, of course it's true.

. . .

After the meeting, Anne-Lise has a headache.

She stops in the library doorway and puts on her winter coat and scarf. The painkillers seem to have had no effect. Her eyes narrow in the Winter Garden's bright fluorescent light. Staring down at the floor, she speaks quietly. "I need to go home. I'm not feeling well. That's why I couldn't concentrate earlier on."

Paul is there too. Camilla smiles at Anne-Lise and makes sure that he sees it. She says in a loud voice that she had no idea that Anne-Lise wasn't focused, she seemed as attentive as ever.

Outside the December weather is cold and gray. Anne-Lise manages to drive along the motorway toward Holte without any problems, but after turning onto Vase Road she almost misses seeing a cyclist in the dim light. She slams on the brakes seconds before hitting his rear mudguard. Without looking around, she swerves the car until it comes to a halt perpendicular to the road. The car behind her does a grinding emergency stop. There's a small shudder as it hits her own car.

The driver leaps out. Together with the cyclist, they shout at her and bang their hands on her car. The driver says that his front bumper is dented and demands her telephone number and insurance details. Anne-Lise obliges.

She manages to park off the road. She and the driver exchange phone numbers. He asks her if she's in a bad way, implying that she's either drunk or high. She tells him that she has a headache. Once he has gone, she sits for a while in her car with her head in her hands.

Eventually she decides that driving is too risky. It's barely half a mile to her house, so she can leave the car where it is and walk the rest of the way.

Anne-Lise walks along a road lined with villas, close to a hedge with long bare branches that form a prickly canopy over her head. The pain is so bad that she can't bear looking up.

A woman's voice calls out. "Brigitte!"

After hearing the name called a couple more times, Anne-Lise glances around. There's only a woman she doesn't recognize, so Anne-Lise starts to walk again, but the woman catches up with her.

"I knew it was you! Camilla's friend! So nice to see you! Do you live near here?"

Anne-Lise cannot think what she is talking about. The woman notices her blank stare. "You don't remember me, do you? The choir. The Copenhagen Postal Choir."

"Oh!"

Anne-Lise feels dizzy. Her headache makes it hard to think. Even so, she knows that if this woman discovers that "Brigitte" is in fact Anne-Lise, Camilla will find out. And then her colleagues will not hesitate to stick the "mentally ill" label on her for good.

The woman is dressed expensively in a blue woolen coat that is almost full-length. The shade of her lipstick is far too bright for her age. Anne-Lise can't help but feel that this woman seems confused and a little disturbed.

"Brigitte, do you live around here too? We do need a choir here instead of in town."

Anne-Lise is only a hundred yards or so from her home. "I'm afraid I don't. I'm just visiting . . . an old friend of mine."

"Not Camilla? Or has she moved out here?" The woman obviously doesn't remember how Anne-Lise's evening at choir practice had ended up.

"No. Not Camilla." Anne-Lise moves out from under the hedge. She knows that she doesn't have the stamina to continue the lies for much longer.

The woman repeats herself. "I live nearby. And we do need a choir here."

Anne-Lise has no idea what she's thinking. "Yes, we do."

"Perhaps you live in the Holte area?"

"No. No, I don't."

The woman wipes her mouth, as if something were stuck there. "I was Camilla's friend once."

"Yes?"

"I was. I stopped seeing her when she started that relationship with him . . . you know, that ghastly man."

"Yes, I know. What was his name again?"

"Dragan."

"That's it. Dragan."

This woman won't stop talking. "Odd name. But he was a refugee. From Serbia, wasn't he?"

"Yes, that's right. Serbia." Anne-Lise forces herself to look at the woman. "It was Dragan . . . ? Dragan . . . ?"

"Dragan Jelisic, wasn't it?"

"That's it. Yes, Dragan Jelisic. Yes, yes. I thought he was really hard to get on with."

Anne-Lise excuses herself abruptly and hurries home.

The next best thing to being able to speak to Henrik would be to talk to no one for the rest of the day. She walks up the driveway, unlocks the door, and goes to lie down on the black sofa, with little hope of the migraine going away soon.

She thinks about Camilla and what it might mean that she once went out with a Serbian refugee and has kept it secret. But the pain in her head makes it impossible to think.

Only the revenge fantasies about Malene and Iben are alive in her mind, as if the images lead a life of their own. A young man in a red tracksuit hauls Malene's body into the undergrowth. The cracking sounds as branches break when her body is pushed down onto the woodland floor. Iben's pale neck, the echoing acoustics of the stairway, the veins that become visible in her neck and under the thin skin beneath her eyes. And in the shadow of the trees, the terror in Malene's eyes when she understands that she is being punished for having ruined another human being's life.

Anne-Lise is determined to think about something that makes her feel like a good person, one who is normal and healthy.

The blood is flowing from Malene's body and soaks into the ground.

She can't tell how much time has passed when she discovers that her head has cleared a little. She is still lying on the sofa, but now she feels able to phone Henrik to ask if he can pick up the children today.

Without moving the rest of her body, Anne-Lise reaches out and takes the phone off the hook.

She can hear voices. Has Henrik come home while she was resting? Since her car isn't parked outside he wouldn't know that she is home already.

It is Henrik. At first she can't grasp what he's talking about. The other voice belongs to Nils, Henrik's brother. She wants to say something but has an awkward moment trying to turn the phone around.

". . . as if I haven't told her that a hundred times already. To tell you the truth, it's all been very tough going."

Nils sounds sympathetic. "Henrik, I believe you."

A pause, but Anne-Lise is so baffled that she can't think of anything to say. What are they talking about?

"But have you thought of speaking to her doctor?" Nils adds.

"We saw him together. And we agreed afterward to do what he advised. It went well. But she's refusing to see him again."

Nils sounds more serious than Anne-Lise had ever thought possible.

"Henrik, you can always phone me. Remember that. And you can always drop by to talk to us, anytime. Stay the night if you like."

Henrik's voice is dull. "Well. Thanks. But there are the children."

Everything filters slowly through her headache.

She screams.

She runs.

She cannot endure the living room now but doesn't know where she wants to be. She's in the hall but can't stand it there either.

Henrik's footsteps are on the floor upstairs.

Anne-Lise runs around as a rush of thoughts overwhelms her.

Why should I have believed that they could bear to live with me? I'm bursting with evil thoughts. All the time! How I've kidded myself! They'll have to move out. No, I'll have to move. They can have the house. I'll go away.

Henrik catches up with her in the kitchen. She has collapsed. He shouts: "I didn't say anything bad about you! I didn't!"

But now the rapist in the red tracksuit leaps out from between the tall rushes. He strikes me. He gets out his small black razor. He holds it against my neck and forces me into the bushes.

Henrik shouts: "Anne-Lise, don't! Don't!"

I must hit my face as hard as I can. I deserve to be punished because I'm a horrible wife. I'm a bad, bad mother.

The rapist's pimpled face is grinning at me. I can see his small pointy teeth.

Henrik is holding my hand in his. I can hit myself with the other hand. He tries to grab it too, loses his balance, and falls over me. His belly on my head. His elbow between my legs.

He shouts: "Anne-Lise, stop it! Stop!"

He holds me around the chest. He has clamped my arms so I can't move them. He presses his cheek to mine. His mouth is close to my ear.

"Hit Malene! She's the one you should hit, not yourself. And Iben! Not yourself. Them!"

iben

chapter 34

Something glitters on the wall at the other end of the hut when it catches the feeble light of the oil lamp. It is the shell of a dead beetle. At first Iben thought the creature was alive, but time has passed since then.

For thirty-five hours or thereabouts she has been looking at the shiny black shell of the beetle. She has touched it and then tried to scrape it free from the wall's cementlike mixture of mud and cow shit.

Iben is the only one of the prisoners who hasn't thrown up. She is only suffering from the diarrhea and the fever. Under normal circumstances they would never have touched the water in the hut, which is kept in calabashes and old plastic bottles.

One of the hostage takers is called Omoro. He has come along to crouch by her several times, asked her if she is very ill, and prayed for her to get better soon.

Through the fever haze she has heard him argue again and again that it was essential to capture them. His tribe must chase the SEC out of the slums of Kibera.

No one contradicts him but still he repeats himself. "Look, we are not criminals. That is not what we are!" He sounds unhappy.

Iben can't make out his features in the darkness.

Omoro is the man with the machine gun who sat next to the driver in the SEC's white truck. Now that he is walking about she notes that he is tall and well built. The lower part of one of his ears is missing.

The fever makes it hard for Iben to think of a reply to his insistent questioning.

"Please, can you not see that we are right to do this?"

She watches the lamplight flicker across the blade of the knife that rests across his thighs. An awful stench fills the enclosed darkness of the hut. The hostage takers won't let their prisoners out except when they "have to go" in the muddy trench just outside the door and, with the sickness, all four hostages are having to go several times an hour. Roberto doesn't always get there in time. Once he didn't even get up off the mud floor—he was too weak—but tried to clean up after himself with a handful of straw. There are more flies and insects crawling about in his corner than anywhere else.

They all shiver, because the night is cold and they are wearing only their T-shirts and trousers. Soon the sun will rise and its furious heat will make the air in the hut even denser.

Iben is lying on her side. She is very still, but now and then she stretches out her index finger and pushes at the beetle, as if it were a button and pressing it could stop something from happening. She knows that the others are awake too, but none of them speaks.

She has never felt fear like this. It is not like a sudden shock, a passing state. The hostages could be taken out and shot in five minutes, or in ten, or in fifteen. Half a night has passed, but the shots might still be fired at any time. Nothing changes. There is no letup in the awareness of danger, only increasing fear.

The fever makes Iben limp and exhausted, but even so, she only manages to sleep for short breaks. The others have had a worse time of it, though. Yesterday she had to clear away what Roberto had thrown up when he was groggy with fever. It seems that the Luos regard her as stronger than the rest and now they turn to her when they need to address the captives.

What does this mean for her chances of survival?

Four other aid workers from another section of SEC had been taken not that long ago. The negotiations to free them had ground to a halt and the hostage takers decided to shoot one of their prisoners, and then one more, before they agreed to let the other two go.

Who from their group would the Luos pick first? Would it be the prisoner whom they regarded as the strongest?

But she couldn't have left Roberto to lie there in his own vomit. Something had to be done. They all have to keep drinking because they are losing fluid fast, but it has meant that their only alternative to thirst is to continually boost their gut infections.

She washed the vomit off his face and helped him out of the hut when he had to go out to the trench. Cathy and Mark, who are partners back home in Illinois, held each other close all through the first evening, whispering how much they loved each other. Now they lie apart without moving, staring into the air or at the wall. Iben isn't sure how ill they really are. Their stillness could be a strategy they've worked out to keep the guards from getting angry with them. On the other hand, it could be instinctive. Shock and fear might have paralyzed them, not illness.

Iben must have slept after all, because the next time she looks at the doorway, light glimmers around the edges of the cloth covering. The windowless hut is always filled with darkness. Only the spaces around the cloth allow air in. The shafts of sunlight hurt their eyes whenever someone pushes the cloth aside to get to the latrine.

They hear men walking past the hut. Many men.

Their movements seem calm and nobody is shouting, so presumably the huddle of dwellings is not under attack.

None of the prisoners has said out loud "When will they kill us?" or "Who will be killed first?"

From the beginning, Iben has thought that they will hold back from killing the hostages they like best, which means it's important to build a personal relationship with as many of them as quickly as possible. The trouble is, it is hard to seem congenial to a gang of hostage takers when you are weakened by diarrhea, fear, and lack of sleep.

The men out there are singing hymns.

The prisoners' eyes were covered when they were driven to this place, but on her trips to the trench Iben has calculated that their hut is part of a group housing about twenty people. All of them seem to be men. There are definitely no children.

Iben recognizes many of the hymns from her father's two LPs, sung by an English church choir. He played them every Christmas.

They sing harmonies in their deep voices, sounding surprisingly organized, as if a conductor were leading them. Iben decides to join in their singing. At the end of each hymn, she repeats one of the verses loudly. She wants to make sure that the men outside can hear her.

It works. She had felt certain religion would be their soft spot.

Now Odhiambo, one of the guards who wasn't present at the hostage taking in Nairobi, comes in to fetch her. They don't want to prevent a believer in Jesus from taking part in their service.

Iben hasn't eaten for more than twenty-four hours, but she doesn't feel hungry. Her fever is going down a little. She is strong enough to walk straight, even though her legs still feel shaky, and if she squints her eyes she can stand the piercing sunlight.

She is outside. A warm wind flutters in her filthy clothes. The smells are not like the stench of the hut. Here is light to see by. Here are colors and trees.

The men have formed a loose circle. These fifteen or so men should care a little more for her once this service is at an end. They start singing again.

Cross of Jesus, cross of sorrow,
Where the blood of Christ was shed,
Perfect Man on Thee did suffer,
Perfect God on Thee has bled!

O mysterious condescending!
O abandonment sublime!
Very God himself is bearing
All the sufferings of time!

Iben can smell the bush around them. It smells of dry, crumbling wood.

She steals a quick glance at the Luo men's weaponry. They all seem to have machine guns as well as knives and all within reach. They must fear an attack from outside the village, because they can't possibly think any of their prisoners has the strength to fight off the guards and run away into the wilderness?

An older man leads both the singing and the reading of lessons. He wears black nylon trousers and a chain around his neck with an amulet knot.

Perhaps illness has weakened Iben, because the sound of these grave, worshipful voices touches a raw nerve and the singing moves her deeply.

Frail children of dust, and feeble as frail,
In Thee do we trust, nor find Thee to fail.

Or is it because she has been forced to stay in the dark for so long? She manages to blink the tears away from her eyes. Something has gripped her, perhaps a combination of the singing, the words, and being able to look far into the distance.

Maybe these baobab trees are the last natural thing I will ever see, she thinks.

O come, Thou Rod of Jesse, free
Thine own from Satan's tyranny;
From depths of hell Thy people save,
And give them victory over the grave.
    Rejoice! Rejoice!
Emmanuel shall come to thee, O Israel.

The prayers between the hymns are more difficult to follow, but Iben mumbles her own words in Danish. Here, outside in the light, she can see how depressed the men are. No one knows how this will end. After all, two of their friends have already died.

The moment the service is finished, Iben begins to speak warmly about the injustices done to the Luo tribe. Thinking ahead, she had reasoned that this would be her best chance of being allowed to remain outside for a while. And, maybe, to get to talk to someone.

Five of the men gather around her. They all agree and work themselves up into quite a state. Having to take hostages to make their point troubles them. Iben asks Omoro directly if he was a friend of the driver who died yesterday.

Yes. She asks about the friendship.

The others are still listening. Iben tries to be genuinely amicable toward all of them. She feels herself turn white, but perhaps they won't notice. If the men know what's good for them they will pack her off to the hut again. Letting her get this far shows how inexperienced they are.

Iben remembers that the first time the Hamburg reservists were ordered to kill the inhabitants in a small Jewish town, each man in the battalion had to escort one Jew to the place of execution in the forest. Once there, he had to shoot the prisoner and then return to get another Jew. These minutes alone with the victim, walking along the forest path, maybe exchanging a few words, were enough to make it much harder to kill, and many had given up. Others were plagued by terrible nightmares afterward.

The battalion officers quickly learned to plan the killings differently. At later massacres, the soldiers never had a moment alone with the Jews. The rule was to make the victims seem like one large, anonymous horde. The German concentration camps were run on the same principle. Shaved, starved, and filthy, the prisoners were bound to be less unsettling to the German camp staff because the inmates seemed not quite human, and this made it that much easier for the camp guards to get on with their work.

Iben knows full well that the brief interlude outside the hut has made it that much harder for these men to kill her. For the moment she feels satisfied with herself.

A short, gray-haired man with scars across his cheeks comes up to her. He says something in Dhuluo that might well mean that she must go back into the hut. Odhiambo says something in reply. What he says includes the name "Phillip," and at the mention of this name the scarred man glances quickly at Iben to check if she has noticed.

Iben knows the importance of keeping her expression blank. Phillip is an unusual name for a Luo, which makes it easy to work out that they are discussing Dalmas Phillip. Although a fairly minor Luo chief, he is much talked about as one of the most active fighters against the Nubians. He is also said to have raped many Nubian women, despite being more than sixty years old.

Iben finds it impossible to completely hide her reaction. The man registers the instant shift in her face. It ruins everything. They can't let her live if she knows the identity of the leader of the whole hostage operation. Iben is suddenly aware of how tired and weak she is. She slips back into the darkness of the hut and, curling up in her place, she cries.

Cathy mumbles words of comfort, but Iben senses a new reserve among her three fellow prisoners. Of course they too can see that the risk of being first in line for execution increases for them the better Iben gets along with the men outside. But then, what can they say? Iben could easily argue that a good relationship with the guards could very well save all of them.

Cathy keeps repeating that they will make it, they will survive. It is the same mantra that Iben has been repeating to herself endlessly over the last two days.

Meanwhile Iben has worked out a twist to the scenario. If the Luos simply wanted to drive the SEC out of Kibera, shooting in the general direction of aid workers would have been quite enough. Considerations of employee security would be sufficient reason to make them close their local office. The Luos' risky decision to kidnap four SEC workers might mean that they want much more. The leaders of the operation may well be angling for a large ransom payment, for instance. And Omoro, Odhiambo, and the others would almost certainly know nothing about it. In any case, the SEC would never give in because the result would only lead to more kidnappings and, in the long term, cost more lives.

Iben hasn't told the others of her suspicions, but now she cannot resist telling them that the guards know that she recognized the name of Dalmas Phillip.

This silences Cathy.

Iben tries to rest on her patch of uneven hardened mud. She scratches at the beetle's back and tries to make herself dream about Denmark. A muscle in her stomach cramps. It isn't painful, but her entire abdomen twitches.

Only three years earlier she was an ordinary student. At this time of day she'd have been sitting at home reading. A smell comes back to her, the scent of printer's ink and coffee that filled the rooms of her female friends when they met to discuss books.

Cathy's voice pulls her out of her dream. "Look, SEC will have to get in touch with our embassies. And if the diplomats threaten to stop development aid, then all of a sudden Arap Moi and the police will be on our side. And then they'll find us." The oil lamp is close enough to Cathy to illuminate the imprint on her cheek of the rough floor. "And when the police come to free us and attack everyone out there, it won't matter if you know about Dalmas Phillip."

It's sweet of her to try to be reassuring. They both feel that to attack the Luos here in the bush is nearly impossible, but neither of them says so.

It has been a long time since they heard anything from Roberto. Iben asks him how he is doing.

His voice is almost gone. "Not too good."

Iben goes to sit next to him. The darkness and the heat do strange things to time. It must be the waiting that makes time move so terribly slowly. Eventually they fall asleep. Their dreams are chaotic.

Iben is in her own corner again when Omoro comes in with a kettle full of the dreadful tea that is available everywhere in Kenya. It is always served mixed with milk and lots of sugar. Most Kenyans love their tea, and it is a thoughtful gesture on Omoro's part. Iben and Cathy thank him profusely and drink, even though the oversweetened concoction somehow swells in the mouth after more than twenty-four hours of hunger.

A little later Omoro brings a dish of dry mush made from ground cornmeal. They eat with their fingers from the dish, doing their best to forget about those trips to the trench. It is a pity that Roberto has no appetite, but it's a relief that his soiled fingers aren't dipping into the food.

Omoro sits next to Iben and whispers in her ear: "If that old man with the scars wants to take you outside, you must try to get out of it."

Iben would like to ask Omoro what he has heard about Dalmas Phillip, but she stops herself. Instead, she tries to imitate the sound made by the Luos when they understand and accept something.

A fly insists on trying to land in her eye. Every time she waves it away it comes back. Mostly the native people don't seem to notice the flies, and Iben doesn't want to disturb the intimacy with Omoro by waving her arms about.

Omoro is silent for quite a while. Finally he speaks. "You saw Ojiji too."

"Yes." Iben knows that Omoro's friend, the dead driver, was called Ojiji.

Omoro sits quietly for a little longer, before saying the same thing again. "You saw him too."

"Yes. I did."

"You saw him in the truck with me."

"Yes." She tries to come across as gentle and friendly. The fly investigates her ear. "Omoro, it was dreadful."

Once more he seems not to know what to say.

Iben mumbles to show her sympathy. Even though she can glimpse his face in the darkness, she cannot distinguish the expression on it. She feels rather than sees that he is crying soundlessly. His breathing is irregular.

Then Omoro tells her about the choir to which many of the men here belong. With the support of a Christian aid organization, they went on tour around Kenya. In addition to the choir, Omoro and Ojiji also sang in a quartet together. Once, all four of them had traveled to Mombasa to sing at an event in the town council building. The mayor of Mombasa was in the audience. They saw the sea. At night they slept in a park, even though it was forbidden.

She has already heard many stories about Ojiji after the service this morning. All the men seem to feel that his death was the most important event of the last twenty-four hours. They mourn Ojiji in a different way from the other dead man, with more sorrow.

Omoro speaks again: "We should never have made him drive the truck."

"Omoro, you believed that it was more dangerous to sit next to the driver, holding a machine gun. No one could have known that it was the driver they . . ."

They talk together for a while longer, speaking into the darkness. Then someone outside the hut calls to Omoro.

When he has left, Cathy stirs. "You're good at this, Iben."

"Thank you. It's harder with the rest of them. I think Omoro and I get along well because we sat together in the truck's cab." Iben feels worn out. She lies down before speaking again. "It can only be to everyone's advantage if I manage to get along with at least some of them."

Cathy lies very still. She is silent.

Then, a long time later, Cathy whispers, half to herself: "I could try to do the same thing. Usually I'm better at it than this."

"Are you still feeling ill?"

"Yes. No. The diarrhea seems to have stopped, but I'm . . . Oh, maybe it's just because I'm so scared."

Roberto and Mark must be listening.

"What about the other two? How are you?"

Nobody responds, except Cathy. "Mark is having a very hard time. Mark?"

A deep sigh tells them that Mark has heard them. Cathy turns to put her hand on his forehead. He whispers "No" and she takes it away.

Iben lifts the small oil lamp and holds it close to Roberto's face. "Roberto, how are you?"

He looks bad. She asks again, but he says nothing.

She feels a cold sweat breaking over her skin. She strokes his cheek. No reaction. She becomes aware of her heart thumping as she bends over him and gently pulls back one of his eyelids. His eye has rolled up in its socket so that only the white part is visible.

"Roberto!"

Cathy's voice is hoarse. "What's going on?"

"I don't know. He's gone limp. He seems to be unconscious. Oh, God. He's fucking unconscious. What should we do?"

Iben moves to the doorway. She pulls the cloth back and speaks as authoritatively as she can manage. "We need a doctor!"

The guard outside the door is new to Iben. She keeps repeating her request. "We need a doctor! Quickly!"

After a while the guard calls another man. He calls out again and soon several men are milling about outside the hut.

The older man who conducted the service turns up. He goes inside to examine Roberto. When he comes out he looks worried and speaks at length in Dhuluo. Dalmas Phillip has joined the group now. The two older men discuss the situation.

Odhiambo explains to Iben: "Ochieng will help your friend."

So Ochieng is the name of the other old man.

"But Roberto needs a proper medical doctor!"

More discussion. It is quite clear that Dalmas Phillip is the man who makes the decisions. As he pronounces his judgment in Dhuluo, he watches Iben with calculated indifference.

Odhiambo interprets. "He says that your friend will not be seen by a white doctor. It is not possible. But Ochieng will help him."

Iben easily picks up that Odhiambo doesn't think much of Ochieng's skills.

Iben turns to Phillip. His smell fills her nose. "It is very important that the sick man is seen by someone who can give him penicillin. And some medicine for cholera."

She tries to catch Omoro's eyes, but can't see him in the group. Then she spots him. He has hurried away from the others and is walking swiftly toward a group of trees outside the perimeter of the site.

She has lost her chance. She is no longer the favorite prisoner. Now she is the one who has stuck her neck out farther than anyone else.

She meets Phillip's eyes.

He speaks English now. "It will be as I say." He falls silent.

There's something about him, about his eyes, scarred skin, and short gray hair. A fast sequence of the things he has done to Nubian women is running through Iben's head. There is nothing more she can say.

She discovers that she doesn't dare meet his eyes again or even look in his direction. Instead, she sinks down on her haunches and waits. She doesn't move until one of the men says something, which she assumes must mean that she is to go back inside the hut. She obeys, unable to fight for Roberto any longer.

Mark and Cathy have heard everything, but they don't say a word. Iben can't be sure if there's not a small part of them that's happy she's the one taking risks.

On her way to sit down she touches Roberto; he seems lifeless. Cathy has rolled him over on his side in the recovery position.

A little later Ochieng comes in. He makes Roberto inhale the vapor from a steaming brew of herbs but seems to know perfectly well that he can't cure him and that the treatment he is offering is only for show.

The night is cold and Iben shivers in her flimsy clothes. It's so pointless for Roberto to die this way, only a few yards away from where she is trying to find enough peace to sleep. I must try to do something to help Roberto. I must try. But she knows that she will not.

Cathy and Mark just lie there, quietly.

Should I move alongside Roberto to warm him with my body? She thinks of how she avoided sharing her warmth with him while he was still conscious. She felt awkward about sleeping with her arms around her sick boss. But now everything has changed—it is not feeling awkward that gives her pause, but the thought of waking up during the night embracing a corpse.

After a little while she moves over to Roberto and makes the others come too, so that all four of them can keep each other warm. She dreams that she's back in the office. Malene, Camilla, and Anne-Lise are hysterical because there is a trail of blood across the floor where someone has dragged a dead body. Somehow Iben knows that the blood is Ojiji's. Other things happen that she can't recall afterward.

The night feels so long that only remembering the dream proves to Iben that she has slept at all. When the gaps around the curtain become lighter, Roberto is still alive.

They are relieved, but Mark has become quite strange, almost aggressive. He moves clumsily back to his own space, bumps into the others, and pushes them hard enough for it to hurt. Iben doubts that he is ill but doesn't dare question him about it.

She can hear the men getting together for their morning service. Should she sing with them again? Should she go outside? If she goes outside, showing anger wouldn't make it harder for them to kill her. The choice is between staying in the hut to demonstrate how unforgivable she finds their treatment of Roberto, or joining them, which goes against every natural instinct.

She thinks to herself: If I do go out there it might persuade them to let a doctor see Roberto.

Iben sings along with the hymns and again adds her own solo verses. Then, for the first time in more than twenty-four hours, she hears Mark's voice. He speaks quietly.

"Shut up, why don't you."

"Mark!" Cathy sounds upset.

Mark continues: "Iben, you won't gain a thing by sucking up to them. Not these guys."

Iben carries on singing regardless. This morning they haven't sent a guard to bring her outside. She gets up and, keeping an eye on Mark, tries to get out through the door. The guard says something incomprehensible, shoves her back inside, and pulls the cloth back in place.

Iben has no tears left. All three lie still and listen.

Then Cathy speaks. "Iben. You're a survivor."

This time there are fewer voices in the choir. Some of the men must have left, setting out early in the morning. Iben manages to pick out seven voices.

No one comes in with a morning meal. Iben is dozing when she is alerted by the sound of running feet. Four shots ring out. Men are shouting in Swahili.

Then nothing.

All is quiet again.

Iben peeps through the doorway. Militiamen are walking from hut to hut, investigating each one. Their uniforms are different from anything Iben has seen before, neither police nor army. Someone must have dispatched a special unit to free the hostages. There are about twenty of them. She can't work out who is the leader until the soldiers haul two Luos from a hut and push them down on the ground in front of a man with glasses. He addresses the Luos and then turns away to give the soldiers new orders.

The guard in front of their hut has disappeared. Iben stands in the doorway and peeps around the cloth, but she doesn't go out. At the far end of the encampment eight unarmed Luos are standing in a line.

Now Cathy and Mark have joined Iben and stick their heads around the other side of the curtain.

Some of the soldiers march the Luos along to the biggest hut and shove them roughly inside. Omoro is among these eight men.

His eyes widen when he sees Iben. He calls to her: "Iben! Iben!"

Silence.

The leader of the special unit walks toward the hostages. He is smiling. "Everything in order?"

Iben finds it hard to look at him and hard to concentrate on what he's saying.

She hears gurgling noises from the big hut. Maybe she replies something to his question. Afterward she can't recall.

The soldiers come out again. They haven't been in there long. Their clothes and hands look clean but Iben notices the tops of their shoes where the leather is stained red.

None of the hostage takers emerges from the big hut.

chapter 35

ben cannot figure out what Paul is up to.

Just after Gunnar left the DCIG, Paul told her to drop her work on Chechnya for the next issue of *Genocide News* and concentrate on Turkey instead. She has no problem with that—except that Paul is also insisting that Anne-Lise is to be her co-editor.

That's simply too much. Anne-Lise has never done anything journalistic, never written or edited anything. She is sure to run to Paul every time she can't grasp one of Iben's decisions, with the likely result that she'll ruin Iben's relationship with Paul and, in the long run, with the board as well.

After the meeting Anne-Lise said she had a headache and went home—something to be grateful for at least. Now Iben has twenty-four hours to get over her annoyance before her new teammate returns.

Paul has closed the door to his office, so there's no need to escape to the kitchen for a discussion with Malene. Camilla can hear what they're saying, but it doesn't matter. Malene acts distant and uninterested. Obviously she is still displeased about Iben's voicing her opinion of Gunnar earlier.

After they chat for a while, Malene says she'll pop down and get something nice for their afternoon coffee. She takes her bag with her, which means that the trip is just a cover for her to talk to Gunnar on her cell phone.

When Malene returns, she has spoken with Gunnar, as predicted.

"He's really annoyed. During the meeting here, Gunnar realized that Paul didn't have a mandate from the board as he'd said he did. It didn't take long for Gunnar to figure out that Paul was trying to use him in some internal power struggle." Malene looks at Iben, not acknowledging that she was right about Gunnar after all. "He turned down Paul's offer of a seat on the board."

When Iben gets home that evening she tries not to think about the project with Anne-Lise. She checks her e-mail and answering machine, and wonders for the umpteenth time if it would be right to phone Gunnar.

She slices a handful of vegetables, pours olive oil on top, and adds some spices. After microwaving the mixture she eats it with pieces of Rye-Krisp while watching TV. She could say that she wants to hear Gunnar's thoughts on the meeting today. She's just a dedicated employee—nothing wrong with that, is there? That's what she could tell Malene, if she asks her.

Standing next to the heavy wine-colored armchair she inherited from her grandmother, she dials his number. He answers the phone.

"Gunnar, I hope this isn't a bad time?"

"No. Not at all. It's good to hear from you."

But Iben doesn't learn much about the meeting because Gunnar says that he's in a hurry, he's on his way out.

Iben feels suddenly deflated. But then she thinks it's just as well to know that he's not interested in her. No need for any more arguments with Malene.

Gunnar explains that he has promised an old friend to go to a showing of the friend's documentary about a development project in Uganda. The filmmaker is going to give a brief talk about his work and afterward the audience will join in a debate about both the film and the project. Would Iben like to come along?

The answer seems to stick in her throat. One of her hands is scratching at the back of the old armchair, her body tense. She feels a familiar shiver, almost like fear. She covers the mouthpiece and breathes a huge sigh. No criminal this time, but she looks around her all the same.

They agree to meet in half an hour at the Nørrebro Street office of the development organization Ibis. When Iben arrives, Gunnar is waiting for her. He looks happy to see her and introduces her to his friend.

The noise of the crowd milling around in the lecture theater is quite different from the earnest atmosphere of the DCIG. The aid activists, and the audience in general, are colorfully dressed, talk in loud voices, laugh, and call out greetings to people they last met on field projects abroad. Almost everyone is tanned.

A few older men wander about, working the crowd. Like Gunnar, these men seem to have many friends and acquaintances in the audience, the majority of whom are young, female, and often strikingly attractive. Three women chatting near a window catch sight of Gunnar and wave. He looks delighted and waves back.

Iben keeps wondering how many of these people have slept with each other. In a hut in Zimbabwe, for instance, or in a shack in El Salvador. Or in someone's apartment, late one night after a party. It follows that some of them might have been with Gunnar. She can't let go of that thought either. She regrets putting on a prim cream-colored blouse, which had seemed so perfect. Still, she can't think what else she might have chosen to wear.

Gunnar introduces her to another "old friend" even though she looks quite young. The woman leans into Gunnar as they talk. Iben can't figure out why this girl's turquoise dress is somehow provocative, given that it is high-necked and not at all figure hugging.

Fortunately Iben hits it off with many of the people she meets. They still remember her from the media coverage six months ago—a Kenyan hostage crisis is especially likely to stick in the minds of Africa activists, of course.

Gunnar has reserved two good seats in the middle of the theater. After a very brief lecture, the film starts up.

Iben and Gunnar are sitting side by side in the dark on the hard wooden seats. They do not touch. Iben leaves one hand resting on her thigh. It's the hand closest to him, only a couple of inches away. Her hand senses the warmth of his body, but neither of them moves. Even the air between them is still.

When the film ends, four people carrying glasses of water and writing pads sit down at a couple of tables at one end of the room. They are introduced as "the panel this evening." Twice they refer questions to Gunnar, saying, "Gunnar, you know all about this issue." Gunnar's answers are lucid and well delivered. He doesn't exploit the opportunity and avoids sounding overly academic. He comes across so well that Iben half suspects that he had it in mind when he invited her here. It makes her happy to think her opinion might matter to him.

Afterward, in the throng of people, Gunnar invites her to the nearby Café Sebastopol. Outside in the night air Iben and Gunnar walk, pushing their bicycles along as they chat about the film. Once inside the café Iben tries to be relaxed but also to maintain a slight distance. Strictly speaking, this isn't a date, she tells herself, and she is definitely not trying to seduce her best friend's would-be lover.

They talk a little about Gunnar's meeting with Paul that morning. When Gunnar and Paul said goodbye, Paul put his left hand over their clasped hands and told him that he would keep Gunnar "informed whenever the situation opened up." Iben and Gunnar have a good laugh about this.

They talk about literature too. Gunnar subscribes to *Granta*. It turns out that they've both read Botho Strauss. Gunnar smiles at a quote that Iben happens to recall: "The silent man, who was sitting at the cleared table in the feeble light of the projector, leaned on his forearms with his body suspended like a heavy, wet dress from between his shoulders."

Gunnar has read several of her articles in *Genocide News* and they talk for a while about the high-ranking Nazis who simulated mental illness in the run-up to the Nuremberg trials. Gunnar tells a story about Karl Dönitz, first commander of the German submarine fleet, later commander in chief of the entire navy and Hitler's successor for the final period of the war. Dönitz used to wander around in prison with his head hung low, making a kind of engine noise. When asked what he was doing, he answered that he was a submarine. It didn't wash, of course. No one was taken in by his performance as a lunatic. They both laugh at the image of the commander rumbling around in the prison yard. Gunnar's hand rests on the table very close to Iben's.

At her front door, Iben fumbles with her bicycle keys. When she tries to shift the bicycle sideways, a pedal hits the knife fastened to her leg. For the first time, it strikes her that she has forgotten about her fear of being ambushed by a professional killer.

Hurriedly she looks up and down the dark road. Far away a broad-shouldered man is standing, looking in her direction.

As she runs up the stairs, thoughts of Gunnar still absorb her. Malene can't simply keep him for herself. She can't have him on standby, just in case Rasmus packs his bags one day. He's too old for Malene; she said so herself. But it would be catastrophic for Iben to have to work so closely with Malene if they were no longer great friends.

She can't fall asleep right away. So she switches on the television in her bedroom and piles up cushions to lean against in bed. Then she goes to the kitchen for marshmallows and a few spoonfuls of ice cream.

Just as she is coming back to the bedroom the phone rings. She runs to the living room and notices that she has several messages on the machine.

Malene is on the phone. "Where have you been? I've been calling you all evening!" She is obviously very upset.

Out of habit, Iben thinks it must be Malene's arthritis, only Malene doesn't sound as subdued as she usually does during an attack. Then it hits her. Iben has an eerie feeling that she knows what Malene is about to say.

"Rasmus has left!" Malene is screaming.

"What?"

"Moved out! He's moved out!"

"Oh, no . . . but where to? Why . . . ?"

Somehow Iben had known. It fits too well. Of all evenings, it had to be this one.

Without thinking, Iben hurls her bowl of ice cream at the nearest bookshelf. Fragments of the bowl shatter across the floor and some of the ice cream splashes onto the screen of the television.

Malene is talking. She says that Rasmus told her earlier this evening that for the last six weeks he has been having an affair. Someone who works as a bartender in Bopa.

"So I threw him out!"

"You threw him out?"

"I didn't want him in my apartment for a second longer!"

Iben knows she has to support her friend, reassure her that she has done the right thing, comfort her by telling her how good it is to have the self-assurance to act on your feelings. But somehow she can't make herself begin.

"And you weren't in, Iben."

"No . . ."

Iben doesn't explain. She holds the receiver to her ear and, with the telephone cord trailing like the lead of a tethered animal, edges over to the bookshelf, where some marshmallows lie among the melting remains of the ice cream. She puts one in her mouth. Then she grabs two more and puts them in her mouth as well.

Malene keeps talking. "So I got rid of him. But I don't want to be here—I can't bear even to look at the apartment." There is a short pause. "Iben, can I stay with you?"

"Malene, why don't you come here?" Iben asks, as if she hadn't heard Malene's question.

When the call is finished, Iben goes to the kitchen, puts the kettle on, and finds Malene's favorite tea. She takes some cleaning fluid out of the cupboard so she can wipe the ice cream off her books and sweep up the bits of broken bowl. And she'd better change back into her work clothes as well.

But she doesn't. On the way back to the bedroom, she collapses on the sofa and weeps, the side of her face pressed against the unyielding arm.

The intercom buzzes. Iben jumps up and runs to release the downstairs lock.

Next she must change her clothes and wipe off her smeared makeup. She runs into the bedroom and pulls her blouse off. No time to change her trousers. The bathroom next. She puts cleansing cream on her face.

When Malene comes in, Iben's face is still covered with cream. "Malene! I'm in here!"

Malene joins her in the bathroom. She seems emotionally drained, but gives Iben a hug. "Iben, I'm so glad to see you . . . you're a true friend."

By the time they sit together on the sofa with their tea, Iben has pulled herself together. She has reminded herself that she isn't the one who has just lost the man she has loved for the last three years. She needs to be there for Malene.

She remembers her one and only experience of breaking up after a long affair. The man was one of her literature teachers at university and almost eleven years older. They spent amazing amounts of time together, especially considering that he not only was regarded as a hardworking academic but also had a live-in partner.

He told Iben practically from the start that he wanted to get out of his relationship, but then the day came when he told her that his partner was pregnant. He didn't seem to feel that this needed to affect what he and Iben had together, but she had put an end to it there and then. It took her more than a year to get over it.

Malene doesn't touch her tea, but talks on in a loud, trembling voice. "And I said to him it was pointless. Shit, she's only twenty-one. What good is that for him? Hanging out with a twenty-one-year-old barmaid. But he said they get along so well."

She stares up at the ceiling, tears streaming across her temples. "*So well*—because she has done film studies for six months. Oh, yes. They can discuss movies. Fucking movies! Must be great to have something to talk about after screwing."

"Oh, Malene!"

"And I asked him if she was healthy. He wouldn't say and insisted, but insisted, that health had nothing to do with anything. Then I said, 'But you can't know for sure, can you? There might be something wrong with her. Like, maybe she's got AIDS. Or MS. Or the Big C. Anything. You can't be sure. You didn't recognize that I was ill, not when you met me. Not when you first said you loved me.' "

Malene leans against Iben, who holds her close and tries to say all the right things even though she knows it won't make a difference. Malene's mascara has run and some of it has rubbed off on her white shirt. She blows her nose now and then but has given up drying her tears. Her voice has become hoarse and she keeps repeating herself.

"We were having such a good evening too. We ate, he seemed happy, and we were relaxing together. And then he just suddenly came out with it. There was something 'he had to tell me, it was only right.' And then it all snowballed from there. What did he imagine? I mean, what did he think would happen when he told me something like that?"

"I don't know."

"Did he think that I'd listen to his story and that would be that? Did he think we would just continue as before?"

Iben thinks back to the moment when she turned to her teacher and told him it was all over between them. They were sitting on a stony beach at the far end of Amager Island. The beach was one of their special places, somewhere no one they knew would ever come. He protested, but it was as if a repairman had told him to buy a new fridge. "Iben, are you sure? And there's absolutely nothing I can say to change your mind? Well, okay. I guess that's it." He had listened to Iben, agreed, and then gone home.

Iben stopped going to his classes. It was tricky to find enough courses to fill the days when he was not in the department. He never contacted her again, but she couldn't avoid hearing on the student grapevine that he had married and had a little boy.

Iben looks around. Her living room strikes her again as ugly, almost repulsive. She hates her old furniture and unframed posters. Hates the cold overhead light.

Later, when Malene is crying a little less, Iben gets up and goes to the kitchen. She makes a fresh pot of tea and puts four frozen rolls into the microwave. While they thaw, she slices cheese for the two of them.

From now on Iben will look after Malene when she has her arthritis attacks. There is no one else, unless a smart new admirer carries Malene off. And if the illness worsens and the admirers vanish, Iben will be on duty for a long time ahead.

Still fragile, Malene has kicked off her shoes and put her stockinged feet up, warming her toes under Iben's thigh. She can't stop tormenting herself.

"I wonder what he's doing now? They must be so pleased. I bet they've been fucking ever since he turned up at her door."

"Malene, don't you think—"

"I bet he's in her arms now. They're naked. And I bet she's happy too because he's taken the plunge."

Very late that night, Iben finally brings a cloth, a bucket of water, and a roll of paper towels to the bookshelf. She starts cleaning up the ice cream.

Malene sits up. "What are you doing?"

"Something made me fling my ice cream at the bookcase when you phoned this evening."

They exchange faint, miserable smiles.

ben is on her way upstairs to Malene's apartment. It's in an old building with stained-glass windows on each landing that run from floor to ceiling, and over time, some of the panes have fallen out of their lead calms and the property manager has replaced them with cheap plain glass. Iben has always thought the stairway rather beautiful, even though the blank fields of glass break up the images.

It is late on Saturday morning. Rasmus has said he will come to collect his belongings but Malene doesn't want to be there. She is holed up in Iben's apartment, so Iben has promised to go and keep an eye on him instead. Rasmus mustn't be allowed to carry off the wrong things or take more than he's entitled to. Iben has a pretty good idea of what belongs to whom, and besides, she can always phone Malene if in doubt.

It will be strange to meet Rasmus now that their relationship has changed. Iben knows that she should be angry with him, but she can't force herself.

Only four days have passed since Malene thought Rasmus loved her. Malene has since tried to convince him that it's all been a mistake, but now he's certain that it's "the right thing" to stay with his new girlfriend.

Malene speaks about the way he shut her out completely. It

was done in a day. He decided to be cold toward her and, right away, he was. Rasmus's behavior toward Malene has made Iben question whether men's feelings are as strong as women's. There's no way of telling. But there is one major difference: men seem to be able to postpone their emotional reactions until it suits them. Even men you think you know well can turn their back on you in an instant, acting more distant than you ever thought possible.

The apartment is on the fifth floor, and when Iben finally reaches the landing she can hear Rasmus rummaging around inside. She is just about to press the doorbell when she realizes that Rasmus doesn't live here anymore. This is Malene's place and by now Iben, the owner's best friend, has more right to be here than he has. She's certain that Malene would prefer her to make a point of this and considers using her key, but then she decides against it and presses the doorbell.

Rasmus lets her in. His hair is all over the place. He must have run his fingers through it several times.

She has never heard him speak in such a serious tone. "Iben! We have to talk. Come inside and have a seat. There, on the sofa."

She follows him into the living room. Many items are already in boxes: a few small pictures, some books and CDs. The music center and the loudspeakers are dismantled and about to be packed, together with the large TV and the folding dining table chairs.

"Would you like coffee? Or something?"

"Rasmus, I'm not sure . . . Maybe we shouldn't . . . I think Malene . . ."

She settles down all the same. She has no idea what he wants to tell her.

Characteristically, he begins to talk about a computer program he's written. Apparently he's devised a long and complex piece of spyware, which he had intended to use in order to trace the sender of the e-mails.

What is he really saying? Is this technical stuff meant to prove how much Malene meant to him, even though he's been unfaithful to her? Whatever the message, he spends such a long time on the details of the programming that her mind begins to wander.

Later on she helps him take his things down to the white van he has borrowed. She does several rounds with bags of clothes, CDs, and boxes full of bits and pieces. She has always liked Rasmus. He's a nice guy; simply not the right one for Malene. His parents, who live in Svendborg, are schoolteachers with a shared enthusiasm for sailing. The pair seem to confirm the argument that people with a background in education are best equipped to bring up happy, stable children.

Malene and Rasmus have given a few parties that their parents have attended, and Iben has never met anyone who didn't immediately warm to Rasmus's mom and dad. Malene used to look forward to the summer holidays in Svendborg, unlike the few days she would spend with her own family.

While Iben helps Rasmus, she tries to think of something pleasant to say to him now that they aren't likely to meet again. She would like to say that she's pleased to have gotten to know him and that he was very good for Malene . . . for a time. Maybe she ought to say that she wishes him well, but that somehow seems disloyal. On her way back upstairs, Iben decides to keep the good wishes until Rasmus is all packed and ready to drive off.

She clutches an armful of posters and calls back to him from the landing: "I'm taking these down now!"

"Iben, wait! Just a moment!"

She goes back in.

"The heavy things should go in first. I'll start with the table."

"Let me help."

"Don't worry. It's actually easier to do it by myself." He walks out, rather unsteadily, carrying the large birch-wood table.

Iben looks around to see if there's anything useful for her to do. She goes to put away some of Malene's glasses that are on the drying rack. While she's at it, she decides to wash up some of the dishes that are still on the kitchen table.

Is that Rasmus's voice she hears from the stairs? Who's he talking to? Isn't that a woman's voice? She turns the water off before the basin has filled.

Is it Malene? For a second, Iben feels sure she heard Malene's voice. What's going on? What does Malene want?

No more voices. She must have been mistaken. Maybe it wasn't Malene. And it's unlikely to have been Rasmus's new girlfriend. Maybe just a neighbor?

Iben stops and listens. Everything is quiet now. She walks into the short corridor outside the kitchen. In the silence of the stairway she hears Rasmus move with heavy steps. Then, suddenly, there is an echoing crash and a scream.

She runs along the hallway and out onto the empty landing.

"Rasmus? . . . Malene? Rasmus?"

Nothing.

The next landing. Nothing.

Another empty flight of stairs and then she sees it.

A large hole has opened up in the wall. At first she can't make herself go any closer. She stands a few steps above the landing, staring at the emptiness that is as tall as a man. It used to be a mosaic of stained glass.

She inches closer. She can see people moving around in the courtyard below and talking in frightened voices. Somebody screams. Iben doesn't have the courage to look at what might be down there. Instead she takes another couple of quick steps forward and discovers at the last moment that the step in front of the broken window is wet. She grabs the handrail with both hands. Her body slips sideways and lands heavily. Trying to get up, she puts one hand down on the step, only to find that her palm slides on the slippery surface. She sniffs at her sticky hand. Someone has poured oil on the floor.

Iben manages to get up and maneuver around the fluid. She runs down into the street and looks around. Rasmus isn't there. And Malene isn't there either.

The door to the courtyard behind the building is locked. Iben fumbles in her pocket to find the keys. It takes so long. At last she gets the door open. She runs through the dark passage.

The yard is divided down the middle by a wire fence, and Rasmus is hanging across it, his body bent double. Iben had no idea a human body could break in the middle like that. One of the vertical steel fencing posts protrudes through his back.

Despite all the blood, Iben can see that Rasmus's face has slammed into the profiled steel. It is crushed. The impact of his body has made the wire fence sag, but its sharp edge has sliced open his abdomen.

Iben backs away, knocking into something on the pavement, and sits back without wanting to. She looks at what she's sitting on. It's a piece of Rasmus and Malene's dining table. It is quite clean and unused, as if the last few days haven't happened, as if Rasmus and Malene and Iben might still gather around it, in this small yard.

Over by the wall a man is speaking on his cell phone. The police will arrive soon. A woman is pushing against a door to the kitchen stairs. She must be trying to keep children away from the yard.

Iben stares at the table fragment. Not long ago it was cluttered with plates, bottles of wine, flowers. She hears the voices around the table. "Pass me the rice, would you? Rasmus, I met Ole from film studies in the bus. You won't believe what happened in the Center today . . ."

A dark knot in the light wood stares back at her, like an eye.

She tries to get up.

was standing on the staircase and called out to Rasmus that I was on my way down with the posters. It was sheer chance that Rasmus asked me to wait until later. He wanted to take large things like the table down first."

"Then what happened?"

"If someone had been waiting in the stairway to pour oil on the steps, that person would probably have assumed that I would be the first one to come down."

"I see. What happened instead?"

Iben breathes in quickly. "Look, where did the rail go? There's usually a handrail across the window. A long strip of brown railing. When was it taken away? It can't be a coincidence—there've been several strange things happening over the last few months . . . anyway, it can't have been an accident. Someone is after me. Or after Malene. It's her apartment. Someone might have thought she was the one on her way down."

Iben and a woman police officer are sitting together in one of three police cars lined up in front of the door to Malene's building. Detectives are cordoning off the stairs and the courtyard and interviewing the neighbors to find out if they saw anything.

"Very well, Iben. Now, I'd like you to take me through what happened again, step by step."

Iben describes how she offered to help Rasmus with the table and how, when he said he'd manage on his own, she went to the kitchen to clear away some dirty dishes. Then the next thing she heard was a crash and a scream. She ran downstairs at once, then slipped and almost shot out through the broken window herself.

Iben also tells the officer about Anne-Lise and her suspicions that she might have some kind of personality disorder. She mentions Anne-Lise's trick of hiding blood in her own office and pouring it all over herself, and her swapping Malene's medication. She knows that Anne-Lise is capable of doing all sorts of things. She might very well have removed the railing and poured oil on the steps.

Iben gasps for air again. She feels she is presenting essential information. It might just lead to Anne-Lise's arrest.

The detective, who is listening quietly, breaks her silence. "We're called out to many fatal accidents. We can't assume that one of the victim's nearest and dearest is a murderer every time someone falls off scaffolding or hits a high-voltage cable."

"No, of course not. But in this case a section of handrail is missing."

"Sections are missing from many stairways in old buildings in central Copenhagen. Accident investigation is my job. Sometimes accidents are the outcome of the most terrible coincidences. But, ninety-nine times out of a hundred, an accident is an accident. It's not like TV . . ."

"Of course I know that. It's just that—"

The detective interrupts her: "I understand your problems with the woman at work—I'm sure it makes sharing an office with her very uncomfortable. But, to put it plainly, it's not relevant to the police investigation."

"But someone took the handrail away and poured the oil on the step!"

Iben might as well not have bothered.

"My colleagues are looking into it right now. Some are upstairs taking photographs. They'll find whatever was left or poured on the stairs and who could have done it."

A male police officer knocks on the car window. He has come to tell them that there was no one else on the stairs at the time. No one saw Rasmus fall.

When he has left, the detective turns to Iben. "Here's my card. Contact me if anything new occurs to you." Her tone of voice suggests that she doesn't mean it.

The name on the card is Dorte Jørgensen. Iben knows that she must make herself sound more logical in order to make Dorte Jørgensen take her seriously.

"I understand that you don't believe me, but honestly, I'm not normally a nervous person. A couple of months ago, before everything I told you about started to happen, I was as calm as you are now."

Dorte smiles at Iben, but Iben can see she's distracted.

Iben raises her voice. "I don't like the idea of going home on my own. Someone has probably just tried to kill me. What will stop her from trying again? Or trying to kill Malene?"

Dorte doesn't respond.

"You must do something about it," Iben goes on.

Dorte gets out, walks around the car, and opens the door for Iben. She climbs out gingerly. Her coccyx and one of her hands are still sore after her fall.

Earlier, while she was carrying things down to the van, she felt warm. After the accident, she hadn't noticed how cold it had become. When Dorte speaks, her breath condenses into little clouds in the chilly air.

"What you have is a typical stress reaction. It's quite natural after an experience like this. Spend the rest of the day with some close friends and take a couple of days off work. Talk to someone about it. And if you still feel on edge you can get free counseling from a trained psychologist because you knew the victim and saw the consequences of the accident firsthand."

Iben thinks that now, for the first time, there's a trace of warmth in this woman's officious way of talking.

"I'd like to help you, but I can't. I'm not trained for it. It's not my job."

Iben walks a few paces behind Dorte toward the door to the yard. Maybe she should give in and accept the opinion of the professionals, but something inside her insists that they're mistaken. What has happened is simply too terrible to be an accident.

She must phone Malene to warn her. Anne-Lise might be on her way to Iben's apartment right now.

She tries to imagine the two police officers telling Malene that Rasmus is dead. God knows how she will react after having slammed Rasmus for several days. Shouldn't Iben get home as soon as possible? Or would Malene prefer to be alone?

Iben knows that she must go back up to Malene's to fetch her jacket and her bag with her cell phone, wallet, and bicycle keys. But first she has to see the yard once more.

Rasmus's body is covered with a pale gray tarpaulin. It looks like a big sack, suspended only by the thin wire netting. The area around it is cordoned off with red and white tape.

The police photographer has left. An officer is keeping an eye on the place, his hands firmly clasped behind his back. It's quiet. Are there faint noises coming from the neighboring apartments? Or is her hearing overly sensitive? Like the moment in Malene's kitchen—did she actually hear the voices?

She moves closer to Rasmus's covered body and looks up at the broken window in the dirty brick wall rising high above her. He landed far away from the wall. He must have slid down the stairs at some speed.

That's how he was. Always in a rush.

When her father died it was cold too. She paced back and forth in the hospital parking lot, across its hard asphalt. She looks at the surface on which she stands now. It's not black—more like a pale gray.

Police tape cordons off the landing where Rasmus fell and the flight of stairs to Malene's apartment. Another officer tells Iben to go back down and then up the back stairs. However, when she explains who she is, he lets her through.

There are no signs of the police having been in the apartment. Everything looks the same as before. Iben uses the telephone to call Malene.

"They've told you, haven't they?"

"Yes." Malene's voice is composed, low, and without any trace of emotion.

After waiting for her to say something more, Iben breaks the silence. "Shall I come home now?"

"How did it happen?"

"Didn't they tell you?"

"Yes. But weren't you there?"

Iben tries to describe exactly how it was. Then she warns Malene about Anne-Lise, realizing she'd rather not go home at all.

When they finish, Iben picks up her bag and her jacket and walks into Malene and Rasmus's living room. She stands there for a moment. There is not a sound to be heard. She walks into the bedroom. It too is quiet. Then she visits every room in the apartment to memorize them. Back in the living room, she calls out in a low voice, "Rasmus, I'm taking the posters down now."

Silence. She slams the kitchen door behind her and takes the narrow stairs back down. Dorte Jørgensen is still in the yard.

"There's something I didn't tell you earlier."

Dorte looks uninterested.

"Something factual."

Dorte turns away from the policeman she was talking to.

"Okay. Let's deal with this in the car."

They go to sit in the police car. Iben explains that she thought she heard a woman's voice. And that it could have been Anne-Lise's.

Dorte pulls out her notebook. "Why didn't you tell me that before?"

"I wasn't sure. It was very faint. A woman's voice, I think."

"Are you sure that it was Anne-Lise's voice?"

"No, I'm not. As I said, I can't be sure."

"It could have been, say, Malene's voice?"

"Why do you ask that?"

"The most common murderer by far is the spouse or partner."

"But I know Malene. She'd never kill anyone."

Dorte looks at her.

Iben repeats herself. "I'm certain she'd never think of doing something like that. She wouldn't. Never."

"Take it easy, Iben. I believe you. You're the one who brought up the idea of murder, not me." Dorte's voice drones on monotonously, as if everything she is saying is routine.

"If you're sticking to this statement, then I have to pursue it. The apartment will be off-limits for quite some time. My superior will call Malene and your colleague to ask them where they were at the time of the accident and if they can prove it."

"Will Malene be questioned?"

"Yes. And if the case proceeds I shall have to call you in to make a formal statement, which you will be asked to sign. Are you aware of all this?"

"Yes. I am."

Dorte might have noticed Iben's hesitation. "You also know that perjury carries a prison sentence?"

"But I haven't said that I know for sure that Anne-Lise was there. All I've said is that I heard a woman's voice. Maybe. And that maybe it was her voice."

The look on Dorte's face gets to Iben. Iben is aware that she's acting in a way that—coming from someone else, and at some other time—would annoy her more than anyone.

Dorte speaks calmly: "Now, you must think carefully about what you did and didn't hear. Take your time." She waits, rolling her pen between thumb and index finger.

"I've said before . . . I'm not absolutely sure."

Dorte puts her notebook away. "Tell you what. Just for now, I won't make this a priority."

She straightens up and starts to open the car door. It's time for Iben to get out of the car again.

Rasmus's parents have arranged for the funeral to take place in six days. Most of his belongings are already packed, which makes things easier. His parents pay off his student loans and Malene takes over what he owes on his Illum credit card. She is allowed to keep the pieces of furniture she and Rasmus bought together. Legally his parents and his brother have a right to claim all Rasmus's possessions, but they let Malene hold on to what she wants from their life together.

No one mentions Rasmus's new girlfriend.

Others are also alert to Malene's needs. Iben talks to her on the phone every night and goes to see her often. She also helps Malene with the many practical issues that she must now deal with. It is her chance to prove to Malene that she is a loyal and reliable friend. Ever since Kenya, when she failed to reply to Malene's phone calls and e-mails, Iben has been unable to convince Malene that she would never abandon her.

Iben finds grief has made Malene less attractive. She has lost weight, maybe more than five pounds, and because she was already so thin, her sharpened features make her look older. Not that it seems to matter to men. Malene still turns as many heads as ever when she walks down the street with Iben at her side.

Gunnar offers to help Malene as well. Before he heard about Rasmus's death Gunnar had left a message on Iben's answering machine: "Hi. This is Gunnar. Good to see you the other night. It was a terrific evening . . ." A pause. When Iben played back his message for the third time, she decided he must have worked out what to say, only to change his mind and improvise something else instead. His voice sounded a little flat at first, as if he had rehearsed what he was saying. "I'm sitting here reading an article in the *Guardian* that reminded me of what you said about the lack of political awareness in American literature. It's an interesting article, but not as interesting as what you said."

During this last sentence his tone became a little livelier. When Iben listened for the last time, she thought it sounded as if he was faintly amused.

"Did you notice there's a poetry reading by Inger Christensen this Thursday? She'll read some of her early work. Would you like to go? Anyway, you know my number."

Iben can't call Gunnar now. She comforts herself by switching off the machine so that new messages won't record over his voice.

It is barely a week after the funeral when Iben and Malene set out for IKEA to look for a new dining table. Even though it's a weekday and they have left the DCIG early, the huge furniture halls are crowded with happy-looking young couples, talking loudly about their future. Many of the women are pregnant and just as many of the men are carrying babies in carriers fastened around their bellies.

Malene doesn't cry, but she is very tense. She examines one of the cheapest tables. It will be some time before she can afford good furniture again. The trouble is that she doesn't really feel like living with any of the cheap IKEA tables. Iben feels Malene probably doesn't want any of the more expensive tables either.

She pats a small birch-wood table for 789 kroner. "Once the flaps are up it'll look a little like your old one."

Malene isn't paying attention.

Iben can't help thinking: What will this table look like when it falls from the fourth floor? Will the corner crack, or the legs come off? Will the top split?

The model rooms along the back wall are not only furnished but also warmly, invitingly lit and carefully decorated with posters in striking colors. There are books on the shelves and plastic models of food ready to be eaten. But the cozy Swedish style extends only about ten feet up. Overhead is a span of concrete beams some fifty feet long. Iben looks up at the colossal air-conditioning units suspended by thin cables from the industrial ceiling. She wonders how much one of these units might weigh. If one of them fell, would it crush a person underneath? Bend him double?

While Iben thinks, she holds on to another flimsy-looking table in white Formica and steel tubing.

It occurs to her: If someone were after us, we'd be easy targets now, walking close together, our attention on things like tabletops, designs, heights, and widths.

Malene's voice breaks into her thoughts: "You know, regardless of whether Anne-Lise poured the oil on the floor or not, he would still be alive if it wasn't for her."

Iben knows what's coming next. It's not the first time she's heard it.

"He'd never have wanted to move in the first place if I hadn't felt so worn out all the time. You know, by Anne-Lise's . . . Rasmus always wanted a low-maintenance woman with no problems. I knew that perfectly well. Instead I . . . it was me who ruined our life together. But it was Anne-Lise's fault. I was always beat after an eight-hour day with her. And I had to explain to Rasmus. I had to. Didn't I?"

Iben has heard all this before and has stopped listening.

"If Anne-Lise hadn't started her warfare . . . it makes me so angry. It's weird. You've never experienced anger like this, Iben; you don't know what it's like. And there's nothing I can do. Nothing at all."

When Malene returned to the office for the first time after Rasmus's death, Anne-Lise expressed her sympathy. She seemed so convincing when she opened her eyes wide and said, "How dreadful it must be for you. It's the worst thing that could happen. The thing we all fear the most."

Paul had told Malene to take as much time off as she needed, but every day off was another day for Anne-Lise to dig her claws into the Center's users. And if the merger happens, Anne-Lise's close association with them—and therefore with the board—will matter when the time comes to decide who should be fired.

The work on the Turkey issue carries on, although Iben and Anne-Lise's collaboration is, of course, strained. Still, Iben has to admit that Anne-Lise isn't completely useless when it comes to newspaper research. She seems to know not to interfere with Iben's writing and editing. Also it's surprisingly helpful when she uses her librarian's skill to check data and chase articles and author names in the databases of foreign libraries. During the last couple of weeks Iben has come to realize that it was rash of her to jump to the conclusion that it was Anne-Lise who murdered Rasmus. So much might have happened on the staircase that day.

Malene and Iben give up on finding the right dining table. In IKEA's restaurant they buy the traditional Swedish dish of meatballs in cream sauce, with potatoes and cranberry jam on the side. They buy themselves glasses of wine as well. While Iben eats, Malene again expounds on what a wonderful man Rasmus was and how miserably wrong her own behavior was. She doesn't touch her food.

"It's like holding a blowtorch in your hand and not knowing what to direct it at. You have no idea what it's like to be this furious."

She fiddles with the food on her plate, pushing sauce and potatoes and cranberries from side to side with small, picky movements. "I tell you one thing. Now Anne-Lise will soon learn what it's like when I can't stand someone!"

Iben doesn't reply.

chapter 38

ben knew the garden would be large, but not this large.

It's three o'clock in the morning. She is walking in the tall, wet grass in the winter moonlight. The trees, bushes, and hedges do not look black, but somehow it's difficult to distinguish the many shades of green and brown that are visible during the day. The only color she can see clearly is the bright red branches of a bush.

The tall, old-fashioned villa at the far end of the garden is also red.

She doesn't feel the cold as she slowly makes her way to stand under one of the old fruit trees. She has on her thickest jacket with the hood up. Above her she can see bare branches and, here and there, an apple silhouetted against the dark sky.

The villa is dark too. No one is up at this time of night along this suburban road. And no one is likely to be awake enough to cycle, as Iben has just done, all the way from Nørrebro to Vaserne, north of Holte.

If a light goes on anywhere in the house, Iben can get away long before they come outside to investigate who is roaming around in their garden. But why should anyone discover her?

She moves closer to the house, walks around it, and peers through the dark windows of the ground floor, trying to make out what is in the rooms. As always, the knife is strapped to her shin, even though she fears Anne-Lise least of all.

Iben should cycle back home after peeking through all the windows on the ground floor. The whole excursion seems a complete waste of time. She can't think what she hoped to find.

A week has passed since she realized that her suspicions about Anne-Lise murdering Rasmus were stress-related. It's different for Malene. She won't be able to move on until she has a clear picture of what happened. Iben came here tonight more for Malene's sake than for her own.

If only she could find something that would help Malene. Then maybe Malene could finally put it behind her how Iben owes her for getting her the job at the Center.

She looks up at the second floor again. Dark, no signs of life.

She places the ladder she found in the garage near a first-floor window and climbs up. The rooms must be unusually high-ceilinged, because the climb is more than twenty feet.

If she and Malene could be back on equal footing, like the old days, then it would be all right for Iben to phone Gunnar.

The window next to the ladder isn't closed properly, just secured with a hook. It's somebody's study. She sees a computer and a shelf full of magazine boxes and folders.

Iben listens for sounds. There aren't any. She won't go in, of course—that isn't part of her plan.

She thinks of what she will tell Gunnar when she calls him. She leans farther across the windowsill. Right in front of the window stands a large desk with stacks of papers and files. It's too tempting. Iben pulls off her bulky jacket and hangs it on the edge of the open window. Then she takes off her shoes and hangs them by their laces on the window hook.

She estimates the distance across the desktop and then from the desk to the door. The seconds spent crawling over the desk are the most critical. Afterward she will put a chair under the door handle. If they try to get in, the chair should hold them off long enough for her to escape.

She manages to climb in without any problems. Her thick black winter gloves feel too warm, but she keeps them on. A wooden chair seems perfect for jamming the door shut, but she checks it to make sure. Putting the light on is out of the question, and it takes time to locate the computer's volume knob in the dark. The bedrooms are likely to be on this floor too and she doesn't want the Windows start-up to wake somebody.

The computer is password protected, and she tries everything she can think of, first pressing Enter, then keying in "Anne-Lise," "Henrik," their children's names, and their initials. Nothing works. She starts checking through the bookshelves. It's difficult to read in the frail light and everything has to be brought close to the screen. Then she finds a lot of odds and ends—some coins, a battery, a plastic bag. Underneath the bag lies a small bicycle LED lamp. Its batteries are low, but the faint red glow it emits is better than nothing.

With the help of the lamp she realizes quickly that everything in here is related to Henrik's job and his finances. There's nothing here. This is as far as she'll go. She knows she should get out now.

She listens at the door. Still nothing. After gently extracting the chair from under the handle, she opens the door a fraction. It moves smoothly on its hinges. She peers through the crack, then opens the door a little wider. The floorboards are bound to creak in a house this old.

Behind one of these doors Anne-Lise is sleeping at Henrik's side. Her two children are asleep behind other doors. Iben hears a few grunts and, for a while, a man's snoring. The noises come from behind the door farthest away.

Only a few steps to the top of the stairs.

If Henrik wakes up and sees her, it'll be easy enough to run back to his study, jam the door shut, and speed down the ladder.

She tries her weight on the floor outside. It doesn't creak. Sweeping the red light around the landing, she can see that they have had a smart new floor laid. She creeps toward the top of the stairs.

From the ground-floor hall she walks into a room that was probably three rooms in the original design. The red light from her lamp is lost under the high ceiling.

The first thing she looks for is a quick exit route. Two large French windows lead out into the garden, but they are locked and she would need a key to open them. The main door probably has the same kind of lock. They make it harder for a thief to get away and a burglar alarm less essential. If Iben needs to escape she will have to break the glass.

She starts investigating the living room. The walls are white and a large sofa covered in black leather has been placed in the middle of the floor. Almost everything is in the style of the 1980s, including the blue Montana shelving system and the large framed Walasse Ting print. Seeing the quality of everything in here, she's certain that the Ting lithograph is an original.

But still nothing to show Malene.

The door to the dining room is open and so is the door between the dining room and the kitchen. The entire ground floor smells slightly of pizza, and the floor is littered with small cars and toys. Iben tries to memorize where the cars are so she won't slip on them if she has to switch her lamp off and run.

Here and there on the tables and shelves are bundles of old mail and other papers. She leafs through them: bills, notes from Ulrik's soccer club, information leaflets from the Pensions Authority, messages from the Association of Librarians, and a handful of old furniture catalogs.

Then there's the telephone. It has an answering machine. It's not blinking, but there might still be some old messages stored. Fumbling in her thick winter gloves, Iben turns the sound down and presses Play.

When the tape starts up she raises the volume just enough to hear what's being said. A slurred woman's voice begins uncertainly: "Jutta. If you . . . Well, I was, you know, talking to a friend and then I thought of you and . . ."

An upper-class accent. She is high as a kite.

"Anyway, remember the time we'd all gone around to . . . what was his name? And we'd just got the trousers, or at least I'd just got them. But she said we should go. And you were so smart and said we'd just arrived from Odense. Ha ha! It was brilliant. I thought about that just now. Because I've been talking to a friend and she didn't think so at all."

The message rambles on for a while longer. Iben can't make any sense of it. It's weird, though. Why is a drunk woman confiding in Anne-Lise over the phone? Has Anne-Lise called her in the same state? Does Jutta know that Anne-Lise hits the bottle too?

No more messages. The house is so silent that Iben has become uncertain about how loud any noise she makes is and how far it will travel.

The stairs creak. She starts as if the sound were an explosion. Is someone coming downstairs? She takes a few long steps to reach the fireplace and grabs hold of the heavy poker. Iben would never use it against anyone—it would be as remote a possibility as pulling her knife on Anne-Lise or Henrik—but she needs a heavy implement to break the French windows. She has a vision of herself running through shards of glass into the dark garden.

She switches off her lamp, takes up a position facing the glazed door, and freezes on the spot, the poker raised. With any luck she'll respond quickly if someone does come in, so that whoever it is won't see anything—just a shadow slipping into the darkness.

She listens intently. Henrik could be watching her from only a few yards away without her having heard a thing. Once more, she's unable to distinguish whether the sounds are imagined or real. Faint noises from the bedroom, perhaps? Whispering? Like the voices she thought she heard before Rasmus fell.

After a while she lowers the poker. Her hand and shoulder ache. Turning around, she tries to make out if someone is standing in the dark room.

No one, it seems.

She really must get out of the house.

Still, she shouldn't miss the kitchen. There might be some sign of Anne-Lise's alcoholism. She peers into the kitchen cupboards. There's nothing as obvious as empty bottles of spirits.

There is a magnetic calendar stuck on the fridge. In the light of the cycle lamp Iben reads all about Henrik and Anne-Lise's dates. It says where they have been tonight. "A + H Meet in nursery. Re Clara." What's that about? Why a meeting about their daughter?

There's nothing else of interest on the refrigerator door.

The rubbish bin is stuffed with folded pizza cartons, but underneath them Iben finds a scrunched-up piece of paper with handwritten notes, partially soggy from the tomato sauce. She flattens the page between sheets of paper towels, which she is careful to put in her pocket.

The writing isn't Anne-Lise's. It is in a small, precise hand with very straight uprights that slope slightly to the left. It must be Henrik's.

Meeting re C.
It upsets us to hear about children hit by C. We want to apologize to their parents.
    What can we do to improve things?
    It is true that Clara has been aggressive toward friends who have come home to play. (Okay, we'll accept that they call her "unusually aggressive"

but will stand for nothing stronger. Do not tell them about the episode with Victor in our house.)

Stress this: Our willingness to cooperate. Remind them that we both turned up for the PTA day in August. (Try shifting talk away from the other meeting.)

Important—remember: we have not had any anger management problems with Clara before and we both believe that she will get over this phase soon.

(Agree with A-L in the car.)

ONLY if necessary: That the family is angry about other matters and it might have affected Clara. Not angry at her. She is not to be blamed.

No problems, that is, apart from her mother's terrible situation at work. Stress that we're optimistic.

We hope that the Center will become part of Human Rights, surely quite soon. Then A-L gets new colleagues. We'll become stronger as . . .

At this point the paper is too stained to read. The only other words she can read are "in confidence."

What a relief. She's found something!

With clumsy gloved fingers, she folds the notepaper and puts it into her jeans pocket too. She becomes aware of an itch on her shin, just above the strap for the knife. She tries to scratch it with the toes of her other foot but her knee bangs into the open door of a kitchen cabinet and it slams shut.

On tiptoe she runs back to the living room and takes up the same position as before, the poker ready to smash the glazed garden doors. She stands absolutely still. Her heart is thumping and her mind is churning with fantasies about Henrik coming into the room brandishing a baseball bat . . . or maybe a gun.

She must get back to the study, unless it's already too late! There is no time to investigate the basement now.

But as she stares out of the window, she discovers that something in the garden has changed. When she stood here earlier, she could see quite distinctly the straight silhouette of the nearest tree trunk. The trunk looks thicker now and its outline is irregular. Either something is leaning against the tree or someone is trying to hide behind it.

Her heart hammers wildly in her chest and her mouth suddenly goes dry. She feels so faint that she is scared of falling over—someone has followed her here. She thinks at once of Omoro's Kenyan friends. And she thinks of Mirko Zigic. He cut the arm off one of his victims and drew on the walls with her blood. He tied a cable around the neck of another woman and tightened it over a hook in the ceiling before he and his men raped her.

Iben feels a cold sweat covering her whole body.

She forces herself to think that she's mistaken: it's a play of the moonlight, or maybe it's a different tree. There will be a simple explanation. Her fears are compulsive, irrational. She moves quickly toward the hall. She is close to the bottom of the staircase when she spots a door to the space under the stairs. Could she barricade herself in there if someone was waiting for her at the top of the stairs?

She opens the door and takes a peek, switching on her little lamp. It's another study. Papers are arranged in very orderly piles. It must be Anne-Lise's workspace.

She should be getting out now, but she can't miss the opportunity. She must have a look. She checks a whole series of drawers. No time to turn on the computer, but isn't Anne-Lise likely to have made a backup CD of her files?

The battery in her lamp is about to die. The red light is fading gradually.

Iben leafs through the stacks of papers, trying to leave them as tidy as before. It's hard holding the lamp in one gloved hand and turning the sheets with the other.

At last she finds a collection of CDs in a drawer. Those marked with dates are presumably backups. She doesn't take the most recent so Anne-Lise won't notice; instead she picks three disks from somewhere in the middle. Now she can leave.

She returns the remaining CDs. A piece of paper has slipped to the back, squashed by all the other stuff in the drawer. She pulls it out. The lamplight is so weak, she can hardly see the letters even when she holds the lamp immediately above it:

> ... *because of the fantasies of revenge against Iben and Malene. But more and more, they are turning against myself. The images are terrifyingly real and I'm part of them now, as if all three of us, Iben, Malene, me, are*

merging. Something deep inside me must have been destroyed when I pun-
ish myself instead of them. As I did that time when I had what Henrik calls
my "breakdown." I would do anything, give anything—except my family—
if I could be sure that I don't completely fall apart before we merge with Hu-
man Rights . . .

There seems to be more papers like this one, but time is running out. Iben stuffs the CDs and the piece of paper inside the waistband of her trousers. Craning to see if there is anyone on the stairs, she suppresses an almost irresistible urge to run up them.

Nobody is at the top of the stairs. Henrik's snoring has stopped. All is still. Once inside the study, with the chair jammed once again under the door's handle, Iben sighs with relief. Soon she'll be outside. She puts the lamp back under the plastic bag and takes a good look around to make sure that she hasn't left the slightest hint that would give her away. Everything looks fine.

Just as she starts to remove the chair, the handle jerks up a little. Someone on the other side has also blocked the door.

The handle doesn't move.

Iben runs toward the window.

A man's voice roars: "Now! Now!" His voice sounds as desperate as Iben feels. He shouts even louder: "Take it away now. Then RUN so he can't hurt you!"

Over by the window Iben realizes that the ladder is already gone.

Just below the window a heavily built man and his large black dog stand guard. The man is calmly talking on his cell phone and is close enough for Iben to hear.

"I'm not running anywhere. Burglars never carry guns. If you're found with anything like that on you, the jail sentence is tripled." The man is wearing a long black coat with pajamas sticking out underneath. He's probably a neighbor whom Henrik called to come over.

The man has brought a flashlight. He shines it toward the study window, but Iben manages to move out of sight just in time. He shouts in the direction of the window: "You there! Looking forward to three months inside, hey? Maybe five! And that's on top of whatever else is waiting for you."

Iben could kick herself. Why did she even think about breaking into the house? She should've known it could only go one way.

The light's beam travels across the ceiling. She takes care to keep out of the way and settles down on the floor, leaning against the wall with her knees drawn up. She is shaking.

Neither of the two men has mentioned phoning the police, presumably because one of them has already done so. The police could be here any moment.

A sleepy child speaks on the other side of the door. It's a boy. "What are you doing?"

Henrik answers his son. "Your daddy has caught a burglar."

"Where is he?"

"He's locked in the computer room."

"Wow."

The next voice is Anne-Lise's. "NO!"

"Why, what? Mommy?"

"You mustn't go so close to the door."

"Why not?"

"Because. Stay over here, next to me."

"Can he shoot through the door?"

Anne-Lise speaks quietly. "No, darling, he can't."

Iben waits until the cone of light leaves the window for a few seconds, then throws herself across the desk and grabs her jacket and shoes from the window hook. The man in the garden hears her and shines the light back in the window, but Iben is already lying flat on the desk.

The boy speaks again. "Why can't I go over there? Is he going to come out?"

"I just want you to stay here by me. I know—let's go into your room."

"No-oo . . . Mommy, I don't want to."

"Yes! Come on."

Iben pulls off her sweater and rummages in the pockets of her jacket for the hood and scarf. She ties the scarf over her face and pulls the hood well down over her forehead, trying to make sure that not a single strand of her blond hair is showing. After buttoning her jacket, she ties the sweater round the bottom of it. The effect she wants is slim hips and a bulky upper body in the hope that she might be mistaken for a man.

She jumps up on the desk and stands in front of the open window. What chance does she have? Everything is so high in this old villa. Even though she's just on the second floor, the ground seems very far down.

The man shouts at her again. "Jumping? Don't do it. You'll break your legs." He pulls quickly at the dog's lead. "And if you don't, Skipper here will get you anyway!"

The police might be just a minute away, but Iben crawls back into the room. There's a mess of electrical cords under the desk. She pulls two extension cords out of the mains socket and ties them together. The result is a kind of rope, at least twenty feet long.

Anne-Lise is apparently still hovering in the hallway, but her voice is at a safe distance from the door. "What if there are two of them?"

"There aren't. I spotted this one downstairs."

Anne-Lise sounds quite different from when she's in the office. "What do you think? Will he jump?"

"I don't think so. Besides, Lars is there with his dog."

Iben opens the upper part of the window and climbs back up onto the sill. Now she grasps the crosspiece between the upper and lower windows and stands with her entire body on the outside of the house. Stretching, she can just grab hold of the gutter that runs along the roof.

The man named Lars calls out: "Hey! Stop!" He speaks into his cell phone. "The man is trying to get onto the roof. I bet he's high on something. It's a little guy. I don't like this. It looks bad."

He calls out: "Get back inside! Prison is better than what you're trying."

Iben manages to place one foot on the upper edge of the open window and heaves herself up. She tests the gutter. It seems solid. She moves one more step along and then tries to propel herself farther onto the roof, but a dangling edge of her sweater gets caught. She hangs on to an attic windowsill while she tries to free herself.

Lars talks to Henrik again: "Better pull down your attic steps. The police will have to get up there to catch him."

She wastes a lot of time fiddling with the sweater, but in the end it tears. She looks at the large hole with relief. Supported by the attic window, she crawls up to the roof ridge, taking care to stay as flat as possible even though she is out of Lars's sight. She can't see him either.

She pulls the scarf down. The wind fans her skin.

The villa is too enormous for Lars to be on the lookout everywhere. It should be possible to find a place where Iben can climb down and escape before he sees her. Then she sees him in front of the house. He has walked farther away to keep an eye on her. He sweeps his flashlight over part of the roof. Hurriedly she pushes the scarf back across her face, just in case.

There are lights on in two neighboring houses. One of them presumably belongs to Lars, but maybe another man is on his way.

Iben knows she needs to use the cords to get down now, but she doesn't dare. Instead she crawls until she is midway along the ridge of the roof. Lars won't be able to figure out where she's going next. But Henrik might open an attic window. And the police will arrive. And maybe more neighbors. More dogs.

Jump now.

Now.

Still she hesitates. Will the knot hold the cords together? She pulls them out of her pocket and tugs at them to check the knot.

She thinks of Rasmus, remembering how she found him.

She thinks of what will happen if her sweater or her jacket catches something—maybe the gutter again—or if she slips on the tiles.

A light comes on in the nearby attic windows. Car headlights are approaching fast. It can only be the police car.

Now.

She slides down to a dark attic window at the back of the house. Supported by its frame, she makes a noose at one end of the cord, places it around the window frame, and tightens it. Holding on to the cord, she descends to the edge of the roof.

She wants to reach the ground quickly, before the others have time to find her, but she hasn't counted on just how slippery the thin plastic cable is. She hits the first knot, barely managing to hold on, and then slides full speed down the next length. Her plan to stop halfway to assess where she is and choose the best spot to land fails.

When she reaches the last stretch of cord, it whips back into her hands and she can't hold on. Iben lands behind the house, next to a washing rack and some garden furniture. Her feet, knees, and hands crash against the flagstones.

I've survived, she thinks. That is the first thought to go through her head, and it makes her feel ecstatic.

She gets up. A tall fence is only a few feet away.

She pushes the garden table over to the fence and tries to jump up. She can't. There's a sharp pain in her right foot. She crawls up onto the table, then onto the fence. She hauls herself down the other side, putting her weight on her arms and her left foot.

She looks around at the unfamiliar garden, but when she hears voices nearby she pushes herself through a hole at the bottom of the hedge to a garden next door. The voices seem to be moving off in the opposite direction.

The pain in her foot is excruciating. Her hands hurt too. Examining her palms, she realizes that the cable has ripped her gloves and even cut into her skin.

When the voices die away it is still dark.

Her bike is hidden in a driveway just down the road.

She gets up and limps toward it, thinking: I have something for Malene. Now we're even.

She's such a liar! It's lies, all of it!"

Reading this stuff makes Iben furious. She kicks her good foot hard against the mattress. She has taken a couple of pain-killers, but the bump in her other foot still causes a shooting pain. This makes her even angrier.

Iben was too much on edge to sleep when she came home. She has brought her laptop to bed and the screen is covered in text:

> *Monday morning. I've been at the DCIG for two months now. I walk into their place. No one asks about my weekend, no one bothers about the trip I told them about last week. Simply nothing!*
>
> *I just say "Hi," sounding relaxed. I'm trying to forget what they were like last week, to give them another chance, a fresh start. Just to do this one little thing: pop into their shared office and—"Hi!" Camilla says "Hi" too. Iben says not a word.*
>
> *They don't bother to look at me. I stand there for a while, hoping for a little attention or something, ready to say a few words about what I've done, what a nice time we had, how the sun shone . . . something, anything!*

It takes three minutes and I'm back where I started. Dumped in the middle of all the misery I had managed to ignore for a while. It's that quick . . .

Anne-Lise's CD is not password protected. Iben takes a deep breath and opens another file.

It's quite obvious that they insist on seeing me as "the librarian," a dull figure nobody needs to take any notice of. They want me to behave in character and are prepared to do everything they can to force me to. It really angers them if I look attractive or say something interesting because it makes it harder for them to cut me out.

During the lunch hour, Iben fought with Camilla. I'm positive that the reason was that she had caught Camilla chatting to me. Nobody is allowed to talk to me; Iben and Malene will see to that, all right.

Every time I've been away I forget how appallingly awful it is. When I'm not surrounded by it, I simply can't believe what it's like. How can anyone be so evil? I just don't understand!

Iben tosses and turns again. Luckily the two large empty mugs and the soup plate are on the small table by her bed. She leans back and wipes the sweat off her forehead with the duvet cover. She still hasn't recovered. It's a quarter past eight in the morning. She hasn't slept and within the next hour she must be at work, behaving normally.

After getting home on the suburban train, the first thing Iben did was to take painkillers and run herself a hot bath. She drank a mug of cocoa in the bath and then made herself a large bowl of oatmeal, mixed with raisins, nuts, and skim milk. Then she went to bed.

As far as she knows, she left nothing behind in Anne-Lise's house that could identify her. No one recognized her—seemingly, no one even realized that the intruder was a woman. But you never know.

She can't risk seeing the doctor today. If her foot doesn't get better in a few days, she'll have to act as if the accident has just occurred. Before then, Anne-Lise will have seen her in perfect shape.

She opens another file, written only a few weeks ago.

I must hold on to the belief that the others aren't justified. I must remember that. They have no right to decide that I should be eliminated. But when they say I don't get on with people, it's true. Or so it seems—I don't, not with the Center's users or my colleagues. It's all such a mess. Once upon a time I thought I was easy to work with, but maybe everyone was just pretending.

At times I think I should phone up my old library and ask if they really did like having me on the team. They would say yes, of course, but would that too be a lie? I'll never know.

Iben's nausea won't go away. It's easy to see from the diary that Anne-Lise is sick—probably some form of paranoia, with attendant delusions. Iben decides to phone Grith this evening and discuss the more precise clinical diagnosis. But even if you know that, it's still shocking to see this distorted view of yourself. The fact that it's all down in writing, and in such a detailed, elaborate way, makes it all the more persuasive.

After failing to sleep earlier, Iben drops off while she's sitting on the toilet. She calls the office to say she'll be in late. Just forty-five minutes, she says, and for once she gives in and takes a taxi to work.

As soon as she steps out on the fifth-floor landing, the security camera will pick up her image. They'll be able to see her and they mustn't realize that her foot hurts like hell. There must be no hint that she's feeling sick and hasn't slept all night or that she's just read Anne-Lise's insane ramblings about herself and everybody else in the office. She stares defiantly at the camera and presses the doorbell. They let her in. Iben smiles and says hello. The piercing pain in her right heel and ankle makes her reluctant to take a single step, but she can't just stand there. She walks to the familiar row of hooks to hang up her jacket as best as she can.

Maybe this is how it is for Malene. She endures terrible pain at times and now she also fights to hide the fact that she barely sleeps for grieving over Rasmus. Before his death, Malene would talk to Iben about her fear of being disabled and alone. Sooner or later she could be wheelchair-bound, unable to get to work or to have children.

When Rasmus died, the future Malene dreaded seemed to close in. She stopped speaking about her arthritis. Instead she carries on endlessly, like she did at IKEA, about how wonderful Rasmus was, contrasting his super-human qualities with her own shortcomings. It was her behavior that drove him away. She follows this up with more attacks on Anne-Lise—

how she ruined their life together and then drove Rasmus to an early death. It was possible, after all, she argues, that Anne-Lise poured oil on the steps and even gave Rasmus a shove.

Okay, it's not likely—but it's possible.

Late one night, Iben had slipped and mentioned to Malene that she thought she had heard a woman's voice in the stairway just before Rasmus fell. Malene returned to this so often and with such fervor that Iben regretted ever having breathed a word about it. After a couple of weeks, these stories were becoming just the tiniest bit irritating.

Crossing the floor, Iben feels that she's putting on quite a good show, even managing to chat about this and that.

But Malene notices at once that something is up. Her eyes widen. "Iben, what's the matter?"

"Oh, nothing."

Iben knows that Malene won't believe her and twists one corner of her mouth in a small grimace that only Malene will notice, to let her know that she doesn't want to talk about it right now. Iben has every intention of telling Malene what happened last night, but now something is holding her back, though she can't think what.

Camilla doesn't say anything, and Anne-Lise is keeping to herself in the library.

"Has Anne-Lise been out of the library?"

Malene looks at her. "Why do you ask?"

"No special reason."

Iben sits down and tries to hide her relief—no need to get up again until lunchtime. She bends down to take off her right shoe. The laces are already very loose, but it still hurts when she eases the shoe off over the top of her foot. She suppresses the sound she wants to make so that it comes out as a very faint gasp.

Is this really what it can be like for Malene, day after day?

She can hear from the tapping rhythm that Malene is writing and then correcting the same word several times. One more mistake. Malene hits the keyboard. It slides sideways and her fingers hit the corner of the large flat surface of the mouse. It must have hurt, because she pulls her hand away at once and rubs it with her other hand. Iben and Malene exchange a smile.

Next to Iben is a stack of documentation on the Turks' killing of 300,000 Pontian Greeks between 1914 and 1922. Although Turkey's extermination of roughly 1.5 million Armenians has eclipsed the mass murder of the Greeks, the issue of *Genocide News* on Turkey will be the perfect place to bring attention to the atrocity. Among other eyewitness accounts, Iben will include a description of how Turkish soldiers drove Greek families, women, children, and old people away from the coast and into the desert. Once their victims were isolated, the militia left and took all the food and water with them.

Iben sits in silence, staring at the desk. She should keep working, but she's having trouble concentrating on the material. She can barely respond when someone talks to her. Instead she reads random back issues of *Genocide News*. A large greasy stain across the top of a front page catches her eye. The headline says "The Psychology of Evil II." It's her own article: ". . . in a war situation, men and women who kill at a sufficiently great distance from the victims are, to the best of his personal knowledge, not traumatized later in life. The closer the soldier gets to the victim, the harder it is to kill."

She thinks of how distant she is to Anne-Lise. If Anne-Lise were to have an accident serious enough to disable or even kill her, Iben's head would tell her it was a tragedy but her heart would secretly be glad to be rid of her. These new thoughts make Iben interpret her writing differently.

"The conclusion must be that simple acts, which in themselves appear to cause only limited damage, can lead to psychological changes that in turn make possible even greater and more destructive acts."

Having read Anne-Lise's journal entries, Iben sees how the following passage also seems to apply: "We tend to exaggerate the similarities of those who belong to our group, just as we exaggerate the homogeneity in other groups and the differences among them."

By now the nausea from this morning has returned. She stares at the broken spring that dangles from her desk lamp, its sharp little tip, and the reflections of the overhead light on the broken metal.

Her thoughts must have been drifting for quite a while when she hears Malene and Camilla chatting about Malene's swimming sessions.

"Of course it isn't just about keeping your body fit. It does something for your mind and your mood as well."

Iben reads on: "Cognitive dissonance makes us like those whom we have helped and dislike those we have hurt."

She hears Malene's voice again: "If you don't stay in good shape by doing something active, like you do with your choir, it's easy to end up just like her in there." Malene nods her head in the direction of the library.

Iben needs to be alone. Just for a few minutes. She quickly bends down to put her shoe back on. Despite her painful foot and upset stomach, she walks toward the restroom. She keeps her face turned away to hide her expression.

It feels good to hear the small click of the lock. She settles down on the lid, in the tall, narrow stall with its melon yellow walls and odor of toilet cleaner. She lifts her sore foot and puts her hand gently but firmly around the taut skin of her swollen ankle.

The last words of her article are still with her: "The more appallingly brutal the acts a perpetrator commits, the more strongly he comes to believe that they are only right and proper."

She asks herself if that is what they've done to Anne-Lise. Is what she says in her diary true?

The throbbing pain has spread. It lurks behind Iben's eyes, in the back of her neck, in the roof of her mouth, in her arms. It melds with images and words of so many genocides that she has pondered over. She can't help returning to the one question that researchers inevitably ask themselves: If I had been born in Germany before the Second World War, would I have supported the Holocaust? Then she remembers Anne-Lise, who might well find her out if she doesn't get back to work soon.

She finds Anne-Lise at Malene's desk, apparently angry about something. Over the last few weeks, ever since Rasmus died, they have all been kind to Malene—Anne-Lise too. Now that seems to have changed.

Anne-Lise is speaking too fast, and her voice has a metallic ring to it. "You were talking about me a moment ago. I heard you say that unless people pull themselves together, they'll end up like me." She sounds as if she's about to have a breakdown. "Running after two small children keeps you fit. Camilla, you know that, don't you?"

Malene is quite calm. "Anne-Lise, I didn't say that about you."

"I heard you. You said 'or you'll end up like her in there.' And you meant me."

"Anne-Lise, you misheard me. I never said that."

Looking at Anne-Lise, Iben is about to chime in, "Malene never said that. I'm positive she didn't." But the words won't come. Malene, who is so used to Iben backing her up, gives her friend a bemused look: What's wrong?

There's a short pause. Iben stays silent.

Malene starts her usual little act that never fails to drive Anne-Lise crazy. "If you are hearing people talking about you, then maybe you should see your doctor."

As expected, Camilla joins in. "A doctor might help you, Anne-Lise. Well, anyway, it's always worth a try."

Malene looks at Iben. Iben feels more and more sick.

Anne-Lise is shouting now. "But you said it! You said it!"

"Anne-Lise, hearing voices is a serious matter. You must look after yourself."

"I'm not hearing voices! You said that!"

"What's your doctor like? You'll need a good one."

"I know there are a lot of helpful sites on the Internet."

Camilla stares at Iben.

Anne-Lise looks withdrawn. Maybe this is what it takes to make her crawl back into the library and hide.

Malene still won't let go. "We haven't even mentioned you in here today. Have we, Iben?"

Iben can't speak.

Malene repeats, more loudly and clearly: "Have we, Iben?"

A quarter of a second passes.

It is like a test. An evaluation of a human being's most important qualities.

Half a second.

It strikes Iben that her situation only confirms what she wrote in her first article about the psychology of evil. Christopher Browning's study showed that what drove ordinary Germans to kill Jews was not the threat of punishment, but peer pressure. The men felt they must not let down the comrades with whom they had endured such dreadful hardships.

Three quarters of a second.

The pressure on Iben has other similarities to the forces that drive people to kill, and kill again. One brief moment can have incalculable consequences and determine which side a person takes for the rest of the war.

One full second.

No more time to think.

Malene is having such a difficult time these days. Nothing should be allowed to add to her distress. If I humiliate her in front of the others, Iben thinks, our friendship may not survive. She'll lose every last ounce of trust in me. She might tell Gunnar. That too could change my life. If only Malene and I could have talked about this alone.

I'm taking far too long. They're all staring at me. How strange it is. I believe that no group has the right to destroy one individual. It's an article of faith for us here at the DCIG. And now I must choose: either my ideology or my best friend. An inner voice tells me to agree with Malene. My human instinct, like the instincts of millions of Germans, Russians, Chinese, Cambodians, demands that other people should be eliminated.

So much would be sacrificed if I were to break with Malene. And how can I be certain that Anne-Lise deserves that kind of sacrifice from me?

I don't want to turn my life upside down.

The Winter Garden is quiet apart from the slight humming of the computers. Iben looks directly at Anne-Lise. She can't remember when she last did that.

"We were talking about you, Anne-Lise." Iben blinks. The light is so bright. She starts again. "You weren't imagining it. Not at all."

Malene slaps the palms of her hands on the desktop. "WHAT?"

Iben repeats it and now her voice is firmer. "We were talking about you, Anne-Lise. What you heard was exactly what we said."

Iben can see Malene losing her confidence.

"Iben, you don't mean what you're saying. Did you really hear what we were talking about? What are you . . . You're not saying that . . . ?"

Iben's eyes fill with tears. It's hard to see Malene. Instead she turns to Anne-Lise, whom she can't see properly either.

"Anne-Lise, listen. You're not psychotic! You're right! Everything you heard was said. We talked about you. We've talked about you before now too."

Iben can hear that Anne-Lise has also begun to cry.

"Are you siding with her?!" Malene is screaming.

"No! No! I'm not on anybody's side. I'm just telling her the truth. We talked about Anne-Lise. We did."

"You're her friend now!"

"No. I'm only saying . . ."

Malene sounds as if she's hardly able to breathe. "I can't bear it . . . You're just . . ."

Anne-Lise is still standing at Iben's side when Malene runs out of the office, slamming the door behind her.

ben rushes out the door after Malene, as fast as she can manage on her sore foot.

Malene is not on the stairs and not on the pavement outside. Iben calls her cell phone. No response. Apart from the endless rows of parked cars, the road is completely empty. The morning air is cold, and Iben hugs herself as she leans against the red-brick wall and tries to collect her thoughts.

Then she phones the Center. Anne-Lise takes the call and sounds quite different. Iben realizes that Anne-Lise is dying to talk about what's just happened, but Iben avoids the issue. All she says is that she has a headache and is going home. She will be away for the rest of the day.

She takes a taxi and calls Malene's home number. After about ten attempts Malene finally answers.

"Iben, so you're backing her up now?"

"No. Malene, I'm your friend, always! But you're not yourself."

Malene interrupts with denials, but Iben continues. "Look, Malene, it's obvious why, with everything that's happened. But I'm worried about you."

Malene is shouting. "I hate to think what you're like when

you really fucking care!" She slams the receiver down and doesn't answer the phone again.

When Iben wakes up, her bedroom is dark. The clock radio shows that it's nine o'clock at night. Nine hours have passed since she lay down on top of the bed.

She limps along to the kitchen and makes herself her usual portion of oats, raisins, and skim milk, and thinks about Malene. Everything has gone wrong. Iben's foot is painful and she feels emotionally drained. She sits down at her desk, placing her bad foot gingerly on one of the old chairs. The laptop is turned on and Anne-Lise's CD is still in the drive. She checks through more files while she eats.

There are collections of photos from summer days in the garden and from a family holiday two years ago in Rhodes. The children are splashing in the sea, and Henrik, whose body looks exceptionally pale and thin, is grinning at the photographer.

Iben knows what she's after and why, but doesn't care. Dozens of experiments in social psychology have proven that, after making a complex choice, people often set out to look for reasons to confirm that they were right. The deciding factors may have been marginal, or even random, but in the experiments, subjects would construct arguments and find information to support their eventual decision. By then they would have shut off other considerations and convinced themselves that their choices were significantly different. Put simply: justification after the fact makes life easier.

Iben has eaten her cereal by the time she gets to older photos of the family, who are visibly happy. Iben feels proud of the stand she took today—her refusal to help destroy this smiling woman. She is well aware that the choices people had to make during the Holocaust were utterly unlike her own. Even so, she thinks that perhaps she might have been part of the small, select group of heroes who refused to obey. In her mind she pictures the survivors in their rooms. She sees a woman at a desk looking at photos of a victim she has saved, her bad right foot resting on a chair.

Iben scrolls through other entries about the daily misery Anne-Lise endured at the Center. In bed later that night, Iben thinks about what she has read. How can it be, she asks herself, that I couldn't see the consequences of what we were doing until I saw them in writing? Somehow, I must have known all along. Malene must have known too.

She thinks about how, in reality, she and Malene were able to hold three utterly contradictory beliefs simultaneously. First, they felt their actions were okay because they weren't hurting Anne-Lise—she was too thick-skinned to notice. Second, their actions were okay because Anne-Lise deserved to suffer for destroying the good working environment at the DCIG. Third, they knew that their treatment of Anne-Lise was fundamentally wrong, although they never dared put it into words or even acknowledge the thoughts. Somehow they sensed that they shouldn't tell anyone outside the office what they were doing.

When Iben comes into work the next morning, Paul is standing at Malene's desk. They are gossiping about some of their German colleagues. Paul looks relaxed and Iben thinks that he has no idea what happened yesterday.

As usual, Iben greets everyone in the Winter Garden. Then, for the first time, she walks into the library to greet Anne-Lise.

"Hi."

"Hi, Iben."

Iben tries to catch Anne-Lise's expression. "How are things?"

"Just fine. Really. Fine. What about you?"

"Oh, fine."

Anne-Lise hesitates for a moment. "You know, I'm actually feeling happy."

Iben nods toward the papers on the desk. "What's all that about?"

"I have to sort out the keywords for this pile of new books."

Iben yawns. "I guess I'd better get to work too."

Anne-Lise says, "Yes." Then she uses one of Malene's phrases: "We'd better be good."

When Iben sits down at her desk, Paul has left, and Malene leans across her desk as far as she can and whispers: "We need to talk."

They go off together to the small meeting room. Iben emphasizes how it would have been so much better not to have been forced to disagree in front of the others. Malene apologizes for this, and for her words on the phone. Because Paul is at the Center they can't spend too much time away from their desks, but they promise each other to have a longer talk later.

Iben needs to work on the Turkey issue. However, as things stand, it would probably be best to avoid Anne-Lise for a while. She sends an e-mail to her instead, saying that she's sure their planned discussion will generate all sorts of exciting ideas, but that she would like to postpone it for a couple of days.

Anne-Lise has enough understanding of what is going on and e-mails back a simple "Fine by me."

Iben turns to Malene and suggests that they work on the delegates' handouts for the conference about the ethnic cleansing of East European Germans between 1945 and 1950. Iben goes to sit next to Malene so that they can go over her draft together. Iben, who has brought her mug of coffee along, takes a sip and starts scanning Malene's text.

The heading strikes her as being in poor taste: "Welcome to the International Conference on Ethnic Cleansing of Germans 1945–50."

Reading on, the very first sentence also seems odd and inappropriate given the subject matter. The next sentence sounds so heavy you just want to run away. She turns to the next page. It's no good either. Then she abandons the second page too. This is hopeless.

Iben tries to recall what she thought of Malene's previous draft. As far as she can remember, it seemed all right. Why does it look so different now? What can she say?

She tries to find something positive before she starts to criticize it.

Iben looks up and sees her best friend watching her. Does Malene sense how Iben feels about their friendship today? Probably not. For the last few months Iben has felt uneasy about it, but Malene appears not to have noticed. But then, why should she? It's not as if Iben has actually said anything.

Luckily, Iben finds something on the last page of the conference papers that works. Now she can praise it with sincerity.

"Malene, I really like this passage at the end. It's so inviting. Friendly."

"I did try to write as if I were writing to a friend."

They smile.

Iben is back at her own desk, preparing to review a new book about Yugoslavia for the the DCIG Web site, but once again she has trouble concentrating.

She creates a new file for notes to herself. Her comments might be part of the groundwork for another article in her series on the psychology of evil.

At least now she's not wasting her time at work. Besides, it's the only subject she can focus on.

EVIL, PSYCHOL III

Just about everyone must have heard a friend praising her great relationship with a lover only to say, soon after breaking up, that she knew from the start that it wouldn't last. She will insist she "knew," even when they had bought an apartment or had a child together.

The interesting point is the friend's claim to have known all along while acting as if she did not. This might be something to bear in mind when trying to understand people who have committed terrible acts that they at other times in their life have claimed they could never possibly commit. It could be that we should stop trying to see every human being as a consistent whole. A better image of the human psyche might be a bunch of grapes: each "grape" is a set of characteristics, worldviews, and moral codes. Subconsciously, we pick one grape or another at different times.

Without being an actual clinical case of split personality, individuals are simultaneously able to hold contradictory beliefs, each one developed and honed by years of experience. This, despite the person being aware of only one state of mind at a time.

Iben adds an NB: "Is this too early to insert references to research into DID? Do I have any other examples to base this argument on? There must be something—but where?"

This interpretation of how people function could explain, for instance, why many Serbian schoolteachers in Bosnia were able to take an active part in the killing of their pupils and their pupils' parents. Parents who survived in most cases declared themselves unable to grasp how the teacher could bring himself to do what he had done. He had always seemed to be very caring toward the pupils. The only explanation seemed to be that he had been lying to them for years.

But he didn't lie. When the war started, he moved to another grape in his bunch. And when the war ended, he went back to the old one. This move-

ment might explain why so many war criminals are without remorse. They resume their prewar life, and everything concerning their actions in the war is hazy. They feel as if it was someone else who went wild, killing innocent children and adults.

Another NB: "Do I lack a good lead-in here? Maybe the next bit should be a different article? Or 'The Psychology of Evil IV'? It's at this point that the perspectives open out."

In God, Gulliver, and Genocide, *the author Claude Rawson (professor of English at Yale) has analyzed Hitler's prewar speeches. They are very vague on the subject of what should be done about the Jews. Should they be deported to Madagascar, or some other course of action? Superficially, the Germans were unsure what it was that Hitler wanted—and yet, at the same time, they knew. Hitler was able to obfuscate the appalling implications of his policy while making its advantages crystal clear to non-Jewish German citizens.*

Similar patterns can be observed in the Rwandan radio broadcasts and the propaganda aimed at German soldiers. No one utters the words "kill" or "murder" outright. But everyone knows what is really going on, and the underlying message is clear beneath all the vague and circuitous language that dehumanizes the victims. Expressions such as "exterminating the vermin" or "cleaning up a village" allow propagandists to consign the very real suffering of the victims to a partly unconscious "mind grape."

An important avenue for future research might be to examine if this obscurity of language in the days leading up to genocide is something more than linguistic. Usage might reflect the dynamics of a central psychological mechanism that is essential to the catastrophic final result. Could it be that genocide simply would not happen without a critical mass of indistinct expressions to support a convenient distribution of mental processes into appropriate grapes? That is, the process culminating in genocide depends on the coordination of several perceptions at the same time—on parallel thinking along multiple lines rather than the single-mindedness we usually believe to be the rule in making life decisions.

Such research could also tell us about the way people think and arrive at their decisions more generally—not just in the realm of genocide.

Iben leans back in her chair. She feels much better now. There is no telling if this piece will ever be published in the magazine, but at least it's safely stored away in the computer.

Malene is staring at her screen and Paul is wandering around their office again. It seems he has decided he should show his face more often and chat to his staff. He wants to be inspiring and supportive, but he does have a tendency to pick the wrong moments.

During lunch he asks Iben what she has been reading recently. Of course, he means articles relevant to her work at the DCIG, but she can't resist mentioning the clinical texts about DID again and tells him about the embryonic article she has just written. After a while she stops, suddenly feeling self-conscious about talking for too long.

But Paul is appreciative. "Fantastic! I mean it, Iben! That's just the kind of discussion we should be having. It's wonderful for you to explore entirely new lines of thought."

He follows up his comments with a series of criticisms, but constructive ones. His aim is to clarify the bunch-of-grapes hypothesis. How well does it fit actual facts? What are the possible applications?

When the break is over, he asks Iben to join him in his office. This makes Iben nervous. Paul sits down and gestures for her to sit opposite him. As he leans back on his chair, she notes that he is growing a small potbelly. The door to the Winter Garden is open behind her. It can't be anything serious or he would have closed the door, she tells herself.

"Look, I hate to say it, but I believe that Robert Jay Lifton has already written something similar to what you're proposing in his book *The Nazi Doctors.*"

Iben smiles happily. Clearly all Paul wanted was to carry on talking.

"In it Lifton introduces a concept he calls 'doubling' to describe what happened in the minds of doctors who would spend their days doing experiments involving the torture and mutilation of living human beings, and then go home after work and behave normally, playing with their children and so on."

Iben is familiar with this. "But Paul, Lifton's theory of doubling is different. It states that under pressure of the special conditions in concentration camps, the doctors developed just one separate personality. And this 'other' was independent of their normal selves, which made them perfectly capable of immersing people in boiling water . . ."

Her voice grows louder than it probably should in a conversation with her boss.

"What I've tried to figure out is if the situation is more complex than just the splitting of a personality. You see, my 'grapes' are not mental strategies created under pressure. They already exist inside all of us."

Paul doesn't reply. He puts his hands behind his head and then removes them again. Iben is afraid that she has said something wrong.

At last he speaks: "I'm not sure I agree with you, but that's not the point. I want you to know that, should we come under Morten Kjærum and shuffle across the road, I'll make it my business to fight to keep you. We mustn't lose you. Taking into account that you're an information officer and not a paid researcher, I must say that you're exceptionally talented. And we need talent. I will emphasize that point to everyone."

Iben feels both relieved and proud. At the same time, she's very aware of the open door; the others are undoubtedly listening.

"Thank you . . . thank you very much. It's kind of you to say that."

The whole morning Paul has tried to create a good feeling by praising each of them in turn, but his declaration to Iben proves that she is now at the top of his list.

She walks back to her desk. Her foot hurts less now and it's easier to move without a limp. Camilla, who is right outside Paul's door, must have heard everything he said. She doesn't let on, though. Iben tries to catch her eye; Camilla is gazing intently at her computer screen.

If there is a merger, Malene, as project manager, would almost certainly be the first in line to be laid off, even though she has been in her post the longest time. The look on Malene's face now reminds Iben of Cathy's, back in that filthy hut, when she realized that Iben had become friendlier with Omoro than the rest of them had. But unlike Cathy, Malene doesn't say anything conciliatory.

Instead, she mimes: "Are you coming?"

They go to talk in the small storage room where, only two and half months ago, they and Rasmus had played around, hunting for Anne-Lise's password.

Malene sits down on the old chair and looks at Iben. "Did you truly believe that we were talking about Anne-Lise?"

"Yes, but . . . you were."

"Of course we weren't."

"But—"

Malene interrupts her. "Anne-Lise is hallucinating. And you didn't seem all there yourself. Like you hadn't slept all night. Are you positive about what you did and didn't hear?"

Someone walks past in the corridor. Anne-Lise? Iben and Malene are silent until the sound of footsteps has disappeared.

"You aren't sure, are you? I can see it in your face."

"Yes, I am sure."

"I can't stand the way we always have to put up with Anne-Lise's paranoia. We've been reasonable. Unlike her, we've acted professionally and done our best to make this place work properly. We tried to help her, even though she shouted at us and Paul refused to give her sick leave."

While Malene speaks she presses the tips of her fingers against the wrist of her other hand. The last time Iben saw her do this was once when they were in Malene's apartment. Malene was lying on the sofa, propped up by a lot of cushions. She had just said, "When I'm resting like this, I can hear my bones crumbling, all on their own."

"I simply don't understand why you're encouraging her by saying that we were talking about her when we weren't."

"But you were talking about her."

"I don't want to talk about it anymore. It's not too hard to work out what you're up to."

"What do you mean?"

"You don't want to admit it, do you?"

"Well, you'll have to tell me what you mean first . . ."

"All this with Paul and jobs and cooperating with Anne-Lise."

"What are you saying? Malene, you mustn't think . . ."

"You know, what that e-mail said about you is absolutely true. I've always thought so. You are self-righteous."

They are back at their desks. Iben isn't sure that they are friends any longer. She watches as Malene types away on her ergonomic keyboard. How can she concentrate? How is she able to write? Like Iben, she must want to go home. But Malene is a survivor too.

What next? Iben has visions of a future when she will be free to spend time with Gunnar. They will have dinner together, their heads close together, her hands in his, intimate.

Iben starts to leaf through the massive pile of documents.

Malene is obviously capable of believing that she hasn't said something she really did say. What other things might she do without remembering them afterward? Pour blood into a box file? Send e-mails full of threats?

Iben watches her old friend. She has no idea of what's going on inside Malene's head. Malene feels Iben is looking at her and ignores her. Instead she seems to be engrossed in a couple of folders that are next to the bulletin board.

It couldn't possibly be Malene's voice that Iben heard on the staircase just before Rasmus fell. Until now, Iben thought it was out of the question.

malene

chapter 41

One of the first times Iben and I went to the cinema together *after she had started at the Center, we were walking across the square in front of city hall and she said, "Isn't our city hall unbelievably similar to the main SS guardhouse at Auschwitz-Birkenau?" And a little later, "Did you see that dog? It's just like the dog that belonged to the assistant commandant at Treblinka."*

Iben hadn't worked long for the DCIG, but she was already thinking constantly about genocide and its psychology. I don't think she has the mental stability you need to work in a place like this; she's too sensitive. Unlike the rest of us, she can't keep her cool. I shouldn't blame her—she is who she is. But it drives me absolutely crazy when she stares at me like she thinks I'm some kind of Nazi officer about to subject Anne-Lise to the Final Solution. What can you do with a friend who thinks that about you?

She hasn't said it straight out, but she keeps insinuating it. I get so angry with her. What she's saying makes a mockery of people who have experienced real genocide. How can she draw a parallel between their suffering and a spoiled librarian's failure to understand why people don't like her? How can Iben see me in terms of a genocidal killer? I think she might be close to a nervous breakdown.

As you may have figured out, I can't help but suspect that it's actually Iben who sent the e-mails and exchanged my pills. I'm certain she's weird enough to hide

The phone rings. Malene gets up from her computer and looks around. She realizes how dark the room has become while she has been writing. Positively gloomy. She'll switch on some lights after she deals with the phone call.

It's Malene's mother. "Malene, you really must change the message on your answering machine."

"Oh, Mom, I know. I know."

"It gives you such a shock, hearing his voice."

"I know. It's just one of those things . . ." Malene rubs her face with the knuckles on her left hand. "You know, I still get bills addressed to him. Like he's still using his cell phone and . . . it's awful."

"But Malene, changing the voice message isn't just for your sake—it's about being considerate to other people."

"I'll do it. I promise."

Should I really spend money on another answering machine? she thinks. She knows she can't bring herself simply to erase Rasmus's voice. Some nights she plays his recorded greeting repeatedly. She might drink a bottle of white wine, sliding slowly into oblivion as she presses the button over and over again.

Her mother cuts into her thoughts. "It matters to people who call you."

Sooner or later there might be a power cut, Malene thinks. Or someone might fiddle around with the cables and then I'd lose his message anyway. I should definitely buy a new machine.

Her mother says that she bumped into a few old friends in Kolding. They'd heard about Rasmus and expressed their sympathy for Malene.

"You must let us know if there is anything that Dad or I can do for you. Anything at all. We worry about you so much."

Malene doesn't reply.

"Are you writing to Rasmus?"

"Mmm."

"That's good. I mean, it's good for you to write down what you feel. I'm sure there are so many things you'd like to tell him."

"Mmm."

Afterward, Malene walks around turning on lights. Someone who didn't know about her arthritis might miss the small signs of her illness scattered around her apartment: a plain metal-framed adjustable chair set among the wooden dining chairs; special knives and other equipment in the kitchen; small toylike objects for exercising her fingers.

She sits down and continues her letter.

I admit that Iben is right about some things. We have been too rough on Anne-Lise. We shouldn't lower our own standards. Yet it was Anne-Lise who started it all. She was the one who convinced Paul to give her some of my most exciting responsibilities. She was the one who maneuvered it so that I would be the first in line to be fired if we merge with Human Rights. It doesn't matter that I've been here the longest and that I'm suffering from this vile, diabolical illness, which could make it difficult for me to get another job. And that I lost you three weeks ago.

Rasmus, can't you understand how awful all of this is making me feel? Bitter enough to do things I'd never have thought I was capable of doing?

Even so, I've always behaved professionally toward Anne-Lise. I wasn't friendly, but I was always polite. Iben made me join in with some of her antics—she thought up some really crazy things. I know I shouldn't have played along, and I regret it now. Yet, to think that Iben told me off, in that smug way of hers, for what she had coaxed me to do in the first place.

Malene hits the wrong keys several times. "I'm too angry to write now. I can't . . ." She gets up, grabs her tea, and drinks half of it before sitting down again.

Of course, I'm not so stupid I can't work out why this is happening right now. Iben needs to think up a reason for getting rid of me, and she probably believes every word she says. That's what self-righteousness will do for you.

Oh, Rasmus, I'm so dreadfully disappointed in her. I can't imagine ever trusting her again.

Malene looks around the room. The remains of her supper are on the coffee table. She sits on the sofa to eat because she never did buy a new dining table.

Now you're gone. Iben says that she thinks our relationship wasn't as good as I remember it, but what does she know? What does anyone know? Except you and me!

I

t is a special day for the DCIG.

A genocide researcher has just completed her Ph.D. thesis and today she will take her oral examination at the Historical Institute of the University of Copenhagen. Anita studied the mass killings during Stalin's Great Terror, a period during which, according to some estimates at least, 4.5 million Soviet citizens died.

Ole, who chairs the DCIG board, was her advisor. At one time Anita spent practically every day in the large meeting room going through the extensive but rather chaotic collection of Soviet documents. Everybody in the Center liked her. A trained nurse and the mother of three children, she started to study history at the age of thirty-three. Now, after ten years and a divorce, she is up for a doctorate.

Ole, Frederik, and several other board members are going to attend the formal public examination. It is an academic occasion, but also a reason to celebrate with the doctoral candidate at the reception afterward. The Center has closed for the morning so that Paul and his staff can go as well.

Malene is rushing along the confusing network of wide concrete corridors at the university's Amager campus. She takes a wrong turn, tries another one, and gets it wrong again. She knows that even former students can't always find their way about this place. Iben once likened it to a web spun by a schizophrenic spider.

Two male students are sitting with their papers spread out on top of one of the fixed concrete seats. They turn to look at Malene, who is wearing a tightly fitted dark green jacket that looks good with her light-colored hair. She designed her new knee-high boots herself, drawing them in detail for the orthopedic shoe maker.

She thinks about when would be the right time to call Gunnar. It would be good to get together again. She phoned him once, but he wasn't in and she didn't leave a message. She knows that his magazine has sent him to Afghanistan, but he should be back by now. Maybe his trip was extended.

At last she sees a group of well-dressed historians at the far end of another corridor. Frederik's blond head is sticking up above the crowd. She goes to greet them.

Ole is there too, in the center of the group. Where is Paul? Have he and Frederik met since the board found out about Paul's anti-Frederik machinations?

Malene says hello to everyone. She and Frederik chat in their usual mildly flirtatious way while people begin to drift into the lecture theater. She looks around for Iben and the rest of the DCIG crew. They're probably already seated.

On her way in Malene sees several other familiar faces. Many have no special links either to Anita or to the Soviet purges, as far as Malene knows. Maybe they've come to get into Ole's good books, or Tatiana's? Still no Paul. It depresses her. As things stand now, he of all people should try to humor the chairman.

Then she spots Iben sitting between Anne-Lise and Camilla. So, how far away should I sit from Iben? Malene asks herself. It would look too obvious to go to the opposite end of the room.

Quickly she squeezes between some tables so that she can approach them from the other side and sit next to Camilla rather than Anne-Lise.

She can hear them talking. Their voices carry. Iben, especially, is speaking a little too loudly.

"Do Dragan and Zigic know each other?"

Camilla turns her head nervously from side to side. She seems as if she would like nothing better than to be somewhere else.

"But Iben, Dragan hates Zigic!"

"Camilla, that's not the point. I asked if they know each other."

"Dragan hates him!"

"But, have they met?"

"No, never. They haven't!" Camilla shakes her head. Something about her body language shows that she's lying.

Malene looks around quickly. How many others are listening in? Most likely quite a few.

Iben charges forth. "We looked up Dragan Jelisic in our database. His name is mentioned in a book called *Days of Blood and Singing*. When I was at the Center this morning, I tried to find it, but it's not in the library anymore, although the record shows that it hasn't been checked out."

Malene sits down and asks what's going on, but they are all too absorbed in their conversation with Camilla to answer her. She asks again and Anne-Lise explains, leaning back behind the other two.

"Last night, Iben saw on the Internet that they've dropped all charges against the Chicago Serb who said he'd sent the e-mails."

"Okay, but what is . . . ?"

Malene can easily imagine how that would have upset Iben. However, she has more serious things to worry about.

"Nobody informed us. Iben decided to phone up people to make sure," Anne-Lise adds.

Meanwhile, Iben continues her interrogation of Camilla. "Do you know where that book might be?"

"No, I don't."

Camilla purses her lips and stares at the tabletop. Why is she so bad at lying? It's like she's asking to be punished.

The murmur of voices around them dies down when the audience sees that the chairman of the examiners has stood up.

Iben's eyes stay on Camilla. "Anyway, someone has been in the Center and has . . ." Then she realizes that she's the only one still speaking.

The chairman welcomes everyone and introduces Anita. In a long blue dress, she looks radiant and very much in charge. She says that she is delighted to see so many friends and colleagues with whom she has worked over the last four years, and adds an apology to those who have had to stand at the back. As Anita starts explaining her thesis, Malene figures out what has happened.

Yesterday evening, Iben found out that the supposed sender of the e-mails wasn't under arrest after all. And until yesterday, Malene would have been the first person she phoned with the news. Not anymore. It could be that she contacted Paul as well as Camilla. But either way, she obviously phoned Anne-Lise.

A while ago, Anne-Lise said she had heard that Camilla had a former lover who was a Serbian refugee. Camilla denied it at the time, and they agreed that Anne-Lise had made it up. Now Iben has clearly changed her mind.

Iben and Anne-Lise must have Googled Dragan's name and checked it out in the DCIG database. Anne-Lise must have been so pleased to be working together with Iben on this.

Asking Camilla to explain herself is out of the question while Anita is lecturing, but Malene can't concentrate on what she's saying. She leans forward a little to observe Camilla, who is sitting very still, almost paralyzed. Malene's eyes meet Anne-Lise's. She too keeps glancing at Camilla.

Iben has put her cell phone in front of her on the table. It blinks but doesn't ring. Iben gets up and tries to leave discreetly, but she's carrying her computer bag and has to push past a whole row of people. The scraping of chairs makes quite a racket. She waves her cell phone apologetically at Anita, who seems unfazed and carries on talking.

The Center isn't putting on a good show today. The chief is playing truant, the staff can't keep their mouths shut, and the information officer gets up and leaves in the middle of Anita's presentation.

Why is the call so important? Something to do with Dragan Jelisic? Even so, couldn't it wait? Ever since Iben came back from Kenya she has been quite paranoid, on and off. By now she's probably imagining all kinds of horrors about Camilla's ex-lover.

There is an interval after the first speaker finishes debating Anita's thesis with her. Crowds of people slowly drift out of the hall, and at the door Malene finds herself standing next to a couple of university lecturers with whom she worked on a project investigating Danish immigration policy during the 1930s. She feels it's only polite to talk to them. Once she reaches the corridor, Iben and the others are already out of sight. She pops her head around the door to the reception area, where wine, cheese, and assorted tapas are waiting to be served. The others aren't in there either. Mikala, another historian, says that she's helping Anita by setting out the party food.

They chat for a while and suddenly Ole and Frederik turn up. Ole has a Coke in his hand. He turns to Malene, who notices there's a minuscule crumb of chocolate stuck in his beard.

"Where's Paul?"

"I've no idea."

"He's avoiding me. I couldn't get hold of him on his cell phone either."

"That's odd. He usually keeps his cell phone on all the time."

Malene doesn't care for the way Ole and Frederik seem to be in cahoots.

"Maybe his battery has run down."

Ole and Frederik exchange a strange glance.

"Oh, I hope he hasn't had an accident," she adds.

Frederik smiles at her. "No, that's not it."

"What do you mean?"

Frederik makes a face and Malene senses that she mustn't ask him any more. She can usually make him tell her everything. Maybe it's Ole's presence that's stopping him.

The talking outside the room has grown to a roar.

Malene manages to slip through the crowd and follows the corridor to the end. No luck. She returns through the crowd and goes to the opposite end. No one here either. Then she turns a corner and hears voices from behind the closed door of a seminar room.

Iben is shouting. "How do you explain this?"

Malene opens the door just as Iben starts to read from the screen of her laptop:

"It is a well-known fact that the lifelong trauma affecting people who have survived severe torture will include vivid, intensely painful flashbacks in which they reexperience all their past suffering. Such recall phenomena are triggered every time they see something that reminds them of the torture. The militiamen entering the Omarska camps manipulated the flashback phenomenon with endless inventiveness. Mirko Zigic, now wanted by the War Crimes Tribunal in The Hague, and one of his soldiers, Dragan Jelisic . . . !"

Iben stops dramatically and stares at Camilla, who can't seem to stop crying. She continues to read: "And one of his soldiers, Dragan Jelisic, thought up the trick of placing bottles of Coca-Cola within sight of prisoners being tortured. For decades to come, survivors of their torture will relive the full terror of the destructive pain they were once subjected to every time they see a bottle of Coke. And where in the world can they hide from the occasional sight of a bottle of Coca-Cola?"

Anne-Lise, who has been perched on the edge of a table, gets up. "This man was your lover!"

Camilla somehow looks like a scolded schoolgirl. "But I didn't know it back then." She looks up at them. "It was dreadful when I found out. That's why I went for the job in the Center. You know me. I think things like that are terrible, and you must know me better than that!"

"How long were you and Dragan together?" Iben asks.

"Four months."

Camilla is weeping even louder now, her head in her hands. Iben makes a move to put her arms around her, but Camilla angrily waves her away.

Now they can only stand and look. They're at a loss. No one has switched on the lights despite the gray day. The dull daylight turns the walls the color of damp cardboard and makes the tabletops look like pools of stagnant water. Iben and Anne-Lise are drained of color too.

Iben puts down her computer on a table and Malene walks over to it. Iben was reading from an e-mailed selection of scanned book pages from *Days of Blood and Singing*, and the source is someone working for the UN Commission for Human Rights in Geneva. The e-mail arrived during Anita's lecture.

Camilla wraps her arms around herself. Her eyes have a distant look and she speaks in a soft, low voice: "He wasn't at all like the way they describe him in that book. I was with him before I got together with Finn. Dragan cared about me even though I'm so fat. He didn't mind my body."

Malene looks from the computer screen to Camilla's body, which doesn't appear to be overweight at all.

Anne-Lise takes up the questioning. "Where did you meet?"

"At a party. He was such a little guy, almost weedy. He looked like he'd never hurt a flea. I felt sorry for him. He was a refugee, chased out of his own country. He said that his three sisters had been raped by Bosnians. They killed the girls afterward. He told me all that, and he seemed so unhappy that I . . . I don't know. Anyway, we met afterward and then again."

Camilla wipes her face on her sleeve. "And he says everything about him in that book isn't true."

Iben is still clearly agitated, but her voice is quieter. "Did it ever occur to you that a man like Jelisic, who has killed hundreds of human beings, might lie to you?"

Camilla doesn't answer. They are all silent.

After a while Camilla speaks again. "He admitted that he had done bad things. Countless people did, that's true. But he wasn't at all like that when I met him. And he didn't want to talk about it. He was so torn up inside."

"Do you still see him?" Iben asks.

"No, I don't . . . of course I don't."

"Have you seen him since you read this book?"

"No."

"But you did ask him if what the book said was true—isn't that what you've just said?"

It's strange to see Camilla like this. She always seemed so sensible. Now it's as if she were someone else. Her crying and transparent lies remind Malene of what Grith had told them about women with DID, especially the part about them being subjected to abuse as children. Often one of their identities tends to be a distressed child.

Iben takes a deep breath. "Are our views of this man really so far apart? When you believed he had sent you that hate e-mail, you seemed terrified. More frightened than we were—and you still are. Why?"

Camilla doesn't answer.

Anne-Lise asks, "Is he still in Denmark?"

Camilla's head is lowered. She pinches her arm in several places. "I don't know."

"But you believe that he sent these e-mails?"

"I don't know."

"But you thought he had sent the one to you?"

Camilla doesn't reply.

Iben takes over. "Do you think that he was responsible for the blood and for exchanging the medicine?"

Camilla looks down again. "I get confused when you're like this, Iben. I just can't . . . It's just that . . ."

"Do you think that he pushed Rasmus?"

"Stop it! Stop attacking me!"

Anne-Lise looks undecided whether to try to comfort Camilla or keep her distance.

Camilla is still shouting. "I want to go home!"

"Of course you do. I know this is tough for you, I can see that. We'll help you find a taxi . . . but first, just tell us this. Do we need to be careful? Will this man try something else? Would he really try to kill us?"

Although Iben is speaking calmly, Malene detects a genuine underlying fear.

When Camilla repeats that she wants to go home, Iben gently replies: "We'll stop after a couple more questions. Can't you see that we are all in this together? We need to figure out as a group how we can best protect ourselves. Don't you agree?"

"Yes." Camilla peers at them. "Yes, you're right. I agree. But I do need to go to the bathroom."

"Of course."

After the door closes behind Camilla, Malene turns on the light.

The break was over long ago. Malene glances at Anne-Lise, taking in her broad, square-jawed face, her dark shoulder-length hair, and her dull, expensive clothes.

No one speaks.

Finally, Iben breaks the silence. "When she comes back we must try to be kinder to her. Perhaps we were a little too hard on her."

The minutes pass, and after a while it becomes obvious that Camilla is not coming back.

Iben stands at the window, carefully scanning the gray buildings and bare trees, as if a Serb militiaman might be lying in wait for her. Malene knows this is exactly what is on her mind.

Anne-Lise goes and looks out the window as well. With the lights on, the faces of the two women, standing close together, are reflected in the large panes against the wintry background outside.

Malene also wants to do what Camilla did: simply slip away.

he hums the bass line of an old Barry White number first: "Daaaum—daum daum—da da." Then he starts the message.

"You have reached Rasmus and Malene's answering machine. Where are we now? We don't know either. So, please leave a message after the tone."

It's evening now and Malene has lit only a few small lamps scattered around her living room. She listens tearfully to Rasmus's message. When she's heard the message a couple of times, she goes to the kitchen and takes a bottle of white wine out of the fridge. Drinking will ruin her night, but she doesn't care. Settling onto the large pale sofa, she plays the message again.

"Daaaum—daum daum—da da. You have reached Rasmus and Malene's answering machine. Where are we now? We don't know either. So, please leave a message after the tone."

She finishes the glass, drinks another one, and then goes to get his pale blue T-shirt. He forgot to pack it because it was in the laundry basket. She hasn't washed it. She lies on her back on the sofa and holds the T-shirt to her chest.

Iben would find this beyond comprehension, she thinks, even though she wouldn't actually ask Malene why she's tormenting herself like that.

"Daaaum—daum daum—da da. You have reached Rasmus and Malene's answering machine. Where are we now? . . ."

Her fingers are tingling. It's from all the crying. She wants some ice cream. Malene pulls herself together and walks in a reasonably straight line to the kitchen. She takes out a pack of vanilla ice cream with cherry swirls. The scoop has the right kind of broad, soft handle, but even so she should leave the ice cream to soften a little. Never mind. She stabs at it, hurting her hand in the process. She wipes a few tears away with her sleeve and returns to the living room.

She is back on the floor in the darkened room, listening to the message again and again. The bottle is empty. She knows she should stop, but instead fills a glass with rum, orange juice, and ice, and recalls what she said to Rasmus the last time they met.

They stood together in the hall. He was on his way to his new girlfriend's place with three jackets slung over his arm. The twisted brass hooks point at the back of Malene's head. Her own coats and jackets hang from the other hooks, without shape or life, like carcasses in a slaughterhouse. The fur collar on her green coat is unpleasantly close to her cheek.

She shouted at him, like she is doing now. "So why don't you just leave! Leave! I don't fucking want you here anymore! You're a liar! A fucking liar! Don't think for a second that I'll take you back when she throws you out!" She hits out with her arms, as if he were there.

He tried to calm her.

"Malene, Malene, please. I'm so sorry . . ."

"Don't! You lost the right to say 'Malene' like that! Just go. Liar!"

He tried again. "Can't we just . . . This is so difficult."

She stamps the floor and strikes the green coat beside her. "You're a total shit! I'll never have you back! Whatever happens to you!"

"Oh, Malene. I'm so sorry."

That's what he said. He'd said, "Oh, Malene. I'm so sorry."

Because he was carrying his jackets, he wasn't able to defend himself when she slapped him. Her hand hurt like hell, but he didn't seem to feel a thing.

All the while she was certain that he would come back to her. He would have come back.

She was also certain that he would have turned around and never come back.

When she drinks some more, the words begin to change.

She stands in the hall. He is there. The empty hooks stick out, shiny and eye-catching.

"Don't leave! Don't fucking leave! I want you here, I do! You liar. I want you!"

"Oh, Malene. I'm so sorry."

That's what he says. He has said, "Oh, Malene. I'm so sorry."

"It's a mistake. A misunderstanding. You do want to stay with me!"

"Yes. I do."

They kiss. She reaches out. With one hand, she grabs hold of one of the short black legs of the coffee table, and with the other, the thick legs of the sofa.

She is still, her eyes closed.

Now that she is quiet, Malene can hear her neighbor in the apartment below making a racket. He's banging on the pipes and howling, "Shut up!"

It's simply too much. He knows that Rasmus has died. Without moving, she screams, "Shut up yourself!"

She watches the pattern of light on the white ceiling. Her hands and feet are starting to hurt. She should take one of her strong painkillers.

She gets up slowly, holding on to the coffee table.

Standing doesn't feel too bad; she's not completely drunk. Her body feels odd, though, like a piece of meat that's been cooked for hours and hours until the flesh falls off the bones.

She moves slowly toward the bathroom; every step causes a burning sensation in one of her feet.

She swallows a pill.

Back in the living room she checks the time. It's only a quarter to eleven. Maybe she'll even escape a hangover.

Her phone rings and displays Gunnar's number.

She decides to answer.

"Hi, Malene. It's Gunnar. Is this too late to call?"

"No. Not at all."

"Are you sure I'm not disturbing you? You sound slightly out of it."

"No, I'm fine. I fell asleep on the sofa and just woke up. I'm pleased it's you."

"I'm back from Afghanistan. I saw you'd phoned me."

"Well, I guess so."

"I thought maybe we could get together?"

"I'd like that very much."

"Should we figure out a date now?"

Malene thinks for a second. "Do you want to come over? Tonight?"

A pause.

"Do you really think that's a good idea?"

"It'd be so nice to see you. You can tell me about Afghanistan. While everything is still fresh in your mind."

"Okay. That sounds good. It should take me about twenty minutes."

Malene picks up the cushions and the wet paper towels, wipes spilled juice off the coffee table, and puts back the candlestick and the books that have fallen to the ground. She opens the windows wide to air the room and changes into a rather revealing dress. She knows she should behave properly, but just thinking about Gunnar makes her excited. Maybe it's the combination of the alcohol and the painkillers.

When she opens the door to him, he glances quickly at her dress. A look of surprise crosses his face. Gunnar is tanned, which makes his eyes appear lighter. He has brought a bottle of wine. Smiling broadly, he hugs her and asks how things are.

Malene is about to start telling him but realizes it could ruin the evening. "Oh, you'll get the whole story, but not now. I want to hear about your trip."

Sitting on the sofa, he doesn't begin to talk about his travels—instead he just looks at Malene with a certain amount of surprise. Does she seem drunk? She hopes not. He's been laying siege to these walls for years, and now she'll let the gate swing open after the gentlest of knocks. He pretends to reach for his wineglass, letting his wrist touch her arm. She meets his gaze. It could be the expression on her face that makes him kiss her.

He's good at it. His body feels warmer than Rasmus's.

She has never been with a man over forty, but Gunnar is more in shape than she thought and surprisingly seems to know her body better than Rasmus ever did. When her breathing deepens, she remembers when she was once far out at sea in a sailboat and had jumped naked into the ocean. The underwater sensation comes back to her now, the light pressure of the water all over her body, her hair streaming out and up around her. She comes up for air, gasping.

She and Rasmus used to swim naked and then surface together, spluttering, spitting salt water and laughing at each other.

She bursts into tears.

Gunnar holds her tight and lets her cry. "Does this feel wrong for you?"

"No. No."

"I know that you must . . . you know, miss him. You must. But I thought that . . ."

"Gunnar, it's all right. We've known each other for years and I'm so glad that you're here tonight. I'm very fond of you."

Gunnar gets the wine and their glasses. They start to talk about Rasmus and Afghanistan. But their attention soon wanders back to each other's bodies.

It's almost three in the morning. They discover how hungry they are and move to the kitchen. Malene takes out olives, bread, a couple of different cheeses, and fruit preserves, and then slips off to the bathroom for another pill. The first one is still doing its job; the second one is just in case.

Gunnar begins to reminisce about when he was younger than Malene is now. He was determined to make a difference in the world, to make it a more just society and improve conditions in the third world.

"We all know that the bottle of wine we've drunk tonight could have paid for vaccinating twenty kids and saving the life of at least one. We're no different from the Germans during World War Two. They knew that Jews were being killed, but they ignored what it meant."

Malene is massaging the knuckles on her right hand. "But it isn't quite the same, is it? The state killed them back then. You're talking about aid for the poor."

"I believe, in essence, it is the same. We put on shoes produced by a child who is being crippled by work. We drink coffee bought at starvation prices."

Gunnar leans across the table, takes her aching hand, and warms it between his hands.

"I very much hope that the world will become a better place. And if it does, our grandchildren may look at us the way young people today regard the generation who collaborated with the Nazis. They'll say, 'I do not understand you.' We will explain that life simply was the way it was. 'Famines came and went and no one did anything about it. People died of hunger to provide us with cheaper coffee.' We'll have to admit that we knew but chose to do nothing about it."

Malene feels uneasy but can't figure out why. She wants to pull her hand back, but doesn't. She has an impulse to say, "You old Socialist," and tease him, but knows she shouldn't.

"The kids will hate us because they have never been in our situation. They will turn on us and say, 'You must've been so different back then. How could you watch a film or eat in a restaurant when you knew that the money you spent might have saved a child's life?' They will say, 'I don't get it. I could never do anything like that.' "

Gunnar looks expectant, waiting for her response. Malene realizes what's making her feel uncomfortable. It's his manner of speaking: the manic rhythm of his words, and his complete absorption in his subject. He reminds her of Iben.

Malene feigns exhaustion, but Gunnar's energy is undiminished. She asks him if he slept on the plane.

"Not much," he says vaguely, and begins on a subject that has fascinated Iben these last few months: the psychology of evil.

"Ignoring the small flash of doubt in yourself—that is what evil is. Nobody thinks of himself as evil, but that deception is part of evil's nature. And you can't lie to yourself all the time. Once in a while, there's that moment when you question if you are doing the right thing. And that's your only chance to choose what is good, to do the right thing. And the moment lasts maybe fifteen minutes every other month, maybe less.

"Most people will immediately decide not to act. The implications of having to change their lifestyle are just too overwhelming, and then it doesn't take long before they forget that there is another option. They're stuck in their old ways—good or bad."

Malene wonders about Gunnar. "Why do you feel so strongly about this?"

"Because I know what it's like to be caught up in evil. Quite a long time ago, I was a hard-core member of the Communist Workers' Party. I spent years fighting for the ideology of people who were responsible for more mass killings and genocides than the Nazis. In effect, we were sustaining those dictatorships. I knew the truth—of course I did. At least, every once in a while."

Malene has never heard Gunnar speak so openly about his early life.

He interrupts her thoughts. "But I have no more to regret than today's neoliberals. Socialists aren't responsible for as many people dying as those who support the policies of the U.S. and Europe, policies that reinforce poverty and economic dependency. And it is happening here and now."

It is pitch black outside the kitchen windows. Malene begins to put the food away. She sees how Gunnar loves to turn arguments on their heads. Iben too. For years now Malene has enjoyed listening to him and to Iben.

The true source of her discomfort is the thought of how well Iben and Gunnar would get along together.

In the morning Malene is tired. Gunnar set the alarm for six because he has an early meeting. She would have loved to call in sick, but doesn't dare to—not when the office is in such a state of flux. Instead she sleeps until nine, then calls the office with a story about a dental appointment and says she'll be in by eleven.

Camilla, who answers the phone, begins to apologize. She goes on and on. "I know I shouldn't have left like that, without a word, but I . . . you know, being in a classroom brought back things that happened to me at school. And I felt terrible about Dragan Jelisic."

Malene is lying on the sofa, wrapped in a blanket. "You really didn't know what kind of a person he was then?"

"No, I didn't. But, Malene, I've been so stupid. I should have told you about him right away. I do realize that. It was wrong and I'm annoyed at myself. Please forgive me. I hope you're not too angry?"

"No, no. Not at all." Malene means it. If she had learned about Camilla's indirect connection to Mirko Zigic a month ago, she might have been much angrier. But now she is much more concerned about how she'll manage her life without Rasmus, as well as preoccupied with Gunnar and her crumbling friendship with Iben and the possibility of losing her job.

There's no room to be terrified of some Serbian mass murderer who might—might—have sent them scary e-mails. She knows it's different for Iben.

When Malene arrives at the Center, Iben is going full steam.

She spent last night phoning people again. First she called Camilla to pump her for more details and persuade her to call Paul and tell him everything about her Yugoslav contact. Then she called journalists and genocide experts all over the world. Listening to the women talk, Malene learns that Anne-Lise has also been finding out more about Jelisic.

I should have checked in on Iben last night, Malene tells herself. Instead Anne-Lise must have called her to commiserate.

They seem to have already discussed the likelihood of Zigic still having ties to Camilla's ex-lover and analyzed various options for finding out more about Jelisic. Clearly they have been sharing their fears with each other.

It isn't long before Malene wants to go back to bed. When Rasmus died, Paul told her she could leave the office whenever she needed to. Only she doesn't want to be alone. It would be great to phone Gunnar for sympathy, but that's impossible now, after having just spent the night together.

She takes her mug of coffee and sits down opposite Iben. "How's it going?" they ask each other. Iben briefs Malene on her Jelisic research and talks about how scared she is of him.

Is this her oldest, dearest friend? She cannot believe how much things have changed between them and that she's losing her just when she needs her most. Still, she must face up to the fact that Iben has changed, possibly for good. How can Iben be so cold and calculating, especially after Rasmus's death? But it seems Malene has become an obstacle in Iben's pursuit of both Gunnar and a new career in the DIHR. Why bother being sentimental over the past? Regardless of the Iben-shaped void in Malene's life?

She listens as Iben calls the Belgrade office of the International War Crimes Tribunal and is passed from contact to contact without learning anything new. Malene looks at the familiar details: the broken spring on Iben's lamp, the plastic troll on her own desk. Then she turns to the board with all its cheery photos of Iben and Malene posing with Tatiana in Prague, sitting next to Frederik and Paul at a dinner table in Odense, and standing around with academics at a conference in Oslo.

She is worn out. Malene gets up and goes to the kitchen. She refills her mug and returns. She prints some information and goes to get it from the central printer next to the library. On the way, she pops in to browse through the large collection of East European documents. She looks for a couple of articles in the magazine boxes behind Camilla's desk. She'd do anything not to be sitting opposite Iben, looking at her pale face.

Later while Malene is hanging out in the kitchen, eating cookies from an old plastic bag, Camilla comes bursting in, obviously not expecting to find anyone. She is visibly upset. Seeing Malene, she quickly tries to change her expression, but it's too late. Malene asks her what's happened.

Camilla paces up and down in the small space. "They won't stop!"

"What do you mean?"

"Now they're asking me about Dragan's friends. 'Are any of them blond?' "

"Really?"

"They started on the phone last night and they haven't stopped all morning. I gave them a blow-by-blow account of every person I ever met with Dragan."

Malene looks incredulous.

"It's Iben, really," Camilla explains. "She is convinced that Zigic is in Denmark and that I've met him without knowing it. She thinks he's here under a false name and she's doing everything she can to find out. But I had to tell her that none of the men I'd met with Dragan looked anything like the pictures of Zigic! But still she picks and picks and picks on me. She says that I must've met lots of former Serbian militiamen when I went out with Dragan."

Malene wants to soothe her and tries to take Camilla's hand, but Camilla brushes her away. She rubs her hands on her blouse and keeps walking around.

"She thinks I'm lying, all the time. She now thinks it was me who was there . . . on the staircase, with Rasmus!"

Her voice becomes whiny. "Malene, you don't think so, do you? Only Iben would dream up something like that—right?"

"No, of course I don't. Not at all." Malene puts the cookies on a plate and offers one to Camilla. "I do understand how you're feeling. It's totally crazy."

Camilla stops and shakes her head, staring down at the plate. "No, I mustn't. But thanks."

"It would do Iben good to sleep more than four hours a night, don't you think, Camilla? And not spend most of it reading books full of descriptions of psychiatric diseases or the murders of millions of people? It could help her, couldn't it?"

This is the first time anyone in the office has heard Malene criticize Iben. They both realize that, starting today, all the old alliances are null and void. Unless Malene wants to become a lone wolf in the office, she'll need to find a new ally: Camilla. She knows that they're too different to become close friends, but that doesn't matter. After all, Anne-Lise will never become truly close to Iben.

Malene tries again to comfort Camilla. She tells her how she feels about the way Iben has behaved these last few days. But there are things about Iben that Malene won't give away. Right after her father's death, Iben would apparently wander the streets in a state of deep depression. She acquired a profound aversion to people, and this antipathy caused such an overpowering reaction that on two occasions Iben had to spend the night in a psychiatric ward.

Now Iben is seen as a very competent person. Few would guess the hidden flaws that Malene knows so well. Or do the others sense something? Could this be the reason that everyone was so amazed by the heroic stories of Iben in Kenya?

When Malene returns to the Winter Garden, Iben still hasn't unearthed any more information about Jelisic. Nothing, that is, apart from the familiar Omarska stories that have already been circulated in the press and reported to the War Crimes Tribunal. Like the ones about how Jelisic and two other volunteer camp guards killed a couple of prisoners by forcing them to drink engine oil, and made fathers bite off the testicles of their own sons. Horrors of that kind.

Iben has no evidence as to where he is and what he is doing. Camilla insisted this morning that, unlike Zigic, Dragan is not a member of the Yugo Mafia, and says he is not in contact with Zigic any longer. But Iben can't hide the fact that she doesn't trust Camilla one inch.

Anne-Lise keeps coming in to tell Iben about her latest phone calls. She's good at pretending that she's as scared as Iben. And when they walk from one computer to the other, Anne-Lise follows Iben like a lapdog—an anxious one who glances nervously from time to time at Malene.

Malene tries to concentrate on reading an article about the expulsion of 3.5 million inhabitants from the German regions of Czechoslovakia. The plan is to publish an edited volume of the delegates' papers about the fates of the 15 million ethnic Germans in Eastern Europe in time for the conference. When the Germans occupied Czechoslovakia they behaved with more restraint than anywhere else, except Denmark, but many of the regional Germans supported the occupation. So, during the war, the future Czech president said he would demand "a radical and definitive solution" to the German problem—he envisaged a "one hundred percent effective extermination of Germans." During the first postwar year, some 270,000 Germans were killed and more than 3 million expelled.

The phone rings. Camilla's strange response to the call distracts Malene. Usually so friendly, she seems hesitant and at a loss for words. "If I can see it's from you . . . yes. I suppose it's all right if your name is on the back."

She catches Malene's eye and makes a face. "I see. Then it's not . . . If I mustn't even mention it to Paul, then . . . yes, but . . . All right, I'll do that. Yes, I promise I'll destroy it. I understand. I'll get rid of it. Bye for now."

Baffled, Malene and Iben stare at Camilla. Anne-Lise turns up at the library door.

"It was Ole," Camilla tells them.

"Really?"

All three of them are astonished.

"Yes. You see, Ole wrote a letter to Paul, but now he says it's vital that Paul does not get it. I'm to take the letter from Paul's in-tray and shred it. I'm not supposed to read it or tell Paul."

"It's the sack!" Iben blurts out. "Ole got the support of the rest of the board for getting rid of Paul and yesterday he wrote the letter of dismissal. But why change his mind today?"

They all agree that it probably means the boot for Paul. Malene tries to figure out the consequences for herself, but has trouble. Possible scenarios tumble around in her mind. She is too tired and weak to think straight. If the tension between herself and Iben reaches some sort of crisis and one of them has to go, Paul will keep Iben. But if Paul has to leave first and Frederik is still deputy chairman of the board, then the chances are he will have Iben kicked out. But if Frederik is no longer on the DCIG board by then and Gunnar has taken his place? Who would Gunnar prefer?

Malene realizes that before she arrived they must also have been discussing the awkward situation of Paul versus Frederik. Anne-Lise says that her husband has a great amount of experience in this because he's sat on so many corporate boards. In Henrik's view, Paul's attempt to eliminate Frederik was such an outrageous maneuver that the board has no option other than to get rid of him.

They discuss who should take over as temporary leader of the DCIG—Anne-Lise thinks Iben is the one who should be Paul's long-term replacement. They talk about what Paul would do next and if his departure would increase the likelihood of a merger with Human Rights. And, of course, they have to wonder why Paul seems so calm about everything, and where he has been these last few days.

Malene has many questions but she can't make herself talk to Iben or Anne-Lise. She can't bear even to meet Anne-Lise's eyes ever since Rasmus died. Instead she turns to Camilla. Does she detect something? Something small. Tiny. As if Camilla is trying to avoid Malene's glance.

This will get worse, Malene thinks. Less than an hour ago, I comforted her when Iben had upset her. But in front of Iben, Camilla knows who is the strongest and has chosen sides accordingly.

Malene hates Iben for this too.

Malene catches a picture of herself in some suburban street back in Kolding, trotting around talking ineptly to groups of acquaintances, just like her mother used to do when Malene still lived at home. Now Malene is the ghost at the party, unemployed, dressed in some dull old sack of a dress and complaining, as her mother did: "It feels as if my old colleagues wanted me dead and out of the way. How can people be like that?"

It seems that nothing she has done or achieved has helped her to escape from her mother's shadow—not moving to Copenhagen nor getting a university degree. And it's Iben's fault.

They must get back to work. Malene is determined not to mention Gunnar.

No more than a quarter of an hour later, Malene smiles at Iben and speaks in the old confiding way, as if she has no idea that there's been a change in their friendship.

"Iben, Gunnar spent the night with me."

"Oh, he did?" Iben manages to look friendly and curious, as if the previous week hadn't happened, as if Malene were talking about any man.

She then hurries out into the corridor, toward the restroom. Malene sighs. She relaxes and smiles at Camilla, who looks questioningly at her. Maybe later Malene will feel bad, but maybe not.

Iben returns. She looks paler than usual. A tiny muscle is twitching beneath the blue skin under her right eye. She sits down. They both carry on reading their articles.

After a few minutes Iben speaks. "I can't concentrate with you staring at me like that."

"I'm not staring at you."

"Yes, you are."

"I'm not!"

Iben gets up again. "I have a lot to do."

"I know that very well."

"So far I've spent the whole day on Dragan Jelisic. I need to finish the Turkey issue."

"I know."

"And you're staring at me."

"No, Iben, I'm not."

"Look, I'm not trying to punish you or whatever it is you imagine. It's just that I can't get anything done when you just sit there and watch me. I assume that you can't concentrate with me here?"

Iben is right, but Malene doesn't reply.

"We'll both do better if I work somewhere else. I'm going to move to one of the readers' desks in the library."

Malene stiffens and almost shouts, "You're going to sit with Anne-Lise?"

"That's exactly how I didn't want you to take it. I'm not . . . 'going to sit with Anne-Lise.' I'm going to sit somewhere where you can't keep staring at me like you're doing now." Iben starts gathering up her papers.

Everything is happening so quickly. Soon the picture of office life will look utterly different.

Malene watches Iben as she marches off with her bundles of paper. She's no longer prepared to fight to keep their old friendship.

Near the end of the day, Malene goes to the restroom.

When she comes back, Camilla has disappeared. Malene stops in the doorway, calling into the empty air: "Camilla? . . . Camilla?"

No one answers.

In the silence, Malene's thoughts move unhindered. Is Camilla in the library? Is she joining the other two in there? Is the idea to exclude Malene?

Malene listens. She hears a murmur of voices coming out of the library but can't tell whether it's two or three.

She goes to the middle of the Winter Garden and then stops. The light from the fluorescent tubes reflects off the large shiny leaves of the plants on the windowsills. She has looked after these plants for ages. She turns, but no one is standing behind her.

Again, she calls out: "Camilla? Where are you? Camilla?"

camilla

chapter 45

Once Camilla eavesdropped on two women sitting behind her in the bus. In the middle of their gossip, one of them said, "You know, she's one of these women who always pick men who're bad for them." Camilla has forgotten whatever else they were talking about, but that phrase stayed with her.

She met Dragan almost ten years ago, at a party given by Lena, who's in the choir. Camilla had turned up in the afternoon to help Lena and Simo, her husband, arrange the furniture, make the salads, and set out the food. By seven o'clock, Camilla was eager to start getting ready for the party. She put on a freshly ironed, loose-fitting dark blue shirt and an ankle-length skirt in a shade of light brown that matched her hair—clothes that flattered her figure. Lena had noticed that she was getting flustered and told her not to worry. Simo's friends always came bumbling along at any old time. Simo was an electrician from Yugoslavia but had moved to Denmark long before the civil war started in his homeland.

Lena was right. Most of the Yugoslavs turned up really late, and their behavior at the party was something of a shock to Camilla. The drinking was much heavier for a start, the dancing was wilder, and the music louder. And all of them seemed to feel that parties were not only for chatting about this and that but also an outlet for their emotions.

At one point during the evening, a dark-haired man with a square jaw stood outside on the balcony and shouted incomprehensibly at people in the street. In the apartment everybody laughed, as if the man's behavior were a normal part of their Saturday-night fun. Some of his friends made him come back inside and sit on the sofa. Camilla started talking to him. His English was very good. He said that his name was Dragan and he had been a schoolteacher in Bosnia. He had come to Denmark a month ago and lived near Lyngby, in a refugee camp for Yugoslav asylum seekers. He looked to be in his late twenties, roughly the same age as she, but he didn't mention anything about a wife or children.

They got up to dance, but it went badly. The music was unlike anything Camilla had ever heard before, a surreal mixture of gypsy melody and punk rock. Dragan was dancing about wildly, with big leaps and flailing arms, but even in all the noise and under the low lights, Camilla couldn't let herself go.

Later that night she went to the kitchen to rest her legs. Two friends from the choir were there too. While they were talking, a spat broke out in another room. There was a terrific crash.

They hurried to find out what was going on. A group of angry Yugoslavs had gathered around Dragan. Someone explained that Dragan had gotten into an argument with a buddy who had locked himself in the bathroom. After some shouting at each other through the door, Dragan had kicked it down. Some of the guests seemed very frightened.

Dragan himself was still very agitated about whatever the man in the bathroom had said and wouldn't stop yelling. Something made Camilla walk toward him. She heard Lena saying to her husband that she was going to throw Dragan out. Simo replied that he didn't want her to.

When Camilla stopped in front of Dragan, he took her in his arms. They stood together for a while. Quite still. He stopped shouting. Then they went off to dance.

A few minutes later Lena came up to them. She said she wanted to thank Camilla for calming Dragan down. She asked if he had ruined the evening for Camilla and if she would like Lena to ask him to leave. Camilla told her no.

They kept on dancing and talking. Later on they made love on his large black coat, spread on the ground in the shrubbery behind a large upmarket block of apartments in Frederiksberg. He walked her home afterward and seemed so different from the way he had acted at the party. He recited long Serbian love poems, which he knew by heart, and spoke about the ideas and characters in books written by Russian authors a hundred years ago.

The next few weeks were special. Camilla had suddenly become a member of a circle of Yugoslavs that included both recent refugees and older immigrants who had come to live in Denmark before the war. She went to dozens of their wild parties, as well as to little get-togethers in asylum camp rooms and down-at-heel apartments with a decidedly Balkan decor. Since the refugees had plenty of spare time, there was a gathering almost every evening.

An apartment belonging to Goran, a stage technician at the Betty Nansen Theater, was a favorite meeting place. Evening after evening Goran's hallway was full of his guests' black jackets, frequently smelling damp because even when it rained his friends would walk everywhere to save money.

They got along well together, the Serbs and Muslims and Croats. Back in the old country, their brothers, fathers, colleagues, and schoolmates were busy killing one another, but here they worked hard to form a community that would help them live with some dignity in what they hoped would be their new homeland.

Apart from Camilla and three Yugoslav women, everyone in the group was male—young men with strong features and, sometimes, muscular bodies shaped by military training. They hung around Goran's, ate hearty soups in his living room, and teased one another. When they watched television, they would become very serious and discuss everything under the sun. And when they thought of something to celebrate, they would pour out shots of slivovitz, a plum brandy that Dragan explained was mostly a drink for old people in Yugoslavia.

Camilla noticed that the others had respect for Dragan. They regarded him as wise and well read. Only when he had too much to drink would his personality change. He would pick fights with the others, shouting abuse and calling them names. Once he threw a television set through the window because of something that was said on the news.

All the same, everyone seemed genuinely fond of him. This was something Camilla realized was part of their culture: you stood by your friends no matter what. You gave each other space to be wrong and explode, unlike the Danes, who would have run the other way. Such resolute loyalty was something Camilla would come back to again and again when she told her friend Anja about her new boyfriend and his world. Camilla heard of only one person who could never be forgiven. That man was Mirko Zigic. In those days she didn't have a clue why Zigic was such a reviled figure. The others never said more than "Zigic enjoys the war, while everyone else suffers." Dragan said he'd kill Zigic if they ever met again.

Dragan moved into Camilla's little apartment just two weeks after the party at Lena and Simo's. Every morning she woke feeling happy and somehow cleansed. Sex with him was wonderful and washed away her past, because he came to her with the same passion that seemed to drive his rage.

He usually stayed in bed while she flew through her morning routines. Often—maybe a little too often—she arrived late at the City Post Office, where she was working as a junior secretary.

One day a friend told her that during his escape from Bosnia, Dragan had lived for a while in a dumpster. He had put a mattress in it and slept there at night, after bolting the lid from the inside so that no one could rob or kill him. Someone else told her what had happened when Dragan had taken a train from Banja Luka. A group of Serb militiamen had stopped the train and ordered the male Muslims to get out and pile into large, locked vans. They also took the young male Serbs, forced them to join the militia after a short period of military training, and informed them that any deserters would be shot. That's why Dragan had been a member of the uniformed militia.

She made attempts to unravel Dragan's past, but every time she tried to ask him about it, he became annoyed and told her to mind her own business. Yet she felt that, as his girlfriend, she had a right to know.

One evening over supper she decided to push again for answers. He started to shout at her and throw things about. Although he didn't hit her, she knew he would have if he hadn't checked himself and rushed out the door into the street. By ten o'clock he still wasn't back. Worried, Camilla called Goran to find out if Dragan was there. Goran's girlfriend, Natasa, said he wasn't. She could hear how upset Camilla was and urged her to tell her the whole story. Natasa reassured her. She had lived and worked in Denmark for ten years and knew both cultures well.

"Camilla, I want you to know that Dragan cares for you very much. It means a lot to him that you appreciate what a warm and wise man he is."

"Oh, I do."

"But, you see, if your relationship is to last, you must also respect him as a man."

"I do, honestly."

"It's hard for him to believe that you do. There he is, living in your apartment without paying anything himself. Just two years ago he was a schoolteacher with good prospects. He had done well for himself in a country that in many ways was rather like Denmark. He wants you to see him as the kind of man who can quote by heart from Dostoyevsky and Borges and Kundera. It was humiliating to have to live in a dumpster. It was humiliating to be unable to stand up against men who marched him off a train and into an army truck. And it is humiliating to live off hand-outs from the Danish state and not be in your own country, defending yourself and your family."

Camilla understood all that perfectly well, but she still couldn't grasp why he was being so secretive.

Later, Natasa came back to this issue: "Perhaps it has something to do with defending your family—or not."

"What do you mean?" Camilla knew instantly that she was about to hear something she'd rather not know.

"Camilla, there isn't one of our friends who hasn't experienced something truly horrific. We don't talk about it, but we all know."

"Yes?"

Natasa took a deep breath. "I haven't spoken about this with Dragan, but everyone in our little group seems to know about it. At one time or another they heard, in confidence from someone else, that Bosnian Muslims raped and then killed Dragan's three sisters."

A silence followed. Camilla couldn't think of what to say. "Someone knows that for sure?"

"Yes. You must remember that everything in Dragan's life would have been different, if only he had been free to decide. Everything!"

When Camilla came home from work the next day, a delicious smell of cooking met her on the landing. Dragan had taken possession of her kitchen after borrowing money from a few friends to buy the ingredients for a casserole and a good bottle of wine.

Neither of them referred to the night before. During the meal, Dragan recited verses in Serbian for her. He explained that they were from a poem written in the 1950s, or maybe the 1960s, by an exiled Serb poet. He had left Yugoslavia because of its Communist government and gone to live in London. The poem was very long, and was entitled "Lament for Belgrade." In it, the poet described his travels to the most beautiful capitals of the world. Regardless of whether he was in Paris or Rome or Lisbon, the foreign cities only reminded him of death and emptiness. He longed to leave those places and return to the Belgrade of his youth, the city between the rivers, full of light and a steely will to fight for self-preservation.

Dragan quoted from the English translation of this tribute to Belgrade:

> *Your blood, like dew, has fallen on the plains again,*
> *To cool the breath of all those whose quietus nears.*

In bed that night, they impatiently made up for the twenty-four hours that they had been apart. Afterward, Dragan lay with his hands behind his head and spoke to her quietly. "I've escaped. That's the most important thing. I risked my life to leave. What's done is done. I must learn to put the past behind me. From now on I'll live properly, like you do. You're so good."

She moved closer to him and kissed his cheek, but he didn't turn his face toward her. In the dark she watched the reflection of a streetlight, like a glowing dot, in his pupil. He was lying absolutely still, staring at the ceiling. She kissed him gently once more.

The last time Camilla had spoken on the phone to her parents, her father handed the receiver to her mother much too quickly: a bad sign. Whenever there was a need for white lies, her father usually let his wife handle it. They all knew she was better at pretending than he was.

Camilla had already drawn the conclusion that they wouldn't like Dragan. Never mind that they had never met him: her parents had disapproved of all her boyfriends. Each time she had taken their dislike to heart. She simply could not escape from wanting to please them.

After she and Dragan had been living together for almost two months, she felt he must meet her parents. They invited Camilla and Dragan for Sunday lunch. Her parents' apartment was in Vanløse and Camilla still hated the place. For the rest of her life she would always drive long, round-about routes just to avoid having to pass within sight of her old school. Their home was crammed with every sort of bric-a-brac, which, in a strange way, made it appear vaguely reminiscent of the old Yugoslav immigrants' apartments.

Her parents welcomed them, smiling. Both Camilla's father and mother did not speak English well, but they tried hard, since Dragan's Danish was even worse. It went well enough. They showed Dragan into the living room first and then led the way to the lunch table. The meal started with toasts of aquavit and explanations about Danish schnapps and its different flavorings.

Camilla knew she had been right all along. Everything was so obviously orchestrated, so perfectly smooth, that there was no way of knowing what they were truly thinking.

During the meal they exchanged the names of various foods in English and Danish and Serbian. Camilla's parents seemed to be endlessly surprised by how different the words were for the same thing and kept bringing up other dishes to talk about.

She watched them. They avoided eye contact with each other and took care never to leave the room at the same time: they knew she would think that they were criticizing Dragan behind her back.

Previously she had told them about the way Yugoslav homes were full of handiwork, so her mother had covered the table with a white lace tablecloth, a family heirloom made by her great-aunt. Dragan praised the fine lace and told them about the different lace-making techniques that had gone into the tablecloth.

Camilla's mother remarked that cousin Susanne was also going out with a foreigner. Dragan at once referred to a song by Leonard Cohen about a Suzanne, who "takes you down to her place near the river." In Cohen's music and lyrics, Dragan had discovered the dark depths he loved in art. He quoted from that song and then from other songs, analyzing the music and the tempos and how they related to the words. Camilla smiled at him to show her support. He was trying so hard to demonstrate to his prospective in-laws what a cultured man he was. In Denmark, his education was his one claim to respectability, but Camilla knew only too well that everything he said went right over her parents' heads. Still, they were trying to make this work, laughing, asking questions.

When Camilla leaned forward and reached across the table for the spiced herring, her mother froze. Something had caught her eye. Camilla knew what it was.

Her mother's chair shot backward and fell over as she jumped up and ran out of the dining room. Camilla hurried after her, pulling at her blouse to cover the oblong blue bruise that crept up to her collarbone.

Standing in the kitchen, Camilla's mother, who also was a little too plump, was short of breath. Camilla stopped a few feet away from her. She wanted to say, "Why do you have to be like this, every time?" or "Why do you always think the worst of every single man in my life?" But she couldn't make herself.

Camilla's mother was in tears. "Please, forgive me. I'm sorry, I shouldn't have run out like that."

"Don't worry, it doesn't matter," Camilla murmured involuntarily.

Her mother hugged her. "Oh, Camilla, thank you. We really try, you know. We mean so well . . . but you have no idea how hard it was for Dad and me when you were with Morten."

"But you didn't know what he was like at the time." Camilla backed out of the hug.

Her mother let go. "We did notice, you know. We realized what was going on. And we were so worried that someone would start abusing you again."

Camilla was furious with her mother and she too was crying. Two months earlier, Camilla would never have dared say anything back. But Dragan had given her the confidence to speak out. "You don't like him. You don't want me to be happy!"

"Of course we do! We only want what's best for you!"

Camilla's knees gave way and she sat down on the small kitchen bench with its hard red cushions. It was where she had sat with her glass of juice and marmalade sandwiches every day after school, trying to pull herself together after yet another day of torment.

Her mother watched Camilla as she sat in silence. "We are pleased that you care about Dragan. I'm sure he's good to you. I didn't mean . . . It's very bad of me."

"Yes."

Again her mother tried to reach out to Camilla. "It's just that . . . well, there have been times when we talked on the phone and when you came to see us here over the last few months and you didn't seem . . . Are you happy?"

Camilla met her mother's eyes. "Yes, Mom. I am."

"Does he make you happy?"

"Yes, he does."

"And you really care about him?"

"Yes. I really do!"

that evening Dragan went off on his own to see some of his friends. After he had left, Camilla phoned her friend Anja to say that she'd like to drop by. Anja was a nurse. She and Camilla had once lived in the same building, but later Anja had moved to a bungalow with her husband.

Seated in Anja and Finn's bright, tidy living room, Camilla told Anja about the awful lunch at her parents' place. She wanted Anja to understand how unbearable her mother was. Anja agreed, but the expression on her face seemed less sure.

"What's the matter?"

"How do you mean?"

"What's on your mind?"

"I'm just thinking about what your mother is like."

"No, there's something else."

"No, that's all."

It seemed that everybody could spot something in her relationship with Dragan that Camilla couldn't see.

"Anja, you're my best friend. If anything were bothering you about Dragan and me, you'd tell me, wouldn't you?"

"I just think it's great that you've met a nice guy. And that you're crazy about him and he's crazy about you."

It didn't matter. Camilla knew that if she hadn't approved of

Finn, she'd never have let on to Anja. While they chatted, Camilla wondered if she had made a big mistake thinking that Dragan was the right man for her. She felt that he had helped her to become braver. Why couldn't other people see this? Or could it be, she thought, that this is exactly what they don't like? Maybe the people around me would prefer me to remain withdrawn and insecure?

Finn came to join them, dressed in torn jeans and a purple sweatshirt. He was a slightly built man, already balding. They smiled at each other. Finn was always kind to Anja's friends. He sat down on the sofa next to Anja with one foot curled up under him.

Camilla watched them. He was the sort of man her mother would like to see her marry. Anja and Finn were so close that they seemed like two sides of the same person. Talking to them, Camilla wondered if they had a good sex life. They could have had Sunday lunch with her parents week in and week out.

Anja was telling her about the camper van they were saving up for, and Camilla kept thinking, Would I be happy with a man like Finn? My life might well be easier. Still, the sex would never be as great. You could never be sure, of course.

When Goran's friends got together to watch videos in his apartment, he always disconnected the aerial from the television. No one wanted to risk catching a glimpse of the news, not even during the brief moment before the video began. The news programs were full of reports from Yugoslavia, and they upset everyone far too much. They would rage against the journalists' lies and become aggressive, Dragan in particular.

Dragan watched a lot of television at home and showed more sympathy for the Serbs and their cause than he did when he was with his Muslim friends. Sitting in front of Camilla's set, he watched the news on TV1 and TV2, as well as the news and current affairs programs on the BBC and CNN. He listened to the radio too, even though it often made his blood boil. He'd run around the apartment roaring, hitting out, or kicking things.

At times his arguments were very convincing. Camilla believed that he had knowledge and experience well beyond what the journalists could draw on.

"Journalists know nothing about history! Idiots! They think this is a new war! But we've been at war for five hundred fucking years! They've got no perspective!"

Camilla learned that she wasn't meant to answer when he was in this mood. She stayed in the bedroom or went out. If she hid in the bathroom, he would stand outside the door and carry on shouting.

"In your history books about the Second World War, do they write about the Croats forcing us into our churches and setting them on fire? Do they? Why not talk about that on TV? Do we burn them alive? Camilla? Camilla, answer me! Do we burn them alive? No! We're moving them to protect ourselves! We're allowed to try to survive, aren't we?"

Camilla stayed very still, hoping that he wouldn't break the door down.

He would turn the volume up so the television reports could be heard all over the small apartment.

"But NATO attacks us all the same, Camilla! They're bombing my country! They're bombing my hometown! What do they want us to do? Commit mass suicide? Do they want us to kill ourselves? Or just let Croats and Muslims kill us instead? Would that please NATO?"

At other times, his frustration at his own impotence would overwhelm him. His emotions seemed to be beyond words, and he could only express himself in a mixture of Serbian curses and raw howling.

Apart from in bed, he only ever hit her after having watched the news.

Camilla had twice made the agonizing decision to end it between them. But each time she thought about what he must have been through, experiences beyond her grasp, and felt she understood that it would take a long time for him to become a normal human being again. When he wasn't reminded of the dreadful situation in his country and of how he had suffered, he was everything she had ever wanted. The war must surely end sometime, and then the tensions would disappear from their relationship.

Before meeting Dragan, Camilla had been determined that she would never again live with a violent man, but they loved each other so much. She and Dragan agreed that he should watch or listen to the news and read the papers only while Camilla was at work, or at least not at home. Two hours before she was due he would switch everything off and put away the papers.

It almost solved the problem.

• • •

Dragan had been living with her for about four months when he and Camilla spent an evening in a bar with some of their friends. A large group of Yugoslavs from another refugee camp also turned up. She started talking to one of the newcomers while she waited at the bar for her order. The place was crowded, and it took some time to be served.

The man didn't seem drunk, yet he spoke English with an odd drawl and looked at her with his eyes half closed. Everything about him was somehow very foreign.

He nodded toward her table. "Look who's sitting over there. There's one who'll never be forgiven."

"What did you say?"

The man didn't answer her directly, just continued his line of thought without any hint of irony. "That man deserves every torment the world can throw at him."

"Who? Why are you saying that?"

"That one, with the square jaw." He stared straight at Dragan.

At once Camilla had a sinking feeling.

"Back home in Banja Luka, he was the leader of a small group of men. They came into my street and raped three sisters. Then they killed them."

"Please, you're wrong. He didn't. It was his sisters who . . ." Camilla stopped and said nothing more. Her eyes were fixed on the man's face, and things began to click into place—little things, from their everyday chatter, little things, for which she had no words.

The man drew back, upset to realize that she knew the person he was referring to.

"Who are you?"

Camilla thought quickly; she wanted to learn more. "I'm a teacher. I teach the people at the table over there."

The man looked at her suspiciously. "You must never tell them what I said."

"No, I won't."

"Never! You must never tell!"

"No. I promise."

The bartender brought the man his beer. It was obvious that he wanted to leave there and then, even though he had spent money on the drink. He looked around and tried to explain. "He will kill me. Dragan will not hesitate, not for one second. He hasn't seen me here. But I know him. I know what he's like."

Camilla smiled and tried to calm him down. "I promise. Really. I won't tell him anything."

Dragan got up and looked in their direction. The man made a jerky movement.

Camilla wanted to hear more. "But I don't understand. He told us in a Danish lesson that he was forced to join the militia."

But the man simply turned and hurried off unsteadily toward the door.

Dragan came over and helped her carry the beers back to their table. Camilla didn't say anything. But later, when she had a chance to speak quietly with Lena's husband, Camilla told Simo about what the man had said.

"Who was he?"

"I don't know."

"You can tell me, Camilla. Don't worry."

"I don't know who he was. Honestly."

Simo went away.

Moments later Dragan pulled hard at Camilla's arm to take her over to a quiet corner. "Who told you stories?"

"I don't know who he was. A man."

"Tell me. Now!"

"Why are you . . . ? Look, it's just something he said. A rumor, a casual . . ."

Dragan shook her and glared into her eyes. "Speak up. Tell me!"

Camilla could tell he was clenching his teeth, the way he did before he hit her.

"If you beat me up in here, I'll have you charged with assault."

That only fueled his anger, and he slammed his fist into the wall next to Camilla. "Don't you threaten me!"

But he didn't hit her. He knew well enough that just a few words to the police and he could be locked up for years. Or turned into a fugitive once more, spending an eternity in airports around the world.

Dragan returned to his friends. Soon afterward, Camilla saw some of them spread out through the bar, talking to anyone who might have been standing near Camilla. They pointed to her and the barstool she had been sitting on.

Five minutes later, four of them got up with a determined air, pulled their coats on, and left the bar without saying goodbye.

Dragan didn't return home until nearly three-thirty. Camilla had gone to bed but was still awake. She was crying.

Dragan came to lie next to her on the bed, still wearing his clothes. He held her and spoke gently to her. "Please don't cry. You mustn't. What you heard is not true. But if he tells lies about me in this country, I risk going to prison. Or expulsion. I'll be sent back. If the two of us are to stay together, that man must be made to stop telling lies."

Camilla looked at him. She felt like such a little girl. "It's not true then, Dragan? It was all lies, wasn't it?"

"Camilla, please. Of course it was all lies." His arm tightened around her and she pressed herself closer to him. She wanted to inhale his smell, and pushed her nose against his chest.

"Lies. All lies. All lies. It's all lies," she repeated to herself.

Dragan broke her litany. "Trust me. When I say something is a lie, it is. But you must also understand that you'll never know what war is like. It's horrific. No one reacts the way he expects to—you wouldn't either. And I didn't. But I got away. I risked my life to get out."

Then he went on to say again what he had told her many times before: "I had to put an end to all that. Now it's over and done. From now on, I want to live a proper life. I want to live here with you and be good, like you."

Camilla clung to him desperately, hardly letting him take off his clothes.

It frightened her to discover that sex was even better now, with the uncertainty about what he had or hadn't done, the uncertainty about what he might do next.

The rapturous feeling of being totally free of the past as well as the future lasted longer this time. She was still glowing with euphoria when, later, she examined her body in front of the big mirror in the bathroom for any new bruises.

In the morning Dragan was sleeping so deeply that he seemed impossible to wake. Camilla couldn't go back to sleep. She was tormented by dreadful images about what had happened to the man at the bar. Whatever happened, it would be her fault. What had they done to him?

After eating breakfast alone, she thought she'd wash Dragan's clothes to get rid of the beer and tobacco fumes. She wanted somehow to make up for having threatened to report him to the police. It was true that she had no idea what had really gone on in that war. All she could be certain of was that Dragan was also one of its victims.

She picked up the clothes he had thrown over a chair and carried them off to the bathroom. When she shook out his brown trousers she noticed there was something in one of the pockets: a small, soft package. It felt like a condom.

Camilla, who was on the pill, had a vision of just how furiously she'd let him have it if it was a condom. She'd fly into a rage and not give a damn if he hit her afterward.

But it wasn't a condom. It was a small, transparent plastic bag containing some white powder.

It looked like the cocaine packets she had seen in films. Christ almighty, how could he afford this stuff? Was he an addict? Perhaps he was a dealer and traded drugs to pay for his own habit—sold it to his friends. But that meant they were users too—people like Lena's husband, and nice, hospitable Goran. Could it be true?

All the time she had thought that Dragan's friends respected him. Were they actually scared of him? Maybe they owed him money for drugs? Or maybe they feared and pitied him at the same time. Just like herself.

She threw him out. He moved back to the refugee camp.

During the days that followed, she investigated Dragan's life in Yugoslavia in every way she could. She realized that there were too many corroborating accounts for all of them to be based on lies and misunderstandings. For instance, it was quite clear that Dragan had, together with Mirko Zigic, volunteered for guard and "interrogation" duties in the Omarska camp. Torture was routinely carried out there, as everyone knew by then.

Leafing through a book that Dragan had left behind, a collection of

Crnjanski's poetry, she found a little note stuck between the pages. It began with some writing that contained the word "Dragan," then more incomprehensible words, and then the signature "Mirko Z."

She still couldn't bring herself to report Dragan as a suspected Bosnian war criminal, or even a cocaine dealer. She didn't want to charge him with domestic violence either; the consequences for him would have been too drastic.

One day she met Dragan again at Lena and Simo's place. By now she was much more frightened of him than she had ever been of Morten; yet, once more, they ended up together on his black coat in the shrubbery behind the Frederiksberg block of apartments. He moved back in with her. She hoped that she would have been quicker to distance herself from his alcohol and cocaine abuse if she hadn't known of his past sufferings.

After a while she threw him out again, only to have it start all over again. When this cycle had repeated itself a few times, she still didn't know how he afforded his cocaine but decided to try some herself. She discovered that she had an addictive personality. She had already become dependent on his cooking and his sex and now, in no time at all, on his drugs too.

Then one day Dragan met another woman. He fell as tempestuously in love with her as he had done with Camilla only six months earlier.

Their affair was finished. Over the following two years, Camilla felt deeply depressed. There was nothing to fill her life, except unbearable visits to see her parents or to Anja and Finn's place for yet another altogether too cozy evening of drinking tea and chatting.

Camilla forced herself to attend choir practice regularly. With the help of her parents and a support group, she determinedly beat her addiction. Finally, she understood clearly that the shrew who had stolen Dragan away had in fact also saved her life.

Camilla and the kids get up at the same time as Finn. He is up early, usually at five-thirty in the morning.

She arrives at the Center about an hour and a half before the others.

The red light on the answering machine glows in the semi-darkness, but it doesn't blink. No messages. Malene has forgotten to switch her computer off. Camilla quickly turns on the overhead lights. They flicker a couple of times and then everything looks normal again. She turns her own computer on and goes to make coffee.

The offices are silent, the book-lined walls absorbing the noises from outside. It's still too early for the morning traffic to have started up. Until recently, early morning was Camilla's favorite time at work, a quiet moment to herself when she could organize her work. But these last few days have changed everything.

Ever since Iben discovered that Camilla has been involved with a war criminal, she's excluded her. Camilla knows only too well what that means.

She returns to her seat and finds a stack of unrecorded vouchers. Before she left home she took two aspirin, but she still feels rotten—especially her stomach.

This is how the mornings were for her a long time ago. In

order for her mother to get to work on time, she would drop Camilla off at school about twenty minutes before the first lesson. For years Camilla would start each day sitting with her knees together on the worn old bench in the school yard, speculating about what would happen that day. How would her classmates punish her today?

Maybe she shouldn't drink coffee on an upset stomach. Anyway, it's probably ready. She goes to pour herself a cup.

Then the others arrive and the first two hours pass just as she knew they would.

Later that morning she decides to change the humming fluorescent light in Paul's office. Paul has been complaining about it for ages, and fixing it gives Camilla a chance to get out of having to be in the same room as Malene.

In the storage room Camilla takes her time pulling out the ladder and finding a new tube. She hurries through the Winter Garden, closes Paul's office door behind her, and sets to work as slowly as possible. While she's standing on the top step of the ladder trying to fit the new tube into place, Iben enters briskly and starts speaking without a pause.

"I've been in contact with a Serb journalist, and he told me that a colleague of his was murdered by your old boyfriend about a year ago."

"What . . . ?"

"Dragan pistol-whipped this man to death, Camilla. Someone who had written a critical article about Dragan's friend Zigic and the Serbian cause. Just as I have."

"But . . ."

Camilla has to get down from the ladder, and takes the tube with her.

"You have to help us. We need more to go on."

"But I can't tell you any more than I already have."

"How come I always have the impression you're lying when it concerns Dragan?"

"I'm not lying. There just isn't anything else to say. Look, I feel just like you. I'm scared that he'll come after us too, but what can I do?"

The muscles around Iben's jaw are twitching visibly. She stands with her feet planted apart. Brigitte, the vilest of the girls in Camilla's class, used to stand like that in front of the teacher's desk. The others would cluster around her. When she found something to throw at Camilla, the others would start throwing things too.

Camilla has to sit down. She sinks into one of the chairs at Paul's conference table and buries her face in her hands, pressing her fingers against her eyes.

Iben's insistent voice comes at her through the darkness. "I'd like to believe you. It's just that your whole manner won't let me. You're such a poor liar, Camilla."

"But I'm not lying!"

Camilla can hear her own voice go thin and shrill. Even with her head down and her eyes closed, Camilla can feel Iben silently watching in her warrior's stance.

Camilla repeats herself. "I'm not lying! I'm not lying! I'm not lying!"

She hears Iben turn and walk away.

Camilla knows that she deserves everything she's getting. They are right to punish her. She has been lying, and it has slowed the search for the man who is threatening to kill Iben. What if Iben is killed, or one of the others, just because Camilla hasn't told the truth? Camilla is still sitting with her face in her hands when she hears Iben's voice through the open door.

Iben is telling the others about her discovery. "I phoned Ljiljana Peric. That's the woman who went to the same high school as Zigic. Remember I interviewed her for my article about him? Through her I got the name of a Belgrade journalist who knows Dragan but is now too scared to write a word about either him or Zigic. The journalist says that, without any doubt, Dragan is involved in drug trafficking, prostitution, and kidnapping. That can mean only one thing: the Mafia."

Iben raises her voice to make sure that Camilla won't miss a word. "I have written about Dragan's senior officer during the war. And Dragan was her boyfriend. It's not necessarily Zigic who killed Rasmus; it could just as well have been Dragan. He could have sent the e-mails. And broken into the office before we got the CCTV installed."

Even if Camilla hadn't already been hypersensitive about bullying, working at the DCIG would have been enough. The way they used to treat Anne-Lise was totally uncalled for. Hundreds of times Camilla had wanted to help, but when she tried to be pleasant toward Anne-Lise, Iben and Malene would start harassing her. And, after all, she had to share an office with them, had to be a good team player to make the office run smoothly.

Once she had spoken up and said that they should treat their new colleague with a little more consideration. Malene had replied, "But Camilla, don't you realize it's different for Iben and me? We're old friends. Anne-Lise is just someone who works in the same place as us."

It was as if they had no idea of the harm their behavior caused, or the effect it might have in the long run. Camilla knew. She had seen enough. Almost every day Anne-Lise retreated to the back of the library, behind the East European collection.

Anne-Lise hadn't been with them long before Camilla began to feel she could no longer look her in the eye. She decided to mention it to Paul. She remembers well how it went.

"Paul, I'm not sure that Anne-Lise is settling in. Could you talk to her? Maybe there's something we could do, something to help her?"

"Why do you think she isn't happy?"

"During the coffee break I thought that she might've been crying, because her eyes seemed bloodshot and she was flushed."

"Come on, Camilla! Haven't you noticed that she looks like that all the time? It's probably something to do with her skin, I suppose."

He was on his way out. Camilla returned to her work and tried to be lighthearted while Iben and Malene poked fun at everything. But now Iben and Anne-Lise are chatting away in the library while Malene is struggling to find a way to cope on her own.

At lunchtime Iben is still going on to Anne-Lise about Dragan. Camilla doesn't feel like saying anything. She still doesn't feel very well and eats her celery sticks in tiny bites.

No one around the lunch table is her old self. Anne-Lise is the only one who looks pleased. Malene is trying to open a pack of rye toasts but fumbles and the whole thing slips from her hands. It falls to the floor and several slices break. No one bothers to make a little joke to make her feel better. No one calls her clumsy either. They simply stay silent.

It wasn't until Camilla was an adult that she learned the main secret of survival. It's simple. When someone is angry, you stand aside to allow the person's anger to pass and hit the next one in line. She only wishes she had realized this many, many years earlier. This past year, the "next in line" has been Anne-Lise. Now it seems to be Malene.

Malene picks up the most damaged slice of toast. She tries to show concern at the new information Iben has discovered about Dragan. Instead, she just looks lost.

Camilla can't deny that, one way or another, she's pleased to see Malene cut down to size. For one thing, she can't stand the way Malene dresses, with her low-slung hipsters and sexy short tops—all completely unsuitable for the office.

Malene is chewing a sandwich. Camilla can see some cheese and bread sticking in between Malene's teeth when she opens her mouth to speak.

"You know, I can't help wondering what else you've been lying to us about."

She's so transparent! Malene is hoping for approval from Iben and Anne-Lise.

Nobody responds.

"Right. We'd better be good."

She's still trying hard to sound like her old self, but even that stock comment strikes a false note. Usually they get up and return to their desks, but not this time. Iben and Anne-Lise are not done eating. Only after several minutes does Anne-Lise pull her chair back. Iben follows her at once. And Camilla does too.

After lunch Camilla starts comparing a selection of Scandinavian hotels. The DCIG is planning to host a small inter-Nordic seminar. Paul has asked her to make a list of the relative advantages and drawbacks of each as well as their prices so that he can make an informed decision. When he finally turns up, that is. She struggles with numbers and foreign-exchange rates. Meanwhile the Center's users keep phoning.

In the midst of everything, Malene is pestering her. Obviously when Malene failed to win the others over by picking on her, she realized her only chance was for the two of them to join forces. So now Camilla hasn't had a peaceful moment all afternoon because Malene keeps coming over to have a chat about this or that—TV shows, or gossip about the board or the users.

Camilla replies as briefly as she can to Malene's chatter and keeps staring at the hotel details on her screen. At least it's satisfying to have a handle on their tricks and know how to protect herself.

When Camilla goes off to fetch a new box of labels from the store-room, Malene soon turns up.

"Camilla, I want you to know something. It's quite important if you're to understand how Iben reacts to things."

By now Camilla is determined to ignore everything Malene says. She pretends to look for something inside one of the shelving units, but Malene continues: "Iben had to be treated by psychiatrists when she was nineteen years old. She isn't anywhere near as stable as she makes out. Back then she was much angrier and much more anxious than she is now. She actually wandered about in the streets with a knife strapped to her leg. Until they started treating her, that is."

Camilla turns to look at Malene.

"You know, it could be Iben who has identity problems," she continues. "A split personality, if you like. What if she's the one who sent the e-mails? Maybe she can't face who she really is and that's driving her against the two of us?"

What Malene is also implying is that Iben could have been the one who poured oil over the steps in Malene's staircase and removed the railing in front of the large window. She just doesn't say so.

Camilla can't get away from the fact that there might be something in what Malene is telling her. It's true that once or twice Camilla has noticed a strange bulge on the inside of Iben's leg. Could it be that Iben has a knife tied to her leg all the time? Is she on the brink of becoming paranoid? And dangerously aggressive as well? Perhaps she has been ill for a long time.

After Malene's revelations, Camilla finds a bit of research to do in the library. Passing behind Iben, she wants to see if there is still a bulge somewhere on Iben's legs and get a glimpse of what Iben has been frantically writing about all this week, between her calls to Yugoslavia and giving Camilla a hard time.

Camilla discovers it's impossible to spot any telltale lumps under Iben's clothing, and every time Camilla walks by, Iben closes the document window. For the last couple of days Iben has been printing out something almost every hour, which is what she typically does when she is writing one of her long articles for *Genocide News*. But as far as Camilla knows, Iben isn't scheduled to send in another article any time soon.

Iben's fervor makes Camilla nervous. Maybe she's making up a blanket of lies about Camilla and Dragan to show Paul when he comes back.

What else could it be? Has Iben ferreted out more about them? Is she going to get Camilla fired?

Camilla can't look through Iben's wastepaper basket for printed pages, but in the evening the cleaners sometimes tip the contents of their baskets into the huge bag in the printer room. She goes to have a look. The container is full. Perhaps papers from the previous day are still there.

The door of the printer room doesn't lock. What if someone comes in and finds her burrowing in the black bag full of other people's waste? What's her story then?

Camilla cannot think of one. She stands still and listens. Not a sound, no approaching steps or voices. But who says she would hear anything? Camilla peeks outside. Just then, Iben looks up from her screen. Camilla smiles stiffly. No response. Iben doesn't smile back, just carries on writing.

Camilla closes the door and gets on with her search. The first layer is made up of wrappers from books that arrived for Anne-Lise this morning, and the next one is reams of database printouts. Then, almost at the bottom, Camilla finds the contents of yesterday's wastepaper baskets. Just as she had hoped.

She leafs through several bundles of printed pages without taking them out of the bag. Then she digs deeper. At the very bottom of the waste there are small pieces of torn-up paper. Someone has taken the trouble to tear up her work before throwing it away. Camilla takes some of the largest fragments over to the window and begins to read:

> *CHOLOGY   VIL IX*
> *We are rats! Experimental rats. Only condemned*
> *run in the labyrinth after social psycho*
> *laws we don't know.*

She puts five more pieces together on the windowsill.

> *y interes*
> *gan when I once read in a newspaper abou*
> *vestigation into traffic in a parking area. People took longer to get out*
> *of their slot if another car was waiting to park there. Men left their*
> *places much faster if the waiting car was a high-prestige brand.*

*Women were indifferent to the brand and to the presumed cost of
the waiting car. None of the drivers knew that they were acting
according to these rules. They just did what they did. We are all
predictable. We are rats.*

Camilla doesn't doubt for a second that it's Iben who has written this.
She cannot think what it has to do with herself or Dragan. The remaining
bits are too small to make sense of:

*murderers among us who don't acknowle
Gunnar some time in the future*

Camilla dives into the bag again. Plastic ties and edges of cardboard
poke into her armpit. But this time, when she backs out she has a whole
handful of torn pieces. Some of them seem to form a text, which she re-
assembles on the windowsill.

LOGY   EVIL X
*was also what Primo Levi wrote about the harsh
ween prisoners when he was in Auschwitz: "It is naive, absurd, and
historically false to believe that an infernal system such as National
Socialism sanctifies its victims; on the contrary, it degrades them, it
makes them resemble itself."*

The style of these fragments suggests an academic article, but it
doesn't seem likely that Iben is writing it for *Genocide News* or the DCIG
Web site. It's so incoherent and repetitive.

*We are slaves of
predicta
errible! We are nothing but rats! How could a human
break out of being*

In the Winter Garden she hears the others calling out: "Hi, Paul!"
"Paul, hello! There you are!"
Then Paul's voice, loud and cheerful. "Party time!"

Camilla hurriedly hides her bits of paper under two boxes and runs out to meet him.

Everyone is there. Paul has stopped just inside the front door. He is grinning broadly and waving a bottle of champagne. "Volunteers, please! Who'll get the glasses?"

But the women are so curious that none of them wants to leave.

"Hey, Malene! Could you get five glasses from the kitchen?"

And then he starts telling them what has happened.

"Frederik has left the board! That's one obstacle to our survival out of the way!"

Iben has to ask: "He's gone? But—"

Paul pats her shoulder and replies before she can finish her question. "That's right, I'm in no position to vote him off. Neither is anyone else, not even Ole. The only way was for him to resign."

Anne-Lise chips in. "He did? And we thought that it might be *you* who Ole—"

Laughing, Paul interrupts her. "Yes, but he can't. If I'm not here as the leader, there's no state funding for the Center. Seems that Ole forgot that momentarily."

Anne-Lise, who is standing behind Iben, moves up a little. "Paul, what do you—"

"An old friend of mine is a spokesman for this sector in the party that holds the deciding vote. And the DCIG receives its grant on his say-so. Or not."

Iben catches on quickly and starts laughing too. "You have a friend who . . . I see! Of course you do!"

Anne-Lise is not satisfied. "Which party is that?"

Paul leans on Malene's desk. "Anne-Lise, guess!"

"Your old friend is an MP for the Danish People's Party? That racist lot?"

Paul smiles proudly. "Yep. That's right."

Then he notices the look on her face. "Whatever we're doing here, we're doing it to serve our cause. That's all that matters."

"I see. But what happens now?"

"We carry on as usual. But now we have a new trophy to add to our collection. And the risk that we'll be put under the DIHR is a little less imminent."

Malene returns with the glasses and tries to catch up. "And Frederik, what about him? Is he going to put up with Ole's decision to let you stay?"

"No. That he will not do."

Malene looks around to catch someone's eye. "Aren't Frederik and Ole friends anymore? Is he leaving the board?"

Paul begins to twist the champagne cork. "Malene, that's exactly why we're celebrating!"

The cork pops and shoots off to land high up on a shelf. Camilla glances at Iben. If she hadn't seen her anger this morning, or heard the story about her past, or read the fragments from her article—well, she would've thought Iben was quite normal. Every time Paul says something meant to be funny, Iben laughs longer and louder than usual. She sounds as if she's been at the bottle already. Camilla sips her champagne and curses the day she first allowed Dragan into her life. Years have passed since she learned all the things that Iben has now found out about him. When she looks back at the men in her life, she is so grateful to Finn. After Dragan, marrying someone like Finn is the best choice she could ever have made.

Malene hasn't touched her champagne and seems uneasy. "Paul, we've been so worried about you. And about the Center too. About all of us. You vanished so suddenly, and then we thought maybe Ole would try and . . ."

Paul watches the bubbles in his glass, tilting it gently sideways to top it up. "I was thinking about all of you too, Malene. But the situation turned out to be more complicated than I'd thought because a group of politicians had just left on a fact-finding trip to Iraq. So I couldn't meet with the people I needed to see—not until they returned. I hadn't anticipated that."

When he finishes pouring his champagne, his eyes meet Malene's. "And if the board is to work together as a team, Ole couldn't have the chance to say the wrong things to me or to send me a letter he'd only regret later. Everything had to be put on hold."

Iben has more questions. "Paul, when you said you hadn't anticipated it, do you mean . . . ? You know, when Gunnar was here and Ole turned up 'by chance'? Did you plan it all along?"

Paul raises his glass to her and beams. "Strictly off the record."

Camilla stays silent. Her attention is slipping. The office atmosphere is suddenly so excitable and she realizes now what a relief it is to have read Iben's jottings, with not a mention of Camilla or Dragan anywhere. She sighs and takes a hearty sip from her glass.

Iben has insisted, day in and day out, that Camilla is lying. But now it seems certain that Iben knows no more about Camilla's past than what she has already announced.

Camilla goes to sit in her own chair. She feels very tired now. It would be a dream if this new, jovial Paul told them to take the day off, but of course he won't. He pours everyone more champagne and splashes some on his black jacket. It doesn't seem to worry him. He's on a high.

"I should've bought another bottle!"

Malene's glass is still full, but Iben and Anne-Lise want more.

How can he miss the way everything has changed while he was away?

He raises his glass in another toast. The third one, at least. "Malene, this celebration is for you too! None of you need to worry anymore. Our Center has a future. We are stronger than ever. This is a good day for genocide studies!"

iben

chapter 48

t all starts without a sign of anything out of the ordinary.

A woman professor from Missouri is speaking to Iben on the phone.

"In my view we overcomplicate the process leading to genocide. Fundamentally, it's straightforward. Once a population group sees advantages in killing off another group, it triggers a sequence of psychological mechanisms. Gradually, suitable adjustments are made in the group's ideology. History is revised accordingly. Highly charged public debates will emerge spontaneously and, step by step, they'll develop the intellectual rationale for extermination.

"In the end, the stark truth is that members of one group murder members of another. The only possibility of stopping them is if the world community demonstrates that it is keeping an eye on the situation and isn't going to condone any criminal activity."

Iben objects, but only to keep the discussion going. Actually, she's so fed up with her own arguments, which sound naive and kind of Danish, that she almost looks forward to being contradicted. The professor obliges.

"You know, with hindsight everyone notices the falsification of history in the lead-up to genocide, the ideology and so on, and decides that this must have been what did it. But just examine the genocides you're more familiar with and you'll see that, when all's said and done, the perpetrators are driven by egoism every time. Never mind the cover stories they use to convince themselves or the world at large. Or their victims."

Later that day Iben feels nauseous and shaky. She's definitely not well and takes two aspirin, even though she can't identify any aches or pains.

The *Genocide News* issue on Turkey has been badly delayed by the upsets of the last few days. She must try to concentrate. Even so, an hour before the end of the working day she can't stand sitting there any longer. She must get home.

This anxiety is no stranger to her—she recognizes it from when she was nineteen and suffered a breakdown: her body seizing up as if she has caught a dreadful illness, but nothing hurts.

She is terrified of being referred to a psychiatric clinic and put back on medication. Many of her former fellow patients are probably able to exist only with the help of mind-bending drugs. Ten years ago, Iben had to fight for her return to stability and real work, and she isn't certain she can do it again.

Before leaving the office she looks out to make sure that there's no dark-haired, square-jawed man waiting down there in the street. It's pointless, though. You can't see properly from up here. Perhaps Dragan Jelisic is there. Perhaps he isn't.

Iben announces that she needs to go home because she has a headache. She quickly checks the on-screen camera image. The landing is empty. The elevator is empty too. Nobody is waiting for her in the street.

She cycles away. For a February day it's not that cold. Then she realizes that her balance is too poor to continue cycling. She locks up the bike just a few hundred feet from the DCIG.

Men, broad smiles on their faces, hold severed human heads in their hands. Archive images drift in front of her mind's eye.

We distort our memories when it serves our purposes. Our thoughts too. Even our senses cannot be trusted; we reshape the messages they send to suit our needs.

How much of what I'm thinking is nothing but the egoistic, post hoc rationalization that the professor was talking about?

When I stood up for Anne-Lise, I believed I was good. Was I lying to myself? Was my choice to risk my job and my friendship with Malene based on nothing more than a notion of what would be to my own best advantage?

Three million corpses scattered over the paddy fields of Cambodia. All slaughtered by their own countrymen, believing they were right—but also because they felt that there might be something in it for them.

Five skulls sticking up from a water-filled ditch. Plants winding their way up, around and between them.

Sure, I might gain from losing my friend. I'd be free to date Gunnar. Also, I'd be free of the duty to help Malene, whose arthritis will only get worse with time.

How could I believe that I was making a sacrifice in order to resist the bullying? But I did believe it. I truly thought it was hard to make the choice I made. I felt heroic. Truly good.

"Hey! Watch where you're going!"

Iben walks with her head down without looking where she's stepping. Now she has almost fallen over a small white bulldog. Whining, it leaps sideways against a wall, obviously thinking that it's about to be stepped on.

Its owner tells her off while he pulls at the dog's long red leash. "You're not the only one on the sidewalk, you know!"

"I'm sorry. I'm so sorry!" She sighs.

Meanwhile a thought has struck her. That's it! Though I've seen myself as idealistic, I've lied to myself. That's the evil act that has been gnawing at the back of my mind all day long. I couldn't figure it out. But now that I know, my nausea will fade and disappear.

The sense of unease and queasiness does not leave her, however. She straightens up and looks around. She hasn't gone very far. No one resembles Jelisic. She scans the street in both directions. Pedestrians are few and far between, but he could be in any one of the cars. The traffic seems unending.

She cannot possibly defend herself against a man in a car.

She cannot possibly go home now.

Jelisic could find her there, no trouble at all—there is no steel-lined door, no CCTV camera. If she did go home, she wouldn't be able to relax.

Crowded streets are her best hiding place. She walks quickly now, taking long, decisive strides. It helps against her tremor, which grows fainter the faster she walks.

No Jelisic at the Vibenhus roundabout or in Tagens Road or Nørrebro Street.

She practically flies along, one street after another, running to get away from Jelisic and from the evil she senses in everyone she overtakes. She knows that at one time in his or her life, each person she passes has done evil things toward another person, but they no longer think about it. They all pretend they're so innocent.

If they thought it would benefit them, they would knife the next man in the back, each and every one of them. Only lack of opportunity determines if they become genocidal killers or not. If their community leaders pressed the right buttons, these people would be off on the hunt right away.

When she gets to Nørrebro, there are more people about and it is harder to keep her distance.

Iben can smell the evil inside a young man cutting in just ahead of her. He is wearing a long coat and carries a briefcase, but she has a vision of him inside a Russian army helicopter, throwing out mined toys to kill children in Afghanistan. Ruthlessness oozes from his pores and the smell prickles inside Iben's nostrils, like the drinks of freshly opened lemonade she remembers from childhood.

She veers to pass him, steps into the cycle path, and hears the bells as two cyclists come up from behind. She leaps back onto the sidewalk.

She lands near a young woman walking her old bike with a child seat on the back. She is the type of person who, as a trained nurse, helped eliminate invalids in gas chambers well before the Second World War. Her brand of evil stinks like the raw meat left in a plastic bag that you forgot to throw out before going away on a holiday.

I'm like a rat, Iben tells herself. My sense of smell is a rat's. A lab rat's.

When they tickle one tiny bit of my brain with an electric current I'll run one way, and when they try another bit I'll run in the opposite direction. Like everyone would. Social psychologists can predict what I'll do next. And when a researcher puts me in a cage with another rat, we will tear and bite each other until one of us dies.

That's what we do, never mind what intellectual ideas we use for display. Razor-toothed rats without free will.

A little boy is strapped into the bicycle child seat. He is asleep, and his head in its little helmet is drooping. His romper is open at the neck, and the smell of evil rises from him like the reek of burning grass.

I am sick, she thinks. It's obvious. It isn't normal to smell people like this. Or to think in this way. The next moment she is sweating copiously under her thin jacket. Her whole body becomes damp and cold.

She knows why. And she knows that she doesn't want to think of what is to come. Her nausea grows until at last she throws up. As she leans against a board advertising a kebab place, her stomach contents pump out of her and into the gutter.

Didn't I have one of these attacks in the office one night? The others had left. I remember how furious I was with myself then. And with Malene. What was I doing there? It was something that eased the pressure. Some people smash china or cut themselves. What did I do?

What was I doing? I know I was writing. When I freak out, I write or I read.

She weeps.

I'm sick in the head. I don't want to be sick. It's hateful. I want to be able to work at the DCIG. And to live with Gunnar.

I want a life.

I won't have one much longer. The others will realize soon enough that I'm the one who's abnormal. I'm the only one in the office who has been in a psychiatric ward. The only one who Frederik called "Batgirl" because he—like the rest of them—can tell that I'm different. I'm the only one who'd willingly walk around for four months with a knife tied to my leg.

She wipes her mouth with the back of her glove and cleans off the vomit. She is still leaning against the board. She remembers that after the evening in the office she had a headache cycling home.

I was sick then. Like now. When I rode along St. Kjeld Street I kept telling myself: "I'm not like that. I didn't do that." Nevertheless, I recalled what it was that I had done. But by the time I had turned into Jagt Street it had become very distant, like hearing about it late one night at a party. Once I reached Tagens Road and home, I had even stopped saying, "I didn't do that."

Her ability to think is gone. She wants to lie down but can't do that on the sidewalk. The next best thing would be to sit on a bench for a while or maybe go into a shop to rest, but that's out of the question too. She feels safer from Jelisic while she's on the move. Now she has to hurry, or he'll find her.

I had such a sense of writing the truth. It felt so right: "You, Malene Jensen, have sworn to your secret evil . . ." And then: "You, Iben Højgaard, are for your actions recognized as self-righteous among the humans."

She strides along, her muscles seeming stronger now that she has thrown up.

Outside Nørrebro Station, she stops. Now where should she go? She'd like to go to Gunnar's apartment. He knows about danger. He'll know what she should do to protect herself from Jelisic. But he mustn't see her this way. At least she has the presence of mind to see that.

The other thing she'd like to do is go to Malene's and tell her how sorry she is. It's a good thought, even though she can't imagine that Malene will ever forgive her.

It has become dark. Lights in shops and cars make a shifting pattern around her. She needs to tire out her brain, dampen down her emotions. Other people might take tranquilizers or splash cold water on their face, but she gets the same kind of effect from working intensely. She must concentrate now to distract herself from all these emotions.

She will formulate an entire article in her head, leaving no room for any other thought. Later, all she'll have to do is write it down.

THE PSYCHOLOGY OF EVIL XXII
Here, the previous articles in Genocide News *are followed up with an account of processes, uncovered by social psychologists, that allow perpetrators to reach the stage at which they are capable of carrying out one murder after another.*

By Iben Højgaard

The social psychologist Albert Bandura recruited a group of students to help him with "an experimental study of learning" that also involved a group of students from another university . . .

She thinks about Omoro in that hut in Kenya.
I'll never have a chance to ask him to forgive me. He died because I

hesitated. And I hesitated because I saw an advantage for myself in holding back. He is dead now.

She tries once more:

THE PSYCHOLOGY OF EVIL XXII
Here, the previous articles in Genocide News *are followed up with an account of processes, uncovered by social psychologists . . .*

Two young women step out from a clothes boutique. Their aura of evil smells like pickled gherkins and rotten fish.

Iben's concentration is going. She leans against a wall and tries to take up the thread.

> *The social psychologist Albert Bandura recruited . . .*
> *His "helpers" were to assist him in an experiment by administering electric shocks to members of the other group when they didn't do well enough in tests. Just as they were ready to start, the helper group "accidentally" overheard a senior assistant speak about the "pupils."*

I know why everybody praised me, she thinks: because I ran back to the policemen from Nairobi and tried to make them help the hostages. The press, as well as my friends, kept going on about how I put my life on the line to save the others. It's because they need to hear such things—to be reassured that goodness exists. They dream of it. They watch it on television. But it's all a lie! Those few seconds only proved that I couldn't conceive of the possibility that the police would beat up or kill a white woman. I believed I was in no danger. My whiteness made me invulnerable, or so I thought.

She recognizes the front door to Malene's stairs. She must ask her forgiveness. Forgiveness would be such a relief. Or maybe it wouldn't?

Malene doesn't reply to the intercom, so Iben uses her key to get in and goes upstairs to knock on Malene's door.

Nobody answers. She could let herself in, but she doesn't. She knocks again.

On her way downstairs she can't see the large stained-glass patterns, because it's too dark outside. A pane of clear glass has been fitted in Rasmus's window.

She must pull herself together. Think of nothing but her article.

THE PSYCHOLOGY OF EVIL XXII
Here, the previous articles in Genocide News *are followed up . . .*

The social psychologist Albert Bandura recruited a group of students to help
him with "an experimental study of learning" . . . We are rats, all of us.
Regardless of what has been written in the magazine previously. We're simply
Regardless of what has been written in the magazine previously, we may
Regardless, it must be admitted that I'm sick now. So dreadfully sick I can-
not think anymore.

Iben, concentrate!

THE PSYCHOLOGY OF EVIL XXII
Here, the previous articles . . .

The many lies presented in our magazine are . . . The truth is . . . We are
also in each other's heads. Murder each other when no one is looking. The
self-righteous theories previously described in Genocide News *are . . .*

Iben cannot walk now. She sits down on a trash bin at a bus stop. She'll
have to throw up again soon. It's all these people that do it—their smells:
fried food, piss, chlorine—decay. She's disappearing. It's so hard to stay in
control. Only work to hold on to, and logical thought.

THE PSYCHOLOGY OF EVIL XXII
Here, the previous articles in Genocide News *will carry on, sickly as ever,*
and . . . unable to think anymore. The reason is that we're all rats and ready
to bite each other's heads off.

I will stay sitting here despite the human rats that smell . . . on top of a trash
bin at a bus stop . . . and on behalf of the Danish Center for Information on
Genocide . . . evil under my nails, making them smell bad, and inside . . .
the early wrinkles in my face. In my cells, in my DNA. In me.

I give up.
Two people in love are waiting for the bus. They don't look my way.
They wear the same kind of long coat in a color like butterscotch and

aren't interested in the slightest in a confused woman sitting on a trash bin.

Now a teenage girl comes along to wait. She has painted names of bands and singers all over her rucksack, just as I did in my teens. She is about the same age as a lot of Cambodia's Khmer Rouge soldiers. I know what she could do to that couple.

What about the lovers? They look so innocent. "Waiting for the bus," that's all.

But close up you see the fat oozing out of their pores—long whitish yellow worms. Those two—their bad smell won't go away, even though they probably wash every day. It shouldn't have been like this. Ever.

I shouldn't have fallen ill again. I should've been with Gunnar, in his kitchen, pottering about with the bread and little dishes for a delicious Sunday lunch. He would come and stand close behind me and hold me tight while he kisses my neck. And his two daughters, who are mine too, would be running about, in and out of the kitchen.

I know this scene so well. That's how it should have been. And we would have been so happy. We wouldn't have killed anyone then, neither he nor I. Neither of us would have suffered from paranoia or been sick in the head.

Now I know it will never happen. I've become too weird for him. It shouldn't—*should not*—have been like this.

A tall man with long blond hair is approaching me. He speaks to me. Does he say that he wants to drop something into the bin? I get up, but he keeps saying things.

I have to speak to him. "Are you trying to use the trash bin? Is that it, the bin? I've moved off it now." Then it dawns on me that the man is speaking English, with a drawling accent. What's that he's saying?

"Now tell me. What's your plan?"

I don't understand what he wants but decide I'd better change to English too and repeat the bit about the bin.

He looks annoyed. "What's wrong with you, Malene? I don't care about that bin. What's your plan?"

"What? My name isn't Malene."

I look properly at him. He could have been an aging rock star, once cool but now on his way out. His skin is in poor shape and he has gone flabby, like men do when they're past their prime. I want him to go away and leave me in peace.

"My name isn't Malene."

He stares straight into my eyes.

"I know who you are, Malene. I've waited for you when you come out of the Center. And when you leave your house."

I shake my head. "You've got it all wrong, I'm not . . ."

It is only then that Iben realizes who the man is.

ike when you're off, flying across the handlebars on your bike. Then, in the fraction of a second before you crash to the ground, all your muscles go tense and your mind suddenly focuses one hundred percent.

How can she escape? She glances about her. Some fifteen feet away from Iben and Mirko Zigic, a strong-looking man stands with his hands in the pockets of his pilot's jacket. When his eyes catch Iben's and he realizes she has seen him, the corners of his mouth twitch slightly—something that is not quite a smile.

And opposite him, fifty feet or so away, another man is standing. He too observes her. His hair is cut very short, and there's something very Eastern European about his matching jeans and denim jacket.

Now she looks at Zigic again, sensing the weight of her knife against her leg. Her heart is pounding. Could she win a fight against him? Of course she couldn't. Are these men armed with weapons other than knives? Of course they are.

Zigic interrogates her. "Who do you work for?"

"The Danish Center for Information on Genocide."

"I know that. Who else?"

"No one." She has no idea what he is after and how she should respond. Should she pretend to be confident? Friendly? Pathetic?

Zigic is already irritated. "You will tell me! Who are they? And what do they want! Or else, no deal."

"I've no idea what you're talking about. I work for the DCIG and nobody else."

He stares as if wanting to see straight through her. Her words only seem to make everything worse. "What? Malene, do you want me to believe you sent that e-mail all on your own?"

"I haven't sent any e-mail."

Iben cannot understand why she didn't instantly recognize Mirko Zigic. He looks exactly like the man in the old family photos unearthed by Interpol. Through a mutual friend, Iben had got hold of the photos from an information officer in the DCIG's British counterpart. The pictures were accompanied by a video and documents about his parents and younger siblings. His family had also made statements, swearing that Mirko couldn't have been the executioner and torturer of the Serbian camps. He was kindness itself, they insisted. They must have gotten him mixed up with someone else. It was impossible that he could have built up his own section in the Serb Mafia.

The video was a grainy black-and-white copy of CCTV footage from a Munich burger bar. As far as Interpol was concerned, it was the last time Zigic had been spotted. Poor-quality images showed him, a tall man with long blond hair, having an argument with one of the counter staff about his change, or something like that. Then Zigic jumps over the counter. He grabs the other man's head, bends his neck back, and pushes the handle of a white plastic fork up one of his nostrils. By driving the fork home, Zigic caused so much brain damage that the man died almost instantly.

The camera records Zigic jumping back and calmly leaving the bar before anyone understood what had happened. Since then, no one has seen him.

Iben picks up a strong smell of male genitals. She can't be sure if it's coming from him or whether her mind is still malfunctioning.

He smiles when he notices her looking around at the men he has posted. Why make such a fuss about an ordinary Danish office worker?

He answers without being asked. "I take no chances, Malene. You've been a very smart girl."

A pause, and he goes on. "I'd like to handle this peacefully. We will do a deal with you and your bosses. But if you and your people won't play along, I'll defend myself—with force. And I can promise you won't like that at all."

"Okay. Let's talk."

"That's better. You're being sensible. Now tell me who you work for."

A bus halts. Zigic edges forward, just enough to ease himself between Iben and the bus. She has no doubt what would happen if she tried to board it with the other passengers.

She watches as the lovers in their long coats, the teenage girl, and a few others disappear into the warm yellow light of the bus. The doors close with a loud sucking noise and the bus pulls away, leaving Iben and Zigic standing in the stench of diesel fumes.

"I work alone."

He laughs out loud. "That's good. You won't tell me who you're acting for. I think I like you. But you must know I'm not stupid. I know what you're saying isn't true. If it were true, I would kill you right here. And you know that too, Malene; you have guts."

As if she has passed some kind of test, he grins at her. She tries to smile back.

"Yes. I suppose so."

She observes how the skin on his face is oddly lifeless. It is exactly as Ljiljana Peric described it: carved in wax. In a horrible way it seems somehow to fit the way he smells. She looks down the dark street. No one is around now except his men.

"I appreciate it that none of my men has been charged. That's good and I understand. You want to do a deal."

Iben doesn't have a clue what he is talking about. Obviously, if she has any chance of getting out of this, she must remain calm and tough. She can do it. She is able to stand still, without trembling; she is able to look him in the eye. "I'm pleased you think so."

"But you know what we want from you."

"Well, no . . . it could be quite a few different things."

He winks. "Come on then. Let's go to your apartment and start your computer. And we'll see what's in it."

He signals to his men, turns, and starts to usher Iben in the direction of Malene's apartment.

"All I need is to get my list of addresses back, along with my diary and all the backup copies. Please. Then you'll be free to go."

As they walk, everything Iben has learned runs through her mind. He apparently believes that Malene got hold of a computer disk that contained not only his address book but also information that would indict everyone whose name appears in it. Without their support, Zigic will no longer be able to escape the clutches of the War Crimes Tribunal. He will wait for the file as long as he believes that she has it. But as soon as he realizes the truth, he will kill her. She's well aware that he has raped and mutilated hundreds of victims until they told him everything they knew.

It's only a hundred feet from the bus stop to the entrance of Malene's building. The man in the denim outfit is posted outside to keep guard.

Iben has her keys ready, but the man in the pilot's jacket wants to show off to his boss. He has already slipped the lock and opened the door to Malene's apartment by the time Iben and Zigic reach the landing.

What if Malene is in there? Perhaps she didn't want to let Iben in earlier. Iben would like to call out a warning to give Malene a chance to run down the back stairs, but there's no way. Besides, if she's at home, they will kill Iben at once and spare Malene.

Iben holds her breath, waiting for Malene's voice. What if she shouts out, "Iben! You can't just let yourself in! You should've handed the keys back ages ago!" Zigic would demand to see their IDs, and the next moment he'd get rid of Iben. He wouldn't use a gun, that's for sure. Something quiet: a plastic fork, a piece of string, his bare hands.

Pilot Jacket goes in first. Zigic gives Iben a push and follows.

The men don't inspect the apartment with their pistols drawn, the way they always do in American films. Instead they wander from room to room, completely at ease but examining everything thoroughly, while keeping an expert eye out for a possible attack. Their movements are silent but coordinated, and within a minute or two their inspection is complete. They have checked all cupboards, corners, and recesses, switched on the necessary lights, and drawn the curtains. It's as if they had practiced house searches from early childhood, Iben thinks, and now they do them as easily as telling the time or tying their shoelaces.

Luckily the apartment is empty, but Malene might just have popped down to the kiosk or the corner shop. Perhaps she'll show up in a few minutes?

Malene's bulletin board hangs on the wall in the hallway. Iben walks on the other side of Zigic and talks to him so he'll look away from it toward her. Four photos of Iben used to be pinned on the board, but when she discreetly glances over Zigic's shoulder, the pictures of her aren't there anymore. Instead there are photos of Malene with Rasmus, which she had originally removed when Rasmus left her.

In the living room Zigic turns to her. "First, prove to me that you have the disk. Then we'll talk about what you want."

"What makes you think it's here? I'm not that stupid. I've kept copies elsewhere. I need to have the money first. And then you get your disk."

"I understand that. How much do you want?"

"I've been told to say one million euros."

"That's not a problem."

Iben would dearly like to say, "Good, let's go get the cash now." Better not.

Zigic is smiling in a way that in another man might be charming, almost fresh.

"Come on now, Malene! Show me. I know you have it here."

"That's not true."

"Of course you have a copy on this computer."

Iben doesn't answer. She tries to look confident.

Zigic is starting to lose patience. "Please turn on your computer."

The "let's do a deal" game is over. But then, the whole suggestion of a deal was never realistic—anyone who has seen the file must die, and she knows it.

The computer boots up. Pilot Jacket tells Iben to type in the password.

Iben knows that Malene's password used to be "lofa," for "lots of future ahead," but she might have changed it.

Neither of the men says anything. She has to try something.

She keys in the letters. This *has* to work. She has only one chance.

Windows opens. Iben suppresses a sigh of relief. Pilot Jacket shoves her out of the way, clicks on Find, and enters "Zigic."

While they're waiting for the computer, Zigic steers Iben over to the sofa and puts his hand on her shoulder.

"Why don't you sit down? Stay here on the sofa. Read a magazine or something. Meanwhile, we'll have a look around the apartment."

For some reason, something collapses inside her. She can't hold back her tears any longer and starts to cry without making a sound.

He stands there. What does he want? He said something about reading a magazine. There is a small pile of *Eurowoman* on the coffee table. She picks up a copy and opens it up, holding it in front of her face. Finally he moves away.

He's over by Malene's bookshelf now. She hears him take out a few books, leaf through them, and toss them to the floor. Iben peers at him from behind the magazine. He raises his arm and his command is like a blow: "Read!"

Iben turns her eyes to the pages in front of her, but the text is blurring. Is there some truth in what he has told her? Why else would he risk coming to Denmark?

It's Malene's fault if I die now, Iben thinks. It's Malene who's been in touch with Zigic, not Camilla. And, despite what the others think, I'm not the one who's been paranoid. In fact, I'm the only one who has faced up to reality.

There's something else: this means that it wasn't me sending those e-mails after all. I did remember writing them, at least I thought I did because it all seemed so real, so vivid and convincing, but that was just a fantasy. Now it's all gone. But then, was it Malene who sent them? Ever since I came back from Kenya she's been full of resentment toward me. Why *shouldn't* it have been her?

Zigic has finished going through the contents of the shelf. He has found a box of homemade CDs, which he puts down next to Pilot Jacket. If Iben heard correctly, Zigic calls Pilot Jacket "Nenad." She has the impression that Nenad is uneasy, presumably because he cannot find the file.

Zigic disappears into the bedroom and starts rummaging. She's alone with Nenad, whose back is turned. Why aren't they taking any precautions to stop her from trying to escape? They haven't even searched her; they don't know that she has a knife hidden away. Maybe they don't give a damn because they are convinced of their own power?

Her common sense is fading. She desperately wants to believe that her executioners are going to let her live—that after all a deal will really be possible. But if her work at the DCIG has taught her anything, it is that genocide perpetrators always give their victims a glimmer of hope that they'll survive if they cooperate and don't provoke anger. This illusion allows the perpetrators to peacefully take the victims' weapons and slowly oppress them until they are incapable of resistance. In the end, their execution is as easy and inevitable as swatting a fly.

Iben urges herself to accept the truth of her situation: there is no hope. After all, the inmates in the Warsaw ghetto and the Sobibor camp revolted only when they faced up to the fact that they had nothing to lose.

Nenad still sits facing in the other direction.

She gets up, slowly and soundlessly. Then she takes a step past the coffee table.

Nenad's voice is loud. "No!"

Zigic suddenly appears at the door. Iben practically falls down onto the sofa and quickly raises the magazine to her face. Blindly, she waits for what will happen next, but when she peeps out from behind the pages, Zigic has returned to the bedroom. She stares at an article about handbags. How did they know? Did Nenad see her image reflected in something shiny on Malene's desk? Was Zigic merely passing by?

A reel is playing in her head showing the landscape of Bosnia, the camps and buildings, the corpses excavated from mass graves—piles of corpses with cracked skulls and cut-off fingers; close-ups of the better-preserved bodies; the black marks of the ties that held straining torture victims to their chairs.

She has spent two years trying to understand men like the ones now in Malene's apartment. Is the smell of evil around them different from the smell of ordinary people? All she can get a whiff of is a mixture of after-shave and deodorant—expensive aftershave and deodorant. Zigic has enough money.

Zigic returns to the living room and walks around testing Malene's chairs, lifting them and shaking them. He slams several of the chairs against the floor, selects one, places it in the middle of the floor, and then turns to Iben. "Do you have any string?"

"There might be some in the fourth drawer down next to the kitchen sink." Iben has no intention of telling him that there's some in Malene's desk.

When he goes to fetch it, she'll be alone with Nenad for a few seconds, her last chance before they tie her down and start torturing her. She has to run for the front door. Losing them in the hallway and the stairwell is going to be nearly impossible, but she forces herself to remember Warsaw. And Sobibor.

Her whole body tenses. She hides her face behind the magazine. They mustn't notice. Now she leans forward. Her heels against the floor.

Only Zigic does not go to the kitchen. Nenad goes instead. "I'll fix some coffee as well."

Zigic and Iben listen to Nenad opening and closing drawers in the kitchen.

"There's nothing here!"

Zigic suddenly remembers seeing a ball of string. He shuffles through the desk contents scattered on the floor and finds it under the radiator. He walks to the chair and turns to Iben.

"Malene, come over here. We've got to leave you alone for a moment. We won't be long. But I'm afraid I will have to tie you to a chair."

It doesn't matter whether she can see through his lie or not, and he knows it. What can she do except hope that her common sense, all her instincts, are mistaken?

While Zigic ties her arms behind her back, Nenad pops his head around the kitchen door. The scene doesn't bother him at all—it must be routine. "Hey, where's your coffee?"

Iben finds it hard to speak; her vocal cords seem coated with thick glue. "In the jar . . . by the windowsill."

Nenad seems to have another idea. He looks pleased with himself and cocks an eyebrow. "You have any cakes or cookies?"

"No."

Zigic tightens the string. It cuts into her wrists and hurts badly— nothing compared to the pain to come. Soon he'll discover her knife.

"You know, there are some cookies. Only three left. He's probably eating them all right now."

Zigic seems to find that funny. He yanks hard at the string to make sure she can't move and wanders off to the kitchen.

Iben, it's now or never. Now!

She kicks her right leg up under the chair as far as it can go, reaches for the knife, and grabs it. It's something she has practiced many times. She nicks herself as she jabs the tip of the knife under the string, but suddenly her arms are free and she can stand up.

Soundlessly she slips into the hallway. She's able to reach the door without being discovered.

Denim Suit, however, is guarding the door downstairs. The moment she turns the deadbolt to the apartment they'll hear it in the kitchen. A couple of deep breaths. Someone in the kitchen throws something; she hears him run.

She turns the lock and almost flies down Malene's stairwell, her feet barely touching the steps. They're only a few yards behind her. As she throws herself around a turn in the staircase, she hits the handrail and almost tumbles into an endless fall. She grabs the handrail with her bloodied hands to stop her body from crashing down the steps. The knife clatters to the ground. The near fall only speeds her descent while she manages to pick up the knife.

The men behind her call out in Serbian to their guard below.

He shouts back: "Okay!"

She's already on the second-floor landing when he comes into view, walking slowly up toward her. He's a big man.

She remembers exactly what the yard looked like.

If, like Rasmus, you're on your way down the stairs and shoot out through the window, your body will take off to the right and become skewered on the fence posts, but if you're on your way up, the angle of the fall should be different. It should be possible to miss the wide steel railings and land on the tarmac, clear of the fence.

Iben takes a few more steps down. Denim Suit is getting closer. She turns around, facing up toward the landing. With her hands, she grasps the rails on both sides of the stairs and pushes off with her arms and legs for maximum speed. Her body flies upward and forward. Back on the landing, she doesn't turn the corner but puts one foot on the guardrail and throws herself at the old stained-glass panes. Protecting her face with her arms against the shards of many-colored glass, she falls less awkwardly than she did that night in Anne-Lise's garden. She is on her feet at once, unaware of how badly she is cut. She runs along the wall to the entrance leading to the communal bicycle storage in the basement. She hears no steps. The far end leads to the street behind Malene's house.

She keeps running. The air is much colder now. Normally, taking in lungfuls of icy air would hurt, but it doesn't. She is becoming conscious of the pain in her hands and feet.

At last, she reaches Gunnar's street.

She throws herself into his arms. Her nose is running and her wrist is
bleeding, making large dark stains on his shirt.

Gunnar carries her inside. "Iben, what on earth . . . ?"

He dries her face gently with his shirt and asks where the
blood is coming from. She is crying so much, he cannot make
sense of what she's trying to say.

He examines her hands and starts picking fragments of glass
from her blouse.

"Iben, listen. You need to get out of your blouse and take a
bath so we can see where your wounds are . . ."

"I want to lie down."

"Of course. You will. But first we need to find out where
you're bleeding."

"*I want to lie down!*"

"Yes, yes. Of course." He helps her to the sofa.

The light is too strong. She closes her eyes, but the bright-
ness won't go away. It seems to make dancing patterns against
her lids. She asks for a cushion to cover her eyes. With her face
partly hidden, she tries to pull herself together.

"We have to get hold of Malene and warn her. It is very
important."

She tries to explain what happened but hears how garbled she sounds.

"Iben, let's phone the police right now."

Iben doesn't reply.

"Are you absolutely sure that no one saw you coming here?"

"I don't think so."

"Yes, we definitely have to phone the police."

"Wait. Just a little."

"But Iben, it's essential . . ."

"Just wait." Her whole body is shaking.

Gunnar gets up.

"Don't go."

"I was going to phone a doctor."

"I've only got a few cuts on my hands. That's all. It looks worse than it is."

"Sure, but—"

"Gunnar, please stay. You're not to phone anyone."

She hears him sit down in a chair next her.

"I need to get some paper towels and a bowl of water. I can clean your cuts while you lie here. That's all right, isn't it?"

"Yes. I'd like that."

"Tell you what . . . I won't phone anyone until tomorrow morning."

"Good. I'm just so . . ."

When Iben takes the cushion away, the first thing she sees is that the room is full of books, just like her own. The apartment is large, with ample space between the pieces of furniture. The effect is somehow unfinished, as if he had been allowed half of the family home after his divorce and let the years pass without buying anything new.

She looks at Gunnar. She wants him to hold her close again, like the moment she arrived. She tries to recall what his warm body felt like. She has found a safe place where Zigic won't find her and where she will be taken care of. She touches Gunnar's thigh with her hand and relaxes. She suddenly burps. They both burst out laughing. She begins to feel well enough to feel self-conscious in front of him.

Slow footsteps. Somewhere. Iben can't quite make it out, but they could be coming from outside the door at the far end of the room.

She reacts without thinking. In an instant, the knife is in her hand. Her other hand, still flecked with drying blood, has grabbed a piece of orange stone that was on the coffee table. Before Gunnar can say a thing, Iben is standing, ready to fight.

Malene steps into the room, a damp towel wrapped around her head. "Iben? What are you doing here?"

Malene looks very sensual. Her hair and body are radiating warmth.

"Oh, no! *My God!* Iben? Jesus, what have you done?"

Iben blinks several times and shouts: "What have *you* done?"

"But . . . didn't I tell you? Gunnar and I are together."

Iben had no idea. "No, what's going on with Zigic?"

"Zigic? What do you mean?"

"Have you stolen his address list? Are you blackmailing him?"

"No! No way!" By now Malene looks terrified. She must think that Iben is out of her mind.

Still, Iben can't stop herself from almost screaming: "You and your tricks! You almost had me killed!"

"What?"

"Who do you work for? Apart from the Center?"

"But Iben, I don't understand."

Malene is so believable—as if she has done nothing wrong. It's too much. Gunnar tries to intervene and calm the two women down.

"You keep out of this!"

He reaches out to hold her, but Iben backs away quickly and raises her knife.

"Watch out! Stay away from me!"

Gunnar and Malene stare at her. Suddenly Iben comes to her senses. "Oh, no, please. Gunnar, I'm sorry, I didn't mean it. You know that I'd never . . ."

Everyone is frozen.

"It's all so confusing."

"Don't worry. I understand perfectly. Come and lie back down."

"I'm not at all like this . . . I don't want you to think that I am . . ."

"Iben, believe me, we both understand. We'll look after you."

Iben fights her suspicion that they are collaborating with Zigic. She must not be paranoid. She notices the bloodstains on the sofa. Gunnar won't be able to use it anymore. She mumbles, "I'm sorry," and lies down slowly, after putting Gunnar's stone back in its place.

Iben begins to tell Gunnar and Malene the story, but more coherently this time. Several times she interrupts herself to ask Malene what kind of contact she has had with Zigic. Malene insists that she has had nothing to do with Zigic or his files. He must have mistaken her for someone else.

Gunnar goes to the kitchen to find something for Iben to eat. Iben starts cleaning her left arm, but Malene stops her.

"Iben, let me do it. Just lie down."

How strange to be looked after by Malene. During the last six years it has always been the other way around.

For the first time Iben picks up the smell of sex that hovers in the air—as if Gunnar and Malene have been on a sexual rampage for days, using every available surface. Iben feels so bitter. Everything is falling apart. The pain is starting to get to her.

Malene must have noticed. She produces two strong painkillers from her handbag. Iben lies still, waiting for the pills to take effect, and looks at Malene's hands. While she was being held captive by Zigic, those hands were caressing Gunnar.

Gunnar returns with a bottle of whiskey, a plate of sandwiches, and mugs of hot chocolate for all of them.

Iben repeats how Zigic captured her all over again.

This time Malene says they ought to phone the police.

"But what if one of the men who chased me saw which street I ran to but not which door? Maybe they're still waiting. When the police arrive, their problem will be solved."

"So that's why you didn't want me to phone earlier!"

Malene starts to mumble. "Isn't it just a little . . ."

But instead, she changes tack. "I think I may know how all of this started. Remember the very first time I called Rasmus on my cell phone to tell him about the e-mail threats? He talked about the possibility of writing a spyware program. He kept working on the program whenever he had time. The idea was to forward it to the sender. It would then copy data from the sender's computer. Anything—like the address book and the calendar—and afterward the data would be sent back to us, to help us trap the criminal. But I didn't know he had gotten that far with it."

"But how would Zigic know who copied his files?"

"I suppose he couldn't—unless he got his own spyware set up after

Rasmus's death. I don't know. But let's say that he found my name from
the subscriptions that I paid for online via Rasmus's computer. Then if he
Googled me he'd have found out that I work at the DCIG and might think
that I had something to do with his computer being infected."

"It's just so . . . It means that if Rasmus's software did copy everything,
there has to be a file somewhere in your computer that could wipe out
Zigic's entire organization—bank accounts, supporters' names, details of
people he is using or blackmailing."

Malene goes and gets the laptop. She logs on as Rasmus, then experiments briefly with whatever other e-mail identities he could use.

They watch her in silence, Iben on the sofa and Gunnar in an armchair. Gunnar is so close that Iben could reach out her arm and touch him.

Suddenly Malene calls out excitedly. "Yes! Yes, look! Rasmus sent
an e-mail with the program attached to lperic@brat.org.yu. It has to be
Ljiljana Peric—the woman you interviewed about Zigic."

"But why send it to her?"

"I don't know."

Iben has an idea. "What if he wanted to see if it would work with the
Serbian version of Windows? That would make sense, don't you think?"

"It would. And it must've worked all right, because the following day
he sent an e-mail to revenge_is_near@imhidden.com. And another one to
zigl@tin.co.yu. That must be Zigic's e-mail address. I wonder how he got
hold of that?"

"What if the spyware program found it in Ljiljana's Contacts list? She
and Zigic were classmates, after all. She probably knows him better than
she likes to let on."

Malene talks while she clicks her way through Rasmus's mail. "Look.
The spyware has returned mail from both addresses. The header shows
that Zigic's mail goes via a Serbian server. The other mail was sent on from
a Danish server."

A wave of nausea flows through Iben, the same sickness that made her
sit down on the bin at the bus stop. The inside of her mouth feels as if it's
coated in thick mucus.

Malene speaks, half to herself. "So, it obviously wasn't Zigic who sent
the threatening e-mails. It was someone in this country. And the name
must be in this file!"

Gunnar and Iben lean forward, straining to see. Iben's forehead is covered in drops of sweat. She tries to speak enthusiastically, but her tongue doesn't seem to move. "Imagine! Rasmus found out who it is."

Malene's voice is dry. "So he did. And then he died."

It happens so suddenly. Something contracts inside Iben and her nose fills with the stench of creosote and rendered pork fat. She can smell evil now.

Iben jumps up from the sofa and manages a few paces toward the bathroom before throwing up everything she ate. She kneels, as if about to dive headfirst. The pool of fluid is brown, darker than the world of evil into which she almost disappeared earlier.

Gunnar and Malene come to help her, one on either side. Malene's hand supports her forehead.

"Iben, you've had such a dreadful day. It's understandable, you just can't take anymore."

Iben's head is churning again with the same thoughts she had earlier: What if my memories were real? What if I sent the e-mails and Rasmus found out? I would have known that he could destroy my life. Everything.

Iben whispers, "I'm not very well."

"We can see that. You mustn't worry."

She closes her eyes and tries to think. Her clammy forehead rests on Malene's hand.

What exactly do I remember about the day Rasmus was moving out? He was very serious and said he had to talk to me. He told me about the spyware and how he had designed it. I had expected him to ramble on about Malene and himself, but he started to lecture me about programming and . . . he lost me. Afterward I helped him carry things to the van. What was the subject he approached so hesitantly? Why was it important to talk to me?

"Iben, come with me. Let's get you back on the sofa."

Malene stinks like piss.

She listened to Rasmus talk about his program, but then what happened? Did I take some cycling gear downstairs? A can of oil without a stopper? Did I spill some oil on the steps, just in front of the only window without a guardrail? Did I tell myself to wipe it up and warn Rasmus? Did I carefully skirt around the oily spot instead? And fail to warn Rasmus?

Did I look at my greasy hands and think: Oh, I'd better wash my hands before I carry anything else down—why am I so filthy? Did I drop something?

Malene looks down at Iben. "It feels so good that I can take care of you, just for once."

"Malene, I feel so . . . confused."

"You're to rest now. Relax. We'll sit here with you and open Rasmus's files."

Iben gags again but her stomach is empty.

Malene double-clicks on the file attached to the return e-mail from revenge_is_near. It doesn't open. A dialog box asks about the correct application for this unknown file type.

"I haven't the faintest. Rasmus created the file type himself. What am I supposed to do now?"

Gunnar makes a few suggestions, but nothing works.

Malene is becoming irritated. "Why is it messing with us? When we're so close to finding out who sent those fucking e-mails that started everything!"

Gunnar has another suggestion: "Maybe Rasmus wrote a special file-opening program as part of his spyware."

"Maybe it's not installed on this computer at all," Iben speaks up.

Malene brightens. "Are you feeling better now, Iben? I'm so glad."

After exhausting all the possibilities, the file is still closed. Defeated, they sit looking at the little machine on the table in front of them.

Iben drinks a whole pitcher of water. No more smells now. Her thoughts are more coherent and she recalls what a good atmosphere there was between Rasmus and herself when she helped him move out. It makes no sense to think that Rasmus accused her of sending the death threats. She makes up her mind that, like the e-mails, she imagined what had happened in the stairwell. As before, her illness made it all seem real. She glances at her friend. Something has changed. The warmth has returned to Malene's eyes.

Malene, however, sounds let down. "What I don't understand is why Rasmus didn't tell me that he had found out who sent the e-mails."

Iben notices that Gunnar seems to withdraw a little every time Malene mentions Rasmus.

"Maybe it's because you had broken up two days before Zigic's data arrived?"

"But all the same . . ." Malene looks at Iben. "And you were with him when he moved out. Why didn't he tell you then?"

Iben struggles to find an answer. Nothing comes to mind. "I don't know. I really don't know."

t's late now. Iben convinces herself that it would be too paranoid to argue that Zigic is still watching the street. She agrees that they should call the police.

Shortly afterward, the intercom buzzes. "Police here."

Iben has an urge to warn them: "Be on your guard! You might be attacked when the door unlocks," but doesn't want the man to think that she's neurotic.

While Malene and Gunnar go to the hall, Iben looks for a way to defend herself. Zigic mustn't find her knife if he does a body search this time. She runs to Gunnar's desk, finds a roll of tape, and quickly tapes the knife underneath the middle of the three armchairs. Zigic won't look there.

She has just enough time to put the tape back and return to the sofa.

Malene screams. The next moment the front door slams and then, with a kind of cracking noise, it is pushed open again.

Iben's heart starts hammering. Driven by an instinct to jump, she runs to the window. They are on the fourth floor, but it doesn't matter. What else can she do? She turns her head to scan the room while she pulls back the handles on the largest window.

Nenad is at her side in an instant. She tries to put up a fight.

But he easily throws her to the floor and orders her to lie facedown with her hands behind her neck. It will be so much worse this time. They will take no chances. She chokes on her sobs. It's hard to cough in such an awkward position.

Gunnar and Malene are led in and ordered to lie on the floor in the same position as Iben. They are all searched. The men are much tougher and more efficient this time. Even so, they give Malene lots of attention and search her repeatedly. Denim Suit is so rough that Malene cries out with pain and fear until she is told to shut up.

Zigic jams his hand up hard between her legs, but looks at Iben when he speaks.

"You wish you got that, don't you?"

She knew it was coming. She knows what he is like. Gunnar and Malene had no idea. I should have acted, Iben tells herself. The phrase sticks. I should have acted. I should have acted.

From somewhere above her she hears Zigic parroting a woman's voice, meant to be Iben's. "Oh, dear! I think I'll just run away from Mirko Zigic."

She raises her head a little. He brings a heavy boot down on the back of her head.

Something cracks—like when a pair of poultry shears cut through a strong chicken thigh. Pain suddenly shoots into every part of her face. Iben screams in agony. In front of her eyes the pale, mottled surface turns a deep red.

Zigic kicks her in the side. "Shut up. I tried to be kind and take it easy on you. You didn't want to cooperate, did you? You forced me to treat you differently."

Nenad has spotted the computer. The open e-mail with its attached file makes him whistle excitedly, which attracts Zigic's attention.

Iben raises her head cautiously and turns it sideways to shift its weight from her broken nose. Now the coffee table is in her line of sight. She can see Nenad is talking and pointing to the screen, and Zigic is smiling, obviously pleased. The new position of her head slows the flow of blood to a steady drip. Iben watches the drops and tries to forget the pain by thinking ahead. Zigic will have to move his prisoners somewhere else, she thinks. Sooner or later Gunnar's neighbors will call the police. And besides that, the police station will begin to worry about the lost radio contact with their men, who are probably lying dead downstairs.

Where will Zigic take them? Some secret place where he can hold them indefinitely. He will need to torture them until he knows who might have seen the file or made copies of the disk. He will make the outside world seem utterly distant and meaningless to them. Will he want all three of them? Three prisoners are harder to control than two, or one. Will Zigic pick them out one by one to find out if they know anything, then kill them if they don't? If he decides to get rid of someone right now, who will he choose?

Zigic lifts the laptop's keyboard and fiddles with the small hard disk until it comes out. He puts it in the breast pocket of Nenad's jacket and addresses him in Serbian.

Then he turns to his three captives. "Okay, now I have one copy of the file. Where are the backup copies?"

No one answers.

"Okay. Listen hard. If there turns out to be any other copies in existence after my visit to Denmark, then things will look bleak for you. Bleaker than you can imagine."

Zigic is in no hurry to leave the apartment. "Even if I can't come back to kill you personally, someone else will. And don't think it is just you who'll die. Your families will die too and anyone close to you."

This little speech sounds calm and considered. It is so tempting to think that once he has secured the files, all will be well.

"Listen, if you want to get out of this, pray to God: 'Dear God, please, please help us to remember to tell Mirko about every little thing. And please, God, don't let us make any tiny little mistake in anything we say to Mirko!' You get my message? You understand?"

"Yes."

Zigic has had enough. "Right. We'd better get out of here, but before we go, tell me this. Are there any more copies of the file kept anywhere else in this apartment?"

"No."

"Good. Next question. We are going to take you to a place we know. Is there anywhere we should stop off on the way, any other copies hiding elsewhere?"

Gunnar speaks up. "Yes. I have a copy in my office."

Iben thinks this a very good idea. The reception at Gunnar's office at the Ministry of Foreign Affairs is open around the clock and is well guarded. The building has long corridors, ideal for escape.

Zigic turns to him. "Is that so? At your office everyone will stay in the car, except for you and one of my men."

He moves until his boots are immediately in front of Gunnar's face. "And if you can't produce a file, we'll kill one of the girls. Immediately. This time, think carefully before answering. Is there a copy of the file in your office?"

"No," Gunnar cries.

Iben is so disappointed in him. He has fallen into Zigic's trap. It's because he doesn't dare not to trust the prison guard. Gunnar needs to believe in the only reassuring option, which is that they might survive if they cooperate.

Denim Suit has done the rounds of the apartment. He returns with a broad grin on his face, waving a used condom, and Nenad joins him in fooling about with it. Denim Suit finally empties the contents over Malene's head.

Iben wants to let Gunnar know he mustn't worry about taking responsibility. "I have a backup copy. I left it in the Ministry for Foreign Affairs for safekeeping."

Zigic moves toward her and repeats his threat. "We'll check. And remember, if it isn't as you say, I'll kill one of your friends. So it's your turn to think carefully and answer me. Do you have a file copy in the ministry?"

"Yes."

When Malene hears this, she gasps and shouts at Iben: "No you don't!"

Iben slips into Danish. "Malene, you've just *killed* me by saying that."

"What?"

"He'll kill me now. If I haven't got a file he'll kill me here. You've just told him to."

Iben's outburst makes Malene break down. She starts crying again.

Zigic kicks Iben. "You're not to speak Danish. If you do, I'll have your families killed."

Malene tries to speak in English but is crying so hard she is incomprehensible.

"But what else . . . Iben, oh, Iben . . . when they don't find it, it'll be me who . . ."

Zigic laughs. He walks toward Iben. Somehow he draws his handgun. It is suddenly there, in his hand. It is the first time she has seen it. A little click as he releases the catch.

Gunnar speaks quickly. "Iben. That copy I gave you. Is that what you did? Deposited it in the Foreign Affairs Ministry?"

"Yes."

Zigic addresses Gunnar with condescending sarcasm. "Listen to you, No-Balls. How interesting. I think I believe you."

He bends over Iben, pushes the muzzle of the gun against the back of her head, and slides it down until it digs into the hollow where the cranium meets the neck.

"I believe you, Mister No-Balls." And he presses the trigger.

Her mind explodes. Gunnar. Malene. Evil. A future. A life. Omoro, who died. Rasmus, who died. Father, who died. A moment in Africa, when she stood on the back of a white pickup truck and decided that everything should be different from now on.

The blood under her cheek. The pool of blackening red is about to seep into her ear. She realizes that there was no shot, no bullet in the chamber.

She looks up at Zigic. He's still standing over her. She's still lying at his feet.

Malene screams, a long howl, with her face pressed into the floorboards.

Zigic speaks quietly to Iben. "No such luck. Not this time. Maybe it will be second time lucky."

Zigic orders them to get up.

Nenad turns to Iben, explains that he is going to clean the blood off her face. Of course—her bloody face would make driving through central Copenhagen unnoticed quite a bit more difficult.

Nenad goes off to fetch a roll of paper towels and, in the meantime, Iben collapses on the middle of the three armchairs. He returns, cleans her nose and cheeks, twists the paper up her nostrils and pushes. It hurts like hell, but Iben thinks how careful he is being. It's a little like being a piece of fillet, lovingly marinated by a top chef, but knowing that seconds later, he might decide to carve you up or tenderize you with a mallet.

While he concentrates on her nose, Iben fumbles a little under the chair. And then she too is ready to leave.

The three Serbs stroll downstairs with the prisoners between them.

Zigic is at their side, with Denim Suit scouting in front of them and Nenad following behind, keeping watch up the stairwell. They have been told to be silent, and when Gunnar tries to catch Iben's eye, Zigic knees him in the groin.

It has snowed. A thin powdery layer covers the dark, abandoned street.

An empty police car is pulled up on the white pavement outside Gunnar's front door. Iben looks around for the bodies, but they are nowhere to be seen.

Zigic orders them to climb into a silver car parked nearby, Iben first. She is to sit in the back, with Malene on her lap. Gunnar is told to sit on the bulge in the middle of the back seat and direct the driver. Denim Suit sits next to him. Zigic gets into the driver's seat and Nenad into the front passenger seat, so he can keep his gun trained on the prisoners.

Iben's broken nose means that she cannot smell her friend, but they are so close that it seems she can taste her. The sweet iron flavor of blood blends with the warm pressure of Malene's body. It is the same familiar body she has hugged so many times, when they met or when something important happened.

Iben realizes that Malene's hand is trying to find hers. She responds, reaches out, despite all that has passed between them. The car's movements press Gunnar's thigh against Iben's, making her sense every slight vibration.

They cross the harbor canal on Knippel Bridge. One left turn to go. Zigic directs a question toward the backseat: "Tell me again. Is there a backup copy at the ministry?"

Gunnar and Iben both answer him: "There is."

"Okay. And you know what happens if we don't find it."

"Yes."

The thin layer of fresh snow makes the streets and buildings look delicate. Iben's face is close to her friend's back. Once, when the car bumps, her nose hits Malene's spine and it feels like being knocked out. The blood must have soaked through the paper twists, because now a red blob stains the pale blue material of Malene's blouse.

Malene's body is trembling and she is crying silently.

They park in the lot in front of the ministry, a grand building that is almost completely dark. Two rows of street lamps cast a faint light on the snowy cobbled yard.

Zigic turns to Iben. "You. Are you ready to come in with me?"

Iben answers at once: "Yes."

Maybe she sounded too eager. Zigic turns to Gunnar. "You know where it is too, right?"

"Yes."

"And you've got a night pass to this place?"

"Yes."

"Good. You should worry more about your pals than that bitch next to you. You come with me. And you know what happens if anything goes wrong? Anything at all?"

"Yes." So it isn't Iben who will have a chance to knife Zigic and flee from him in the long corridors of the ministry. It is to be Gunnar. Unarmed.

Iben winks at him when he climbs out. It's all she can do to try to tell him that he must feel free to do whatever he can, because when he returns to the car Iben and Malene will be either dead or gone.

Denim Suit gets out too. He starts pacing up and down restlessly away from the car. Perhaps he's beginning to worry.

Malene moves to sit next to Iben. Nenad watches them. His gun looks different from anything Iben knows. It's longer than other handguns, the muzzle cross-section is square, and there is a bulge below the stock in front of the trigger.

He keeps an eye on them, but can't see everything. Iben's knife is hidden in her underwear, across her buttocks. She scratches her bum. The next moment she has the knife in her hand, hidden behind the back of the driver's seat.

Malene sees it. Her face turns to stone, but she stays quite still.

Iben watches the pulse on Nenad's neck. It beats in a slow rhythm. Da-dum. Da-dum. Da-dum. It is alive. Nenad's life is there. She stares. Da-dum. Nenad is good at computers. He likes his coffee and cookies. Nenad treated Iben's nose with real care. There it is. That small beating thing, the spot that her knife must hit. Just there. And his life will be spurting out of him.

She leans forward, shifting the knife to her right hand behind the back of the driver's seat. Her leg muscles stiffen in readiness to leap.

She waits. The best possible moment may not be now. Maybe it will never come. Maybe Denim Suit will return any second.

It might have been Malene's quickened breathing that alerted Nenad, or the frightened look on her face. He moves over, craning to see. He will soon find out what Iben is hiding.

She throws her body across the small car and raises the knife with both hands. She plunges it in, straight into the life-sustaining pulse.

His blood sprays all over Iben and the car. His eyes roll up. His lips draw back over his teeth and his arms begin to shake. Still his eyes stare at her. Then slowly fade. He falls.

She grabs the gun from his lap. Denim Suit, who has been about thirty feet away, must have heard something and runs back to the car. Iben doesn't lower a window, just shoots at him through the rear window. She only touches the trigger, but a volley of shots ring out. It is some kind of miniaturized machine gun.

Malene's face is white. She might be about to faint. Iben shouts at her, "Get out! Out! Out!"

Iben shouts, "Run!"

Malene runs.

Iben searches Nenad's pockets but can't find a spare car key. She'll have to get out and run too.

She's only gone a few steps when Zigic and Gunnar come out through the brightly lit main door of the ministry. Zigic sees her. He doesn't turn toward Gunnar, but thrusts the knife sideways with an instant backhand stroke. The blade is driven precisely into the center of Gunnar's chest, and he slumps to the ground.

Malene has reached the other side of the short channel of dark water flowing between the complex of ministry buildings and draining into the harbor canal. She shouts that she has seen a taxi. Iben runs after her, following the waterway.

She is in time to see the taxi on the far side of the ministry compound. Despite Malene's flailing arms and shouting, the cab drives off.

Zigic is closing in on her. It is the worst conceivable place for running. The cobbled quayside is deserted. Tall, dark warehouses on one side; on the other, the black, freezing water of the canal. Where can she hide? There is nothing. She runs on.

Zigic is fast. Iben turns to shoot at him, but after a short burst the magazine is already empty. It is much smaller than a real machine gun. She throws it into the snow and runs.

Only one brightly lit object stands out against the dark—a large white shape: a houseboat. It is moving away from the quay. The mooring ropes have been pulled in and its decks seem completely abandoned. It is about to sail away, to leave them, but it is slow. They can still leap on board.

Iben overtakes Malene, whose arthritic feet must be hurting her badly. A few seconds more and then Zigic will be almost on top of them and everything will be over for them both.

Iben reaches the dock and leaps. She lands on the deck. Now rescue Malene. There's only one short moment to spare. She turns to reach out for her friend.

Iben has a vision of a scene set in Gunnar's apartment. Malene and Gunnar are together, damp with sweat, in his bed.

Does she hesitate for just a moment too long before reaching out? She doesn't know. How long before she acts? Two seconds, or three? She doesn't know. Perhaps she doesn't hesitate at all.

And now the distance is too great. Malene can't jump.

She screams.

Iben stands under the bright spotlight on the small area of the deck. In front of her, a white steel wall with one door set in it. She pulls at the handle. It's locked.

What? Fucking what? The houseboat is only ten feet from the quay, moving so slowly it's practically standing still.

She runs the few steps to the other side. The deck is barred there and she can get no further. She runs back. Barred again. She hammers on the door.

This boat will not mean freedom and survival. It is a floating cage. She climbs up a ladder welded to the white wall. She hangs on to the ship's flank, illuminated, like a black dot on a huge sheet of paper. She is just a few yards from Zigic's gun.

She keeps climbing while she looks over her shoulder. She watches. Zigic stops a couple of feet behind Malene. He raises his gun and aims. Iben moves on up, but it takes time to climb so many small rungs.

He is so close she can see his finger bending to press the trigger.

He has her now.

iben

malene

anne-lise

camilla

ben shows up in good time. Today looks like one of the first proper days of spring. The brilliant sunlight brings out every crack in the pavement where she stands. Weeds will soon push up through the gaps.

Malene's parents are the only other people who are present. Like Iben, they wait in silence, staring down the long one-way street. Cars should be coming into sight soon.

Over the last five days Malene's mother has phoned Iben almost every evening. Malene's parents arrived in Copenhagen yesterday and Iben went to meet them.

Not one day will pass when Malene's parents won't wonder why it was their daughter and not Iben. Even now they must lie awake at night, thinking that it should have been Iben.

As for herself, Iben watches Animal Planet and eats bowls of ice cream with marshmallows night after night. She thinks about what Malene did. In bed she twists and turns and thinks about what she herself did.

A green car shows up at the bottom of the street. Malene's father and mother wave. When the car draws near them Iben recognizes Malene's aunt and her three children, whom she has met on her visits to Kolding with Malene.

Another thing that Iben has been pondering: Should she go into therapy again? But then, how will it help now?

More cars pull up. She must not be so nervous. Zigic can no longer come anywhere near her.

A whole fleet of police cars responded instantly to the shootings. Zigic was easy to arrest, hemmed in by the icy water and holding an empty gun. The disk Zigic had removed presented a much harder case. Detectives searched Zigic, his car, the wastepaper baskets and corridors of the ministry, the trash bins in the yard, and every other possible spot. Police divers combed the bottom of the canal several times. The disk was never found, but the man in the denim suit survived Iben's gunshot and told the Serb police where to find Zigic's computer. The data it held was sufficient to round up almost the entire organization.

Malene's aunt hugs her parents and, after a few quiet words, moves on to Iben.

"Iben, this must be hard for you."

"Yes. It is."

"And you have much to be grateful for."

"Believe me, I know."

The uncle talks to her too, as do other members of Malene's family. Iben looks down at her feet. Do they see anything in her face? What are they thinking?

Frederik gets out of a taxi and catches sight of her. He walks quickly toward her, stumbles on the curb, and saves himself by taking a couple of running steps.

Everyone has come: Malene's friends as well as colleagues, Rasmus's family, and of course Camilla, Anne-Lise, Paul, and members of the DCIG board.

A transport van pulls up to lower two women in wheelchairs. Iben has never seen them before. Presumably they knew Malene from the Association for Young Arthritic People.

At last she spots Gunnar climbing out of another taxi. She observes his black suit, which looks new and expensive. His eyes are bloodshot and so swollen that his whole face looks different. She has been visiting him at the hospital over the last few days. Iben walks inside the chapel with Gunnar. She knows the music and hymns that Malene's mother has chosen. All of them echo inside her head.

. . .

"What happened on the quayside was an exception and I'm perfectly aware of it. In principle, it shouldn't have happened. Her every instinct would have urged her to save her own life. So, what she did was—exceptional. Incomprehensible. Against nature."

It is the day after the funeral and Iben is seated in the DCIG's small meeting room. There is only one other person in the room: Dorte Jørgensen, the plump woman detective who spoke to Iben after Rasmus's fall.

Dorte frowns and closes the door firmly. Iben is being interrogated. She doesn't intend to cave in to the tension that the detective is trying to create, but continues her line of thought.

"It was nothing short of miraculous. The way human beings behave is subject to natural laws. Then, suddenly, from one moment to the next, an exception occurs. That I am alive is precisely because of such an exception, as extraordinary as an apple rising from the ground to attach itself to a branch on an apple tree. Or a malignant tumor regressing and disappearing without trace. Or blood dripping from a statue of Christ."

"Interesting. Now, do you have any explanation for how the hard disk from Rasmus's computer could've disappeared?"

"I guess Zigic must have thrown it away somewhere in or around the ministry."

"You see, it contains data about his organization. We have searched everywhere. And I mean everywhere. Even the bottom of the canal. We've drawn a blank every time."

"Well, I really can't . . ." Dorte is getting on Iben's nerves.

"That hard disk contained not only data on Zigic. It also held the name of your e-mail sender, who is based here in Denmark. It's not too hard to see what I'm thinking, is it?"

"I'm afraid it is. I don't understand."

"I should have thought it was pretty obvious. The man you killed in the car could've had the disk in one of his pockets. And you could have taken it before you ran. In all that excitement, nobody searched you."

"But I'd have no reason . . ."

"Well, now, that's questionable."

"What do you mean?"

"One possibility is that it was you who sent the e-mails and that a file on the disk proved it. Rasmus might even have told you he knew when you helped him move."

"But . . . why would I send anyone threatening e-mails?"

"Why indeed? Why should anyone?"

"I had no reason at all."

Iben has heard from Malene's mother that the police have sealed Malene's apartment and that they can't start clearing it yet. And with the discovery that Zigic was in Denmark, the police are now considering the theory that Rasmus may have been murdered.

Dorte pauses deliberately before continuing. "The special something I sensed between you and Gunnar when you were both at the station—am I wrong about it?"

"What do you mean?"

Iben knows that Dorte can see something in her face, and she scratches the bandages on her nose.

"If before the e-mails were sent you had already fallen in love with the man who was Malene's lover . . . it could've caused bad blood between you, couldn't it?"

Iben can't reply. She takes a deep breath.

"Maybe you regretted sending the e-mails. Or maybe you didn't. One way or the other, the spyware found you out and Rasmus told you."

Does Dorte do this to other people she interrogates? Is making wild accusations part of her method, just to see if one of them hits home?

Iben tries to prevent herself sounding strained. "Look, it doesn't make sense! Rasmus and I had a good time together that day. I helped him carry some of his things. There is no way we'd get along so well just minutes after he accused me of e-mailing death threats."

Dorte's eyes are still fixed on Iben. "You might have told him that your laptop had been left in the office and that Anne-Lise had access to it. That would calm him down. After all, Anne-Lise is the one you people tried to pin the e-mails on."

Iben can't think what to say.

Dorte rests her arms on the table. "But, if Anne-Lise did *not* have access to your computer at the time when the e-mails were sent, that could have been established the following day. And you would have lost your job, your old friend, and all hope of Gunnar ever becoming your lover."

It's unbelievable. This woman, Dorte Jørgensen, is installed here, in their lunch room, calmly accusing Iben of having killed her best friend's partner! Certainly she doesn't go that far with everyone?

Iben feels like waving her arms about and shouting that this is all totally insane. Living through these last few weeks has upset her terribly, and somehow she feels that Dorte might even be right.

She pinches her thigh to wake herself up. She must concentrate.

What did happen? Should I give myself up? Should I say I did it and serve a life sentence in prison?

Once more her mind conjures up an image that has recurred since the first time she met Gunnar. She is in his kitchen, cooking lots of nice dishes; he stands behind her and puts his arms around her. And his daughters come running in, laughing, from the living room.

Iben is not herself during the rest of the interrogation. When Dorte gets up, opens the door, and walks into the hallway, she turns and speaks over her shoulder.

"Well, Iben, we'll take a look at that. It's a good idea. Malene's mother has mentioned that Malene kept writing letters to Rasmus after his death. We are definitely going to follow up that line of inquiry."

O n the pavement a little ahead of me a man in a wheelchair
*was being pushed along by his wife. I caught up with them. They
both seemed quite elderly and were deep in discussion. Just as I
passed, the woman spluttered with laughter. A little later I
turned to look at them and they were both still talking at the
same time, apparently sharing a story that they enjoyed hugely.
And I came to think of Iben.*

*Rasmus, you were always loving and kind, helping me when-
ever I needed it. But I couldn't help feeling that I was a nuisance
to you. It was never like that with Iben.*

*At times when I couldn't do a thing for myself and needed
hospital treatment and had to be hauled downstairs to the taxi,
she never acted as if she was sacrificing herself. I didn't feel I was
a problem. Or when she went shopping for me, helped me
dress—things like that. For years she was with me and saw more
of me than even you did. And all the while we had such a good
time. We laughed a lot.*

*I hate her now for what she has made me suffer over these
last few months. That's a fact. But I'll never find a friend like her
again. She really was special: an exception.*

• • •

I remember one time when I was in the living room and you were in the kitchen. And suddenly I heard a crash.

At first I actually felt pleased. He's dropped something, I thought. Maybe he's poured boiling water all over his feet. Just for once, I thought, he'll know what it's like not to have full control of your hands. But it didn't take long at all before I started to worry.

I called out to you: "Oh, God! Rasmus? Did you drop something? Did you hurt yourself?"

Of course you didn't know what had been going on inside my head. In its own small way, that moment seemed like the sort of dissociative identity disorder that Iben was always talking about.

Rasmus, I am so very sorry about what happened on the stairs. I simply don't know what came over me. You are the only one who knows how bad I feel about it. You are the only one who can understand.

God alone knows how much Iben heard. It wasn't my intention to push you out through the window. I have no idea why it made me so blindly furious when you insisted that your spyware proved that I had sent those e-mails.

I gave you a shove. Nobody can be sorrier than I am now. Am I truly sick in the head, Rasmus? Is that it?

they're sweet now. They speak to her and laugh with her. Everything has changed completely—so much so that Anne-Lise finds it hard to believe the way things were not so long ago.

Paul is different too, quite unlike his old self. He is in the office much more and is suddenly of the opinion that it is "simply natural that the functions of the DCIG and the DIHR should be coordinated." He is no longer prepared to fight to maintain the independence of the Center.

Anne-Lise cannot make him out. Only recently he did everything he could to help the Center survive, even trying to force Frederik from the board. Was that some kind of macho thing? Could the reason be that any organization only has room for one man of their kind?

The office was closed for the day after Malene's death. The following day Iben brought in a red rose, which she placed on Malene's desk. The next morning Iben replaced it with a fresh rose and again the next day. It was as if Iben believed that Malene was a saint and that her desk and chair were sacred.

When people turned up to use the library, Iben lectured them at length about how her own survival had been due to a "psychological miracle." Paul told her repeatedly that if she felt like staying at home she should, but Iben didn't seem to get the hint. Perhaps she wanted to be at work.

Every day people phoned to offer their condolences and find out what happened. At times, it became too much for Iben, and Anne-Lise took over.

"Iben was climbing this ladder on the houseboat, so she couldn't follow what happened on the quay. But a lot of the warehouses have been converted into apartments, and people were watching from their windows because they had heard the shot Iben fired at Zigic. The witnesses all say that Zigic was aiming his gun at Iben. But at the moment he was ready to pull the trigger, Malene called out. No one knows why. She threw herself in front of the gun. Iben was then able to reach the roof and that saved her. The metal ridge protected her."

At some point in every single phone call, the person would wonder about Malene's brave act. They wanted to know more, and Anne-Lise's replies became more and more precise.

"Yes, it's true. Quite remarkable. I've never heard of anything like it . . . Of course, but what Iben did in Kenya was different. She says so herself, you know. After escaping, when she ran back to the hostages, she didn't think of it as taking a risk. She simply couldn't imagine that the Kenyan police might side with the hostage takers.

"Yes, how true that is. Malene was very special. We were so proud to have worked with her. No, I suppose we didn't realize that she had this in her." Anne-Lise isn't completely sorry that Malene is dead.

Sometime after Malene's funeral, Iben puts a large portrait of Malene on the bulletin board. She stops bringing in roses and also suggests to Anne-Lise that the two of them should leave their desks in the library and move into the Winter Garden.

Taking over Malene's place so soon after her death makes Anne-Lise uneasy, but Iben says that it's okay with her. Paul and Camilla agree.

Malene's things are put away on a shelf behind Iben, and Anne-Lise takes the seat opposite her. Anne-Lise puts her photo of Henrik and the children almost exactly where Malene's plastic troll used to be.

Until a new project manager is appointed, Iben takes over Malene's tasks. They stop speaking incessantly about Malene during the breaks and move on to other things. As they continue working together on the special Turkey issue, the talk flows easily between the desks in just the way Anne-

Lise used to dream it would. Everything is as she hoped it would be when she left Lyngby Central Library. The only problems troubling Anne-Lise are rooted inside her own mind.

Look how they smile, she thinks, sweet as pie, as if they never tried to drive me insane. Of course they tell themselves that never happened. It makes them feel good. And how much better would it be if I managed to forget everything as well? But how can I forgive them? How will I ever be able to trust anyone the way I did just a year and a half ago?

One evening she agrees to go with Henrik to a tasting arranged by his wine club.

He beams and gives her a kiss. "You're my old Anne-Lise again!"

The tasting takes place in a large specialist wineshop in Østerbro. It is crowded, and everyone seems to be in a good mood. Some come straight from work and are still in their suits. Others, like Henrik, have changed their clothes.

A couple of Henrik's old friends from university started the club and most of their circle joined it, mainly because it was a nice way to keep in touch. Henrik and Anne-Lise usually meet many of their old gang.

Nicola rushes up to greet Anne-Lise. "It's great that you'll be at Jutta and Stig's! And thank you so much for the invitation to your place. I'm so pleased that you're your old self again!"

Anne-Lise and Nicola see much more of each other these days.

The shop's proprietor introduces the first wine and the first round of glasses are being filled at the long, French-style dining table in the middle of the room.

As one wine follows another, several people come over to say how delighted they are to see Anne-Lise. They must have been talking about me more than I ever realized, she thinks. It's as if she's been away in the hospital with a disease or something.

It all becomes too much for her. She finds Henrik and nods toward a narrow passage between two walls of boxes of wine. They slip away from the others.

"Henrik, listen. It's good that nobody has noticed anything different about me, but it isn't right what they're all saying: I'm not 'the old Anne-Lise.' "

Henrik looks stunned, taking a step back and hitting his head against the protruding corner of a box. She must have sounded much more adamant than she intended.

"I'm trying to behave like a good person, but it's such an effort. I'm so bitter."

"But Anne-Lise, darling."

"My head is bursting with fantasies about revenge. You have no idea! And they won't stop. I can't cope with it! I'll never, ever be my old self again!" Anne-Lise's lips are tightly closed, and she sinks down on a spindly wooden chair.

Henrik sighs, drags a box along to the chair, sits down, and puts an arm around her. He speaks to her gently. "You will be yourself again, Anne-Lise. Of course you will. It just won't happen overnight, that's all."

"No. Iben is right. Other people shape who I am. I can't make myself into who I want to be. We all have it in us to be murderers and executioners and war criminals."

Henrik's arm tightens around Anne-Lise's shoulders. "What are you saying?"

"Henrik, for God's sake. I wouldn't be the woman I am now if I could choose. But Iben says we can't choose. Other people determine who we are."

Henrik shifts the box so he can sit facing her and takes her face in his hands.

"Please, explain this to me slowly. Try to help me understand what you're saying."

Anne-Lise feels like throwing her glass of red wine on the storeroom floor.

"It's like this. Iben watches nature films and says that people behave the same way as animals. She says that there are patterns of behavior that everyone conforms to because they are instinctive and predestined—psychological laws of nature. She's been studying developmental biology and social psychology and research papers about the psychology of the perpetrator. And she has written two articles about evil called 'The Psychology of Evil I' and 'II.'

"I hate those articles of hers and her lectures too. Iben's outlook is so grim and black. I've heard her say things like 'The more I learn, the more convinced I am that we would all act in exactly the same way as the perpetrators if we were in their situation.' "

"I see. What do the others say to all this?"

"No one in the office ever argues with Iben. And I realize now that she's right."

"She's wrong, you know."

Anne-Lise mustn't start sobbing now, when all their friends are within earshot. She tries to be as quiet as possible. "I don't want to be like this, Henrik. I'm evil." She looks into Henrik's face and senses him thinking: Oh, God, will this never end? He deserves so much better.

"Anne-Lise. You are not evil."

"But I wasn't sorry to hear that the back of Malene's head had been blown to bits, was I? If the others had died as well, I wouldn't have minded. Does that sound like 'the old Anne-Lise'? Does it?"

Anne-Lise drives Henrik's large, dark blue car home from the wine tasting. He asks her to stop just before they reach the house where Anne-Lise's parents live. Her mother has looked after the children, but he would prefer them to wait a little before picking them up.

"I've thought about what you said. Remember what Malene did. She was the worst of them; nonetheless, she did something that Iben's theories couldn't explain in a thousand years.

"To sacrifice your life for someone who is not your child—how would Iben get around that? She can't. And if Malene can do something like that, then there is something in all of us that is both unpredictable and potentially good. It exists in you. And in me."

They sit together in silence. Anne-Lise moves close to Henrik and rests her head on his shoulder. He puts his arm around her.

One week after the police interrogated everyone in the Center about Rasmus's death, Camilla starts pressing Iben to find out how the investigation is going. She feels nervous about her sessions with Dorte Jørgensen and is keen to know what is going on.

When Iben puts down the receiver, her hand is shaking. "I spoke to Dorte Jørgensen. The investigation is closed. Malene wrote on her home computer that she was aware of having a split personality. She admitted to having killed Rasmus."

All work ceases. It seems unbelievable at first, and then Malene's image changes in an instant. They decide to phone again to make sure Iben hasn't misheard. Anne-Lise makes the call.

Iben is shocked, but then, they all are. They had put together a shared memory of Malene, like a jigsaw puzzle. Now it has come apart and every piece takes on a new meaning.

The rumors about Malene spread rapidly through the world of human rights. Anne-Lise hears Iben speaking to one of the callers: "Naturally I'm deeply grateful for Malene's self-sacrifice. Deeply. But I did wonder. It didn't fit somehow. It's understandable now. She was tormented by her guilt over having killed Rasmus. And, perhaps, she was mentally ill. That would explain a lot."

Iben listens to the voice at the other end of the line, and then continues.

"Absolutely. What she did wasn't the response of a healthy human being. In fact, her self-sacrifice in no way contradicts the theories I discussed in my articles in *Genocide News* on evil."

chapter 55

P aul opens the front door with a bang and steps into the office, beaming happily at everyone. He's barely over the threshold before he starts announcing his news. "At last, I can tell you all!"

"Hi, Paul! Tell us what?"

"It's such a relief to be able to tell you. I promised not to whisper a word before it was official. Today's the day! Morten Kjærum has accepted a post at the United Nations in New York. His directorship at Human Rights will be advertised soon, possibly as early as May."

Iben gets in first. "Is it yours for the asking, then?"

"So far, that's impossible to tell."

"But you seem over the moon, right?"

Paul slings his jacket over one chair and sits down on another. "Put it this way: to be honest, the heavyweight contenders are Frederik and myself. I'm the boss for this place as well as a member of the board at the Center for Democracy. We've been very active at the DCIG, organizing things like conferences and other stuff that's kept us in the public eye—quite unlike the Democracy Center. Take that successful Yugoslav conference at Louisiana—Frederik's people didn't have a chance, organization-wise. It means that I have the edge. Also,

Frederik removed himself from our board not long ago. One way or the other, he's lost quite a bit of power."

"How long have you known this?" Anne-Lise wants to know.

"Two weeks."

Iben, Anne-Lise, and Camilla exchange glances. It's suddenly clear to all of them why Paul has behaved so strangely over the past few weeks. They pretend to be pleased for him, but it doesn't take Camilla long to see that the news is to their advantage too. Paul obviously wants to stay in charge of the DCIG and will set about merging it with the DIHR as soon as possible.

Iben will get a whole crew of intellectuals with whom she can argue all day long.

Anne-Lise will have other librarians around her. She'll want that, even if she and Iben make a great show of getting along so very well. Camilla can clearly see that Anne-Lise would love to have other colleagues to talk to. Now her dreams will come true, and without the hassle of looking for a new job.

Only one of them has any reason to worry, and that person is Camilla herself. She knows that when this kind of place merges with another one, the bosses will always try to save on secretarial posts.

It's only three o'clock, but Iben starts clearing her desk. She seems very happy these days and has stopped staying late at the office every night. Apparently she sees rather a lot of Gunnar Hartvig Nielsen.

Her bag is packed and on her desk when that seedy old fusspot Erik Prins ambles in. As usual he stops at Iben's and Anne-Lise's desks for a chat. He starts telling them about a new book he has come across. Talking about it reminds him of Iben's articles.

He continues in his high-pitched voice: "You know the way everyone harps on about how odd it is that concentration camp officers would go home from work and behave like decent loving fathers? What's so odd about it? We're all like that."

Iben nods and says she agrees. It seems she's not in such a great hurry to get home after all. They chat away and then she launches into one of her spiels.

"We let rip with idealism and grand words, but it's nothing but rationalizations of our own egoistic behavior. Not only do we lie to others; we also lie to ourselves. Each one of us lives inside a house of mirrors—our own instinctive self-righteousness distorts the way we view reality so that we can justify our actions to ourselves. And there's no way we can escape."

Iben and Erik are completely on the same wavelength. Camilla, however, can easily see how badly Anne-Lise takes it, and feels she can't stand much more of it either.

Earlier Camilla might have shouted, "What about Malene? Everyone is capable of choosing to be an exception from your theories! Otherwise life wouldn't be worth living." But there's no point in saying, "What about Malene? If you're a guilt-ridden murderer and sick in the head, then you can be an exception."

Anne-Lise suddenly gets up and hurries off to the restroom. She's behaving just like she used to.

On her way home Camilla collects Dennis from an after-school club and takes him with her to the supermarket.

When they arrive home, Finn's car isn't there yet. They're just inside the door when the phone rings. She puts the shopping bags down and runs to answer.

A man's voice is speaking English. "Hi, Camilla."

She recognizes the voice instantly. The skin down the back of her neck and spine seems to contract. If he's using his cell phone he could be nearby. Right outside the door, for all she knows! He's capable of anything. He might get inside her home. It wouldn't matter a damn to him if Finn were there. She concentrates on hiding her fear from her son and covers the mouthpiece of the telephone.

"Dennis, it's for me. Why don't you run along to play CounterStrike on your dad's computer?"

Dennis shouts, "Yeaaah!" and rushes away upstairs. With Dennis out of earshot, she speaks to the caller.

"What do you want?"

She knows already, of course. He wants what he always wants when he's in Denmark and has the time.

"I hate you!" Camilla shouts. "You sold yourself and all your chances in life. Zigic had your name on his list. I know the kind of things you've done for him. You've worked for him for years."

He only makes a snorting noise.

It upsets her even more, but she tells herself to remain cool or Dennis will hear her. She musters all her self-control.

"Dragan, remember that I know you well. I know that you don't have to be like this."

"And you know that I can get into your house anytime I like. Or turn up where you work. Camilla, for all you know, I could be in your bedroom now."

She takes a deep breath. "You think that when you say things like that you'll make me want you. I don't. It's no good. I think you're a loser."

Dennis is standing in the doorway. "Hey, Mom, who are you talking to?"

"No one special, sweetie."

"It's got to be someone."

"Yep, that's right. Look, why don't you go out and play ball in the garden?"

"Why?"

"Because I'd like you to."

"Can't I play CounterStrike now?"

"No, not anymore. Go to the garden."

"Aw, Mo-om."

Once she is sure her son has gone outside, she whispers into the mouthpiece: "I don't want you anymore. You don't understand me at all."

Dragan laughs. "I'm staying at the Plaza and I'll be in my room tonight. My name is Guido Pirandello."

She can see Dennis. He runs up to the window, presses his face against it, then grimaces and giggles. She tries to smile back at her little boy and speak to Dragan at the same time.

"Dragan, I'll report you. I'll tell the police where you are. Don't phone me again!"

She slams the receiver down. Afterward she collapses on the sofa and cries, listening for Finn or Dennis at the door.

Finn doesn't return until about an hour later. She hugs him and kisses him warmly. They chat, mostly about the pipes Finn is supplying for the office kitchen in a large clothing company. She has made fishcakes for supper, served with boiled potatoes and her own homemade sour cream and mustard dressing.

When Finn has helped with clearing the table, they brew a pot of tea and settle down to watch *Good Evening, Denmark* and *News & Views* on the television.

Later on, as she makes her way to the Plaza Hotel, she thinks: He's the devil! Her head is full of images of Dragan. I haven't hated anyone so much since I left school.

She's told Finn that she's going over to Vibeke's to practice a few songs for the choir. "You'd better put the kids to bed," she told him. "I might be a bit late."

She imagines her children grown up, and when they somehow learn what their mother got up to once or twice a year, she can hear them ask, "Mom, is it true? When we were little, did you really make love to a murderer?"

As the hotel elevator ascends, Camilla can feel her skin crawl as she thinks about her answer.

"No, no, I didn't. I'd never do that."

"So what did you do together? You were unfaithful to Dad, weren't you?"

"Goodness, where do you get such dreadful ideas? I wouldn't dream of it. How can you? I'm your mother!"

chapter 56

t is half past one in the morning. Iben is leaning against the head-
board of Gunnar's big bed. He is next to her and they are both
writing on their laptops. Documents and books are spread all
over the duvet. They are both absorbed in what they're doing,
but now and then one of them tells the other about a thought or
a piece of text. Or they touch, kiss, and wait to see what will happen next.

Quietly, in the light from the bedside lamps, their minds play
with each other in a private game they both love. Their bodies are
at rest, as if as they were floating in a warm swimming pool.

Gunnar's chest bears a small pink scar from Zigic's knife.
Iben covers it with her hand, as if she could protect him now,
one month too late. Her hand moves on, slipping through the
hair on his chest, and her other hand lets go of a book about the
Armenian genocide.

Iben and Gunnar stay awake most of the night, but at the
DCIG the next morning Iben is bursting with energy. She will
always remember Malene and respect her memory, but it's a fact
that the office is running much better without her and there are
no more problems with people not getting along. Anne-Lise has
flourished in a totally unexpected way, and Paul turns up every
morning in top form.

Iben's only worry concerns the Turkey issue of *Genocide News*. It has been a source of anxiety for her ever since she learned, on one hand, that Paul is pretty sure he will be the next head of the DIHR and, on the other, that he is chummy with a representative of the nationalist Danish People's Party.

All of a sudden Paul whipped the planned Chechnya issue off the schedule, meaning that a study of Christians killing Muslims went down the tube. Instead all the Center's resources are to be brought to bear on Turkey—including how Muslims killed more than a million Christians.

Paul's stated reason was that Turkey was up for discussion in Brussels. Still, these days no one talks about the genocide carried out by the Turks. Inevitably, the suspicion comes to mind that Paul has made some secret agreement with influential figures in the People's Party, who are against all immigrants but the Muslim contingent most of all. They already stopped Ole from firing Paul. Maybe their next move is to install him at the top of the Human Rights Institute?

And, if so, does Iben's work serve, above all, to fan the fear of Muslims and the growing hatred of them? Is she perhaps doing her bit to target the large Turkish community in Denmark? Naturally Paul would never tell her so straight out. She has no choice now, except to make the Turkey issue as good and comprehensive as possible, supporting the Center and the cause in general.

After work she goes to Gunnar's place. Every second week his daughters are there too. Iben has liked them immensely from the very first time they met. It seems that they like her too. At a stroke Iben belongs to a family—a brand-new one, but a family all the same.

It's incredible that less than half a year ago Iben and Gunnar met for the first time. At Sophie's party. Three days later, she and Malene received threatening e-mails.

She is sitting on the bed in the oldest daughter's room, listening to music, looking at the girl's latest download of pop-star photos from the Internet.

When the intercom rings Iben answers. It is Dorte Jørgensen.

"I hope I'm not disturbing you?"

Iben pulls herself together and smiles even though no one is there to watch her.

"Not at all, Dorte. Come straight up."

All in all, Iben is happy. During the last few weeks she has discovered how much she's capable of. Although she's felt close to the edge once or twice, she's realized that it's best to stay in her own apartment during those moments. She doesn't want Gunnar or the girls to notice anything odd about her.

Whenever Dorte turns up, her feeling of being in control begins to slip. Lurking at the back of Iben's mind is the fear that one of these visits will provoke an anxiety attack—and the agonizing fear that she might give things away about herself.

Iben says hello and welcome, calls Gunnar, and offers to make coffee. The daughters wander in too and they all gather around the coffee table. Gunnar's bloodstained sofa has been thrown out and replaced by Malene's elegant designer one, which her mother insisted that Iben should inherit although she has no room for it in her apartment.

Dorte looks around with an expression that seems to suggest that Iben's staying here is suspect. Iben serves coffee and asks Dorte what is on her mind this time. They will try to help in every way.

Keeping an eye on Iben, Dorte explains that she has been examining Malene's confessional letter to Rasmus. "Everything about it is consistent with her other letters to Rasmus. With one exception. All the other letters have been saved repeatedly. It seems that Malene was a nervous writer and kept hitting Save every five minutes. But, if you check the Statistics option under File Properties for this particular letter, it has been revised only once."

"I see. What does that mean?"

"The significance is that the letter might have been written by some-one else. Not by Malene and, therefore, possibly after her death. It's easy to add a false Save date."

"Really? Do you think . . ."

"Well, we've been wondering about it. Interestingly, we established that someone did boot up the computer and use it after the police had sealed Malene's apartment."

"So it could only have been one of you . . . or . . . ?"

"That's always possible, of course. Given that there seems to have been no break-in, it's the likeliest answer, I suppose."

Iben feels that she's still herself. But the girls look worried. Maybe she's more transparent than she imagines. Iben glances at Gunnar, who under-stands at once.

"Hey, it's time to start fixing supper. Off to the kitchen we go."

Dorte begins from where she left her interrogation of Iben last time, renewing her verbal attacks from every angle. "With regard to the e-mail you received, whoever wrote it called you 'self-righteous.' Did that person know you? What do you think?"

"I really couldn't say."

"You must have an idea. However vague it might be."

"Malene has confessed to it, but it's . . ."

Iben's heart is beating hard. The pressure is on now. It will make her focus. Make her mind clear and calculating, like in Kenya. And in Anne-Lise's house. And when Zigic caught her. I'm changing now, becoming a "survivor," she thinks.

But somehow it doesn't happen. Is it because Malene is dead? She can't focus. She cannot save herself.

Dorte continues: "Iben, you have to live with your past. Your actions will affect you. And affect your husband too. The first month might be easy for you. And the next one, and the next one—but sooner or later what you have done will catch up with you. Why do you think I'm so certain of that?"

Iben doesn't want to answer but replies as she must: "I don't know."

"Because we're responsible. We have to take responsibility for what we do. In the end, you alone decide how to act. Look at Malene. No one would have predicted that she'd sacrifice—"

"Malene was mentally ill. She wrote that herself."

"That's what you say."

Iben leans back and sighs. "I must say, you do check everything thoroughly. It's very reassuring. I'd be happy to help in any way."

Dorte nods. Her eyes don't leave Iben for a second. "That's good to know."

Iben gets up. She walks over to Gunnar's wall of pine shelving and then back.

"Look, would you like to examine my computer? You can look for Rasmus's spyware, or e-mailed threats or drafts of Malene's confession."

Dorte has it in her to smile at this. "Thank you! I'll accept your offer, thank you."

"Your theory is a bit far-fetched, if you don't mind me saying so. I doubt whether it's convincing enough to get you a search warrant. I just hope you realize that I've nothing to hide."

"Of course. Do you use any other computers?"

"No. I take my laptop to work."

"I'll have to get independent confirmation of that."

"I understand."

Maybe Iben leaves the room a little too eagerly. When she returns from the bedroom carrying the computer, Dorte sounds kind.

"Both of you must miss Malene a great deal?"

"Yes, we do. And what she did was extraordinary."

When Iben hands over the laptop, Dorte produces a CD from her pocket and asks permission to install the useful little search program she has brought along.

Iben agrees, noting that Dorte expected to be given access to the computer.

As they wait, the program searches through the items on the hard disk. Dorte breaks the silence. "Do you feel that your work affects you a lot?"

Iben thinks that this might be another attempt to get at her when her guard is down. "I don't know. But we are constantly reminded of how frail the bonds are that restrain our instincts and prevent us from doing terrible things."

"Perhaps working day in, day out on such things might blunt your sensibility?"

"That could be true. Yes."

The search program has stopped. Dorte keys in a few commands, narrows her eyes, and leans toward the screen.

Dorte had tried to sound casual about the program she "had in her pocket," but Iben quickly spots that the detective is far from a computer buff. It could be sheer desperation that made her come this evening. Probably, the consensus back at the station is that the case has been closed ever since Malene's confession came to light. Dorte won't have a leg to stand on unless she finds something in the computer. And she won't.

Iben listens to Gunnar and his children having fun in the kitchen. She feels much better now and returns to the previous subject.

"But on the other hand, working at the DCIG might have the opposite effect. That is, not to blunt our perceptions, but to make us more appreciative of the lives we're privileged enough to live."

Dorte keeps staring at the screen.

"We have been allowed to believe that an orderly, day-to-day existence and our care and respect for each other are givens. Our work shows us that they are not. It also opens our eyes to the importance of goodness. Precisely because it can vanish so quickly."

At last Dorte looks up from the screen and states the obvious. "Not a trace of anything."

Just as Iben tells herself that the worst is over, Dorte has another thought.

"By the way, do you know of anyone who might have a key to Malene's apartment? Or someone who might know the password to her computer?"

Iben must think quickly now. It's a test. She lifts the lump of orange mineral on the coffee table. "Not as far as I know. Malene never told me her password. I didn't have a key, and I'm pretty sure nobody else did."

"The thing is that whoever wrote the confession must have been someone who had a key. Key or no key, you've got to be very cool about breaking and entering an apartment under regular police surveillance, especially if the next thing you do is settle down to a bit of computer work."

They talk for a little longer, but Dorte begins to look tired. She gets up to leave and puts her CD away.

"I'm sorry to have disturbed you. Hopefully it wasn't too uncomfortable for you."

"No, not at all. I mean, you obviously must investigate every possible lead. We owe that to Malene and Rasmus. Please feel free to call anytime."

Iben escorts Dorte to the door and then goes to the kitchen, where Gunnar is puttering about making lots of delicious dishes for a buffet-style supper. The girls are preparing a big bowl of salad.

Gunnar asks how it went. Iben mutters noncommittally.

She goes to stand behind her man, who is frying little slices of pork fillet in butter. She puts her arms around him and leans her head against his back, sensing his warmth against her cheek.

The two girls smile at her. Iben's ear is pressed in between Gunnar's shoulder blades, and she can hear the beating of his heart.

This is exactly how I wanted it to be, she thinks. Like this.

acknowledgments

A list of the people in Denmark to whom I owe thanks would take up several pages, and so for the American edition, I'll just mention the people at the Danish Center for Holocaust and Genocide Studies in Copenhagen: in particular, Torben Jørgensen and former research director Eric Markusen (now at Southwest State University, Minnesota). When I first called the center in the summer of 2000 and told them of my plans to write a novel about a fictitious genocide information center and the severe office harassment problems among its staff members, they could have reacted in so many ways. What they did, however, was to recognize immediately the possibilities for information on genocide in this novel. They invited me into their midst and supported my work more than I could ever have hoped.

In the United States, I thank Professor James Waller at Whitworth College. Our discussions at the biannual conference of the International Association of Genocide Scholars, as well as our correspondence afterward, helped me write the articles that are part of this novel.

I am also indebted to Yale University's professors Ben Kiernan and Claude Rawson. Our talks during my visit to Yale's

Genocide Studies program helped me enormously to formulate Iben's thoughts on perpetrator behavior.

Thank you, too, to my friends Doritt and Joseph Linsk, of Atlantic City, New Jersey, who put a roof over my head for several weeks as I worked on the chapters about Iben in Kenya.

I cannot give enough thanks to my editors Lorna Owen at Nan A. Talese/Doubleday, New York, and Kirsty Dunseath at Weidenfeld & Nicholson, London. I've been amazed, witnessing their complete devotion to transferring my novel to the very different English language.

And then, I am grateful indeed to my first and best reader, Mette Thorsen.

Christian Jungersen's first novel, *Thickets*, won the Danish Best First Novel of the Year Award. *The Exception*, his second novel and the first to be translated into English, won the Danish Golden Laurels prize, and has been a huge bestseller across Europe. Born in Copenhagen, he now divides his time between Dublin, Ireland, and New York City.

a note about the type

This book was set in Minion, a neohumanist font created for digital technology by the American type designer Robert Slimbach and issued by Adobe in 1990. Minion is an original face inspired by the humanist forms of fifteenth- and sixteenth-century Renaissance type.